FINAL BREATH

ROBERT F BARKER

Want to know what started it all?

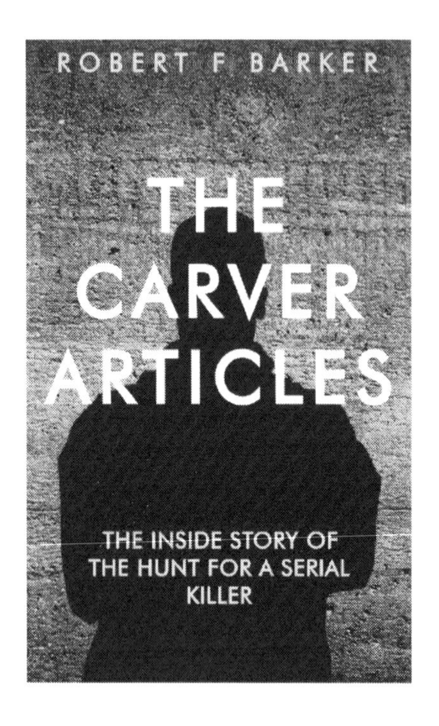

Sign up for the author's V.I.P. mailing list and get a free e-copy of, *THE CARVER ARTICLES,* the series of articles that kick-started it all - as featured in LAST GASP

To get started, visit:-

http://robertfbarker.co.uk

By The Author

The DCI Jamie Carver Series;

LAST GASP
(The Worshipper Trilogy, Book One)

FINAL BREATH
(The Worshipper Trilogy, Book Two)

First published in Paperback in 2017

Kindle Version first published in 2017

ISBN-13:978-1979036528

To my family for your endless encouragement
To my good friends, Sue and Keith, for your patience, honesty, and valuable feedback on my early, woeful, attempts.
To all members of the excellent Vale Royal Writers Group –
whose invaluable feedback and support keeps me rooted

Prologue

1

As has become his habit, the man waits until late evening when most have gone, to progress the work that plays on his mind more and more these days. Soon, he will have to make others aware of the time-bomb on which he is sitting. Before then, he needs to know how far the fall-out will spread, more importantly, who he can trust.

Tonight, he is working his way through more of the video files stored on the hard drive they recovered from the bottom drawer of the filing cabinet that now stands over in the corner. In doing so, his focus is less on the *what,* than the, *who*. Some he has identified so far - those who like to see themselves in the gossip mags for example - may not be overly-concerned about aspects of their lifestyle being revealed. They may even revel in it. For others, it would spell disaster, personal *and* professional.

As he finishes typing-up the file note on the clip he has just watched and clicks 'save', he checks the time. It is coming on ten o'clock, the limit he set himself for that evening. The hours he devotes to the work have expanded in recent weeks. In part, it is due to his desire to just get on and be done with it. But he is also conscious of the urgency of the task. When the shit hits the fan, he doesn't want to be the one accused of feet-dragging. He is also mindful of the effect it is having on other areas.

The woman with whom he shares his life for instance.

Like him, she still bears the scars of what they went through. He knows how she feels his absences. Once before he lost someone because he failed to pay attention to things that matter. He is determined that it will not happen again.

About to close-down and clear away, he pauses. He still has ten minutes. Provided the next clip isn't too long, he should still be home in good time. He hesitates, then clicks on the icon. Almost at once, he realises his mistake. The telling factor is the quality. Most of the stuff he has seen is amateurish, filmed on hand-held devices, the sort of thing people put up on social media every day.

Not this.

The stillness of the frame suggests a mounted camera of some sort. And the first edit, a few seconds in, shows at least one other is being used. Lit, staged and, by the look of it, maybe even scripted, it is of a different order to the others he has seen. A couple of the others are almost, but not quite, of this standard, the activities depicted, the sort that cater to a very narrow range of tastes. As he waits to see what the focus of this particular scene will be, he holds his breath, gaze locked on the screen. It doesn't take long for things to become clear, and when they do, his stomach starts to churn the way it does when he knows he is about to witness something it will take him a long time to forget.

It starts with the girl being led into the room. It is not so much her nakedness and the blindfold that worry him - it is a common motif in such productions - but her hesitancy, and age. The first could be down to good acting. But whilst her figure suggests someone of at least consenting years, it is clear she is not yet fully mature. His guess is late-teens, which means that regardless of whether she works in the industry or not, she is exploitable. Such exploitation takes many forms. Money, drugs, physical coercion, even the sex. His instincts tell him that in this case, the middle two are most likely.

It is when the camera pans and he sees the wooden beam with the noose hanging from it, the low stool set up beneath, that real fear starts to replace the churning. He knows how these days, visual trickery, clever editing, even CGI, can achieve the desired effects. But something tells him that what he is about to see may not involve such techniques.

For the next few minutes he sits and watches the scene play out. In many aspects, it mirrors the sort of 'edge play' that those whose tastes run in such directions can access on-line any time they wish. Only the girl's reactions, and the clip's provenance, tell him that what he is witnessing is not, in any sense of the word, 'play'. Tears of fear are hard to achieve in such circumstances, especially in one so young.

The end, when it comes, is not so much an anti-climax, as a confirmation of expectation. He has seen it coming, pictured it in his mind, from the moment he saw the noose. His own experiences of many months before helps in this regard, and he is far from unaffected. In this case, familiarity does not lead to immunity, the reverse in fact. Having seen it before, experienced it, he is uniquely placed to empathise with the girl's terror, to feel her pain. And though he closes his eyes, tight, towards the end, it does not lessen in any way the overall impact. The shaking that began in his arms early on before spreading through the rest of his body, continues throughout. And when, after a period of silence, he opens his eyes and sees the blank screen signalling the clip has ended, he knows that he does not have to wait until he can steel himself to watch it all the way through, to know *how* it ends. The same for its significance.

To this point, he has been comfortable responding to queries about his evening activities by referring to it as, 'research'. He has done so in the belief that the case that almost cost him his life - others were not so lucky - is now closed, that the matters he is 'researching' are historical. He knows now he was wrong.

The case is not closed.

In reality, it never was.

It merely continues.

And it is all going to happen again.

2

'I'm Xena,' the dark-haired girl says.

'I see,' the man says. *Zeena? What the Hell sort of a name is Zeena?*

'And I'm Gabrielle,' her blond companion says, giggling.

'Of course.' *I'm missing something.*

"Xena" steps back to give the man to whom she is talking a better look. 'Is this okay?'

His eyes slide down to her boots and back again. *You've got to be joking.* But when he sees the hopeful look in her eyes, he chickens out. 'It's er... very original.'

Gerald Hawthorn has a vague notion that the girls' outfits - all gold bracelets and dangling fronds of leather and suede - are inspired by an old TV series. One that achieved cult status way back. Some swords-and-sandals romp about a mythical warrior-princess. But he and Barbara have never really done TV, and he doesn't like to ask, in case the girls think their attempts to comply with the club's strict dress-code aren't up to scratch. It was why he opted for a polite-but-neutral, 'Interesting outfits, ladies,' when he'd approached to introduce himself and welcome them to, Josephine's.

In truth, Gerald thinks the pair have missed the mark. Whilst his carefully-worded guidance allows for some interpretation, it doesn't run to any form of 'fancy dress'. Especially as the range of interests catered for at the venue he and Barbara have worked hard to establish as the foremost of its kind outside London, are quite narrow.

But it is the girls' first visit, and so he doesn't say anything. They will see for themselves as the evening wears on. And if they become regulars, they will soon pick things up. So he keeps conversation light and, whilst the older couple they came with chat to friends at the bar, he goes about making sure they don't have any wrong ideas, as he likes to do with first-timers.

Eventually, conscious he is nearing the point at which a couple of twenty-somethings may start to misconstrue the attentions of a man old enough to be their father - *grandfather?* - he decides it is time to move on. He hasn't sought to discover what they are into, other than themselves, but he suspects he'll know before the night is over. Wishing them a pleasant evening, he excuses himself.

As he moves away, they huddle into each other. And before passing out of ear-shot, he just catches the word, 'cutey', which brings on a smile. Gerald Hawthorn knows he is wearing well for fifty-five, and that women half Barbara's age still admire his combination of boyish good-looks, healthy tan and still thick, steel-grey hair. But he never tries to capitalise on his good fortune. He learned that lesson years ago. Nevertheless, as he heads off, the girls' murmurings lend his saunter an easy confidence that falls just the right side of arrogant swagger.

As he ncars the club's newest feature, a faithful reproduction of the stocks on display in the Tower of London's Black Museum - it cost an absolute *fortune* - Gerald's nose tells him the evening is starting to get underway and that it is time to check for, 'spoilers'. Many years in the club business, Gerald lets his sense of smell, as much as his other senses, tell him when things are livening up. Usually an hour or so after opening, it is when the lingering odours of furniture polish, disinfectant and Carpet Fresh give way to a heady cocktail of perfume, alcohol and pheromones. Loitering next to the stocks, he lets his practised gaze roam the room, seeking out anyone who looks like they don't belong. A lesser man may have difficulty completing the task. But though Gerald isn't blind to the sights on offer, he is professional enough not to let himself be distracted -an immunity built up during their Soho years.

It being a second Friday – Intermediates' Night - he takes his time. With so many new faces, the chances of someone out to cause trouble, or worse, a reporter working on an exposé, are raised. But they have several journalists on the books now, and they assure him that these days, the tabloids won't look twice at a place like Josephine's, not unless it involves a 'celeb', and he and Barbara are always careful about those.

As he completes his sweep, he relaxes. Apart from some new couples gathered in the middle of the room, already sharing excited introductions, he recognises most of the faces. And those he doesn't, seem sufficiently at ease to suggest it is not their first visit.

It is a good crowd for a Friday. In fact, the place is as full as it has been since Christmas. People finally seem to be getting over the brooh-ha of, The Trial, and all that followed. He hasn't heard *Her* name mentioned for months. Tonight there is even something of the old buzz in the air. It is mixed with outraged and, in some cases, embarrassed laughter as people compare outfits, or out themselves for the first time. As usual, the majority are second, or even third-timers testing things out one last time before graduating up to first and third Saturdays - 'Seniors' Nights.' He glances across at the bar where

Greg and Nichole are only just coping. A couple of minibuses have arrived together, and for several minutes the reception area is chaos as everyone seeks to get in out of the cold. Most of the women's outfits - some of the men's also – do not lend themselves to standing outside on wintry February evenings while the door staff check IDs. It makes Gerald think about the design for the new reception area lying on his desk. Barbara could be right, maybe it should be bigger. Across the room, Carmen, their accomplished Meeter-And-Greeter, is doing her thing. A willowy red-head, she looks stunning, as always, in her green bustier. About to join her, a touch on his elbow stays him. He turns.

A blond woman, hair coiffured and back-combed into a golden mane, is at his shoulder. She is wearing a white halter-neck dress, the front and sides of which plunge over her still-ample cleavage to her waist, where they are nipped by a thin, gold belt. Below it, the dress flares open from just below her crotch, allowing glimpses of well-toned leg sheathed in glossy, white hose. In her strappy-heels she stands an inch or so above him - a Goddess - and he feels the familiar stirrings. She kisses him, lightly, on the cheek before draping a tanned arm over his shoulder. Her gold bangle sparkles under the lights, and the five-diamond ring he bought for their tenth anniversary twinkles blues and yellows.

'How're things looking?' she says, as she casts her gaze over the assembling guests, as he had been doing.

'Should be in for a good night,' he says. 'Or we will be, once Alison shows up.' He checks the bar again where Greg and Nicole, are earning their pay. 'This is the third time this month she's been late. I'm going to have to have words with her when she gets here.'

Barbara Hawthorn gives her husband a sideways

glance. 'I'll do it,' she says. 'You'll have her in tears.'

Staring into the lively blue eyes, he feigns surprise. 'Who? Me?' But he cannot keep it up. She knows him too well.

'I see Arthur's back,' she says. 'We've not seen him in a long time. Who's the girl?'

'Where?' He turns in the direction she is looking, which is when he sees her.

Leaning with her back against the far wall, near to the entrance to the Theme Rooms, she is talking to the sixty-plus corporate accountant they haven't seen since the scandal broke. He wonders how he missed her. He'd seen Arthur earlier as he'd circulated, and spoken to him, though only briefly. She must have been in the ladies. Wearing a shiny black dress which seems moulded to her, she is tall, even allowing for her heels. And the glossy, sandy bob looks real, rather than a wig, as many like to wear. As she and Arthur lean in to each other, conspiratorially, her gaze sweeps the room, falling on groups of guests, drinking them in, before moving on. Her undisguised surveillance, coupled with her confident manner - she looks as at home as a Saturday-Nighter - sparks Gerald's interest.

'I don't know her,' he says, staring across. 'He must have found himself someone new. Looks interesting, wouldn't you say?'

The hand on his shoulder flicks his cheek. 'Down Rover. You go help Carmen. *I'll* say hello to Arthur.'

She sets off across the room, exchanging nods of recognition and words of greeting with those she passes. As heads turn to follow her progress, Gerald takes pleasure from witnessing the effect she has on people - of all ages. At fifty-three, Barbara is even better preserved than he is.

As he joins Carmen and the newbies, now arranged on the sofas in the middle of the lounge, some of Gerald's attention stays on the trio across the room. Arthur's partner smiles as Barbara says something to her, then passes comment to Arthur, at which he laughs, heartily. Barbara turns, seeking him out, and points. The girl sights along the outstretched arm and for a split second there is eye contact. Gerald's pulse quickens. But then he hears Carmen saying, 'And this is Gerald,' and he turns to give his guests his full attention. There will be time for eye-games later.

'Gerald is one of the club's co-owners,' Carmen says. 'I'll introduce you to Barbara later.'

For the next few minutes he goes through the drill. Being welcoming - it isn't an act. Showing just the right amount of relaxed charm to put the women at ease, without alienating their partners. Mirroring the firmness, or lack of it, in the men's handshakes.

He asks how they have come to hear of Josephine's.

'Through your web-site,' says a woman with jet black hair and fingernails to match.

'From a guy I work with,' the male half of a younger couple says. 'He's been coming for years. I didn't believe him at first.'

'We saw your advert in Skin Two' a middle-aged man says, nervously. Then he remembers, and looks up, sheepishly, at the older woman perched on the chair's arm above him. Already in role, she glares at him. But it is early in the proceedings, and she lets it go.

Through it all, part of Gerald's interest stays on what is happening across the room. And though he cannot see their faces - Barbara's back is to him – his built-in antenna tells him that the mood has changed. Huddled into each other, the jokey chatter and smiles seem to have disappeared, replaced by earnest expressions and hand gestures. At one stage, as Carmen is explaining to her group the rules governing how to go about checking whether a scene is 'open' or 'closed', Gerald turns, to see how they are doing. He just catches the quick glance Barbara casts in his direction, before turning back to hear whatever it is the girl is saying. He isn't sure, but he thinks Barbara looked rather tense.

A few minutes later, Barbara breaks away and he sees her mouth to the couple her usual, 'Enjoy your evening.'

But the smile that goes with it isn't her normal one. And instead of coming back to him, she makes her way to the office next to the bar. As she opens the door, she turns, sending him a look he reads as, '*We need to talk'.* A feeling of disquiet begins to make itself felt in his stomach. A minute later, Gerald excuses himself to go join her.

As he enters, she is pouring herself a Glenfiddich. Usually, she is even stricter than he is about sticking to their, 'No Alcohol While Working' rule.

'What is it?' he says.

She tosses the drink back, then turns to him. Her face is flushed, but it is too soon for it to be the whiskey.

'You won't believe it.'

'Who is she?'

She re-fills her glass, then turns to him once more. 'She's Arthur's niece.'

'And?'

'And she's police.'

He waits. It isn't as if she's the first.

'And she's asking about, *Her*.'

As the reason for his wife's early imbibing finally becomes clear, Gerald Hawthorn feels the world around closing in on him once more, just as it did all those months ago.

CHAPTER 1

The call came in the early afternoon. It interrupted Q's dictation, and lasted only seconds.

'Tell me where, tell me when,' the man said.

Q thought he sounded weary, as if resigned to the inevitable. His podgy features broke into a sly smile as he made his reply, which was equally short. But despite its brevity, the exchange was enough to ensure that for the rest of that afternoon, Quentin Quinlan had to fight even harder than usual to keep his mind on his work.

As luck would have it, it was Wednesday, the day, 'Q', as he was universally known, liked to keep free of his more important engagements, just in case he needed to take some mid-week time-out to indulge his other interests. That particular afternoon he had scheduled only two appointments. The first was with a naive but not-bad looking middle-ranking oil company executive. Recently come out, the man was convinced that his Chairman's failure to grant him a place on the board was clear evidence of, 'blatant homophobia.'

Q's second client was a titled Cotswolds landowner. Six months earlier he had sold several acres of paddock to a couple of thirty-something, city re-locators. For no good reason Q could discern, the landowner had taken a belated dislike to the couple, and was now looking for Q to find a legal means through which he could steal his land back.

One thing Q was good at – the bedrock upon which his firm's reputation as one of the South West's leading litigators was built – was his ability to make his clients believe he shared their problems. That he was as committed - no, more committed - to righting the wrong they have suffered as themselves. In reality, he found most of the problems his clients brought him boring in the extreme. As he listened to them droning on about whatever 'grievous injustice' they believe themselves to have suffered, he often liked to imagine throwing them from the window of his executive office on the third floor of Cheltenham's historic Corn Exchange Building. Unless they were particularly interesting, when he imagined other things.

This afternoon, Q's eloquence was such that by the time both meetings ended - sooner than either client had been expecting - both left satisfied that their particular case was top of Q's High Priority List. They also believed that their cause was being pursued with all the vigour Quinlan and Quinlan's considerable resources could muster, and that they could look forward to early resolution.

In both cases Q waited until the door was firmly closed, bcfore returning the papers to the, 'Special Attention' pile on the shelf behind him, and from where he had retrieved them only minutes before the clients had entered.

It meant that by four o clock he was free. Remembering to transfer the documents and other items upon which his future now depended, from his safe to his briefcase, he left the office, locking the door behind him. As he passed the temp with the yellow hair and dark roots, who had been his PA for the past month, he dropped his voice recorder onto her desk. He barely looked at her as he said, 'I'm heading over to Wilding's for a pre-meet before tomorrow's hearing. I won't be back today.'

Abi Forshaw watched her boss's overweight frame as it waddled its way through towards the Reception Suite. The way Q was leaning to his left, she wondered what could be in his briefcase that was so heavy. She didn't believe his story about going to Wilding's for a second. In the short few weeks she had worked at Quinlan's, Abi had come to understand why Q had had to make do with agency PAs for so long. And like those before her, she had come to decide that she'd had enough of his complete lack of consideration for those he employed. She had already set a mental reminder to not miss the following day's Evening News, the one with the jobs supplement. With her experience, she didn't need to work for someone to whom the word 'ethics' was a shorthand reference to an inappropriate joke he had circulated on the office e-mail concerning a lisping prostitute and a punter from Clacton-On-Sea.

In mellow mood following the telephone call, and with the rush-hour traffic yet to build, Q took the back road through the countryside to the Gloucestershire village of Newent. It was going on five when he swung his Merc onto the parking area in front of the former vicarage on the village outskirts which, twelve months earlier, had been redeveloped into three, single-floor Executive-Apartments. Driving home, he had been buoyed by the thought that soon, he would no longer have to worry about the exorbitant lease payments.

Q's apartment was on the first floor which, as there was no lift, and given his physical condition, was as well. Nevertheless, he was breathing heavily by the time he reached his front door at the top of the stairs. Unlocking it, he stepped inside, dropped his briefcase, and turned to the keypad on the wall. As he punched in the alarm-code, he called, 'I'm home Jezebel. Come to Daddy.'

He turned towards the kitchen but stopped as the keypad gave out a series of beeps. Thinking he must have entered a wrong number, he tried again. About to turn away, the beeps returned.

'Now what?'

Three times in the past month he'd had to call out the engineer to rectify faults in the supposedly, 'state-of-the-art', alarm system. He checked the panel, and was surprised to see the orange light blinking. Hadn't the man said that meant the system was in standby-mode? Puzzled, he stared at the display, but could not make sense of it. He was certain he'd set it when he left home that morning, and Mrs Rogers didn't clean on a Wednesday. Something else. Jezebel hadn't appeared to greet him, either.

Beginning to feel something wasn't quite right, but unable to put a finger on what, Q decided to leave sorting the alarm out until later. If he had to call the company out again, he would be giving them a piece of his mind. Switching the system to, 'disabled', he went in search of her.

He headed through into the kitchen, expecting to see her lurking under the table, but there was no sign. Calling her name in the sing-song she always liked, he shuffled through the chintzy lounge and into the master bedroom. But her welcoming voice and silky caress remained absent. Lifting the bed's counterpane, he bent to check underneath - one of her favourite hideaways.

'*There* you are,' he said. '*Whatever* are you doing you silly girl?' He reached for her, but to his surprise she recoiled, backing towards the wall, mouth wide, as if about to give one of her hisses. He was shocked. She never reacted to him that way. She loved him.

'Goodness, Jezebel. Whatever's the matter?' As he reached further under the bed, his large head and shoulders disappeared beneath the counterpane. And as he stretched towards the frightened animal, labouring from the exertion, he wondered about what could possibly have made her so nervous.

A noise from behind made him stiffen. A light bang, like a cupboard door closing, followed by soft footfalls on carpet. A voice he'd heard once already that day, though only briefly, said, 'You did say your place didn't you Q? About five?'

Panic rose within him. He forgot all about Jezebel.

And as Quentin Quinlan began to back his considerable frame out from under the bed, the thought came that he may have miscalculated. Badly.

CHAPTER 2

It was a glimpse of something that DCI Jamie Carver liked to think could one day be a more regular part of his life. A neat patio, fronting a tended garden. On the lawn, Jason, being helped to get used to his new bike by Aunty Ros. Nana-Sue, smiling, whimsically, at the sight of her grandson enjoying himself.

Normality.

On this occasion, Carver didn't have time to reflect on why, for him, 'normal' remained so elusive.

'She's good with him, isn't she?'Susan Kendrick said.

Carver turned to the woman to whom he owed the sort of obligation that can never be repaid. He nodded. 'She's from a big family. She's used to kids.' Too late, he realised his slip.

But if the woman whose own family had been reduced in the most terrible way possible saw any crassness in his words, she managed to ignore it. 'Would she like children, one day?'

'Maybe,' he said, guardedly. 'When she's ready.'

'Of course, 'then after a pause, added, 'I suppose that after what happened, she'd rather just focus on her singing.'

'That's part of it.

'How is her voice by the way? Is it fully recovered yet?'

Carver nodded. 'Pretty much. She's due some final tests next week, so we're crossing fingers. There's a folk festival coming up in Lisbon in a couple of weeks and she's hoping to be there if everything's okay.'

'Good. I'm pleased for her.'

Carver didn't need to check that she wasn't being ironic. If Angie's mother ever resented the fact that Rosanna had survived, where her daughter had not - and who could blame her if she did - she never let it show. It reminded him of how Angie was, after Edmund Hart did what he did to her - stoic. But Sue wasn't quite done fishing yet.

'If she's from a big family, I expect she'll want some herself, someday.'

'Like I say, when she's ready.'

Sue got the message.

A minute passed, then, 'So. What about you?'

Carver reached for his coffee, relieved that at that moment, the boy on the bike was wobbling down towards them.

'That's great, Jason. Keep going.'

As Rosanna helped the six-year old make the turn, Carver threw her a smile. And he was surprised when the one she returned triggered the sort of buzz he used to get when looked at him that way. But that only made him realise how long it had been, and guilt swooped in to temper the moment.

In no rush to answer Sue's question, he waited until pupil and teacher were heading back up the garden before turning to meet the gaze he could feel, waiting. For a split second, it was like seeing Angie again. Her eyes, the mouth. And he had to work at not reacting the way he sometimes did those occasions they had Jason, and his brain played tricks and let him imagine that the woman playing with him was his mother, not Rosanna. He sometimes needed a good hour before the effects of such episodes fully passed. This close, he could see, clearly, the sadness that would now always be there, though she was getting better at disguising it. Still, he wondered if it was just a little less pronounced. For all that she, her family, had been through, Jason was a happy kid.

As he thought on words that might give her at least some of what she was seeking, he realised that for all its apparent innocence, her, *'what about you?'* was like quicksand. On the surface innocuous, but beneath, undercurrents that would drag him down. In this case, there was only one, but it was already clawing at him.

To be fair, it was coming on three months since she'd last broached the subject that had hung like a pall since the horror of Angie's death. During that time, it had grown heavier. Jason would be entering Year Three at school in a few months. His future could no longer be planned, 'on the hoof'. Decisions needed to be made. The question was, who should make them? And before that, another to be answered, one that was for him and him alone - as many sleepless nights could attest.

It hadn't mattered when Angie was alive. That was clear from the day she learned she had conceived around the time of that fateful night she encountered Edmund Hart. Catholic, like her mother, termination was never an option. Carver tried raising the subject, but only once. He didn't try again. By then, whatever they'd had together was already diminishing. Hart had seen to that. But Angie was strong, and determined. For her, the father's identity wasn't important. Jason was hers, and that was all that mattered. He remembered his surprise when he first realised that, despite the life she had led, her faith was still so strong within her. Besides, by then a new life beckoned, courtesy of Witness Protection. And though she made clear that Carver, being the other candidate, could play a part in it if he wished, she didn't insist. In the end, unsure what was best for either of them, confused by her apparent willingness to embrace single motherhood, he fudged it. He promised her all the support he could give her, but in the absence of any signal that she needed more, went no further. Since then, he'd reflected on it, endlessly. There were times he thought he'd done no more than give her what she really wanted - a new life, free of him. Other times, he cursed whatever had stopped him taking the steps that would have eliminated all doubt, and provided the certainty to which they were both entitled. Of course, he could point to what he was going through at the time as excuses for his failure, but deep down he suspected that was all they amounted to. Excuses.

And it was clear the day of Angie's funeral, that the matter would have to be resolved, one day. Coming away from the crematorium, having declined Sue's invitation - gracious in the circumstances - to join the family back at the house for refreshments. Angie's father, Paul, collared him on the car park. Carver had known that Paul Kendrick was struggling since the day Carver turned up on their doorstep to deliver the terrible news personally, having made it his duty to do so. And when Kendrick came up behind him on the car park, grabbed his arm and spun him around to face him, Carver knew his suspicions were right. Kendrick was a man on the edge, his grief and anger in danger of spilling over into something worse. And Carver didn't shy away when Kendrick put his face close enough that he could feel his spittle as he voiced his feelings.

'You killed her, Carver. I don't care about that bitch you've charged, or what happens in court. As far as I'm concerned, you were responsible.' He followed it up with his equally bitter demand, reinforced by a jabbing finger. 'And it's time you did what you damn-well should have done years ago. Take a fucking paternity test. At least then we'll know which bastard is his father, you, or that murdering psycho.'

It was a shocking accusation, brutal in its intensity. And it had a profound effect. Not only did it rattle Carver enough that he barely managed a couple of hundred yards before he had to pull off the main road while he waited for the shakes to go away, but it rooted itself and stayed, defying all attempts to dislodge it. And though the atmosphere that now prevailed whenever Carver visited Jason was less charged than it once was - Sue Kendrick was a born conciliator - her husband's words that day were never far from Carver's mind. Whether by design or chance, Sue made sure he and Paul were never alone together.

But for all that Carver was yet to put all that had happened into any sort of frame of reference that made sense, her mother's question deserved an answer. The trouble was, however much he wanted to be able to give her some clarity, the best he could offer right now was another 'fudge'.

'I'm not there yet, Sue,' he said. 'I'm getting there, I think. I just need you to bear with me a little while longer.'

She nodded, slowly, turning her gaze on the pair careering about the garden before coming back to him. 'I'll be sixty this year. Paul's sixty-seven. He wasn't in the best of health before… Now he's … Well, let's just say I've always been the strong one. We can give Jason what he needs, for now. But there'll come a time when-'

'I understand,' Carver said.

'I'm not trying to pressure you, Jamie, not like Paul. But I… We… *You,* need to make a decision. It can't wait much longer.'

He looked deep into her face. He wanted her to know he understood. He said the words softly. 'I know.'

She bit her lip. 'Well alright then.' She returned to her grandson's play.

Carver looked at her a while longer, thinking on whether he should say more. But he had no words. He drank his coffee.

Heading home, Rosanna broke the silence.

'So what were you and Sue talking about?'

He stared ahead of him, tried to make it sound innocent. 'When?'

'When I was helping him on his bike.'

He rocked his head from side to side. The conversation was still bouncing around inside it, yet to settle. 'She was just asking about Jason.'

'What about him?'

'You know…' He shrugged. '…Stuff.' *Jesus Christ. Is that the best you can come up with?*

'Stuff?'

'Yeah, just… stuff.'

She sighed, turned square on to him in the passenger seat. 'Now tell me what you were actually talking about.'

He tried to bluff it. 'What do you mean? We were just-'

'I saw the look on your face, and hers. Tell me.'

He shook his head. Thought about blocking her. That never worked.

'She wanted to know if I'd made a decision yet.'

'And have you?'

'You know I haven't. We've talked about it.

'No. You've avoided it. You're still avoiding it.'

'No I'm not.'

'Yes you are. You're avoiding it right now.'

'I'm not.'

'So tell me then. What's your decision?'

'For Chrissakes Ros, I-'

'Don't blaspheme, just answer the question. If you're not avoiding making a decision, then tell me what it is.'

'I've not actually- I'm still…'

'Yes?'

He sighed. 'Look, there's work I'm doing that still… has a bearing on things. When it's finished-'

'What sort of work? Please do not tell me it involves *Her*? I thought all that was finished?'

'It was, is. This is just some… loose ends. It doesn't involve her. Well, not directly. Like I say, when-'

'Whatever work you are doing, it cannot be more important than Jason.' Then she added, 'Or us.'

About to pick up where she'd interrupted, he stopped. He turned to look at her. Her face was set. In that moment he realised.

When he first agreed his secondment to the National Crime Agency's Intelligence Unit, it had made perfect sense. After all he'd been through - the Worshipper Enquiry, Angie, Megan Crane, what she did to him and Rosanna, the trial - an intelligence role seemed just the sort of time-out he needed to get his head straight. And a mainly office-hours desk-job meant he was ideally placed to take on the other analysis that needed doing.

'Important and essential work,' they'd all said. 'Highly politically sensitive,' was another phrase. Considering the names being bandied about at the time, they were bang on. And given his history, no one was better placed than him. So he agreed. That was twelve months ago. A lot had happened since. But they were right. What he had discovered - was *still* discovering - *was* 'politically sensitive', more than anyone could imagine. It *was* important work. It *did* need doing. But whether it needed doing by him any longer, that was something else.

He thought about what Rosanna had said.

He thought about Jason.

He thought about her, *'Or us.'*

Which was when the dull throb in his temples that he knew would stay and worsen over the course of the rest of the day, began to make itself felt.

CHAPTER 3

'This is *sooo* fucking weird.'

Acting-Detective Inspector Gavin Baggus paused in his appraisal of the solicitor's body to glance up at the man who had spoken. The look on D.S. Stu Willoughby's face recalled his own first encounter with the form of death they'd been called to assess that late afternoon. Back then, he was a lot younger than Stu was now, still in his probation in fact. He remembered how the dark imagery, not to mention the confusion it triggered, had lingered for weeks. At least Stu had heard of it, before seeing it the first time. Then again, Stu was one of those rare things in CID. A church-going, straight-as-they-come, family man.

Might take him a while as well, Baggus thought.

Baggus had known Stu nearly all his service - close to twelve years now. Up to six weeks before, they'd shared the same rank, DS, in the same CID unit. That changed when their DI of the last two years reported sick with a viral infection which everyone knew was actually a breakdown brought on by a messy discipline enquiry threatening to ruin his retirement. Baggus was moved up to fill in pending his return, though the rumours he'd heard about the evidence now emerging about his former boss's connections with the Jameson clan, meant that was looking increasingly doubtful. And though Baggus and Stu remained friends, they were both still trying to get their heads round their redefined relationship.

Like now.

Baggus knew that right now, he should be pointing out to his colleague the tell-tale signs - just as someone did with him, all those years ago. Even now, some ten years on, Baggus could remember how he'd had to work to keep the panic out of his voice when he'd radioed his Control Room to let them know the, 'Sudden Death' he'd been called to had all the markings of a possible, "Number One", the official Home Office Crime Classification for Murder. The Detective Inspector who arrived at the scene shortly after, had wasted no time putting him right.

'Any signs of a forced entry?'

'I haven't found any.'

'Any signs of violence?'

'Er, no. But the way he's tied up-'

'Any signs of a struggle?'

'None that I can see, but-'

'So what do you think was cause of death?'

'Looking at him, suffocation, I assume.'

'Caused by the plastic bag over his head.'

'Well, yeah.'

'So you think someone tied him up, put a bag over his head and left him like that?'

'What else could it be?'

The DI pointed to the small key on the end of the length of string dangling an inch or two above the handcuffs around the man's wrists. 'What do you make of that?'

Baggus stared at it. He'd seen it of course, but having no frame of reference had promptly ignored it. Something for the CID to work out. 'Er… dunno.'

'Do you think he might have been trying to reach for the key when he died?'

'Possibly.'

'So who put the key there?'

'Er… whoever tied him up?'

'At least we agree on one thing. And who do you think that was?'

Baggus shrugged. 'How would I know?'

'Have you checked the body?'

'Only for vitals. There aren't any.'

'What about between his legs?'

'What?'

'Have you checked between his legs, his dick?'

'What for?'

The DI bent to the body, beckoned Baggus to join him. Careful so as not to disturb anything, he eased the body onto its side, exposing the naked underbelly. 'What do you see?'

Baggus stared down, trying to work it out. 'He's… got a hard-on.'

'And why do you think that might be?'

Baggus shook his head, trying to think of something that would make sense.

At that point, the older Detective Sergeant who'd arrived with the DI and had been snooping around the bedroom as they spoke called to them. They both turned. He was standing next to the man's bed, holding up a plastic bag. Baggus could see it contained magazines, DVDs, even some old videotapes. The DS took out one of the mags, held it up for them to see. The cover showed a man tied in a manner not dissimilar to the dead man, even down to the plastic bag. Baggus vaguely remembered seeing stuff like it during his initial training. Very different to the sort he and his schoolmates used to laugh over behind the gym. He had found it… disquieting.

The DI turned to Baggus. 'Ever heard of Auto-Erotic-Asphyxiation?'

'I'm, er, not sure…'

'Well you have now.'

Baggus had listened, as the DI explained. It was one of those times when a secondary school-educated son of a production worker, whose main interests are beer and rugby realises he's now in a job where he's going to come across stuff most never get to hear about, never mind have to deal with.

'So is this typical then?'

As Stu Willoughby's question echoed his own of all those years ago, Baggus snapped back to the here and now. He was about to answer when a voice from across the room beat him to it.

'There's no such thing as, 'typical', Sergeant Willoughby. But if you mean are there features that are commonly associated with cases of Auto-Erotic Asphyxiation, then the answer is, yes.'

Both men turned. Over by the window, next to Clem Squire, the uniformed sergeant who'd called them to the scene, a slightly-built Asian man with bucked teeth and wearing a loud, check-jacket, was writing into a small notebook. Baggus turned back to Stu.

'In other words, it's typical.'

The man stopped scribbling to glower at them. 'I'm afraid to have to say, Mr Baggus-Sir, that *that* is typical of the lazy thinking that nowadays characterises so much police investigation work in this primitive country of yours. It is no wonder that so few crimes are prosecuted to conviction when those charged with carrying out a thorough investigation apply reductive phrases that infer assumptions that are not supported by actual evidence.'

Willoughby looked at Baggus. 'What's he talking about?'

Baggus shrugged. 'Haven't a fucking clue. He's Maldivian.'

Willoughby made an *Oh-I-See* face. 'I thought he was a Police Surgeon.'

The uniformed sergeant chuckled.

Baggus shook his head. 'There was a time when Police Surgeons spoke English.'

The Maldivian turned to Clem Squire. 'You see, Sergeant? That is an example of the sort of racist bullying that we are told we must report to the officer's senior manager.' He turned back to Baggus, pen poised. 'Please tell me the name of your superior officer so I can write it down in my little book.'

'Fuck off,' Willoughby said.

'Mickey Mouse,' Baggus said. *Time to move things along.*

'Now, *Mister Qasim Ibrahim-Sir,* when you've finished writing in your *little book* perhaps you can apply your British Government-subsidised medical training to this case and give us your thoughts, so we can wrap it up and call the undertakers?' Opening his jacket, he showed the ticket stubs with their distinctive Gloucester Rugby Club logo, lodged in the inside pocket. 'I need to be at Kingsholm by seven.'

The surgeon, shook his head, gravely. 'I can never understand how a supposedly rational human being can choose to waste precious hours of his limited time on this planet, following a crap team like Gloucester. Now Saracens, that is different.'

'Just get on with it.'

'Yeah,' Willoughby said. 'What are these, 'features' you mention.'

With a sigh, the police surgeon slipped his notebook into his jacket pocket, then crossed to stand next to the detectives, looking down at the body. Suddenly, all trace of humour evaporated. Ibrahim eyed both men, then began.

'For the record. In my opinion, the way the body is tied, in what I believe is called a hogtie position? And wearing a woman's stocking over his head, and what look like female panties, there seems to be clear evidence of some sexual motivation having been present prior to death.'

'That's fucking brilliant,' Stu said.

Ibrahim ignored it. 'The presence of the magazine in front of the body, open at a page showing a photograph of a man tied in a similar manner, would support that observation.'

'Agreed,' Baggus said.

'Looking at the rope running from his neck to the doorknob, I note that the knot at the back of the neck is not a slipknot. That would suggest that the deceased did not intend to strangle himself, which would tend to rule against any intent to commit suicide.' He paused to look at the two men, both silent now. Baggus nodded.

'The scissors on the floor next to the man's right knee is in the sort of position where it might fall if it had been in his hand at some stage, but slipped from his grasp.'

Willoughby shot Baggus a look.

'To cut the rope,' Baggus said.

Willoughby shook his head. '*Jesus*. How fucking

dangerous is that?'

'*Very* dangerous, Mr Willoughby,' The surgeon said. 'If it goes wrong, as may be the case here, and he drops the scissors, there is nothing he can do. And although it is not a slipknot, he will not be able to keep his head up more than a few minutes, especially a man like him who is overweight and probably not very fit. Eventually the pressure on his windpipe will increase and he will strangle as effectively as if he'd hung himself.'

Willoughby gave a shudder. 'Crazy.'

'Absolutely,' Ibrahim said. 'But it is more commonly practised than most people think.'

'Not by me,' Willoughby said.

Baggus gave a wan smile. The look of distaste he'd seen in his colleague's face earlier was back. He turned to the uniformed sergeant.

'Any signs of forced entry, Clem? Doors, windows?'

The sergeant shook his head and in the west-country drawl for which he was famous, said, 'Narthin' at all, young Gavin.' Baggus allowed himself a smile. Squire was often described as, long-in-the-tooth. To him, everyone was 'young', including, on one memorable occasion, an Assistant Chief Constable. 'Waz his cleaner found him when she let hersel' in,' he concluded.

'No signs of a search? Nothing disturbed?'

Squire shook his head. 'Narthin'.'

Baggus turned to the police surgeon. 'What's the body say?'

The Maldivian looked down. 'I have not yet finished examining him, but there does not appear to be any signs of-'

'FUCK.'

Squire's shout came as he leapt back, followed by the others, as a blur of black and white shot from under the bed and out through the gap in the door. A moment later a yelp from the female PC on the front door indicated its trajectory.

'His cat,' Squire said, calming. 'Just his cat.' He breathed out, as did the others.

After a moment, Ibrahim said, 'As I was saying-'

Baggus held up a hand. 'Hang on.' He turned to Squire. 'Did you know the cat was there? Had you seen it before?'

'No,' the sergeant said. 'It must have been under the bed all the time. Bloody nearly shit myself.'

'Do we know he owns a cat?' Baggus said.

'Dotes on it, according to the cleaner,' Squire said. 'She said there was no sign of it when she arrived. I was wondering where it'd got to. Bugger. Now we'll have to catch it before we lock up. I'll go and tell young-'

'Hang on,' Baggus said. Positioning himself in the middle of the room, hands on hips, he flicked his gaze from the body to the bed and back again. Willoughby checked Ibrahim. His airy manner had also vanished.

Baggus turned to Squire. 'You said earlier that the bedroom door was closed when the cleaner got here and she only found him when she pushed her way in?'

'S'right,' Squire answered. 'What're you thinking?'

Baggus didn't reply, mind whirring. Eventually he said, 'I'm thinking, what sort of cat-lover shuts himself in his bedroom with his pet while he plays these sorts of games?'

For several moments, there was only silence as they all tried to imagine how the mind of someone who likes to suspend himself from a door handle with a rope around his neck, works under the circumstances.

'Maybe the cat's part of it?' Willoughby said.

As the pitying looks came his way he shrugged his

shoulders. *Any better ideas?*

But Baggus seemed to give it serious consideration. 'It would have to be the best trained cat in the world to not get in the way while he's doing this stuff.'

'There's something else,' Ibrahim said.

Baggus turned to see the surgeon down next to the body, reaching under the dead man's belly. He looked up at Baggus. 'You said you've seen two before like this?'

Baggus nodded.

'Where they erect?'

He nodded again. Turned to Willoughby. 'They call it "Angel Lust".'

'Mine too,' the surgeon said. 'You see it often with hanging victims, even judicial executions. In some, it lasts until the post-mortem.'

'And he's…?' Baggus waited.

'Ice cream,' Ibrahim said, coming to his feet.

Baggus threw him a puzzled look.

'Mr Softy,' he explained, the toothy grin showing.

For almost a minute Baggus stared at him. The others waited. Eventually, he remembered the tickets nestling inside his jacket.

'Ahh, fuck.'

CHAPTER 4

As the silence stretched, so did Ellen Hazelhurst's feeling of discomfort. As Governor of Her Majesty's Prison Stigwood, she had put the proposal to the inmate sitting across the other side of her desk as her duty required her to. It was now the other woman's turn to speak. Ellen had expected she would reject it outright, at the very least come back with some blistering comment. But so far all she'd done was sit there, wearing the patient half-smile Ellen had seen before. It triggered doubts that made Ellen wonder if the offer was so way-off it didn't warrant a response at all, and that the inmate was simply waiting for Ellen to catch up and realise it. *So bloody annoying.* A bit like the way she always managed to look like she'd just come straight from some salon, rather than the high-security block that was now her home. It wasn't the first, nor even second time she'd made Ellen feel this way.

That very first day, when Ellen had her paraded in her office so she could deliver the address she gave to all all new lifers, she'd found the woman's self-composure off-putting. And this was right after she'd been through the normally humbling experience of medicals and body searches. Her second one-to-one a few weeks later, to introduce the Minnesota thing, went no better. As before, Ellen came away feeling she had failed in her objective; to make clear that here at Stigwood, there was room for only one authority figure - herself. Nor was she alone in finding the woman, 'difficult'. Even the normally unflappable Board of Trustees seemed to lose their intimidating edge the day they made their surprising - and still controversial - decision. Normally they only considered written pleadings for Special Concessions. In the case of the woman sitting opposite however, they somehow found reason to waive the rule and allow her a personal hearing.

As she waited, Ellen was conscious that she needed to be careful. It was important she avoid saying or doing anything that might undermine her hard-earned reputation as someone who treated her charges fairly, but could still clamp down when circumstances dictated. In this regard, she liked to ensure that those under her care learned, early, that if they failed to respect the trust she was always prepared to give on first meeting, they would see the side to her that said, *You had your chance, my turn.* And the P.O.s who worked for her were happy to ensure that during prisoners' 'settlement periods', her messages were reinforced, as forcefully as circumstances dictated. But right now, Ellen had the sense that, several months into her seven, concurrent life sentences, Megan Crane was yet to take those messages on board.

Wary that if something didn't happen soon, her discomfort may start to show, Ellen gave things a push. 'Is there anything I've said that isn't clear? Would you like me to go over any of it again?'

Megan Crane's response was to let the patient smile

fade, replaced by the sort of frown someone wears when they are working through a problem that is particularly sensitive. Eventually, she spoke.

'Let me check if I've got this right. This researcher-' She leaned forward to check the name under the signature on the letter Ellen had slid across the desk for her inspection.

'Lydia Grant,' Ellen prompted. 'Doctor Lydia Grant.'

'Doctor Lydia Grant,' Megan said, as if Ellen had not spoken. 'She wants to come here with her needles and probes, wire me up to her machines, and try to find out what makes me tick. Is that the essence of it?'

Ellen shifted in her seat. The woman had a way of twisting things so that even the most straightforward situations could be made to sound sinister. 'I think, 'needles and probes' is a bit of an exaggeration, but-'

The striking eyebrows arched upwards. 'You think so? How else do you think she intends to get inside my brain? A nice chat over tea and cupcakes?'

'Well, I imagine she will-'

'Have you ever met this, Lydia Grant?'

'No, but she's working on behalf of the Home Office, so I assume she's-'

Oh I see. So because she's working on behalf of the Home Office, that means her methods are fully approved, does it?'

'What I'm saying is-'

'Forgive me, Ellen- You don't mind me calling you Ellen, do you? My understanding is, it doesn't matter what you say. It's what I say that matters here, whether or not I am prepared to be a subject for this-. What is it exactly, a study? A project? Some sort of experiment?'

'I would say it's a study rather than a project. But I'm not sure it matters whether its-'

"You're not sure? Dear me. Ellen, you're the Governor of this establishment I believe?'

Ellen stared at her.

'That being the case, I'm not sure you should be admitting to inmates that you are not sure about things, especially when they may have a bearing on an inmate's well-being.'

About to reply, Ellen realised, and stopped herself. *There. That's exactly what she does. And I'm bloody falling for it. Again.* She took a deep breath, eased herself back in her chair. As she did so, Megan Crane eased back in hers, the half-smile returning.

For long seconds, the two women remained still and silent, both aware of the game they had just played, and who had been on top when it ended.

Wary of exposing herself further, Ellen put on her most professional face. She sat up, nodded. 'I've explained what Doctor Grant is proposing, Megan. At least as far as I can based upon the information in her letter. At this stage I cannot assist further as regards exactly how she will conduct her study. All I can say is that these days, the Home Office is as strapped for cash as everyone. If they are funding her research, they must think it is important.'

'Important to whom?'

Ellen paused, recognising the need for caution again. Before the meeting, she had resolved that however much she might favour cooperating with the Home Office - word was that the London-based 'Central Resource Coordinator' role she had her eye on would be coming vacant in the coming months - she needed to be seen as neutral in the matter.

'Important to society's wider understanding of why some people engage in types of behaviours that society classifies as, "criminal".'

Just for a second, Megan Crane looked as if she was about to break a smile. 'Bravo, Governor. You managed to put that in such a way that even I find it difficult to take offence.'

Ellen waited, careful not to acknowledge what could be a piss-take as much as a compliment. Eventually she said, 'It's your choice Megan. You can either agree to take part, or tell me you are not interested.'

Ellen waited. The silence stretched. Eventually the woman spoke.

'If I do agree, what do I get out if it?'

Again, Ellen hesitated, but she saw the glimmer of an opportunity to claim back some ground.

'You've been here now, how long? Seven months?' Megan nodded 'And this is your first time in prison.' Another nod. 'So tell me. How do you think we run things here? Not just Stigwood, but prisons generally?'

Megan's eyes narrowed. 'When you say, "run things", what are you talking about?'

'I mean how do we keep things running when, in places like this, there are clearly far more inmates than guards? I'm talking about how people in my position, my staff, those in authority, how we maintain order and discipline.?'

'Go on, I'm listening.'

'Give and take, Megan. It's as simple as that. Or if you prefer, you scratch my back, I'll - we'll, scratch yours.' The smile again. This time Ellen took it as a positive sign. She continued. 'Take parole. There's no automatic right to time-off for good behaviour anymore. However, the decision whether to grant an inmate parole after serving a proportion of their sentence can still be affected by prison reports. It may be that when the time comes, it would be in an inmate's interests to make sure those reports are favourable.'

'In my case, I rather doubt that the question of parole will ever arise.'

'Maybe, maybe not. But there are other considerations.'

'Such as?'

'Such as… your current detention regime.'

'You mean this Minnesota thing?'

Ellen tried to sound matter-of-fact as she made her point. 'As you are aware, the Minnesota Study showed that when long-term prisoners are granted a degree of autonomy over the routines and conditions governing their detention, not only do they benefit as individuals, but the pressures on prison staff also ease, quite considerably it seems.'

'I am aware. How is it relevant to this discussion?'

'The Prison Department chose Stigwood as one of the evaluation sites to see if the Minnesota findings can be replicated in UK prisons. However, the decision as to which inmates take part, rests with me. Right now, you are one of them. It doesn't necessarily follow that will always be the case.'

Megan Crane's features morphed into an expression of mock-shock. 'Why, Ellen, surely you are not trying to blackmail me?'

Ellen waved the accusation away. 'Nothing of the sort. I am simply helping someone who is new to the prison system understand the complexities of detention decisions and the factors that may have a bearing upon them in the future.'

Megan Crane gave a thoughtful nod. Eventually she said, 'Would I be correct in assuming that you have some personal interest in my agreeing to cooperate with this Lydia Grant's research?'

Ellen played it straight. 'I assure you, I am entirely neutral in the matter.'

'Of course you are,' Megan said.

Ellen returned her a blank stare.

After a further period of silence, Megan drew a long breath. 'Alright. I'll do it.'

Ellen remained still. Despite her pointing out the realities of prison life, she'd have laid money that, given Megan's grudges against the Powers That Be, she would never go for it.

'On two conditions.'

Here it comes. Ellen leaned forward. 'And they would be?'

'In return for allowing access to my 'rather singular psyche,' as you so tactfully put it earlier, I want a full set of make-up. My specifications and I'll pay for it.'

Ellen sat back, thought about it. *What the hell*. 'And the other?' She was still unsure if the killer was being entirely serious.

'I want the services of a decent stylist instead of that topiarist who comes here once a week.'

'That's all? Makeup and hair?'

Megan smiled one of her seductive smiles. 'Life in HMP Stigwood may have its restrictions, but that's no excuse for not looking one's best during the time one is here.'

For all that Ellen Hazelhurst's thoughts were turning more and more these days to her career post-Stigwood, she was experienced, and good at her job. Another day and in other circumstances, she may have read in Megan Crane's words an intimation - slight perhaps, but discernible to someone paying attention - that she had not yet accepted the fact that, for her, there would never be life beyond prison. But Ellen was already thinking about how nice it would be to re-visit her old haunts around Prison Department HQ on a more regular basis than her infrequent conferencing trips to the capital presently allowed for.

Ellen's face, which for the most part had remained expressionless throughout the meeting, split into a friendly smile. 'I can't see any of that being a problem.'

CHAPTER 5

Carver's mobile had only two caller-specific ring tones. He was responsible for neither. One was the opening bars of *Rapsoda No 1*- one of Ros's favourites. The other was the theme tune to the sixties TV classic, *The Avengers,* which he found particularly embarrassing and wanted to change, but wasn't sure how. It was the latter that started playing as he watched Ros disappear through Manchester's Terminal Two Departure Gate Twenty-Three, having wangled himself an air-side pass through an old Airport Police colleague. He was glad it hadn't rung moments before. Ros's first time away since it all happened, he'd never known her so emotional before a trip. He'd found it more unsettling than he expected.

He tried to sound normal. 'Hey you, what's happening?'

'Where are you?' Jess Greylake said, clearly picking up on the background noise.

'The airport. Just seeing Ros off to Lisbon. She's going to a music festival.'

'Singing?'

'Yep.'

'That's great. I'm glad to hear she's so much better-'

Voice maybe. Not everything.

'How's the house-hunting going?'

He stifled his initial response. 'Don't ask. I'm beginning to wish we'd stayed where we were.'

'Oh.'

He was glad she knew enough not to delve, and wasn't the, '*Told you,*' type. Looking for a new home because you need something bigger is one thing. Doing so to escape what they'd been through, is something else.

'What's up?' he said.

'I got a call off a Gloucestershire DI yesterday. He's got a death he thinks is a bit iffy. Someone you've flagged on PNC.'

'Who is it?'

'A solicitor. Quentin Quinlan?'

Carver recalled the name. When he first came across, 'Q', he'd wondered if it was a cryptic reference to some sort of James Bond connection. 'I remember him. What're the circs?'

'On the face of it, accidental A.E.A. But he's not sure. A bit like the Nottingham thing, I guess'.

Carver nodded. A couple of months before, another of his 'Of-Interests' had died when his car left the road one night in the middle of Sherwood Forest. It rang alarms until a blood test showed the man was three times over the limit.

Jess continued. 'He wants to run it past us. Just for an opinion, he says.'

'Fair enough. When?'

'He's coming up the day after tomorrow.'

'Do you need me there?'

'Not unless you want to be. The way he describes it, I suspect he's chasing shadows. I can give you a call if I think there's anything in it, if you like?'

'Fine with me. Everything else okay?'

'If you mean, is the Northern Area CID coping without you, then the answer's 'yes'.

He gave a, 'Humph,' but couldn't stop the wry half-smile. Jess was aware of his mixed feelings over his move, even if it was supposed to be temporary. That said,the different mind-set required for Intelligence work, was actually proving useful in his other, Analysis Project.

'Give Alec my regards,' he said.

'I will.' She hung up.

As he headed back to the Security Gate, Carver's mind sifted through the images Jess's call had conjured. Sections of a chart projected onto the wall of an office down the corridor from his swam before him. In his head, he located Quinlan's box in a the lower right quadrant. Several connectors ran from it, joining with others, before moving on. He followed them. One of the strands led to a box he'd added only after lengthy consideration, and with some degree of trepidation. But it was part of the big picture and, whatever misgivings he had about acknowledging the individual's connection with the matters he was charting, he could not afford to leave it out. As Intelligence People like to point out, *Good or Bad, Intell is Intell.* He still liked to think that time would prove it to be the product of someone's over-active imagination. Either that or a libellous lie.

But now, as he thought about 'Q', and what it could mean if it turned out his death wasn't as accidental as first thought, he felt the first stirrings of a familiar tightness in the pit of his stomach.

CHAPTER 6

The burly, Scottish DS who collected Baggus from Warrington Police Station's Reception seemed a man of few words. It wasn't until he gained the first turn of the wide, stone staircase, following the sign for, "CID Suite", that the man who'd introduced himself simply as, 'Alec,' showed any real interest. Without turning, he tossed the question over his shoulder.

'Werdjya say yer frae?'

'Gloucester,' Baggus said.

'Issat near Chelt'nham?'

'Close.' Baggus said.

'Aye,' the Scot said. 'Bin there once.'

'Gloucester?'

'Chelt'nham. Bit snooty for ma taste.'

Baggus managed a half-smile, not sure if the dour-Scot thing was real, or for effect.

'Ha'e yer met her before?'

'No. We've just spoken on the phone.'

For the first time, the D.S. paused in his plodding ascent. Turning, he looked down on the younger man. The look on his face set Baggus in mind of a father checking out his daughter's new date.

'Yer'll probably find her interestin' then.'

As the man resumed his climb, Baggus regarded the broad expanse of back, spotted with sweat patches. *What does that mean?*

A minute later, the DS showed him into an empty office.

'She's with the gov'nor. Be w'you shortly.'

Left alone, Baggus took in his surroundings. One of those nowadays rare, red-brick, Victorian police stations, Warrington evokes images of gas-lamps and chin-strap wearing Dixon-of-Dock-Green types. But so far, Baggus was finding the inside surprisingly unimpressive. Apart from the stairs and high ceilings, there was little of the Victorian grandeur that he'd expected. The office he was now in was a case in point. Plain, square, and simply painted in yucky-green, it wasn't so different to his own in Gloucester's Area HQ building - a boring, seventies' concrete and glass affair. Nothing about it told him anything about its occupant. No wall pictures. No pot plants. The only 'desk paraphernalia' was a framed photograph of a late-middle-aged man with grey hair and smiling eyes. As he wondered about it, he realised something else. For a working DI's office, there was a marked absence of paper. His own office was awash with the stuff. Most days he drowned in it. The scourge of modern-day police work. Yet he couldn't see as much as a single crime file. In fact it was probably the tidiest CID office he'd ever been in. He crossed to look out of the window, but the only view was of a sloping roof covered in grey slates. Another difference. His looked out over Gloucester's bustling Dock Basin.

'Nice view, isn't it?'

He turned.

Framed in the doorway, Acting Detective Inspector

Jess Greylake looked sharp and business-like in a dark blue suit and white blouse, set off by a simple gold neck-chain. Her sandy hair was shoulder-length and cut in a style that was practical, but feminine. Tall and slim, he sensed that, unlike some he knew, she wasn't the sort who felt the need to play on her good looks.

'Gavin Baggus?' He nodded. 'Jess Greylake.'

As he came forward to take the outstretched hand, her smile caught him, along with the hazel eyes she immediately used to give him the once-over. Straight away, Baggus realised. She was not at all the battered-around-the-edges divisional DI he had been expecting. As he settled in the chair she indicated, and she made a point of taking the one opposite rather than sitting behind her desk, he noticed her shoes. It made him wonder how she managed if she ever had to chase someone.

For the first few minutes, they went through the, Do-You-Know/Have-You-Met? routine detectives often play when they first meet - a by-product of all the training courses. She offered him coffee, and he was surprised when she picked up the phone and spoke to Alec, asking if he'd mind? When Alec arrived with two mugs a few minutes later, Baggus wasn't sure if the look in the Scot's face when he said, 'Widjer like anythin' else Ma'am?' - was tongue-in-cheek or not.

'That's all for now, Alec. Thanks.'

As he closed the door behind him, he threw Baggus a wink.

Turning back, Baggus found her wearing an expression that made him wonder if there was some game going on between her and Alec to which he wasn't privy. And as they spoke further, swapping pleasantries and touching on the difficulties that come with Acting-up before getting down to business, he began to find her open scrutiny unsettling. The way she kept cocking an eyebrow at things he said, as if doubting his word, was almost off-putting. But then his experience of women wasn't as extensive as a thirty-five-year old, single, Acting Detective Inspector's might be. Perhaps his brother and sister-in-law were right when they said he should devote less time to rugby and more to finding a girlfriend. Eventually, conversation turned to the matter that had brought him north.

As he unzipped his document case he said, 'Is DCI Carver not around?'

She shook her head. 'He's on attachment right now. NCA Intelligence. That's why we're all acting up.'

'You're expecting him back?'

There was the slightest of pauses. 'Hopefully.'

He noted the uncertainty. Before coming, he'd read as much as he could concerning the 'Worshipper Case,' and the man around whom, according to the accounts, it had all revolved. Fascinating though they were, he suspected that what wasn't recorded was probably even more so. It made him wonder about the reasons behind his 'attachment', especially considering how Carver had nearly died.

He dug out a bundle of photographs and passed them across. 'This is how we found him.'

She took a minute to study them.

'It *looks* classic, AEA,' she said.

Baggus nodded. 'My boss still thinks it is.'

'What makes you think otherwise?' She sat back in her chair. *Convince me.*

Baggus drew a breath, then described what they'd found at the scene of Quentin Quinlan's death. As he spoke, she held his gaze in a way which, again, he found unsettling, though wasn't sure why. When he finished, he sat back and waited, glad it was her turn to show herself.

To Baggus, it was the sort of thing any detective worth their salt would get. If she was just some high-flier being given a taste of CID so that when her Chief needs someone to shake the department up, he can point to her 'experience', she would probably see it as all in his imagination, like his own Detective Superintendent, Wilf Robinson had. But she had sounded okay on the phone, and so far, he had the impression she knew what she was talking about. Nevertheless, Baggus was conscious that something about her seemed to have awoken some prejudice he didn't know he had about the sort of women who make good investigators. The thought came that her main interests had to lie outside police work.

'A cat?' she said, eventually, staring at him. 'You called it as sus because of a cat?'

Baggus didn't let her doubtful tone throw him. Robinson had reacted the same way, others too. Baggus replayed the response he'd given when Robinson called him back to the office to explain, 'Why the fuck,' he had called forensic without informing him first.

'That and the lack of-'

'An erection,' she finished. 'Yes, you mentioned that too.'

The look in her face prompted a moment's self-doubt. It wasn't the first. For what seemed minutes, her gaze wavered between him and the photographs he'd produced as she chewed on her bottom lip and tapped her nails on the desk. Watching her, Baggus felt a certainty growing which he couldn't explain. She *was* seeing it - maybe as clearly as him - which was good.

But just as strong, was the sense that she was reluctant to acknowledge it, almost like she was scared to, which had to be bad. It made him wonder what there was to be nervous about. After several minutes' chewing, tapping and musing, she rose and crossed to the window looking out over the slate roof.

'Okay.' She folded her arms. 'Let's assume, just for a moment, someone did him.' She span round so fast he nearly jumped. 'What makes you think it has anything to do with Megan Crane?'

He swallowed. 'The marker on Q's PNC record refers to him being of interest to Operation Kerry. That's why I contacted you in the first place.'

She nodded. 'We flagged several members of her circle prior to the trial. We were trying to put the full picture together. Still are in fact. So he knew her. It doesn't mean there's a connection with his death.'

'Not directly. But we know now he had money problems and his PA is convinced he was involved in something shady. The week before he died he took some strange telephone calls he was keen she didn't overhear.'

'Wouldn't that be normal for a solicitor?'

He nodded. It wasn't any single thing. It had to be looked at in the round. 'And he was keeping something in his safe he wouldn't let her get near, let alone see.'

'Solicitors keep all kinds of confidential stuff for their clients. I don't see how it suggests anything, shady.'

'She also says he lied about his movements. Not just to her, but his partners as well. She knows because she tried to contact him a couple of times and he wasn't where he said he'd be.'

'But you said yourself he had some strange interests. Maybe he-.'

'I think he was blackmailing someone.'

Whatever hypothesis she'd been about to propose seemed to slip away as her eyes narrowed. She returned to her chair.

'Go on.'

'His PA overhead snippets of two conversations. Both times when he was using a mobile instead of his office phone. During the first, he told whoever he was talking to, "Think about the consequences." She's positive he wasn't giving legal advice.'

She stuck her bottom lip out. 'The other conversation?'

'The day he died he was using a voice recorder when he took a call on his mobile. The first part of the call recorded.' Her eyebrows lifted. 'It was a man. All we got was him saying, "Tell me where. Tell me when," which sounds a bit unusual.'

'Have you still got the recording?'

He shook his head. 'His PA wiped it. She didn't know anything had happened until the following day. It's with the lab, but even if we retrieve the message, it won't give us its origin.'

She picked up a pen, started to turn it, slowly, in her fingers. 'Anything else?'

He nodded, sat forward. 'When he left that afternoon, his briefcase was full. It was empty when he was found. And though we recovered a mobile, we know he had another, which is missing.'

She nodded. 'So you think there could be something in Megan Crane's affairs that will shed light on his death?'

'I heard there was a lot didn't come out at the trial. My understanding is that the sort of things she was involved in are the sort some might be keen to keep out of the public eye.'

For long seconds, they regarded each other across the desk. Two DI's - *Acting* DIs -checking out how far to trust the other's instincts. If there'd been mind games before, there were none now. He wondered what was so hard. All he wanted was information. But she was no longer challenging his theory that Quentin Quinlan may have been murdered.

As he watched, her gaze turned to the photograph on her desk. She reached out and picked it up, studying it closely, as if it might contain answers to whatever questions were running through her mind. He was wondering about its significance, when she put it down. She sighed, then blinked, as if coming out of darkness into bright light. Then she pinned him with a stare that brought back memories of Mrs Lunt, the High-School Sciences teacher he and his fellow adolescents used to hold in awe.

'There are still some sensitivities around the Worshipper Case. Leave it with me. I'll get back to you.'

CHAPTER 7

Jess Greylake stared out at the grey roof beyond the window, remembering the times she'd caught Carver doing the same. She knew now what the attraction was. The blank landscape was conducive to pondering. And Gavin Baggus had given her much to ponder.

She'd never forgotten Carver's warning, soon after she joined the Operation Kerry Investigation. 'If you stay with it, this enquiry will change you, and in ways you can't imagine.' When she pressed him to expand, all she got was, 'You'll see.'

Well she had seen, and he was right. She *had* changed. For one thing, she was single again, despite Martin's attempts to come creeping back the week before the trial, begging forgiveness for his, 'little slip.' Martin being a TV documentary producer, the timing wasn't lost on her. When he realised that his old tricks no longer worked and that she had grown impervious to his charms, he even remarked on it. 'You're different,' he told her that final meeting. 'There's a coldness about you.' *Towards you maybe,* she had thought, but didn't deny it. By then she was already realising that the things she had seen, what she had learned, *had* affected her - maybe deeply. What she didn't know back then, was just *how*. Even now, eighteen months on, she was still finding out.

Certainly, her interests had changed. Same with the people she liked to hang out with. Somehow, the nights out with friends that used to be the ideal antidote to work, no longer drew her like they once did. She had discovered other places, more interesting, more stimulating, than the pubs and clubs she used to frequent.

Then there was the fall-out from the trial. 'It will go on for a while yet,' Carver had said, this right after she'd moaned about the string of requests for interviews, background information, and 'personal insights' into matters connected with the Worshipper Enquiry - for which read, Megan Crane. It was as well her finances were more or less stable - *Thanks Dad*. Some of the hints left dangling had been ridiculous. And Gavin Baggus was far from the first to turn up with some story about a crime, a suspect, a witness to a crime, or just a rumour which they believed connected with the case that held the country in thrall during the six weeks the trial lasted - and a similar period after.

During the time Megan Crane was pursuing her, "interests", she became known to many, either directly, or by reputation. Since the trial, several of her former "associates" had come forward, each with their own juicy tale to tell about some dark deed they believed the police may wish to investigate further. Up to now, they'd all proved baseless, driven either by agendas around money and/or sex, or rooted in fantasy. As she discovered after following up on some of the early stories, the sort of people who inhabit Megan Crane's strange world have fertile imaginations. Before meeting Baggus, Jess had expected that his story would prove similar. That having learned of a "Megan Crane connection", he had added two and two and got five. But within minutes of them meeting, her thoughts took a different turn.

For a start, Quentin Quinlan *did* have a strong connection with Megan Crane - and others of her circle. Carver had confirmed as much in an email earlier that morning. Furthermore, the circumstances of Q's death bore features that brought it within that circle's range of interests. Soon after Carver began delving into the material they recovered from her cellar, he had shown her a selection of the clips off one of the hard drives. His intention was to give her some idea of how far Megan's interests extended beyond those they saw during the Worshipper enquiry. She was shocked, and horrified. Up to that moment, Jess had believed she had the dominatrix more or less sussed. But after seeing the clips, she realised, her level of understanding barely scratched the surface. And having listened to Baggus, she had to admit, Quinlan's death *did* raise questions.

The other thing that was different, was Baggus himself.

Since first being drafted onto Operation Kerry, Jess had found that conversation about the case - particularly with men - tended to follow a pattern. Invariably they started out professional, focused on facts, evidence, cold analysis. All very, adult and professional. But at some stage - and it varied according to the rank and experience of the other party - an element of nudge-nudge, wink-wink would creep in. At some point - usually when talk turned to the sort of practises BDSM enthusiasts like to engage in - the knowing looks and leery smiles would begin. Eyebrows would raise. Double-entendres she had heard so many times would slip out. For all the changes in detective work in recent years, CID still attracts a high proportion of alpha-males. And as she had been reminded several times, disappointingly, many are incapable of talking about such matters without either, reverting to adolescence, or hinting, in some way, towards their, "prowess".

But Gavin Baggus had displayed no such tendencies. In relating the circumstances of Quentin Quinlan's death he stuck, rigidly, to the facts. If he had a personal view about those who practice AEA, he kept it himself. Same with his questions about Q's connections with Megan Crane. Clearly, he had done his research before coming to see her. He was well-informed about Operation Kerry, the trial, and as far as someone not closely connected with the case could be, Megan Crane herself. But Jess had got no hint that he regarded a connection with Megan as anything more than a chance to shed light on a so-far-unexplained death. If he was fishing for some juicy detail or salacious piece of gossip about the dominatrix that the media had somehow missed - her experience was that many did - he'd hidden it well.

And as she reflected on the Acting Detective Inspector from Gloucestershire, she decided that unlike many of his kind - young, ambitious, out to make a name for themselves - Gavin Baggus was that rare thing in CID these days. Someone who is interested in one thing and one thing only. Discovering the truth. And though she couldn't put a finger on why, she already had the sense that she could trust his instincts.

As she reached for her mobile, a knock came on the door. Looking up, she saw Alec in the doorway, a DC at his shoulder. The DC was carrying what she recognised as a set of Committal papers, and looking stressed.

'Can we hae a quick word Ma'am?' Alec said, not

waiting to be invited.

She beckoned them in, sensing normality intruding. She wasn't altogether ungrateful.

It was late in the evening before she finally managed to ring Carver.

'How'd your meeting go?' he asked when he picked up.

'I think our friend from Gloucestershire may be onto something.'

'Tell me,' he said.

Jess recounted the facts as Baggus had to her. When Carver asked, she gave him her thoughts about Baggus, then her own on Quentin Quinlan's death. Then she waited, phone in hand, while he digested it all.

Eventually he said, 'I need to check a couple of things. Give me a couple of days. I'll get back to you.'

'Okay.' But before hanging up she said, 'Jamie?'

'What?'

'I'm sorry.'

There was a pause, then, 'Don't be. It's not your fault.'

After he'd gone, she turned to look out at the grey slate, still visible in the light from her office.

Carver was right. It *wasn't* her fault. But she was already thinking about what her call would be triggering in his mind. And the fact it wasn't her fault, didn't make her feel any better. She repeated her apology to the grey slate that was more rightly his.

'Sorry, Jamie.'

CHAPTER 8

Thirty miles down the M62, Carver was a mirror image of his former partner. The only difference was, his skyline included Manchester United's Old Trafford Stadium, which, as a Liverpool fan, he was fed up of hearing people describe as, 'iconic'. It took a good ten minutes before he jolted himself out of the gloom that settled in the wake of Jess's call.

Reaching down, he opened his bottom desk-drawer. Taking out the bunch of keys attached to a heavy brass fob, he left his office and made his way down the corridor to the back of the building. At the far end was a plain door secured with two locks. He unlocked the mortice lock first, then the Yale. Behind it was another door, with a keypad. He punched in the number, waited for the green light and the click, then entered.

The room was about five meters square. Along one wall was a desk with a printer, a basket containing documents, and an old-fashioned, brass desk lamp. Next to the desk was a stand with a projector. The only other item of furniture was a grey-metal, four-drawer filing cabinet. It was bolted to the floor at the base. A stout iron bar ran down, through the handles, attached to other welded-on fittings by heavy padlocks and a thick chain. He removed the locks and bar before unlocking the cabinet itself. From the third drawer down, he took out a laptop, placed it on the desk, attached the lead and booted up.

Two minutes later, he hit 'enter' and sat back as the projector threw the image onto the once-green wall he'd had repainted white. The room lit up as the wall filled with a series of geometrical shapes connected by lines and annotated flow-diagrams. The shapes varied according to content. Squares contained names. Circles, locations. Triangles showed dates. Points of interest were captured within cartoon-like thought balloons. It was all colour-coded. Question and exclamation marks appeared at various places.

The fruit of nine months' late-evening labours, the schematic charted what Carver knew, or had discovered, to date about Megan Crane's complex network. It had been slow work, slower than he'd anticipated when he reluctantly accepted the undertaking. And there was still much to do. Although he'd trained, years before, in the ANACAPA - 'Analytical Capability' - methodology, he'd never found it that easy. Nevertheless, it had revealed many previously unrealised and interesting connections, and was continuing do so. Most of it was yet to be shared with those who had tasked him, and he had grown used to fielding their weekly probings about his findings, their, 'likely implications'. Despite the growing pressure, he was in no rush to report. He knew what the response would be when he did. And he needed to know he'd seen everything before it all disappeared into some black hole – as it surely would, once its existence became known.

As he had done that day Jess first rang to alert him to Q's death, Carver focused on the box containing

Quentin Quinlan's name. He pulled his chair forward so he could more easily follow the linkages flowing to and from it.

His mobile rang. Seeing 'ROS', he hesitated before answering, taking a few seconds so he would sound normal. She always spotted tension in his voice. Her musical training, he assumed.

'Where are you?'

'Jus' abou' to go on,' she said, her accent thickening as it always did when she was nervous. 'I am las' this afternoon but I have another spot tonight'

'They'll love you,' he said. She gave a self-deprecating snort. For all her fiery passion she was surprisingly modest of her talent. 'Just be yourself and enjoy it. You were great the night before you left.'

Carver had never visited Lisbon's famous, Teatro Nacional de Sao Carlos. But as he fed her further words of encouragement, he imagined her, waiting in the wings of an ornate stage, wearing her fabulous, white, 'performance' dress, her flaming hair falling around her shoulders. It was pure coincidence that this year's International Festival of Folk Music was being held in Rosanna's home city. She was desperate that her appearances over the fortnight did justice to her beloved Fado - the distinctive folk music that is to Portugal, what the Tango is to Argentina. As the time had neared to her leaving, he had assured her that the, 'disaster,' she foresaw was purely imaginary. But her impending performance wasn't the only thing on her mind.

'Have you managed to get around any of them?'

He could almost hear the longing in her voice. But as he visualised the pile of brochures and estate agent's fliers lying on the coffee table back at the flat, his stomach tightened.

'Not yet, but I will. This weekend.'

'How much longer Jamie?' she said. The question he was hearing more and more these days.

'I've told you. As soon as we find the right place…'

'I thought we had the right place.'

He bit his lip as the image of a pleasant-looking cottage, set back from the road and with a large garden swam before his eyes, tugging at him. Surely she didn't want to go over it again, not now?

At the time, he'd convinced himself that their decision to move was a joint one. That after what happened neither of them could ever settle there again. But as the weeks passed with no sign of the 'dream-house' he'd promised they would find, 'No trouble,' he had come to recognise his own dishonesty.

Surprisingly, Rosanna seemed to get over what had happened relatively quickly. Once her voice-box healed – no permanent damage the doctors said, thank God – her voice eventually came back as strong as ever. And he now realised that those nights when he'd come in late, anxious about her being alone, she'd actually been fine. It was him, not her who kept re-living it.

The trouble was, it wasn't just the memory of when he rushed in and found her tied to the chair with *Her* looming over her - Jesus, I can't even *think* her name - that wouldn't go away. It was everything else that had happened round that time as well. The mistakes that returned to haunt him, the realisation that even after all this time, he was still vulnerable. And of course, there was poor Angie, the greatest horror of all… *and Jason…* When he first suggested to Rosanna they move closer to Manchester, he'd countered her uncertainty with, 'My roots are there. And don't believe what you hear, you'll love it.' Which was why she went along with it. Not a word of argument. Not even when it came to selling the cottage. Nor did she complain about the dilapidated state of the Rushton flat they took when he gave in and accepted his secondment, along with the task of analysing the cabinet's contents that came with it. But they still hadn't found what they were looking for. Now, hearing the way she recalled their lost hideaway, he sensed her need for hope.

'I'll find somewhere soon, Ros. Trust me.'

'I hope so....'

The fall in her voice reminded him that right now, downbeat was the last thing she needed.

'Look, stop thinking about it. You just go out there and knock-em dead. By the time you get back, I'll have found us a new home and I'll take you to see it.'

She brightened. 'Promise?'

'Promise.'

As he hung up, he experienced a moment's panic as he realised the task he'd set himself. He'd been through the latest batch of brochures the night before. Nothing in them roused his interest. And the prices. He was beginning to think they'd be better off staying in the sticks after all. There are plenty of other nice places in Cheshire - Derbyshire even - that fitted with their dream. Then again, Derbyshire was a bit close to a certain prison establishment.... It reminded him what he was supposed to be doing.

Pushing thoughts of house-hunting to the back of his mind, he concentrated again on the task in hand - Quinlan's box. As he'd remembered, several lines ran to and from it. He followed their trails, noting connections, remembering names and places. As he took it all in, Carver breathed deep. It was as he had thought when Jess first mentioned his name.

He focused on one particular box. To begin with, when he first pictured the linkages, he hadn't been sure. But there it was. Okay, it only linked via a dotted line, and there was a question mark alongside it. There were others with whom it was more strongly associated. But it was enough.

Over the next hour Carver returned, again and again to Quinlan's box, retracing lines, looking at linkages, thinking about those with whom he connected, what they might stand to lose if, as Baggus seemed to suspect, Q had been blackmailing someone. The picture was complex, the possibilities many. And the more he read and considered, the more certain he became. Getting to the truth, would not be easy.

By the time he closed down and put everything away, a dull pain throbbed at his temples. By the time he locked up and returned to his office, everyone had gone.

CHAPTER 9

Sophia's Coffee House stands on Bold Street, just off Warrington's bustling Sankey Street. Friday nights it closes at nine. When Carver arrived shortly after eight and took a table at the back, business was already slowing. It meant that the young girl in the black T-shirt with 'Barista In Training' on the back was able to leave things in the hands of her older colleague and join him when she brought him his coffee.

Taking the seat opposite, she said, 'Just a sec.' She took out her mobile.

As her thumbs danced across the screen, he waited. Eventually he sighed. 'Rosanna sends her regards.'

She smiled, but didn't slow. 'That's nice.'

Carver shook his head. He was still never sure when she was being genuine, or simply polite. As he waited some more, he used the lull to study her further.

Eighteen months had passed since the night she'd saved his life. During that time Kayleigh Lee had changed. A lot. Gone was the punkish fifteen-year who, intelligent and mature beyond her years was then still prone to bursts of childishness. Like smuggling a fart-cushion into court and secreting it amongst the defence team's benches. The Judge hadn't been pleased, the defence even less so. Now, just turned seventeen, taller, slimmer, and calmer thank God, the young woman she was turning into was more apparent each visit. There was still no mention of boyfriends, or girls for that matter, but it couldn't be far away.

The sooner the better.

A minute later, she stopped typing, put her mobile away, folded her arms and turned to him. He waited until he was certain he had her full attention, before starting.

'How are you doing?'

But instead of answering, she cocked her head to the side and raised an eyebrow.

'What?' he said. But when her face didn't change, he knew he couldn't keep it up. He shook his head, put down his mug. 'Oh for God's sake. Happy birthday for last week.'

The look changed to one of disappointment. 'Well that sounded sincere. Card in the post is it?'

'I don't do birthday cards.'

'I bet you do for her.'

He pinned her with a look, *Don't...*

'What?' Her turn to feign innocence.

He shook his head again, drank his coffee. Eventually he dug in his jacket pocket, pulled out the small package, placed it in front of her.

'Ahhh… Is this for me?'

'I meant to drop it off last week, but I was busy.'

She pulled off the wrapping. The purple-velour box was square and flat. She opened it, took out the silver chain with a Saint Christopher. As she looked up at him, the delight in her face made him wonder how many of her previous sixteen birthdays had brought any joy.

'And before you say anything, it's from both of us.'

But there was no trace of sarcasm when she took it from its setting, draped it across her hand and said, 'It's lovely. Thank you. And tell Rosanna thank you as well.'

Carver nearly choked on his drink. Rosanna was only ever, '*her*' or '*she*'. But as she lifted it to her neck, he saw what was coming - and realised his mistake. Sure enough, she turned in her seat. Without saying anything, she lifted her hair at the back with one hand, offering him the ends of the chain with the other. He had no choice but to accept, and was thankful when he managed to work out the fastening and do the necessary with the minimum of fumbling. Though quiet, there were still several customers and he checked to see if any were looking. But only the woman behind the counter, her supervisor, seemed to be paying them attention. Turning back to him, she showed it off, waiting.

He managed a smile, nodded. 'Looks nice.'

She checked herself using her mobile. 'It's beautiful. Thank you.'

But as she leaned towards him and he saw what she was about to do, he drew back, glancing towards the counter. 'Don't.'

'What's up? I'm only saying 'thank you'.'

'I know. I'd rather you didn't.'

She sank back in her seat, gave a terse, 'Tch. You're weird.'

'Even so.'

They sipped their coffees.

After a while she said, 'You don't *have* to keep doing this, you know?'

'What?'

'This. Dropping in every few weeks to, "See How I Am Doing".'

He nodded, thought about it. 'Would you rather I

didn't?'

She shrugged. 'S'not a problem for me.'

'There you are then.'

'But it would be nice if you were a bit…'

'A bit what?'

'I was going to say, *relaxed*. You're always on edge.'

'That's because I probably shouldn't be here at all. At least not, uhh, alone.'

'Why bother then?'

'Because I want to. And, I owe you.'

She gave a sly smile. 'I know, but don't worry. It don't mean we're engaged or anything.' She paused, then placed her hand on his before adding, 'Not yet anyway.'

He snatched it away like he'd been stung. He glared at her. '*Stop* doing that.' He looked around. A middle-aged woman a few tables away dropped her gaze back to her magazine. 'Do you *want* to get me in trouble?'

She turned sullen. 'You're no fun.'

'I'm not here for fun. I'm here to make sure you're okay.'

'I'm fine. It's you needs sorting out.'

He ignored it. 'Tell me. How the job's going. How's college, the family?'

She gave one last, petulant look, then gave in and brought him up to date.

Her new evening job was going, '*alright*', with one rider. 'They treat you like you're brain-dead. There's a script for everything. Even making toast.' Her dad had finally settled into his bin lorry job after some, 'early difficulties.' *Like getting up mornings.* When she described how her mother had started making kid's clothes again and was selling them on-line, Carver had to cover his amazement. He'd known Paula Lee nearly all his service. As a young PC patrolling the Town

Centre, he'd used to come across her regularly, usually in the early hours, in shop doorways - and that was *after* her first three kids. But he was pleased to hear that her studies - Psychology and Law - were going well, and that she was actually enjoying college, especially since moving out of Carnegie Avenue.

In the weeks and months following Kayleigh's life-saving heroics, the debate about funding was one of the more protracted issues the Lee Family Project Steering Group had to grapple with. In the end, it needed Carver to remind them of the Trial Judge's words during summing-up. Referring to the young girl whose identity he'd ordered be protected, and whose timely intervention had prevented two more deaths, he said, "This young girl, only fifteen years of age, showed remarkable courage, initiative, and a level of resourcefulness that did her, and her parents, great credit. The court hopes that those responsible for ensuring her future welfare will wish to recognise and take steps to develop those qualities.' Within forty-eight hours, like magic, the cash materialised.

Finished her update, Kayleigh became suddenly serious. 'I've just thought. I never really thanked you for what you did.'

'What did I do?'

'You know. College. My house. Sorting it all out.'

'Nothing to do with me. I was off the project by then remember.'

'So Rita tells fibs does she?'

'About what?'

'About you speaking to certain people?'

He sought cover in his coffee. 'Like I say, nothing to do with me.'

'Yeah, right.'

Finishing his drink, he said, 'I'm just glad to hear everything's going okay.'

Her silence alerted him. He looked up to find her waiting. 'What?'

To begin with, she was reluctant. *Not your problem.* But after some cajoling, she caved.

'It's our Billy.' The *our* came out, *are*, the way they do in Liverpool - *Are* Jimmy. *Are* Susie. 'He's getting himself in shit.' She went on to describe the crowd with whom the brother twelve months her junior had become involved. The family name - Gilligan, resonated with Carver. *No wonder she's worried.* The main problem, obviously, was drugs. The Gilligans lived on the Charnock estate. Which meant crack and amphet - though not exclusively.

'How long?'

'Couple of months now. But it's getting worse. *Are* Jesse says he's staying out most nights. And he's had the push from his job.'

'Has anyone tried making him stay home?'

'Anyone like who?'

'Your Dad? Russell?' Soon to turn twenty, Russell was the oldest sibling.

'Dad? You must be joking. He never knows what any of us are doing. Never did. Never will. And since Russell got himself supposedly engaged, there's only ever one thing on his mind.'

Carver nodded. *I can imagine.*

'Leave it with me. Let me make some enquiries.'

Her head bobbed. *Thanks.* After a pause she said, 'Can I ask you something?'

'Go on.'

'Do you-' She started again. 'Do you ever, like, think about… *her?'*

'Only every day. Why do you ask?'

'And do you … ever worry about what might happen if she ever got out?'

'Escaped from prison, you mean?' She nodded. He shook his head. 'That'll never happen, so no, I don't worry about it.'

'But how can you be sure? People do escape from prison, sometimes, don't they?'

'What's made you suddenly start thinking she might escape?'

More hesitation. 'Well it's just that… She tried to kill you because she blamed you for her boyfriend's death, didn't she?'

'That's right.'

'And… I stopped her from killing you and Ros, didn't I?'

'Yes, thankfully, you did.'

'So now… won't she blame me for saving you both from her?'

In that moment, Carver saw what he'd been missing since the day Kayleigh stood at the back of the court and listened as the Judge sentenced an emotionless Megan Crane to seven concurrent life sentences. Carver had always imagined Kayleigh as scared of no-one. Her street-wise ways and cocky independence pointed to it. Certainly, her actions the night she saved their lives seemed to confirm it. But he realised now he was wrong. Kayleigh may be brave, but she wasn't stupid. The Forensic Psychiatrist who gave evidence for the Crown categorised Megan Crane's pathological state as, 'severe'. He also described her as one of the most dangerous individuals he'd ever met. Coming from someone who had made a career out of assessing prison psychos, it was saying something. Since the trial,

Kayleigh would have had plenty of time to read up on the likes of Megan Crane. She would know exactly what she was capable of, and she'd had more insight than most into how the mind of a serial-killing psychopath works. And she was right. Megan Crane almost certainly *would* blame her for spoiling her plans. And as Carver could testify only too well, when Megan Crane bears a grudge, she *bears a grudge.*

He leaned forward, putting his weight on his elbows, looked her square in the face. 'Now listen. Megan Crane is in a maximum security prison. She is guarded, day and night. When the Judge sentenced her, he recommended that in her case, 'life' has to mean 'life'. Whatever she may, or may not, be thinking about you, me, Rosanna or anyone else, she will never, ever, set foot outside of a prison again. She will never, ever, be a danger to us. Do you hear what I'm saying?'

She gave him a long look. 'Yes.'

'Do you believe me?'

Another pause. 'Yes.'

Carver sat back in his chair. Then he thought, W*hat the fuck.* Reaching out, he took her hand, squeezed it.

She smiled.

A few minutes later Carver left, satisfied that he had done a good job of reassuring her.

He couldn't know how wrong he was.

CHAPTER 10

Carver was studying an Intelligence Report concerning a new face on the Organised Crime Scene, a Croatian by the name of Jadranko Kisic, when his desk phone rang.

'DCI Carver? This is Geoff Medwin from the Nottinghamshire Collisions Investigation Unit. You left a message about a fatal in the forest, a bloke called Gordon Halsall?'

Carver closed the report on Kisic, sat back in his chair.

'Thanks for coming back to me Geoff. I believe you supervised the accident investigation?'

'That's right. How can I help?'

'I'm interested in what you made of it. I've read your report and know the Coroner ruled Accidental Death with a rider about Halsall's blood-alcohol level. Was there anything else, or was that it?'

Medwin took his time answering. 'I'm... not sure what you are asking me, sir. Are you investigating a complaint?'

The first thing they think of. 'Personal interest, that's all. I know someone who knew the deceased.'

The Sergeant remained wary. 'The report says it all.

He was alone in the car. No other vehicles involved. It was late at night. He'd been drinking. The road was-'

'Where?'

'Where what?'

'Where had he been drinking? A pub? Somewhere public?'

'At his home, we concluded. We found an empty whisky bottle and a glass.'

'Any witnesses? To his drinking, I mean.'

'No, he lived alone. Bachelor type.'

Carver gave a low, 'Hmm.' There are bachelors, and then there are men like those whose names appear in Megan Crane's archive. 'Did you find out where he was going? You mentioned it was late?'

'His mother lived in Brighton. We think he was on his way to visit her.'

'Late at night?'

'It's an easier drive than during the day.'

'Did he have a bag?'

'What sort of bag?'

'An overnight bag, or a suitcase. If he was going to visit his mother he'd have taken one, wouldn't he?'

Medwin's response was slow coming. 'No… I can't say I remember seeing a bag. Look, I'm not sure where this is going. If someone has concerns about the investigation, then they need to raise it officially. As far as I was concerned, it was all pretty straightforward. A single vehicle left the road while the driver was pissed. I'm not sure what else anyone can make of it.'

'That's what I need to know, Geoff. How long have you been in A.I.?'

'Twelve years. Why?'

'Because twelve years makes you an experienced traffic detective. And sometimes detectives get a feel for things.'

'What sort of things?'

'Like when the evidence in a case seems clear, but something doesn't quite add up.'

'Okay…'

'So?'

'So what?'

'So was there anything about this case that, for you - forget the evidence, I'm talking your gut - didn't quite add up?' When no response came, Carver added, 'I'm not trying to screw you, Geoff. From what I've seen, your investigation was by-the-book. No complaints, no criticism. But there may be an aspect to the case you weren't aware of, and which may have a bearing. All I'm asking is, are you one- hundred-percent happy that all the questions were answered to your satisfaction?'

There was another long pause.

'Geoff?'

'Well, seeing as you mention it…'

It was twenty minutes later when Carver rang Jess on her mobile. She picked up immediately.

'You may be right about your Gloucester friend,' He said. 'I think you ought to arrange another meet. This time, I'll join you.'

CHAPTER 11

The fourth time Baggus set out the case for Quentin Quinlan's death being suspect, he'd already decided there would be no fifth. He was as sure as he was on Day One it was no accident, but he was growing tired of being accused of seeing things. As a DC, he'd once worked for a soon-to-retire DCI who kept one wall of his office as a shrine to the young mother whose murder, seventeen years before, he'd failed to clear up. That wasn't going to be him. If those further up the chain were happy to accept Quinlan died playing with AEA, then he wasn't going to embark on a crusade to prove otherwise. Driving up to Warrington that morning he'd told himself. *If they don't get it first time, that will be it. There's plenty other stuff needs doing.* By the time he rounded off his presentation and closed with a matter-of-fact, 'That's it,' he was ready to gather his papers and walk if the two men hearing it for the first time responded as some others had.

In the silence that followed, Baggus wasn't sure just what the response was going to be. But as it stretched, his instincts told him he wouldn't be racing off back down the M5 just yet. Jess would hardly have asked him to come back if she'd harboured doubts, and his audience's body language, or rather, lack of it, was telling.

To begin with, the man whose view he was most interested to hear - Carver - didn't shift from the position he'd adopted soon after Baggus began. Feet up on a chair, head resting on a fist, gaze riveted on the presenter. If it hadn't been for the occasional blink, he could have been in a catatonic state. Baggus hoped it was the pose of someone reappraising what he thought he knew. But until he said something, he couldn't be sure.

At the far end of the table, Detective Chief Superintendent John Morrison, the man who'd led the Operation Kerry Investigation from start to finish, was also giving little away. Baggus had heard the others refer to him as, 'The Duke'. He wasn't sure why. Something to do with the film actor, John Wayne, apparently, though he couldn't see any resemblance. Morrison also remained still and quiet during the presentation, though his bulk rendered him incapable of matching Carver's statue-like state.

Eventually Carver moved. Swinging his feet off the chair, he turned square on to the table. He looked down, examining the backs of his hands, as if answers to questions needing them were written there, before turning to look up the table at Morrison. Had Baggus not been paying attention, he may have missed the exchange of nods.

Morrison - 'The Duke' - cleared his throat. 'Thank you, Mr Baggus. I'm grateful for you taking the time to come back and share the facts of this case with us. I found your presentation… enlightening.' He paused as he made eye contact with each member of his team -

Carver, then Jess, followed by the Scottish DS, Alec Duncan, Baggus had met before. Whatever messages the exchanges contained, they seemed to decide him. His gaze returned to Baggus.

'I understand Wilf Robinson, doesn't share your views about all this?'

Baggus nodded. 'That's correct.' He could have said more, but to be fair, Robinson hadn't stopped him coming back to meet with them all.

The Duke stroked his top lip. 'I believe you also used to work for Derek Hutcheson?'

Baggus nodded again. The former head of Gloucestershire's CID had mentored him during his early CID days.

'Hutch and I go way back,' The Duke said. 'It seems he has more faith in your judgement than Wilf does.'

Baggus's eyebrows lifted as he realised he'd been vetted. But again he said nothing. The now-retired Hutcheson and still-serving Robinson were both well-regarded in South West CID circles, though for different reasons. Hutcheson's investigative achievements - he was Detective Sergeant at Gloucester when the Fred West Case broke - were legendary. On the other hand, the way Robinson cleared out Cheltenham CID a couple of years ago had cemented his reputation for ruthless, but fair, leadership. Baggus wondered which one 'The Duke' placed most stock in.

'Before we proceed, I need to be clear on something.'

Baggus came upright.

'The matters we are about to discuss are… sensitive. I need your word that anything you hear will not be shared beyond these walls with anyone. And that includes Wilf Robinson. Do you understand?'

Baggus's pulse quickened. 'You have my word.'

'In that case-' The Duke turned to Carver. 'Jamie?'

Carver lifted his head, sent Baggus a long, hard stare, then began.

Baggus listened as Carver led him through the investigation which, thanks to the media, people only ever referred to now as, The Worshipper Enquiry. Most of it he already knew, or had heard about. Carver described Megan Crane's involvement with the late serial killer, Edmund Hart. He spoke of how she'd vowed to avenge Hart's prison suicide by killing those she held responsible - Carver and the former High Class Escort who helped him bring Hart to justice. To that point Baggus only knew her as, "Witness A", but now Carver gave her a name - "Angie" - and his mood darkened, visibly, when he spoke it. But other aspects came as a surprise. Such as the fact that Megan Crane had managed to 'distract' some of the investigation team - *Carver?* - enough that at the crucial moment, they were blind to her manipulations. Such as how Carver's fellow DCI - her final victim - had been attempting to blackmail his way into Carver's shoes when he died. The fact that both Hart and Megan Crane were suspected to have claimed many more victims than was ever referred to at court. At this point he subjected Baggus to a searching look - *Checking me out one last time?* - before continuing.

'Originally, Megan Crane told us she didn't keep records of her activities. She lied. After she was arrested, we recovered a filing cabinet from her cellar. It contains details of what she and her circle got up to, going back as far as when she and Hart were active together.'

Baggus started. 'I didn't know that. I read the trial transcript but I don't remember reading about her keeping any records.'

'You wouldn't,' Carver said. He paused, then added, 'It was never disclosed.'

Baggus froze. 'What? Not at all?'

No none moved. The expressions on the faces looking at him were all blank.

'Fuck me.'

Carver gave him time to digest it. He needed it. The law on disclosure is clear. Investigators ignore it at their peril. Evidence - in fact *any* information relevant to an investigation - *has* to be disclosed, both to the defence *and* the court - no exceptions. The list of cases – serious ones amongst them - thrown out by Judges because the rules weren't followed is a long one. And *deliberate* non-disclosure could be seen as - no, not could be, *is* - a crime. As in Five-Years-In-Prison-type crime. As the reason for the The Duke's warning finally became clear, Baggus found himself repeating the expletive he was in danger of over-using. 'Fuck me.'

Eventually he recovered enough that his investigative impulses kicked in. 'But why the hell would you not disclose? If it ever gets out, then you're all going to be… I mean… *Jesus.*'

Carver opened the manila folder that had lain in front of him throughout, took out a sheet of paper, slid it towards Baggus. Baggus picked it up. As he scanned down the list of names, his eyes grew wide and he had to fight to stop more, 'Fuck me's escaping

'These names all show up, in some form, in Megan Crane's archive,' Carver said. 'They are, or were, associated with her at one time or another. It's not a comprehensive list. There are others I've yet to research. If you're anything like me, you probably don't watch much TV, so you may not recognise a lot of them.'

Baggus shook his head. 'You're right. But I catch the odd film and I like sport. Is this the real-?' He stopped as he saw Carver nodding.

'They're all who you think they are. For some reason, actors, premier league footballers and politicians seem to like this sort of thing.

'Bugger me,' Baggus said, for a change.

'Hence my concern to keep things within these four walls,' The Duke said. 'You see our dilemma? How long do you think it would remain out of the papers if that list was made known to even a handful of people?'

Baggus didn't reply. He'd been involved in a couple of cases where disclosed material had leaked back to people who should never have known. Nevertheless…

'So… No one knows about this… at all?'

Carver cleared his throat. 'We're in the process of bringing the Security Services in on it through the National Crime Agency, but slowly. When they know the full extent of it, we think they'll step in and take the lot. And when that happens we'll have nothing. If there are any more deaths, or incidents-'

'Like Quinlan,' Baggus said.

'Like Quinlan, we wouldn't know where to start. Once I've finished analysing it all, they can have it. Destroy it for all I care. But the intelligence will stay with us.'

'Isn't that risky?' Baggus said. 'If the Security Service people ever find out you've retained the intelligence, they'll-.'

'The Security Service won't find out,' Carver said, flatly.

Baggus didn't pursue it. He was a divisional jack. Right now he was happy to not know how these things worked.

Over the next quarter hour or so, Baggus learned more than he'd ever heard before about Megan Crane's astonishing lifestyle and the partnerships she forged – some fleeting, others more lasting - with those who shared her interests. He was incredulous when Carver described the way she kept people as her semi-permanent 'house-slaves', sometimes for days on end, and embarrassed to learn that the phrase, 'Twenty-Four-Seven' had uses beyond Tesco opening hours.

'She sometimes had as many as a dozen relationships on the go at any one time,' Carver said. 'In most, she played the dom. But sometimes the roles were reversed, as with Edmund Hart. Some of her relationships were even more ambiguous. In fact some where… Well quite frankly, we still aren't sure what they were.'

'So what about Quinlan? What is there on him?'

'During the time she was with Hart, Quinlan was one of a group who met with her on a regular basis. Most of them were subs, like him. She refers to them in her notes as, "The UF", whatever that means. The interesting thing is, most of her records are pretty explicit. But apart from recording dates and places of their meetings she never actually describes what went on when this 'UF group' got together. And she doesn't name any of them directly. It's as if their activities were too outrageous, or potentially damaging. For her, that says something.'

'Kids?' Baggus said.

Carver shook his head. 'She doesn't do children, or animals. She always claimed that sort of thing disgusts her.'

Multiple murder being okay, of course.

'We can't rule out that some of her contacts may have had interests in that direction, but I know she would never let herself be connected with it, in any way.'

'Whatever this 'UF' got up to,' Baggus said. 'If she took care not to write about it, then presumably it could involve something that might be worth blackmail?'

Carver nodded slowly. 'The analysis isn't complete yet, but there's one reference that could mean something.' Baggus sat up again. 'The initials, 'VR' keep appearing where she mentions them. But it appears as a sort of cross-reference, sometimes with an exclamation or question mark, like they have some special meaning. She doesn't reveal who it is but he or she seems to be associated with something that happened not long before the group stopped meeting. Soon after that, she seems to have dropped her association with them altogether. Listen to this.' He picked up another sheet of paper from the folder, read from it. '"UF are all talking about VR. I cannot believe it. HG says-".' Carver looked up, 'I don't know who HG is yet. "HG says they are scared in case someone talks. I think The Man is mad".' Carver stopped reading. '"The Man", is written in capitals. Whether she means VR or not isn't clear.'

'Is Quinlan linked to this VR?' Baggus said.

Carver picked up another sheet, passed it across the table. 'This is Quinlan's last letter to Megan. It relates to a meeting they were planning. There's a note at the bottom….'

Baggus eyes scanned down the sheet. Every now and again he stopped and blinked, before moving on down. Certain words and phrases kept grabbing his attention. *For my punishment... whipped... ...to use as you please... totally subservient....* Eventually he came to the note and looked up. 'It's in a different hand'

'It's her writing,' Carver said.

Baggus read it aloud. 'Q keeps talking about VR.

They don't trust him.'

'I'm not sure when she added it,' Carver said. 'I would guess sometime after she stopped seeing him.'

Baggus read through it again. When he looked up, all eyes were trained on him. 'Would you not all agree, this appears to support my blackmail theory?'

For a while no one moved. Then Carver leaned back in his chair and locked his hands behind his head.

'Actually, we've been expecting it.'

Baggus gave him a pointed stare. 'Expecting it?'

'Once we began to realise the sort of people she was involved with, we thought it was only a matter of time before someone tried to capitalise on what they knew.

'Can't we just ask her about all this?' Baggus said. 'Presumably she would know what's it's all about.'

Carver threw a glance at Jess and The Duke before coming back to him. 'We're not sure Megan Crane is the best place to start.'

'Where then?'

Carver looked across at Jess. Baggus followed his gaze.

'Where she and Quinlan first met,' Jess said.

'Where's that?'

She paused, to let a sly smile form. 'Have you ever heard of a place called Josephine's?'

Baggus looked up from Jess's laptop to find her waiting for him. She looked like she was trying to stifle amusement. He guessed it came from watching his reactions to what he'd just seen.

'You're joking, right?'

Her response was blunt. 'No, I'm not.'

As realisation dawned - *No fucking way* - he found his gaze being drawn back to the screen. It wasn't so much the images woven into the website's design that pulled at him - the intention was to entice rather than arouse - as the need to confirm to himself that such a place actually existed. *And* that it was as open about the activities and interests for which it caters, the facilities and services it offers, as any service-provider. Certainly, the website seemed as professional and whizzy as any he was familiar with.

'And we're going there?'

'You want to find out what Quinlan was into, don't you?'

'Yes, but….'

'So what's the problem?'

He glanced up at her then, realising he was blushing, turned his eyes back to the screen.

'You say you've… been there?'

'A couple of times. Background work before the trial. Don't worry. It's not as full-on as it looks.'

He swallowed. 'So you say.'

'Just look on it as a new experience.'

Not sure if he'd heard something in her tone, he looked up just in time to see the smile disappearing. In its place was a look that said, *Any questions*? He shook his head. *I don't believe this*. But what he said was, 'What does 'Dress-Code' mean?'

CHAPTER 12

Megan placed the document, carefully, on the desk before turning to the woman whose gaze had stayed on her as she'd read through it. 'It's not as detailed as I'd expected.'

Doctor Lydia Grant nodded. 'This is just our starter-inventory. We use it to capture initial data, case details, background, personal history, that sort of thing. The detailed analysis comes later. We like to start slowly with these sorts of studies, so we don't put the subjects off.' Then, as if realising what she'd said, she raised a hand to her mouth. 'I'm sorry, I didn't mean to-'

Megan waved it away. 'Don't worry. I don't mind at all being a 'subject'. It's not as if I have a lot to worry about in here.'

The researcher gave an appreciative smile.

As Megan returned it, she wondered again about what Lydia Grant's little slip said about her experience dealing with *actual* offenders - as opposed to the 'Crime and Justice Research Projects' listed in the CV Ellen had shown her. If they reflected experience 'in the field', she should be practised at avoiding traps like the one she'd just fallen into. Right now, it suited Megan's purpose to play along, but she could think of plenty she'd met inside whose hostility towards the 'establishment' would only harden if they thought they were being patronised.

It was a bit like Lydia Grant's appearance.

From what she'd gleaned from Ellen, Megan had imagined a fusty, middle-aged academic. But Lydia Grant was far from that. Megan would put her in her thirties, either that, or she was well preserved for her age. Whichever, it was obvious she looked after herself. As they shook hands, Megan had noted the strong grip as well as the athletic build and toned features that mark someone who works out. Without the glasses and with her hair down, she spied an attractive woman lurking beneath the disguise. Which only made Megan wonder, *Why?* The prospect of unravelling the mystery was one of the reasons she was already looking forward to wherever Lydia Grant's 'research' may take them - at least for however long her sojourn at HMP Stigwood was destined to last. It was a shame about the hair, though. She had an in-built suspicion of bottle-blonds. *Just what are they trying to prove?*. But then, not all women are blessed with hair like hers; coal-black, thick, and glossy.

Such questions apart, Megan was actually enjoying their initial, 'exploratory meeting'. She had listened with genuine interest as the psychologist laid out the parameters of her research, detailing the programme of interviews, discussions, tests, and measurements - physiological as well as psychological - she would seek to use. The aim, Lydia Grant confirmed, was to gain insights into the key motivators that drive those the Justice System labels, 'repeat offenders', but whom the media like to call, 'Serial Killers'. As always, Megan was finding the opportunity to test herself against someone who was nearly-but-not-quite her equal, invigorating. Tiring also, she now realised, - *I'm definitely out of practice* – but invigorating all the same. Come to think of it, she hadn't felt so challenged since her sessions with Jamie Carver, though the comparison wasn't altogether apt. Back then, her careful planning and secret knowledge meant that he'd never really stood a chance. Even so, he turned out to be a more formidable sparring partner than she had expected. Certainly, in the latter stages, she'd had to work doubly hard at keeping her agenda hidden. It prompted her to wonder how Lydia Grant would fare in that regard.

As she reflected on it, her mind went back to a sunny afternoon in her kitchen when, alone with Jess Greylake, she'd pretended that until their first meeting, she had never heard of him. It was the day when Jess – poor, foolish Jess - her tongue loosened by wine and brandy-coffees, had gone on to spill all she knew about him, like some star-struck schoolgirl describing her dreamy teacher to her best friend. It included some of his past experiences, a couple of which Megan *hadn't* heard about, and which she simply added to the profile she had already drawn up. And it wasn't any fault of hers that her plan was foiled at the last minute. It was simply bad luck and unfortunate timing that led to the discoveries that were her final undoing. In fact if Jess hadn't discovered her cellar and its secrets when she did, she'd have….

She stopped herself. She had been over it many times. Doing so again would not serve any purpose. Besides, the way things were going, and from what she was hearing, she had a feeling their paths may cross again sooner than even she had anticipated. And when they did, she was determined things would turn out differently.

Her thoughts returned to the woman sitting across from her. However her CV read, Megan had already concluded that Lydia Grant was not from the top-drawer of Forensic Psychologists. If she were, she would hardly be researching on behalf of the Home Office. Earlier, as they'd talked around what she intended, Megan had been surprised to see signs that she may not even as well-versed as herself in what she had long ago learned where some basic tenets of human behaviour. She'd have thought that any psychologist worth their salt would be familiar with how subliminal signals indicating sexual attraction can be used to deconstruct a subject's mental self-image and, over time, replace it with one more conducive to the practitioner's purposes. After all, wasn't that exactly what those over-paid Harley Street psychiatrists did with their more-money-than-sense-clients? Yet Lydia Grant seemed to have little feel for the subject, not even when they spoke of the 'myths' that had grown around the events that led to her incarceration. She'd have thought the researcher might pick up on it as being key to understanding how her would-be-subject's mind works, and therefore of fundamental importance to her research. If she did, she gave no sign. It put Megan on her guard, and she made a mental note to be less accommodating at their next meeting. If she gave away too much of herself too soon, the sessions may not last long enough for her to achieve her purpose. And that would never do.

'So what happens next?', Megan said.

Lydia Grant smiled the smile Megan guessed was designed to put her, 'subjects', at ease.

'You complete this initial inventory, sign the consent forms - she indicated the buff folder on the desk - then pass it back to me through the Governor's office. I'll set you up on our database, then come back with a proposed date for a first session.'

'And what will that involve?'

Lydia Grant gave a vague wave. 'Oh, I expect we'll just talk a bit. I may need to explore some of your responses in more depth, just so I'm sure I have a proper understanding of your situation, your thoughts on why you are here, that sort of thing.'

'And when you do?'

She became more serious. 'Well… it's hard to say, but sometimes I like to start by trying to turn the clock back. Take a look at your childhood experiences perhaps. But only if you are willing of course. As I am obliged to keep reminding you, all this is entirely voluntary. If at any stage you feel threatened by the process in any way, we will stop and re-evaluate.'

Megan smiled. 'I don't think it's likely that I'm going to feel threatened.'

'Perhaps not, but I'm always careful during these early stages. People are not always aware of what they are carrying around in their heads, and don't like it when they come to realise.'

Megan pinned her with a stare. 'Lydia- You don't mind if I call you Lydia? Some people like to describe me as a Dominatrix. Have you researched any dominatrices before?'

'Mmm, No.'

'Well if you had, you would know that people like me probably spend more time than most thinking about why we are the way we are, what has made us this way. Not all the time of course, but certainly in the early stages.'

'I can imagine.'

'I may be wrong, but I don't think I am carrying much in my head that I am not already aware of. True, some may see some of it as disquieting, shocking even. But I like to think I came to terms with it long ago. Do you understand what I am saying?'

'You're saying you won't be surprised by anything that comes out.'

'Correct. Or is that what all your subjects say?'

Lydia Grant suppressed a smile. 'Let's just say, "we'll see", shall we?'

Seeing her starting to gather her papers, Megan had one last question.

'You mentioned something about doing some sort of brain-scan. How would that work?

'The programme includes neurological analysis. We're interested in comparing subject physiologies. But again if you feel-'

'But how could you do it? They don't have those sort of facilities here, surely?'

'No, we'd do it at our lab. In the University.'

Megan looked doubtful. 'You'd never get permission.'

Lydia Grant's head rocked from side to side. 'It's not impossible. We've done it before.'

'With inmates?'

'Oh yes. It's the Home Office's study. If they want results then they have to let us have access.'

'To my brain you mean.'

'Yes Megan, to your brain.' She stood up. Put out a hand. Megan took it. 'I look forward to working with you,' she said.

'Likewise,' Megan said. She turned to look down to the far end of the room where the Prison Officer who had been present throughout was doing her best to hide the magazine she'd been pretending to not be reading throughout the session. 'We've finished, Collette.'

P.O. Collette Bright rose from her chair and showed the set of teeth that went so well with her name. Turning to the door behind her, she rapped on the window and twirled a finger to let her colleague the other side know they were finished. A loud click echoed through the room. She turned back to Megan's visitor. 'My colleague will escort you out,' then to Megan, 'I need to get you back. It's nearly dinner time.'

'In that case, let's go,' Megan said. As she made to follow after the young P.O. she was coming to know so well, she turned a conspiratorial smile on her visitor and whispered, 'Mustn't be late for dinner now, must we?'

And when Lydia Grant smiled back, Megan Crane knew.

She had her.

Later, lying on her bed, Megan Crane reflected on her meeting with the woman who would soon be poking around inside her head. *And good luck with that,* she thought.

It had actually gone better than she'd expected. There was nothing about Lydia Grant that made her think she may pose a problem. And for an academic, she seemed quite personable, not at all as dry as her CV read. In fact she'd been surprised to realise, she had actually enjoyed the two hours she had spent in Lydia Grant's company. That said, there was still something about her she hadn't quite managed to put her finger on, and which explained the nagging feeling that still lingered. It was the sort of feeling she experienced only rarely, the feeling she might be missing something. She remembered her hair… But no. Something more than that, surely.

As the thirty-minutes-to-lights-out buzzer sounded,

Megan pushed the unanswered questions about Lydia Grant to the back of her mind. There would be plenty of opportunities over the coming weeks to dig beneath the surface and see what lay there. And she was looking forward to doing so. At the end of the day, even psychologists have their secrets, especially ones as interesting as Lydia Grant.

Swinging her legs off the bed, she rose to see to her bedtime ablutions.

CHAPTER 13

The voice in Baggus's head was saying, *This has to be the weirdest set-up ever,* when another said, 'Tea, Sir?'

Looking up, he found Sally, the blonde, girl-woman - he was having trouble gauging her age - holding the cup and saucer at a level that seemed designed to draw his eyes to her crotch. Her short, black dress reminded him of the French-Maid outfit Dina Fahey, one of the more outgoing female DCs, once wore to a boozy CID Christmas party.

'Er, thanks,' Baggus said. As he took it off her, he did his best to ignore the backdrop of stocking-clad legs, tottering on ridiculously high heels.

Squatting, uncomfortably, on an armchair in the Hawthorns' sitting room in their well-appointed Sutton Coldfield home, Baggus was facing the sofa where Gerald Hawthorn had settled next to Jess. Jess had described Gerald as, a 'Silver Fox', and he could see why. But while his gaze was turned towards the pair, the greater part of his attention was on the woman sitting elegantly upright in the chair alongside his, and who was the source of most of his discomfort. Baggus thought that for a woman her age - she had to be well into her fifties - Barbara Hawthorn looked amazing. He was conscious that each time she addressed him, he felt himself colour. He wasn't sure why, but suspected it was something to do with the fact that every time he turned to her, he found her piercing blue eyes - the sparkliest he had ever seen, he thought - already trained on him.

They were waiting for Sally and her male partner - assuming they were partners - to finish serving the teas and biscuits. The man was a Mediterranean type – tanned, swarthy complexion, dark hair pulled back into a ponytail. He was wearing a colourful waistcoat and tight, leather trousers of the sort Baggus imagined might raise questions amongst his rugby mates. Though considering the attention he was paying Jess and Barbara, they'd be wrong. Baggus was surprised to realise that Jess knew the Hawthorns well enough to be on first name terms. And the way they greeted her with kisses when they were shown into the lounge by 'Christo,' the bloke in the trousers, they seemed to think a lot of her.

Baggus still wasn't sure what was going on. But in the ten minutes since they had arrived, he had concluded that the relationship between the older and younger couple was strange in a way beyond his understanding. *If this is how they live, what the hell's this Josephine's going to be like?* The Hawthorns kept issuing terse instructions to the couple, even going so far as to criticise their efforts in a way Baggus found embarrassing, especially as there seemed little to complain about. As far as he was concerned the tea was fine.

Stranger still, was the fact that Sally and Christo - he had picked up their names though there had been no introductions - didn't seem to mind being treated in such a way. And while the pair studiously avoided eye contact with their employers, they had no such qualms as they served him and Jess. There was a definite twinkle in Sally's eye each time she approached him. 'Milk, sir?' 'Sugar, sir?' 'Biscuit?' as if she was deliberately trying to provoke him into something. As far as he could tell, Jess was getting similar treatment from Christo. He was also aware that Jess seemed to be watching him with some amusement. In fact he had the feeling they were *all* gaining some amusement at his expense. He hoped it wasn't a foretaste of things to come.

Eventually, Barbara dismissed the couple, unceremoniously. 'That will be all, Sally, Christo. I'll ring if we need anything.' At which point they hurried out, Sally throwing him a last, mischievous look as she left.

When they had gone, Gerald turned to Jess - 'It's lovely to see you again, Jess,' - and patted her knee. Baggus was surprised when she didn't react to his touch, and glad he didn't leave his hand there. 'You've been neglecting us of late.' Baggus half-expected her to glance across to see if he was reading something into Gerald's words. But she didn't and just smiled warmly at the man who was now leaning into her, eyes twinkling. 'But come on, we're dying to know. What is this is all about? You sounded very mysterious on the phone. How can we help?'

As her husband spoke, Baggus sensed Barbara's eyes on him again, but didn't dare turn to her. It was beginning to make him wonder if Carrie - the only girl who'd ever put up with him for more than a few months - *'If I want a relationship with a rugby team I'll hang around the changing room,'* - had been right after all. Maybe he did have a thing about older women.

He'd also noticed that Barbara shared at least one of Jess's qualities. Though oozing self-confidence, on the surface she could seem distant, until the moment she released a smile and everything changed. It even made him wonder if they might be related. But whereas with Jess there were times when she seemed decidedly more down to earth than the 'DI-In-Charge' role she played, Barbara Hawthorn was different. Although he had known her less than half-an-hour, he already had the sense hers was no act. Whatever her background, her proud-yet-friendly manner seemed real. He suspected that if he were to drop in on her any time of day or night, he would find her the way she was now. Correct, but with a flirtatious edge, charming, and utterly captivating.

Jess returned her cup to its saucer, then half-turned to face the couple. She got straight to it. 'We're interested in one of your former members, Quentin Quinlan.'

'Q?' Gerald said. 'Not seen him in a long time. Can we ask what it's about?'

'He was found dead at his home, a week ago.'

Gerald paled, while Barbara sat up straight as her hand went to her mouth. Baggus thought it was the most elegant response to shock he had ever seen.

'Gavin here-.' Baggus felt Barbara's gaze again. 'Is investigating his death. He'd like to speak with some of the members who knew him, with your permission of course.'

Gerald looked between Jess and his wife, struggling to maintain his composure. 'But why…? Of course… But how…?' He stopped and took a deep breath. 'Oh dear. Poor Q. This is shocking news.' Jess didn't press, and Baggus waited. She obviously knew these people enough to respect their feelings. Gerald continued. 'Can you tell us what happened? How he died?' He turned to Baggus. 'If you are investigating his death, does that mean… it wasn't accidental?'

'That's what I'm trying to find out,' Baggus said. 'There're a couple of aspects I need to look at before I can be sure one way or another. That's why we are here.'

For the first time, Barbara spoke up. 'What 'aspects', exactly?'

Baggus turned to her, trying not to react to her scrutinising gaze. Not sure how much to reveal, he threw Jess a glance. But she seemed relaxed enough not to keep anything back.

'His association with Megan Crane for one,' Baggus said.

Barbara froze.

'Ah!' Gerald's face registered understanding. 'Ooohh dear.'

Baggus wasn't surprised by their reaction. Jess had spoken of the enquiries she'd made at Josephine's as background to the prosecution case prior to Megan Crane's trial, verifying her history, checking names and dates, confirming associations. It had been a worrying time for the Hawthorns. They'd feared that if Megan Crane's connections with the club got too much attention, it would panic the membership and ruin their reputation, perhaps even put them out of business. As it happened, the matter got barely a mention in all the press reporting during and following the trial. But the Internet boards, social media and chat-rooms were full of it. Club attendance figures rocketed and remained high for months. Wisely, the Hawthorns never sought to make capital out of it, and pretended not to hear whenever they walked past some huddle of members and caught the name, 'Megan Crane', being mentioned in hushed tones. Now the name had resurfaced to haunt them once more.

Barbara fixed her gaze on Baggus in a way that made him feel like she was weighing how far she could trust him. Eventually, she turned to Jess.

'What do you need from us?'

CHAPTER 14

The Right Honourable Alistair Kenworthy, MP ended the call, then stood in the middle of his expansive living room, staring into space. The news he'd just received wasn't *too* troubling, but it *was* a reminder that he still needed to proceed cautiously in the matter that occupied his thoughts more and more these days. Not for the first time, he derided himself, shaking his head and reiterating the oath he'd made many months before to never again leave himself exposed this way. Suddenly, he remembered Anne, and spun round to face the open French windows, half expecting to find her standing there, a look of horror on her face. When he saw her still out in the garden, inspecting her beloved roses, he gave a relieved sigh. He really should have checked *before* answering his mobile. But in his eagerness to receive Hugh's update, he had neglected to do so. Another mistake.

'You need to get a grip,' he muttered to himself, turning away. 'Before it all goes to rat shit.'

'Everything alright, dear? You look like you've seen a ghost.'

Turning again, he saw her slightly anxious expression. His mutterings must have carried. He gave a reassuring smile and called back, 'Everything's fine. Nothing to worry about.'

Accepting as always, she nodded, before returning to her dead-heading.

About to head off to his study to give the matter further thought, Kenworthy stopped. Mid-September, the day was bright, the sun warm. As she'd turned away, the sun had caught her in profile, highlighting some of the features that, though less striking than they once were, had drawn him all those years ago. Through the lens of thirty-metres, the lines that, close-to, spoke of too many cigarettes, too much wine and not enough sun-screen were barely visible. Similarly, her flowery summer frock disguised the shallowness of her breasts and all-but covered the inky-blue lines that crazy-paved the back of her calves - her late mother's only legacy. In that moment, lured by a late-summer-day's promise and a train of thought triggered by the telephone call, Kenworthy was struck by something he hadn't thought on for a long time.

Anne Kenworthy, wife, mother, Women's Institute Secretary and - most importantly - sole heiress to her industrialist-father's fortune, was still a fine-looking woman. For all that had happened, the figure that once graced the catwalks of London and Paris was still there, more or less, as was the bone structure that had made her so famously photogenic. Right then, looking at her in the sunshine, Kenworthy experienced a flashback. It took the form of a reminder of the stirrings that had, in his younger days, been a constant in his life - themselves a symptom of the testosterone-fuelled drives he had inherited from *his* father. But then came another realisation, and the stirrings vanished as quickly as they had come.

However she may look, Anne Kenworthy was, nowadays, an empty vessel. The verve, ambition and *passion* that had made her the woman she was, had departed long ago. He understood why. He also understood, and accepted, that he, largely, was to blame. Nevertheless he felt the familiar sense of resentment that arose every time he thought about it. True, what had happened was, with hindsight, stupid, ridiculous - and dangerous. Little surprise then, she had changed. But he still harboured the suspicion - no, stronger than that, the belief - that had she tried harder to put it behind them, spent less time blaming him and nurturing the hurt, anger and all the other stuff she threw at him in the years following, she might, just might, have reclaimed the qualities that had made so special. If she had only been willing to listen, to see things from his point of view, they might even have rekindled some of what they'd once had. But she wasn't, and they didn't. Now, that hope was gone, a distant dream of what might have been. Which was why he'd sought what he craved elsewhere, and how he'd found himself drawn into a situation almost as bad as the one that left her so damaged in the first place. And now, from what he was hearing and in terms of potential damage, it posed as big a threat to his ambitions as any of the skeletons that rattled around in their various cupboards.

For several moments he stood still and quiet, giving what Hugh had told him more consideration than Hugh would ever know it merited. Hugh may be his PA, but that didn't mean he needed to be privy to everything going on in his life, *or* his thought processes. In fact given recent events, the less Hugh knew about these matters, the better. Nevertheless, though Kenworthy was satisfied there was no need for any real concern, he was glad Hugh had thought to ring him. *Forewarned is forearmed.* For a few moments more, he turned things in his mind, weighing possibilities, considering outcomes. Eventually, he relaxed. The bases, as Americans like to say, were all covered. Even if they had missed any, it would only require a light touch on the wheel to bring things back on line. Yes, he thought proudly, the situation was under control, testimony to his ability to operate under pressure. Exactly what the country needs in a Prime Minister.

'Who was it, dear?'

He turned. This time his wife *was* framed in the French windows, a posy of flowers in one hand, garden scissors in the other, a glaze of perspiration reflecting off the finely-hued features. The pang of regret returned. Once, the way she looked now…

'Only Hugh,' he said. It wouldn't signify anything. Hugh often called out of hours. 'Nothing serious.'

Anne looked relieved. 'Good. I thought I was going to have to handle dinner on my own again. The last thing I need today is some Parliamentary crisis.'

Crossing to her, Kenworthy took her by the arms. 'No need to worry my sweet. We're going to have a lovely evening.'

He hugged her to him. Over her shoulder he checked his watch. Not yet two o'clock. Plenty of time to manufacture the urgent phone call from the Whip's office that would force him, regrettably, to give his apologies to the old farts who made up the District Rural Reclamation Committee. Then he'd be free to….

The line of thought trailed off as Kenworthy experienced something that was almost as unexpected as some of the other developments he'd heard about of late. Thinking on what he had to do, part of his mind had turned to the evening ahead. Images of a woman, waiting in a semi-darkened room had sneaked their way into his thoughts. And standing there, with Anne in his arms, something strange had happened. Suddenly he found himself, *stirring.*

'Ohh,' Anne said. 'Why, Alistair. Is that you?' Swapping the flowers to her other hand, she reached down to check she wasn't mistaken.

Fuck, Kenworthy chided himself.

His mind went into overdrive as he searched, desperately, for a way out of this latest, unforeseen predicament.

CHAPTER 15

Josephine's lies just off the main A452 Birmingham to Coventry road, more or less midway between. Baggus saw the sign in good time coming up on his left. "Josephine's - The UK's Premier Private Event Venue." The word, *Josephine's,* was picked out in pink and done in some fancy scroll-script. As he slowed, then swung in through the entrance - no gates, just a couple of white, concrete posts that could take a chain - he was already looking forward to the end of the night. By then at least, he may have answers to some of the questions around Quentin Quinlan's death. But thoughts of what he may have to go through to get them, weren't filling him with enthusiasm.

In front of him was a long, rectangular building. Painted white and with dark-wood window frames and terracotta roof tiles, it had a vaguely Spanish air about it. High hedges to either side screened the outside areas. A sign pointed right to the car park. Driving on, Baggus noted it looked to have been recently re-surfaced, spaces neatly marked out with fresh, white paint. He hoped it was a positive sign. More often than not, the clubs he usually frequented - work purposes of course - had rough, open-ground parking.

He parked up as close as he could to the stone steps leading up to the glass doors with "Main Reception" written on them. Cutting the engine, he paused, hands still on the wheel, to look across to where people were already filing in. The entrance was well-lit. Not everyone was wearing a coat, and some of those that were hadn't bothered to button them up. As he got his first inkling of what the phrase, "Dress Code" actually covered, he let out a breathy, 'Jesus Christ.'

Reaching across, Jess patted the back of his hand. 'Stick with me. You'll be fine.'

He turned to her, but for once he was out of light remarks. He shook his head. As he stepped out, he thought on what his rugby mates might say if they could see him now. In Black Tie and escorting a woman wearing a dress made from some shiny-red material into a place full of characters straight out of a fetish-porn flick.

As he headed towards the steps, conscious he was already blushing like a traffic signal, he tried to remember some of the stuff Jess and Barbara Hawthorn had covered in his 'crash-course'.

Before the Hawthorns took the lease, twelve years ago, Josephine's had been a restaurant and private function venue; weddings, parties, etc. Even back then, a 'bit of kink' was already coming to be seen as an acceptable part of, 'Consensual Adult Play.' Since then, interest in the sorts of activities that were once the sole preserve of the BDSM Community had surged. Two factors accounted for the change. One was the ready availability of 'on-line adult resources' - Web Porn. The second was the huge growth in popularity of what Barbara termed, "Literary Erotica" - which Baggus had been quick to disclaim having ever read, unlike Jess, he noted.

'Slow up, Gavin,' Jess called from behind. Catching up, she pulled at his sleeve and looped her arm round his to check his pace. 'I'm in heels remember. And calm down. It's not like you're going to bump into your mother or anything.'

'Please,' he said. 'Don't even mention my mother. It's bad enough as it is.'

Ten minutes later, they were standing in the middle of the bustling lounge area, sipping coke and mineral water as Gerald pretended to welcome them as new guests. Given his surroundings, and despite Jess's attempts at reassurance as they'd waited for Gerald to join them, Baggus felt more uncomfortable than ever.

'Apart from their sexual interests, they're just normal people enjoying a normal night out,' Jess had said. 'The psychos we deal with wouldn't last a minute here. Just think of it as a club where they meet like-minded people.'

Baggus didn't look convinced. 'Like Megan Crane you mean?'

Jess gave him a rueful glare. 'She was a one-off.'

Baggus scanned the room. 'Says who?'

Whichever way he turned, he found himself staring at some outlandish garment of rubber, leather or both. One couple appeared to be dressed as babies - *What's that all about?* But while several of the women were certainly attractive, some of the men who had opted for something other than black tie – especially those who looked in late middle-age or even older - were making him squirm. He kept finding himself staring open-mouthed at, or spinning rapidly away from, what was for him, some ghastly spectacle. The constant turning was making him nauseous.

'I've already spotted a couple of guests who knew Q,' Gerald said. He seemed to be enjoying his 'furtive guide' role, pretending to be pointing things out, whilst exchanging nods and smiles with the regulars. 'Most of his crowd stopped coming around the time he did, but there's one behind you at the bar now. The chap in the tee-shirt and collar.' He nodded over Baggus's shoulder and turned in the opposite direction to give them a chance to look.

As Baggus's gaze swept the bar, he had no difficulty identifying the man. Fiftyish, and seriously over-weight, he was wearing ridiculous, tight-fitting, shiny-black trousers, a white tee-shirt and a black leather collar. His flabby features spoke of too much good living. Sipping at a green cocktail through a straw, he was talking to a younger couple dressed in Arab garb. He was wearing the flowing robes of a Sheik, while she appeared to be playing his 'harem girl.' The man had the look of someone from the middle east anyway, leaving Baggus non the wiser as to whether he was 'in role', as Jess put it, or had simply chosen to ignore the, Dress Code.

Normal people enjoying a normal night out? Yeah, right.

He turned back in time to catch Jess's eye. She didn't seem in the least phased by the sights on offer.

'Who is he?' Jess said.

'Jeremy Blackstock,' Gerald said. A Birmingham barrister. I always had the impression he and Q were close. You may want to speak with him.'

Baggus brightened. Like some of his colleagues, his views on barristers swung between utmost respect for those who prosecuted and did it well, and contempt for those he considered made too-good a living helping the guilty get off. He had no idea if Blackstock even practised criminal law, but he was happy to pigeon-hole him in the latter category. The idea of button-holing him in what could be professionally embarrassing circumstances, while getting into his ribs over a friend's connection with a convicted serial killer, appealed. Maybe the evening wouldn't be so bad after all.

'Excuse me a minute,' Gerald said. 'I'm needed.'

They watched as he made his way over to the reception desk where one of the doormen - 'Dwain', Jess had called him when he greeted her at the door with a friendly kiss of recognition - was embroiled in a heated discussion with a middle-aged man. The man was waving a document at Dwain, urging him to take it. But Dwain was having none of it, shaking his head, and showing his palms in refusal. During their earlier visit, Barbara had explained their Admissions Policy. Visitors were allowed to enrol as members at the door, provided they produced two forms of identification, one showing a permanent address. 'Some try it on using false ID. They think we're some sort of brothel where they can just walk in and act out their fantasies. It's not what we are about. We like to keep things intimate. A family and friends atmosphere.'

At the time, Baggus was sceptical, suspecting she was putting a gloss on what was, essentially, a seedy operation. But now, as he looked at the way Gerald dealt with the situation, calming the man down and ushering him and his partner - a scantily-clad black girl - into the office behind reception, he wondered if he'd been too quick to judge. Like the Hawthorns themselves, the staff he'd met so far seemed professional and genuine. And from what he was seeing, everyone seemed interested only in having fun. In fact, the atmosphere was more akin to a country club on a party night, than a place where people met to pursue their interest in things many would find shocking, if not downright *weird.* Apart from the outfits - and the stocks – he'd seen nothing overtly sexual at all, though the sign above the double doors at the far end, 'Theme Rooms This Way,' gave some hint.

Alone again with Jess, he made an effort to relax. 'Well it makes a change from Kingsholme.' He forced a smile.

'What's Kingsholme?' she said.

Not into rugby then. Shame. 'Gloucester's ground.' The puzzled look remained. 'The rugby team?'

'Right. Is that the one with the egg-shaped ball?'

Unsure, he looked at her askance. Eventually a smile broke. He nodded. 'I'll give you that one.'

'Good of you,' she said, hazel eyes flashing. Unlike him, she seemed right at home. As if to emphasise it, she dug into her shoulder bag, drew out a length of chain attached to a collar. She held it out to him as she turned, casually, to face towards where Blackstock was standing. 'When I tell you, put this on me then lead me over to the bar.'

'*What?'*

'We're supposed to be members remember. If we want to get people talking, we need to be convincing.'

Baggus looked pained. 'Can't we just-'

'No. Do it now, he's looking this way.'

Baggus took the items off her. 'Ah shit. This is soo-'

'Just do it.'

As he placed the collar round Jess's throat, she added, 'But don't let this give you any wrong ideas.'

He didn't answer, and avoided eye contact, but was aware of the faint smile that played about her lips as he went about buckling it up. 'Now what?'

'Now lead me to the bar. And try and make it look like you're in charge.'

Baggus took a deep breath. 'I feel like a right perv,'

'Stop complaining. You had the chance to play it the other way round and you passed. Live with it.'

As they headed to the bar, no one gave more than a second glance at the attractive couple - him in a smart evening suit, she in a red-rubber dress that wasn't long enough to hide the tops of her fishnets. No one apart from Christo that is. He was serving drinks to arriving guests and hadn't taken his eyes of Jess from the moment she'd walked in.

CHAPTER 16

Carver banged the near-empty bottle of Jameson down on the coffee table and reached for the TV control. He wasn't used to being home alone on a Saturday evening. Nor had he realised until tonight just how much he was missing her. He'd thought about ringing, but didn't relish hearing people in the background having a great time - like he wasn't.

He channel-hopped a while, but found nothing of interest. As he tossed the control away he thought again about cancelling his subscription. What he was paying each month for the privilege of catching the odd Liverpool game was ridiculous.

His eyes flitted to the pile of brochures and property specs he had spent the day gathering in an effort to keep his mind off what Jess and her new partner were up to. But seeing them brought it all back. He didn't want to think about what would happen if they drew a blank - or even if they didn't. He'd spent hours imagining scenarios that might result from their venture into Megan Crane's old territory. None of them ruled her out of things. Okay, it still didn't necessarily mean he would have to get involved himself. Jess had said she was happy to handle it, and the way she had come on the past eighteen months, she was certainly up to it. Operation Kerry had taught her a lot.

Yet the doubts that lingered were still capable of bringing on some of the old fears - the ones he thought he had put to bed, until the day he found himself staring at the body of a woman tied to a post, her hands super-glued out in front of her. A shiver rippled through him.

Don't go there.

You're over it.

You proved it, to yourself and to Rosanna.

So how come she's not here?

'NO.'

He swung himself up and onto his feet, swaying slightly as the blood rushed from his head. It was a sign of how much he'd drunk that he'd had to say it aloud to convince himself. 'I'm not going to do this. It'll be fine. Jess and wassisname will bottom it. And Rosanna will be back. Soon.'

He gazed about him. The flat was small. Not enough room even for the dining table - still in storage, along with her music, and cooking stuff, his books, and all the rest. All of a sudden he saw why Rosanna hated it so much. And in that moment he hated it more. He hated its narrow confines, its restricting walls. He hated the dull, flowery wallpaper. He hated the noisy neighbours. And he knew he had to get out. To be somewhere where there were people.

Work, he thought. There's always something happening there. He could…. He stopped. No, there isn't. He wasn't an operational detective any more. He was an, 'Intelligence Officer.' Someone who sifted papers and read things. A desk man. It wasn't twenty-four-seven like real police work. There was down time. Like Saturday nights.

He checked his watch. Ten forty-five. Jasper's, the bistro-pub at the end of the street, would still be serving. He grabbed his jacket off the chair, checked for his keys, and went to the door. He was about to leave when he stopped and turned in the doorway, looking back at the dismal surroundings that were slowly driving a wedge between him and the woman he loved.

'Bear with me Ros,' he said, then turning, he slammed the door behind him and strode out into the night.

CHAPTER 17

Returning from Barbara Hawthorn's 'personal tour' of the club and its facilities, Baggus felt like he'd been on one of those simulators that take you on a roller-coaster ride through some alien landscape; in desperate need of firm ground and time to let his senses readjust. He got neither. As she led him back through to the main lounge, he spotted Jess over in the far corner. She was with Blackstock and the couple from the Arabian Nights. The Sheik's wife/harem girl, a long-limbed blonde wearing not much more than see-through veils, seemed as interested in Jess as her partner. All four were talking animatedly, and laughing.

It had been Jess's idea that things may go better if she got stuck into Blackstock alone, at least to begin with. When they first approached him at the bar and Baggus threw a casual-seeming, 'Busy tonight isn't it?', Blackstock's eyes nearly popped when he saw Jess on the end of the leash. As conversation developed, it became quickly obvious he was excited by the prospect of something new. From what Baggus could see going on over in the corner, it looked like her plan was working.

Barbara had happened along as Blackstock was

ordering drinks enabling Jess to suggest that she may like to show Baggus round, 'Before things start getting serious.' Barbara seemed to jump at the idea, and though it left Baggus feeling like a novice-detective on the fringes of a major enquiry, leaving things to the seasoned pros, the thought of time in the company of the older woman didn't exactly fill him with dread. As Barbara led him away, his last sight of Jess was her leaning into Blackstock and whispering in his ear. Whatever she said, it made his eyes widen further.

After spending much of the day with Jess, Baggus thought he finally had his head round how things worked. From nine o'clock, members and guests assembled. For the first couple of hours the place operated like any private club. Drinks, conversation, a bit of dancing, getting to know people. It was after the buffet-supper that the serious stuff began.

According to Jess, most of the regulars would arrive having already planned how they saw their evening progressing, what sort of second-half-of-the-night activity they were up for. Others were happy to go with the flow, wait and see who was there and what they felt like doing - depending on the opportunities on offer. However people played it, after supper was cleared away, the focus shifted away from the bar-lounge to the Theme Rooms and the private and semi-private suites located on the first floor.

A couple of the suites were already occupied when Barbara showed him round and she made a point of not disturbing the occupants. 'Respect for others is a major part of our philosophy,' she told him. It didn't detract from the tour, and the website - and Jess - had given him a fair idea of what to expect anyway. He knew that the Theme Rooms were where people gathered to take part in, or watch, a particular type of activity – usually involving some form of D/S action. But as Barbara showed him into the first and, according to her, 'most popular,' "Theme Room", Baggus felt a chill run through him.

It was kitted out with an array of dungeon equipment that looked like it belonged on the set of some Gothic-horror flick. The size of a small gym, the range of equipment on display - wooden frames, stocks, chains, racks, strange looking chairs - together with the mix of harsh and soft lighting and lots of mirrors, made it impossible to see far into its sinister depths. Not yet in use - *Thank God* - Barbara led him inside. Arm still linked through his, she began talking him through what the various pieces of apparatus were for, telling him - rather proudly he thought - how they had come by some of it.

'We found the paddling chair-' she indicated a strange looking contraption over by the right hand wall. '-at Bygone-Days.' Baggus looked blank. 'That place outside Leicester. It sells all sorts of old furniture and bric-a-brac. It's amazing what you can find.'

'I'll take your word for it,' Baggus said, staring at the piece but not sure what he was looking at. With two seats arranged one above the other, it looked like a cross between a set of steps and a commode. The upper 'seat' was tilted at an angle and the lower had a large round hole where someone would normally sit. He couldn't work out whether it was for sitting in, kneeling on, or both.

'The man selling it thought it was some sort of kitchen stool, but Gerald recognised it for what it was soon as he saw it.'

'Good for Gerald.'

As she leaned forward to look into his face, he saw the smile again. 'Would you like to see how any of it works?'

His panic must have shown as she burst out laughing. Given the surroundings, the warm sound felt out of place. Baggus wished they were in The Shady Oak and that she was laughing at some joke he had cracked, rather than his discomfort. She seemed to sense it.

'I'm sorry. That wasn't fair. I promise I won't tease anymore. Come on, there's lots to see.'

He was glad when she switched off the lights and led him out, but as she steered him towards the next set of double doors he became aware of a feeling he experienced only rarely. For the first time in a long time, he was completely out of his depth. Yet he felt comfortable in the company of this older woman who seemed so at ease in this strange environment. And despite the teasing – he believed her when she promised not to do it again - he felt safe in her hands.

The next half-hour was a blur of images and feelings that mixed amazement and creepiness in equal measure. A room laid out like a schoolroom, complete with desks, a blackboard, a dunces cap and, lying across the teacher's desk, a set of bamboo canes. Another, spotlessly white and immaculately clean, was part-dental surgery, part-hospital. The dentist's chair was real, not some mock-up, and the two beds were as neatly-made up, the sheets as well-starched, as any hospital. The last room was done-out like an Arabian harem, all billowing nets, sumptuous pillows, cushions, mattresses, and of course – he was expecting it by now – the obligatory shackles, dangling from walls and pillars. He remembered the couple he'd seen earlier.

Moving upstairs, Barbara showed him the Private

Rooms. Some mirrored the themes he had seen downstairs, but less well-equipped. 'We only allow a maximum of four in one room at any one time.' She said it the way a seaside landlady might warn a frisky young couple, "No bouncing on the beds". But as they returned downstairs, Baggus realised that everything he had seen was scrupulously clean and ordered. The rooms were tastefully decorated, and the feel of the place was nothing like the seedy brothels and other places his work occasionally took him to. Barbara described how club rules only allowed 'full sex' to take place in the Private Rooms, and they were always booked well in advance. 'Some people don't realise that Josephine's is strictly a place for trying out new ideas and meeting people. Anyone who turns up thinking they can jump straight into some orgy will be disappointed. It does happen you know.'

Baggus didn't doubt it. He'd thought exactly that when Jess first described the place.

Now, as he looked across at Jess putting on an act for her fan club - he *assumed* it was an act- he felt Barbara squeeze his arm.

'She's quite attractive, isn't she?'

'Who?' he said.

'You know who.'

He felt himself redden, again.

'How long have you known each other?'

'Not long. We're just helping each other out.'

'Of course,' she said. 'Perhaps you should go rescue her before Jeremy drags her off somewhere.'

He started to move away before she started teasing again, but felt a pull on his sleeve and turned back. Clear blue eyes that more rightly belonged to a teenager bore into his, as if searching for something.

'I'm sure you're a very experienced detective, Gavin. But there are things you know very little about. Do please be careful.'

Unsure whether to take it as criticism or a warning, he was about to bat it off when she did something totally unexpected. Leaning forward, she kissed him, lightly, on the cheek. Flashing another of her smiles, she turned and headed across the room to join her husband at the bar. As she approached, Gerald raised a glass in Baggus's direction and he realised. Gerald had been watching them. Acknowledging Gerald's toast with a brief nod, he moved to join Jess's little group. As he set off, he let out a long, 'Sheeesh.'

As he neared them, he saw Christo hovering behind Jess's chair, making a meal of collecting empty glasses and arranging them on a tray. Seeing Baggus approaching, he moved off elsewhere.

'You're back,' Jess said, smiling.

As she introduced him to the others - 'Gavin's my partner for the evening,' - he shook hands, and checked their faces. They all read the same.

Lucky bastard.

CHAPTER 18

'Quentin Quinlan?' Blackstock stopped his glass halfway to his mouth. 'You know Q?'

Baggus nodded, sipping at his tonic water. It had taken some twenty minutes to get Blackstock to pay him attention. The Arabian Nights pair had wandered off soon after he'd arrived, disappointed to learn that Jess already had a partner. After Jess asked his permission to be excused to freshen up, and which he 'granted', he found common ground by getting Blackstock to hint at his professional background - 'Legal work,' - then mentioning the Cheltenham-based Solicitor he claimed to have known.

'It was Q put me onto Josephine's,' Baggus said. 'I believe he used to come here regularly?'

'He did indeed.' Blackstock said, relaxing a little. Knowledge of Q's association with Josephine's implied a certain closeness. 'What line of work did you say you were in?'

'Sports-ground equipment,' Baggus said. 'Rugby posts, track and field gear, lights, that sort of thing.' One of his mates was in the business and he knew enough to waffle. He guessed Blackstock wasn't much into sport. He was right.

'Photography's my thing. Anyway, tell me more about your lady. Is she pure sub, or does she switch?'

Baggus tried to take the question in his stride and hoped he remembered enough of Jess's 'training' to make it sound authentic. 'Mainly sub, I think. But I'm not entirely sure yet. We're just trying each other out.'

'I see….'

As Baggus took another drink, he could almost hear cogs whirring inside Blackstock's head.

'So…' Blackstock tried to make it sound casual. 'Will you both be playing later?'

'Possibly.'

'Open, or closed?'

Almost caught out by his directness, Baggus remembered Barbara mentioning another of the club's principles. *'Openness and honesty at all times.'* He looked around, hoping to see Jess coming back to rescue him. But she was over the other side of the room talking to Christo. The way they were leaning into each other, Baggus wondered what they could be talking about. He turned back to Blackstock.

'That would be up to her,' he said. Sensing a quagmire ahead, he took the initiative. 'But if she's in the right mood, I might be able to get her to….' He rocked a hand. *Know what I mean?*

Blackstock shuffled forward in his seat, forehead beading with sweat. 'Is she… good?'

'Let's just say she's had some… training.'

The barrister's eyebrows arched upwards. 'How wonderful.'

A few minutes later, Jess re-joined them and Baggus settled back to listen as Blackstock did his best to get her to open up about herself and her 'interests'. Baggus was impressed by the way she kept drawing him in with a few well-placed hints, then fuelled his interest by becoming reticent. After several minutes Baggus caught her eye and nodded over his shoulder.

She made a show of seeing someone she knew. Lowering her gaze she said to Baggus, 'May I be excused for a few moments?'

Baggus feigned impatience. 'If you must, but don't be long.'

As she disappeared into the throng of guests, Blackstock murmured, as much to himself as Baggus. 'What a fascinating young woman.'

By now, the buffet was being laid out, and Baggus sensed the atmosphere becoming more charged. He steered conversation back to their mutual friend, leading Blackstock to ask, 'So how is the old stick these days anyway?'

Baggus feigned surprise. 'I'm sorry, I thought you knew.' With appropriate regret, he described hearing of Q's death in some sort of accident at home. He didn't know details.

Blackstock seemed genuinely saddened. 'How terrible. Poor old Q.'

'Interesting thing was,' Baggus continued. 'I bumped into him a few days earlier and mentioned I was coming here. We arranged to meet for a drink. He said there was something important I needed to know if I decide to start coming regularly.'

Blackstock looked wary. 'Didn't mention my name I hope?'

'No,' Baggus said easily. 'But he spoke about that court case that was in the papers a while ago. That dominatrix-woman who murdered several people? What was her name… Melanie… Mary…?'

'Megan Crane,' Blackstock said, lowering his voice.

'She used to come here. Q met her a few times.'

'Really? Good God. I suppose he wanted to make sure I didn't tell anyone he knew her.'

Blackstock lightened. 'I doubt it. He didn't care who knew, quite proud of it in fact.'

'In that case, it must have been something else.'

As if reflecting, Baggus picked up his glass and turned toward the bar. Through the throng, he could see Jess, talking to a group of guests. He turned back to find Blackstock staring in her direction. As he did so, his tongue emerged to run around his lips. Eventually he transferred his gaze back to Baggus. The pair stared at each other. After several seconds, Blackstock checked around, as of to make sure no one could hear. He leaned forward.

'There was… something.'

'Something?'

'Something I know Q was worried about. He mentioned it to me a few times.' He turned to look at Jess again, before coming back to Baggus. 'I might be persuaded to share it, but only with someone I'm close to.'

Baggus let his gaze flick towards Jess. 'Oh, I suspect that after tonight, we'll be *very* close.'

Blackstock's flabby features broke into a wide smile. Straightening up, he tossed his drink back. 'In that case- But you need to get me another drink first.'

Baggus took his glass. As he headed to the bar he caught Jess's eye and nodded.

We're in.

CHAPTER 19

Baggus had no difficulty spotting the wary looks the Hawthorns kept passing each other as he recounted what he'd learned. Earlier, as the buffet was being cleared and the guests were beginning to drift off towards the Theme Rooms, he'd spotted Jess slipping into the office next to the bar. When Blackstock went to the Gents, he followed. Gerald and Barbara were already there. For the first five minutes only Baggus spoke. Now, as he put the question to them again, he imagined Blackstock running from room to room, searching for them, rather, for Jess.

'So, neither of you have any idea what this 'incident' was?' He glanced at Jess. Her gaze was fixed on the couple.

Gerald crossed to the drinks cabinet, started dropping ice into tumblers. 'As I said, I can't imagine. To my knowledge, nothing's ever happened in the club that would embarrass us with the authorities.'

Baggus checked Barbara, but she was following her husband's every move. As Gerald returned and handed her a glass, another look passed between them.

It was at that moment that Jess finally broke her silence. Her tone was one Baggus had not heard before.

'Sit down Gerald.'

Gerald came around to sit next to his wife on the sofa. They huddled together, like school children who knew they were in for a telling-off.

'You both know I'd never do anything to hurt you, or your business.' They stared into their drinks. 'But it's obvious there's something you're not telling us.' Neither moved. 'I can think of no reason why Blackstock would lie about Q telling him about some incident he was worried might bring trouble on himself. So, let me be clear. I will do whatever it takes to find out what this incident was.'

Baggus kept his eye on the Hawthorns. If he'd had any lingering niggles over Jess's CID credentials, they'd just evaporated. She continued.

'You have a choice. You can either tell us what you know, or we can start visiting your members. And if that sounds like a threat, then I'm sorry, but we need to know.'

Barbara groped for her husband's hand. As he turned to her, she nodded. Gerald drained his glass then rose to refill it. When he returned to the sofa he gave her one last look, then began.

'When I say we don't *know* what happened, I'm telling the truth.' He took a drink.

Barbara must have sensed their scepticism, and chipped in. 'Believe us, Jess. We wouldn't lie to you.'

Gerald rested a hand on her thigh. After a few seconds he continued. 'Up to a couple of years ago, we used to let members rent the club for private functions, events, parties, special occasions, that sort of thing. Sometimes we would be around to help out, clear up, etc. Other times it was a strictly private affair. We'd give them the keys and they would arrange everything themselves, including cleaning the place and locking up afterwards.' He paused to take another drink. 'I suppose we always suspected that some of these functions were rather more… shall we say, hardcore, than what goes on at club nights?'

'Suspected, or knew?' Baggus said.

Gerald gave him a straight look.

'Carry on Gerald,' Jess said.

Gerald took another drink. He seemed to be having difficulty swallowing.

'We began to hear stories about a group of members. They referred to themselves as, The Upper Floor. We think Q was part of it, but we're not entirely sure. We heard their interests were rather… specialised. We never got to hear details of what went on, but there was one occasion, after one of their functions… One of our cleaners found a bag of waste in the bins that had split open. There were items of clothing, men's and women's, that were ripped and torn. There were also several towels, cleaning cloths, tissues.' He paused.

'So?' Baggus said.

'They were blood-stained. Some, quite heavily.'

Baggus felt his skin crawl. He glanced over at Jess. Her face was blank. But then, she'd worked on the Kerry investigation. 'Did you report it to anyone?'

Gerald shook his head. 'We talked about it, but no one complained. Our policy back then was, so long as everything's consensual and legal, we didn't have a problem with it. And scarification isn't exactly rare.'

Baggus checked with Jess. 'Scar-if…?'

'Scarification. Knives. Cutting, that sort of thing.'

Baggus winced, nodded. 'Has your policy changed since?'

Gerald shot a glance at his wife. 'Yes. It has.'

'Go on.'

'Not long after, we began to hear rumours that something had happened at an Upper Floor function. No one would say, but it was obvious people were scared. We tried asking around, but nobody would talk to us about it. In the weeks following, some members stopped coming. They haven't been back since.'

'What do you think happened?' Jess said.

Another glance at Barbara. Another nod. 'We're not sure, but we suspect someone got hurt.'

There was a short pause, then Jess said, 'How serious?'

The couple stared at each other. Without taking his eyes off her husband, Barbara said, 'Fairly serious.'

Baggus said, 'How about, *very* serious?'

There was a longer pause. Eventually Barbara said, 'Possibly.'

'Did you do anything? Tell anyone?' Jess said.

Barbara turned to her. 'What could we do? We still don't *know* anything happened. It was all just rumour, speculation. Josephine's thrives on stories and fantasy. People like to make stuff up.'

'But you didn't think this was made up.'

Barbara returned her stare. 'As I say, we weren't sure.'

Gerald took up the running again. 'Whether real or made up, we stopped the private functions. Eventually people stopped talking about it. We've never heard mention of it since, until tonight.'

Baggus gave Jess a hard look. *How far can we trust these people?* 'What happened to this Upper Floor crowd. Do they still meet?

'We don't know. If they do, it's not here.'

'Then tell us who was involved.'

Gerald looked apologetic. 'If we could, we would. Q must have been, as he made the bookings. But beyond him-' Gerald shrugged. 'People tend to keep things away from us. In case we bar them from membership. And people have always been paranoid about naming names, particularly if it involves something on the edge. Everyone who comes here is in the same boat. Nobody wants publicity.'

There was a quiet cough. Everyone turned to Barbara.

'We do know one person who was part of this Upper Floor group.'

'Who?' Baggus and Jess said together.

Barbara turned to her husband. After a moment's pause, Gerald nodded.

'Megan Crane,' Barbara said.

Baggus was about to say something when there was a knock at the door. Christo poked his head into the room.

'Sorry Mr Hawthorn. There is a problem in one of the rooms. Can you come?'

'Excuse me,' Gerald said.

As he left the room, Barbara asked Christo to bring coffee.

'Of course, Madam.'

Baggus noticed how, as he closed the door, his eyes were on Jess.

A couple of minutes later, Gerald returned. 'It was nothing. Sorted itself before I got there.'

Christo brought in the coffee, accompanied by Sally. Baggus wondered where she had been all evening. As Christo started to pour, Barbara touched his arm. 'That's alright, Christo. I'll do it.' He turned to her and Baggus saw the long look that passed between them. Eventually he put the pot down and, after giving Jess a similar, long stare, he and Sally left.

'What's up with him?' Baggus said.

'Probably knows something's going on,' Gerald said. 'He's very protective of Barbara. You too, Jess, I'd say.'

Jess tried to ignore it, but must have sensed Baggus looking at her. She turned to meet his stare. He didn't say anything. She turned back to Gerald.

'Is there anyone else here tonight would know about this Upper Floor lot?'

'No one I know of. Even if there was, you would have to pressure them to say anything. Like you've done with us.'

Jess pulled a 'hurt' look. 'Now don't be like that, Gerald. I told you what to expect when we first met.' Rising, she went over and kissed him on the cheek. He brightened. She did the same with Barbara.

Baggus stayed put.

A few minutes later, having released the Hawthorns to their hosting duties, Baggus turned to Jess.

'So where does this leave us?' He suspected he knew the answer. They'd gone over the what-ifs and maybes on the way there.

'We need to speak with Jamie.'

Baggus nodded. 'Right. In that case I suppose we'd better call it a night.'

For a moment, she looked undecided, then said, 'I'm going to hang around a bit. See if I can pick up anything else.'

Baggus sighed. In truth, he'd had enough for one night. But he wasn't about to abandon her.

'Fair enough. Where do you want to start?'

'Me, Gavin.'

'What?'

'I said *I'll* hang around. You've done your bit. Let's see what I can find out.'

'Don't be-.' But before he could finish, she rounded on him.

'Go home, Gavin. You don't need to be here.'

CHAPTER 20

Carver had been at his desk less than five minutes when Jess called.

'How'd it go?' he said.

'Interesting. We may have something.' She recounted what they'd learned at Josephine's.

Carver was interested to learn that 'UF' stood for 'Upper Floor' and when she described the mysterious 'incident' they were yet to bottom, his thoughts went to the video clip in Megan Crane's archive that had turned his stomach the first time he'd watched it.

Finishing, she said, 'What do you think?'

He paused, letting it settle. 'It *could* fit, but it's speculative. We need to verify it.'

'That's what I thought.'

'And?'

The pause before she answered was enough to bring him on guard.

'It won't be easy. I hung around last night to see what else I could dig up. It was like the Pioneer, all over again.'

'Ah.'

Over the years, the infamous promotion-do at Crewe's canal-side Pioneer Club and the Professional

Standards enquiry that followed, had assumed legendary status. The Investigation Team eventually managed to trace and interview around eighty officers and staff they could place there. All the smokers insisted they were puffing away outside when the strip-o-policewoman was engaging in a sex-act, on stage, with the male celebratee. Everyone else – including bar staff - were in the two cubicle/ two urinal toilets. Carver was a Detective Sergeant at the time. He was in the Gents, along with thirty-plus others.

'What about the Hawthorns?' he said. 'They must know.'

'They say not. I believe them.'

His first instinct was to challenge it, but resisted. There'd been occasions the past twelve months when he'd wondered about Jess's relationship with the couple. But he was sure she would never let it cloud her judgement. She'd been 'close' with Megan Crane by the time that all ended, and still never put a foot wrong. He actually closed his eyes as he asked the question he knew she would be expecting.

'Any suggestions?'

'Only one.'

He waited. He knew what it would be. And when it came, his head dropped, along with his stomach.

CHAPTER 21

By two o'clock, Carver was resigned to getting no more sleep this night. He'd done his best to knock himself out with several doses of Jameson, but with all that was going on in his head, he wasn't surprised he'd spent the past two hours tossing and turning. For once, it was nothing to do with Rosanna.

When he arrived home that evening, the package he'd ordered on-line was waiting on the doormat. A plain, cardboard box with a stick-on address label, it bore no hint as to its contents. But he waited while he prepared and ate some supper - a microwaved lasagna and a can of Stella - before giving it his attention. Placing it on the table in front of him he stared at it the way he might a suspect letter-bomb. In one sense, it could be exactly that.

'Fuck it.'

Grabbing a kitchen knife he slit the top along the dotted line, emptied the contents out onto the table, then sat there, staring down at them. They consisted of a couple of plastic tubes marked with bar-codes, some self-seal plastic sample bags, several medical swabs, a sheet of instructions and a pre-addressed padded envelope. After staring for close to a minute, he became aware of his thumping heartbeat, and realised that just thinking about it was threatening to trigger a mini panic attack. Knowing how physical movement helped at such times, he rose and made his way as far as the kitchen. There he collected the Jameson and a glass, before returning to his . He poured a generous measure, took another long look at the items in front of him, then knocked it back in one. He began to read through the instructions. He got half way down the numbered sequence before stopping and letting the sheet fall.

He shook his head, let out a long sigh. 'Not now.'

Gathering the items up, he stowed them back in the box, then turned and opened the top drawer of the sideboard behind him. He slid the box inside, then shut the drawer. For all that the issue the kit was supposed to resolve was important, it was not the most urgent. That honour was currently given to another matter, and right now it merited more forethought than DNA samples.

Grabbing the bottle and glass, he retired to the sofa. If he was going to spend the rest of the evening thinking, he may as well be comfortable.

The other matter was the trip he now knew he would soon be making - more to the point, the individual he would meet. The last few days he'd come close to convincing himself it may never happen. That the threat had passed. That Baggus, with Jess's help, would find what he was looking for. That his further involvement would not be needed. He realised now, he had been kidding himself. With the clarity that drink often brings, he saw that just the matters he was still discovering, meant it would have to happen sooner or later. There was too much at stake for it not to. The only question was the form it would take, whether it would be a formal interview under caution, maybe as part of a wider criminal investigation, or a fact-finding 'consultation' of the sort he had engaged in before. His preference would be for the former. At least then he would be in control, and she would be less likely to attempt the sort of game-playing that was her favourite pastime - *maybe*. But he knew now he would have go the other route - and he wasn't feeling good about it.

It had to be done of course. If Gavin Baggus turned out to be right, there was a good chance others could die, in which case they had to do whatever they could to prevent it, and that included meeting with, *Her.*

But knowing it was the right thing to do - and that it had to be him - didn't make it easier. And it made no difference whether it happened today, tomorrow, weeks or even months from now. The result would be the same. Beforehand, sleep would disappear, as it had done this past week. And afterwards..? Truth be told, he had no idea what the impact would be of renewing his acquaintance with the woman who had once wished him dead, and for all he knew still did - Rosanna as well, and probably Kayleigh also come to that. But for all the uncertainty, he was in no doubt as to what his gut was telling him. Whatever the future held, the quality of his sleep wasn't set to improve any time soon.

He lasted another hour, before heading for bed, only to discover there was no respite there from the thoughts and images looping through his brain.

Now, as he rose to head downstairs to put the kettle on, he wondered on how long people can go without a decent night's sleep before it begins to affect them in other ways.

CHAPTER 22

At the back of the houses, high, wooden fences lined both sides of the alleyway. Carver waited in the shadows, chiding himself. In the days when Early Morning Knocks where an almost daily occurrence, thick socks, gloves and warm outer clothing came as second nature. Since then, he'd forgotten that even in September, the hours before dawn can be bloody cold. Seeing the five-strong Rear Entry Team togged up in their Tactical Cover-alls and combats, he wondered if they took his hand-blowing and foot-stomping as a sign he was one of those who'd clawed their way up the ladder without ever having done any real police work. *And what's the saying about when police officers start looking young....?*

At least the kit he'd borrowed so he would blend in when the time came, was helping, even if the crash-hat was a bit on the tight side and the fleece with, "POLICE" on the back, two sizes to big. He checked his watch again. Four-Twenty-eight. He turned to look back down the alley to the far end where his Golf waited. A few years ago, he'd have thought twice about risking it on an op such as this. He hoped his optimism was justified.

One way or another, The Charnock Estate had featured in Carver's career almost from day one. During his probation, it had been mainly muggings, assaults, burglary and, every couple of years, the odd murder - usually domestic. Since then, social deprivation, prostitution, drugs and, of course, the gangs had become the dominant themes. But recent years had brought change. Some said it was higher levels of home ownership that had led to slow, but measurable improvement. Whatever the cause, crime rates were down, employment, up. Eighteen months ago the estate had been given a makeover, houses painted, shells of abandoned cars cleared away. If nothing else, it was a lot tidier. But it wasn't all good news. There were pockets were things had barely improved at all, some were they had even worsened. Osprey Close, the row behind which they were now waiting, fell into that category.

At tap on his shoulder was followed by, 'Ready Boss? Two minutes.'

He turned to see Andy Edwards, the Team Leader, adjusting his visor and tightening his helmet strap. He nodded an acknowledgement. He'd known Edwards since he was a probationer, and was reassured when he heard the Briefing Officer announce him as i/c Rear Entry. Now an experienced TAC Advisor, he would make sure everything happened the way it was supposed to.

Around him, the rest of the team were carrying out their final kit checks. There was still no intell. to indicate they may meet any resistance, but these days, Tactical Search and Entry Teams are trained so they go through *all* the drills, *every* time. As the Briefing Officer had pointed out, most of the Gilligans were now flagged on PNC as a, "Level 3 Risk" in respect of Premises Entry. Twelve months earlier, a PC had taken a baseball-bat to the side of his helmet during a bust at a Gilligan squat. He recovered okay, but only after several weeks in hospital.

The shuffling of feet and flexing of limbs signalled they were ready. Earlier, Carver had listened to the various confirmations coming in over the radio. The PCs with the Water Authority guys reported the drain bags in place. Forward Control at the RV point confirmed the ambulance and dogs were on stand by. When control gave out the latest known room-locations of the three targets, Alpha, Beta and Gamma, Carver took it that the source in the house must have kept her end of the bargain, and sent the agreed text. Everything was good for Go.

At the front of the line, nearest the back gate - presently locked-shut, but not for long - PC Greg Ryan turned to give Carver a cheery thumbs up. 'He'll be right out Boss,' he said, softly.

Carver nodded, and returned the thumb. God he missed all this.

A voice sounded in his ear. 'Charlie Hotel to all Foxtrot-Mike-Ones, Stand-by, stand-by, stand-by… And its.. three, two, one. Go-go-go.'

A distant banging and shouting, echoing over the rooftops, marked the required, 'Request For Entry.' It was followed, almost too quickly, by the enabling radio confirmations. 'Noises inside. Entry refused. Breach to point.' There was a series of dull, 'thwumps,' then a loud crash. 'Breach on White. We're going in.' Hearing it all, Carver gave thanks that for most of his early service, he'd never had to worry about Real-Time Recording.

As entry was being made at the front, two officers at

the back gate raised their crowbars to the gates' hinges, inserted them into the gaps, and pulled back. At the same time, Ryan put his boot to the latch. The gate popped out and fell into the garden with a loud clatter. As bangs, shouts and screams began sounding inside, they filed through into the 'garden' - a square patch of bare earth littered with broken furniture and plastic bags full of God-knows-what. Carver was last through. Though the senior rank present, he was merely a passenger on this one - piggy-backing on the Drug and Vice Unit's op. It gave him a strange feeling.

The next minute passed in a blur.

Lights came on all over. The back door opened suddenly. A young man, bleary eyed, shit-scared and panicking looked out. Seeing them all stood there, he froze for a second, then tried to slam it shut. Too late. A reinforced boot lodged between the door and the jamb. Someone inside tried to help him close it. The PC with his boot in the doorway called a warning. 'STAND AWAY FROM THE DOOR.' Greg Ryan stepped forward and did what he'd just done to the gate. The door flew back as the wood around the hinges splintered and the lower glass panel shattered. Inside, someone cried out in pain. A call of, 'FUCKIN' BASTARDS,' echoed.

Everyone was moving now. Through gaps between bodies, Carver saw people inside, some in uniform. Yells and calls echoed within.

'STAND STILL.'

HANDS DOWN'

'FUCK OFF.'

Over the radio, he heard, 'Target Alpha at White One. Repeat, Alpha at White One.'

Carver pictured the man whose photograph had been

passed around at the briefing, standing at the front-top-left window, looking for an escape route. Seconds later came, 'Alpha secure. Repeat, Alpha secure.' So much for that.

By now, Ryan and two others of the Rear Entry Team had moved inside. Carver hung back, awaiting the call. From somewhere along the alley where they'd waited, the sound of a dog's barking, loud and furious, signalled the K9 Unit moving into place to help secure the site. Then came the message he'd been waiting for. 'Passenger Fifty Seven. Rear Sitting Room please.'

'On my way,' he said.

As he clambered over the shattered door and through the kitchen, he bumped shoulders with two PCs, a male and a female, who were trying to calm a young woman. Close to hysterical, she was pressing her fists to the side of her head and screaming, 'MAMMA.' In the hallway, two more of the team were pressing a younger man Carver thought he recognised, to the floor. Carver didn't pay too much attention to their methods, but put his head down and carried on through. With his visor down and kitted up, it would be a miracle if someone clocked him, but he'd rather take no chances. Turning right, he entered the back room. Another time, he may have been interested to note anything new amongst the usual array of bongs, spoons, lighters, roach clips and other paraphernalia. But he was there for one purpose only, and right now he was lying, half-out of his sleeping bag, on the manky-looking couch, Greg Ryan standing over him making sure he wasn't going anywhere.

In answer to Ryan's questioning look, Carver gave a confirming nod. Ryan didn't hesitate. Grabbing his subject by the scruff of his crumpled shirt, he hoisted him out of his bag and onto his feet. The lad had time for a quick, 'HEY. WHAT THE FUCK-', before finding himself being half-carried, half-pushed, back out and through the kitchen. Carver followed, pausing only to grab the purple and orange, *Nike* rucksack he'd spotted peeping out from under the sleeping bag and which he recognised.

As he exited into the garden - he'd been in the house less than a minute - Carver couldn't help but be impressed, and made a mental note to feed back to the Inspector in charge of the Entry Operation. As far as his side of things was concerned, the objective had been speedy extraction with a minimum of fuss so as not to arouse suspicion amongst the den's occupants. Given the uncertainties before they went in, a minute was pretty good.

They carried on through and out into the alleyway. By now lights were showing in several houses. Ryan headed down to where it was darker, and quieter. His captive was still going through the motions of struggling, but not too seriously. *Probably shitting himself,* Carver thought. As they went, he heard Ryan update his control. 'Romeo Bravo One. Target Beta, secure and out to black. Repeat, beta secure and out to black.' The acknowledgement came back, 'Roger that, Bravo One,' as Ryan stopped halfway down. Holding the lad by the shoulder while pressing him to the fence, he turned to Carver. 'Is this okay Boss?' he said.

'Hang on,' Carver said. Slipping out of his helmet, he brought his mobile up to his face for light, and leaned in. 'It's me, Billy. Jamie Carver. Can you see?'

Billy Lee's eyes went wide. Whatever he'd been expecting, it certainly wasn't Carver. It took several seconds for his brain to engage, which wasn't surprising. Less than a minute before he'd been in a substance-induced stupor. When things finally clicked, he remembered that whatever has happening, he ought to show he was not happy.

'Whadda fucks going on? 'Wasappenin'?' He turned to Ryan, tried knocking his arm away - 'Get the fuck off me. ' *An ant trying to move a gorilla.*

Ryan growled. 'Quiet shithead, or I'll put you back inside.'

Billy switched his attention back to Carver, right now, the lesser of two evils.

'Why are you- What's this-'

'Shut up and listen.' Carver echoed Ryan's tone. Billy shut up. 'I'm taking you out of here. And I don't want any nonsense, understand?'

'But where-? Why are-'

Ryan leaned in again. 'He *said*, do you understand?'

Carver thought about telling Ryan he could ease off. Billy Lee was sixteen. Kids his age have to blow of. He'd never found him a problem. But a bit of fear wasn't always a bad thing. Billy looked from Carver to Ryan, then back again. He made his decision.

'What do you want?'

CHAPTER 23

After five minutes' surly silence, Billy Lee said, 'Where we going? What's this all about?'

Carver said nothing. They were driving through Bewsey. He was pretty sure Billy would have guessed by now. Ahead, on the left, was the Farmer's Arms. He pulled onto the car park - deserted apart from a couple of motors over by the back entrance. He twisted round to face the young man for whom he'd given up on a night's sleep. Eventually Billy stopped looking anywhere but Carver's face, and paid attention.

'Half of them back there will end up in cells tonight,' Carver began.

'So?'

'You're lucky you're not one of them.'

'Couldn't give a fuck if I was.'

Carver slapped him, across the face, just hard enough he might listen. 'How long have you known me, Billy?'

Billy hesitated, looking wary. 'All me fucking life, it seems.'

'You're not far off. You were nine when I first locked you up. That house at Grappenhall, remember?'

'So?'

'So, did I ever screw you over?'

After a few seconds, 'No.'

'Your Dad's been inside, several times.'

'What of it?'

'And your older brother's done two detentions.'

'So?'

'Stop saying, "So". Do you want to go the same way?'

'Who the fuck cares? S'my life.'

Carver slapped him again, harder. This time shock showed, eyes turning glassy. He continued. 'Three years ago, you and the rest of your family were this town's biggest problem. Your Dad was heading for another stretch, a long one. Your Mum was snorting like there was no tomorrow and lining herself up for the mortuary. Remember?' Billy nodded, finally listening. 'Russell was involved in all sorts of crap, and the rest of you were being lined up for foster-care. Then we started the project. Remember?'

'Yeah.'

'Who pushed it?'

'You did.'

'And what happened?'

Billy sniffed, hacked up what was in his throat. Carver lowered the back window. He gobbed out. 'You kept us together.'

'Me. And Rita. A couple of others as well. We all worked damn hard so you could stay as a family. So don't tell *me* no one cares. Right?'

Billy looked sheepish. 'I s'pose this is all down to my fucking sister is it?'

Just for a second, Carver thought about hitting him again. He counted three. 'Eighteen months ago, your, "fucking sister" saved my life, and my girlfriend's. Like it or not, you Lees and me, we're involved, God help me.' As they regarded each other, Carver thought he saw something come into Billy Lee's face he hadn't seen before. 'If you think I'm going to sit back and let shits like the Gilligans fuck your life up, you've got another think coming. Right?'

Billy nodded. 'Right.' After a few seconds he said, 'So where you taking me?'

'To a halfway house.'

'What's a half-way house?

'Halfway between where we've just come from, and Carnegie Avenue. Your "fucking sister" wants a word.'

After twenty minutes listening to Kayliegh Lee talking to her brother the way a mother might to an eight-year old who'd nicked a pound from her purse, Carver decided he wasn't needed. If Billy's apparent remorse was an act, there was nothing he or Kayleigh could do about it. But he suspected it was genuine. Billy wasn't daft. He would know where associating with the Gilligans was taking him. The raid gave him - others as well - the excuse he needed to find an alternative hang-out. And just in case someone managed to access the record, all it would show was that an unidentified youth had done a runner while being taken outside to be searched. End of.

Draining his mug of the not-bad coffee she'd had waiting when they arrived, Carver made his way to the front door. Kayleigh followed him down the hall.

'Thank you, Jamie. I don't know how-'

He held his hand up. 'It needed doing. Don't worry about it.' He nodded behind her. 'What are you going to do with him?'

'I'll keep him here a few days, just to be sure. Then

I'll take him home.' She shrugged. 'It's up to Mum and Dad then.'

Carver nodded, acknowledging the risk. 'I think he'll be okay. He obviously listens to you.'

'You think so?'

He smiled at her. 'I'm sure of it.' As he opened the door he remembered to ask. 'How are you? Still worrying?'

She looked embarrassed. 'Not so much. Not since we spoke last.'

'Good.' He hesitated, debating, then said, 'G'night Kayleigh.'

'G'night Jamie.'

Driving home, Carver thought on how many times in his service he'd encountered a forty-year old woman in a seventeen-year-old body.

The answer was, none.

CHAPTER 24

Jess had visited many prisons, but this was her first time at HMP Stigwood. As usual, entering involved lots of steel mesh, security windows, and, wherever she looked, cameras. The big difference was its Heart Of Derbyshire Peak District location. Set in open parkland, Stigwood suffers none of the problems that afflict city prisons where lack of space means visitors invariably have to park off-site and walk in.

A ring-road surrounds the main prison complex. Around its outer fringe, clusters of buildings and fenced compounds house maintenance and other functional facilities. 'Business' visitors - as opposed to 'friends and family' - are allowed to drive in and park close to whichever part of the site they are visiting. However, vehicles are often searched. Depending on the current Security State, that can take anywhere between ten, and sixty-plus minutes - which rather negates any 'convenience' factor.

On this occasion, Carver and Jess were lucky. When the Gate Team Supervisor pressed the button on the Random Search Generator - a black box on a pole next to Gate Reception - the green light came on. He waved them through to the secure area where they waited while the outer gate closed behind, the metre-high ramps in front folded down and the inner gate swung open. After being checked, registered and cleared for entry, they were allowed on their way.

Thirty yards on, Carver turned right at the T-junction onto the ring road, following the signs for 'Main Prison Reception' and 'Village Annexes'. Only then did Jess get her first inkling of just how different the set-up at Stigwood was, compared to her previous experiences.

As the road curved left and up, towards the main prison building, she found they were driving along an avenue, lined on both sides with sycamore trees. Behind the trees, wire-fencing ran parallel with the road, effectively turning it into a secure corridor. But it was what lay the other side of the inner fence that grabbed Jess's gaze. Rows of sandstone houses and cottages stood behind manicured lawns with well-stocked borders and laid-out flower beds. It reminded Jess of her visit, years before, to Port Sunlight on the Wirral, the model, 'Garden Village' built by William Hesketh in the nineteenth century to house his soap factory workers.

She turned to Carver. 'This is a *prison?*'

His poker face told her he'd been expecting just such a reaction. She'd heard him speak of visiting Stigwood several times, but never to describe it. He nodded at the house they were passing.

'They were built as care homes for Manchester orphans in the nineteenth century. During the world-wars they housed refugees and later, prisoners-of-war. The Prison Department took it over in the early sixties. Nice, isn't it?'

Jess didn't answer. She was too busy checking off the names on the decorated signs in the middle of the lawns. "Greenwood", "Cloverbank", "Riverside". Apart from the sturdy grills over the windows and doors, they could be driving through some quaint village. 'I wonder if they take holiday bookings?'

'These are just the annexes. The main prison is more conventional.'

Rounding another bend, they started to climb. On raised ground, overlooking the site, several red-brick buildings poked above a concrete wall, topped with razor-wire. Jess felt reassured. She'd been wondering about what people might say if they thought murderers, drug dealers and prostitutes were serving out their sentences in such idyllic surroundings.

Twenty yards in front of the Main Entrance, at a point where the 'avenue' intersected with another fence running parallel to the prison wall, there was another set of gates. There, a security guard led them through a further round of ID and document checks. Satisfied, he motioned to a colleague in the cabin on the other side. As the gates started to swing open he waved them through.

'Enjoy your visit,' he called.

Just like Centre-Parcs, Jess thought.

Carver stood at the window looking out over the prison complex. In the far distance the Peak District's rolling hills and crags formed a dramatic backdrop. To his right, Ellen Hazelhurst was trying but failing to hold his interest as she pointed out key elements of her domain. None of it was registering. Breaking off suddenly, he returned to his seat. Jess followed. Forced to abandon her Visitor Orientation Presentation mid-flow, Ellen returned to her desk.

'Tell me again,' Carver said. 'This psychologist you mentioned. What is it, exactly, she's researching?'

Ellen's wave seemed surprisingly vague. 'Something to do with criminal profiling, I believe. I understand the Home Office are looking at setting up some sort of Serial-Offender database? Something like that.'

Carver held his surprise in check. He would have expected someone as crisply efficient as Ellen Hazelhurst appeared to be to know exactly what a Forensic Psychologist working with her most infamous inmate was researching, particularly if it was as, 'ground-breaking' as she'd mentioned. He was also intrigued. Still in occasional touch with some of his old College of Policing contacts, he'd heard nothing about any new Serial Offender initiatives brewing. And he was still coming to terms with the Governor's revelation that the woman they'd come to see was actually *cooperating* with the programme. *Maybe she's changed...* But he knew a few academics who had done work for the Home Office.

'What's her name again?'

'Lydia Grant,' Ellen said at once, as if pleased to have it at her fingertips. Carver didn't recognise it. 'I could get her to give you a ring? I'm sure she'd be interested in speaking with you.'

'Likewise.' He dug out one of his cards and passed it across the desk. 'Now if you can just point us towards where we have to go, we'll get out of your hair.'

Ellen pressed a button on her desk telephone. As she waited, she said. 'If I wasn't so busy I'd show you down there myself, I could do with the change of environment.' Someone answered and she said, 'Toni, is Sue there?'

As Ellen arranged their escort, Carver and Jess exchanged wary looks.

As she hung up, Ellen realised. 'I'm sorry, didn't I

say? She's not here. She's down in Cloverbank.'

Carver froze as the governor's words sank in. 'Come again?'

'I don't believe this,' Carver muttered.

As he took in his surroundings, he knew his sense of deja-vu was more than that. It could be no coincidence that the arrangement of sofas, chairs and coffee-table mirrored, almost exactly, the comfortable lounge where he and Jess had once sat, listening like idiots as Megan Crane lured them into her web. The vinyl upholstery and cheap fabric furnishings were a bit of a come-down, but they were comfortable enough - allowing for the garish purple and reds. And the faux-velvet curtains masking the window grills completed the illusion that they were sitting in some suburban sitting-room, rather than a place of confinement. At the far end of the room, near where they'd entered, a laminated dining table with eight chairs had given Carver further cause to ponder. *Dinner parties?* Across from where they were sitting, a breakfast bar fronted a basic kitchen. A large-screen television was set in the wall above and behind them. Around the room, standard lamps stood in corners, with occasional tables handily placed. The fact that none of them appeared to be fixed to the floor was making Carver even more nervous. He wasn't used to visiting those he'd put away surrounded by furniture that moved. A smell of disinfectant mixed with furniture polish hung in the air.

'If this is someone's idea of maximum security, they need their head examining,' he said.

Jess said nothing, as non-plussed as him, it seemed.

To begin with, Carver had wondered if Ellen Hazelhurst was serious when she described the experimental regime under which some thirty, 'carefully selected' inmates were being held. 'Don't worry,' she'd said, before handing them over to the escorting PO. 'It's all quite proven.' According to Ellen, The Minnesota State Penitentiary Study showed, 'quite clearly', that, 'the more control long-term inmates have over their environment, the less disruptive they are.' Having described the tensions that erupted following Megan Crane's initial arrival on the prison's main wing - territorial disputes, simmering violence, sexual jealousies - Ellen's pride at having restored Good Order and Discipline showed as she described the Prison Department's ground-breaking – that word again – decision to trial the Minnesota Study recommendations. Carver didn't bother hiding his concerns.

'So the only thing between Megan Crane and the public is some window-mesh and a wire fence?'

At this point, the welcoming face Ellen Hazelhurst had shown thus far, waned. She would not be used to her judgement being questioned, certainly not in her office. Carver was aware that many Prison Service professionals believe most police officers' understanding of Penal Theory goes little beyond, *'Lock'em up and throw away the key.'* The look she gave him, he suspected she'd just fitted him to the stereotype.

'Give us some credit, Chief Inspector,' she said. 'Each annex is monitored and fully alarmed. Inmates are tagged, and, take it from me, the 'window-mesh and wire fence' you refer to are more effective than they may look to the layman.'

'Do the other annexes also house Class A inmates?'

Her impatience began to show. 'With the exception of Cloverbank, where for reasons I won't go into, Megan Crane is the only one, each annex houses two lifers and a range of other inmate classifications. Dispersal of disruptive risk depends upon a visible inmate-hierarchy generating a stable, self-regulating regime.'

He wasn't impressed by her ability to quote the jargon. 'You mean the lifers are top-dogs?'

The cold look deepened. 'Don't get the wrong idea. There is twenty-four-hour supervision and staff are in charge. But they work in collaboration with the inmates in a cooperative, rather than controlling, way. Some see it as radical, but I believe it works.'

As she showed them to the door, Carver thought, *And I will, when someone proves it.*

The views of the older PO, Sue, who drove them down to 'The Village' in a golf-cart style electric buggy, contrasted with her governor's. Waiting until they were clear of the main prison, Carver made a point of speaking to Jess about, 'This Minnesota Thing,' in a voice laden with scepticism and pitched to provoke comment. It worked. Sue leaned back so they could hear her above the rattling.

'I've been in this job eighteen years. These fancy schemes only ever last as long as it takes for the wheel to come off. Then all them who pushed it as the way forward start ducking for cover. You watch.'

But the attitude of the younger woman who locked them in Cloverbank's vestibule-airlock as she checked their ID and passes was more positive, and reflected her name.

'I'm PO Bright, but please, call me Collette. Welcome to Cloverbank.' Her eyes had a slight downward turn that gave her a bit of a sad look, but the smile was ready-enough. 'If you'll just wait in here-,' she pressed the buzzer that opened the door into the homely sitting room - 'I'll see if she is ready for you.'

Half-a-minute later, hearing her climbing stairs, Carver turned to Jess. '*Ready for us?* Who the Hell's running the show?'

'I'm beginning to wonder,' Jess said.

A few minutes later, as Carver completed his mental inventory of the room's contents, the alcove under the stairs echoed with the sound of two sets of footsteps. One was markedly more pronounced.

So far, Carver's unease had been based upon a nagging concern that an experimental regime was being tested on prisoners who were not just dangerous, but devious in the extreme. It was coupled with a suspicion that such a system could only work as long as the inmates did not try to take advantage. As the door opened and Carver got his first sight of Megan Crane since seeing her disappear down the dock steps following sentencing, that suspicion disappeared. It was replaced by absolute certainty.

It hit the moment she locked eyes on him, beamed and said, 'Jamie. Jess. How lovely to see you both again.'

CHAPTER 25

Barbara Hawthorn handed Baggus his glass, then settled in the chair facing.

'It's nice to see you again, Gavin. But you really didn't need to come all this way. A telephone call would have done.'

Baggus sipped the whiskey he'd accepted, rather than ask for a beer. *She's right.* And as the unfamiliar liquid burned its way down his throat he wondered what the hell he was doing.

'I'm just on my way back from seeing Jess,' he lied. 'I thought I'd drop in and see if you've come up with anything on this VR character?' She looked puzzled. He prompted her. 'The initials? Gerald was going to check your membership records?'

It took her a moment. 'Oh yes, VR.' She chuckled. He had no idea why, but it gave him a warm feeling. 'Gerald did look, but he couldn't find any VR. I take it you're no closer?'

He shook his head. He didn't like to ask where Gerald was in case she got the wrong idea. *About what? I'm just following up on a routine enquiry. Nothing wrong with that.* But on his way there, he hadn't dared ask himself why he was driving up the M5, when a ticket for that evening's game was nestling in his pocket.

He wondered if she was reading his mind when she said, 'I'm sorry, you've missed Gerald. He's picking up some new equipment with Sally and Christo and won't be back until later. I can get him to ring you tomorrow if it would help?'

He nodded, drained his glass.

'Same again?'

Before he could answer she rose and took it off him. He thought about asking for the beer this time, but didn't. As she made her way to the drinks cabinet, he wondered if Jess might be wrong about her age. She seemed as toned, her skin as unblemished, as a woman ten - no twenty - years younger. When she came back, he made sure not to let his gaze fall on the glimpse of cleavage her lounging robe showed as he reached for the glass. But he caught a whiff of her fragrance. As she turned to find her seat again, he ran a hand through his floppy hair. It came away damp. *You tosser. You're making a right prick of yourself.* He imagined his rugby mates, jeering, *Should have come to the match.* And as he realised, he shook his head at his own stupidity.

'Tell me,' she said.

'Sorry?' She was back in her chair, crystal eyes locked on his. His stomach churned.

'Something's amused you.'

'Just a bit of wind,' he said. *Christ. Now I sound like Basil Fawlty.*

Over the next few minutes, and in response to her gentle probing, he talked, first about his work, then himself. She seemed interested that his father was a production worker, and not a policeman. He asked about her background, but other than mentioning she had graduated from Cheltenham Ladies' College, she didn't expand on the brief description of her work career. 'Pub and club work, mostly.'

After fetching him another refill, she joined him on the sofa. 'So, tell me, Gavin. What do you really think of our little business?'

He gulped the whiskey down in one.

CHAPTER 26

The last time Carver faced Megan Crane with nothing between them, she'd tried to kill him. Now, as he stared at her, he realised. He was woefully under-prepared for their meeting. As a detective, he should know how memory plays tricks. In her case, it had played him a corker.

The problem he'd always had - hell, they'd *all* had - was her appearance. Glamorous, poised, and alluring in a way no one meeting her for the first time could fail to notice. During the period she was killing, the combination masked those other qualities which, if you looked long and hard enough, were also there. The smile that could turn into the rictus grin he only ever saw once, and then terrifyingly. The hardness around the eyes that didn't always fit with the smile. The feline quality in her movements that gave the impression she may spring at any moment. Together, they should have screamed, 'Danger.' Only no one noticed. Not even him. Not until the night he burst in to find her holding a knife to Rosanna's throat, anyway.

Afterwards of course, during all the wash-ups, debriefs, postmortems and other assorted reflections on how they had all come to be deceived, everyone agreed.

The signs *were* there, it was just that, well, at the time they were all just.. *too busy.* Some excuse. In the weeks before the trial, Carver reflected on it all, deeply. On the last day, when the Clerk asked her to, 'Please stand,' so the judge could pass sentence, he knew exactly how dangerous she was. Which was why he arranged for two burly members of the forces PSU Team - read, Riot Squad - to don suits and stand, incognito, next to the Judge's bench. Just in case she decided to show how she would never be cowed by seeking to add the Judge to her list. As for himself, Carver made sure he stayed primed and ready, in the event she might look for a second chance.

It never happened of course. But as he stood there, unflinching in the face of the glare she trained on him throughout sentencing, he remembered what he'd felt as he'd stood on a chair with a noose round his neck, knowing with absolute certainty that he and Rosanna were about to die. Stark fear and sheer bloody terror. After she had been taken down to the cells, he disappeared off to the Police Room where he deep-breathed for ten minutes while waiting for the juddering in his legs to pass. Beneath his suit jacket, his shirt was soaked.

In the weeks and months following, as he came to accept that Megan Crane would never again threaten him, Rosanna or anyone else, the fears abated, though slowly. The process was entirely natural, as well as rational. When damaged, the mind, like the body, seeks to heal itself - like trauma victims who lose all memory of the event itself. Sometimes it happens quickly, other times it can take a while. In Carver's case it happened over a period of several months. Bit by bit, he came to forget how facing her had brought back the fear, the terror. As more time passed, the predominant memory of Megan Crane came to be little more than the face everyone remembered. Which was how he tricked himself into believing that, other than refreshing himself regarding the contents of her cellar filing cabinet, he didn't need any 'special preparation' for their first meeting since the trial. And how it was that when that moment came and he suddenly found himself face-to-face with her with nothing between them but air awash with the whiff of polish and disinfectant - *What's the bloody PO doing behind her?* - it all came back. The fear, the terror. The *guilt.*

As Carver stood there, silent and unmoving, Megan Crane's gaze flicked towards Jess before coming back to him. A faint smile played about her lips. Suddenly, she frowned. 'Are you alright Jamie?'

He didn't move.

'Jamie?' Jess said.

Later, Carver would recall how in those few seconds he came within, 'a midge's dick', of bolting for the door, pressing the buzzer, and demanding to be let out, *Right Now.* Since that night, he'd all-but forgotten what panic felt like. But the sudden return of feelings he thought were in the past, triggered a sickening realisation. *I can't do this.* It was followed, swiftly, by, *I'm not ready.* As the waves washed over him, he held himself rigid, just as he had when they'd held each other's gaze during sentencing. Adrenalin flowed. His options were, fight or flight.

He fought.

With an effort of will, he remembered his post-Hart counselling. He concentrated on slowing his breathing, counted, silently. *One… two… three..* It worked. His heart-rate started to settle. The panic eased. His feet stayed where they were.

When he was sure he had control, he responded to The Woman's question with a slow nod, and he made sure he met her gaze when he said, 'I'm fine. Shall we get on with it?' The warm smile she returned him put him in mind of a Lady of The House, welcoming guests. And it wasn't yet over.

'It's so nice of you both to come,' she cooed. 'Mind, it's not as far now that you're working in Manchester, is it Jamie? How *is* the new job by the way? Not too frustrated away from the mainstream I hope?'

He said nothing. He had no idea how she knew about his move. That she did, added to his discomfort. But he was determined not to let himself get caught up in her games.

'I take it you've met Collette?' She gestured at the Prison Officer at her shoulder.

He nodded again. 'Just.'

'Collette's our Housemother, aren't you Collette?'

The PO said nothing, but Carver noted the way she glared at her charge, as if trying to pass some message. Megan continued.

'She looks after all our needs, and we all love her to bits.' An edge came into her voice. 'Don't we Collette?'

'If you say so, Megan.' As if to escape the dominatrix's gaze, Collette turned away and pulled up one of chairs from around the table.

What the hell's going on here?

Megan turned back to them. 'Shall we sit?' She gestured at the sofas.

Taking their seats, he wondered if Jess was thinking the same as him. *This is how it all began.*

As they settled, the detectives next to each other on one of the sofas, Megan in the chair opposite with

'Collette' off to her left at the other end of the room, Carver's confusions were compounded by another realisation. This time it was to do with her appearance.

Carver could not claim to have extensive experience of women's prisons. Most of his previous visits to Stigwood had come a few years earlier, while investigating the near beating-to-death of an inmate serving eight years for child neglect and manslaughter. During her trial, she had admitted letting her boyfriend rape her three-year old daughter during the months before she died from the abuse and neglect they managed to keep hidden from social workers. The experience taught Carver that when it comes to violence, drug abuse and pent-up passion, women's prisons are even more of a pressure cooker than men's. He certainly didn't see much in the way of 'glamour' though there are always some – usually sex workers - who like to behave provocatively, and dress accordingly. But real glamour? No. He assumed it was because the levelling effect of prison applies as much to looks, as it does status, wealth and power. Not that he expected to find Megan Crane had let herself go. Women like her will always do their best, whatever the circumstances.

What he wasn't expecting, was to find such little difference between this Megan Crane, and the one he'd known before. He didn't know what restrictions applied to things like make-up, and the stuff women use with it - scissors, nail files, tweezers. They could all be used as weapons and would, presumably, be banned - *Wouldn't they?* Similarly, while he could imagine there being some sort of on-site hair-dressing facility, it could never be of the standard she would be used to.

Yet looking at her, it was hard to believe she'd spent

close to two years inside. Her hair was as glossy, black and full as he remembered. The make-up, including the signature red-lipstick, as painstakingly applied as it always had been. Same for her clothes. In UK prisons, women don't wear uniform, but surely there were *some* guidelines? Whatever sort of work-programme she was on - *was she on one?* - he couldn't imagine it suiting the thin cream blouse through which a lacy black bra showed, or the black skirt and heels. But as he lifted his gaze and found hers waiting, along with the knowing smile, he reminded himself to be careful. He made a start.

'Before we-'

'I must say, Jess, you're looking extremely well, and I do like what you've done with your hair. Do you do it yourself or do you go somewhere?'

There was an awkward silence. Carver looked at his shoes. Jess shot him a glance before replying.

'I go somewhere.'

'I'm impressed. You must give me their number.'

He waited several seconds, before trying again. 'I was about to-'

'I'm just sorry I can't say the same for you, Jamie. You look a bit pasty, if you don't mind me saying? Are you getting enough sun?'

He gave her an even look. It wasn't easy. Her eyes flashed as if to say, *There you are. Hello Jamie.*

'We're not here to talk about us, Megan. Or you for that matter.'

She pouted.

'We're grateful you agreed to see us, but we're not here to play games.' She effected an admonished look that recalled his meetings with Kayleigh Lee. 'We're here because there are matters we'd like to speak to you about involving people you know and may have an interest in. But if you're going to fuck us about, then we'll end this meeting now and we'll go elsewhere.'

Her expression changed to one of boredom. 'You're no fun anymore Jamie Carver. Do you know that?'

He said nothing. She slouched back in her chair.

'If that's the way it's going to be, you'd better get on with it.'

He produced the paperwork for her to sign agreeing to be seen without her solicitor present and she squiggled on it. 'He's a waste of space anyway.'

He began by asking if she remembered Quentin Quinlan.

'I do. And before you say anything, I heard about him killing himself. Stupid. He always was a risk-taker.'

Carver didn't ask how she'd come to hear. It hadn't made the national news. 'What about Gordon Halsall?'

'What about him?'

'Are you aware that he also died recently?'

She hesitated. 'No, I was not. How?'

'Six weeks ago. Car accident. Late at night. No one else involved. He'd been drinking. Supposedly.'

For long seconds, she stared at him. Eventually she said, 'The Gordon Halsall I knew wasn't the sort who drinks and drives.'

'That's what the officer who investigated the accident told me. Apparently, he went through half a bottle of whiskey before getting in his car.'

More hesitation, then, 'As far as I recall, Gordon was a gin-drinker.'

'He told me that as well.'

As the silence returned, Carver realised he was witnessing something rare. It took a lot to throw her, but the news about Halsall clearly had. When she spoke, it was as if she was thinking aloud rather than to them. 'Gordon and Q. Dead within a few weeks of each other… That's… a coincidence.'

He nodded. '*If,* it's a coincidence.'

She stared at him. 'What do you mean?'

'We think Q may have been blackmailing someone.'

'Who?'

He shook his head. But he could see she was rattled. 'That's why we're here. We thought you may have a take on it.'

About to say something, she suddenly stopped herself. Her mouth snapped shut. Her eyes slid away left, towards where the P.O., Collette Bright, seemed intent on staring, hard, at the magazine spread out on the table in front of her. A second later, she shifted, so that her whole posture changed. As Carver had spoken of Halsall's death, she had grown tense, sitting upright, then leaning forward, as some do when they receive disquieting news. But now she executed a reverse, resurrecting the flippant manner she had displayed at the start. Leaning back, she crossed her legs and let her arm fall across the chair's back.

'What makes you think I may have a take on it? I've had no contact with either Q, or Gordon for a long time. I'm sorry to hear they both met with such horrible accidents, but it's of no concern to me.' As she spoke, she held Carver's gaze, like it was in a vice. It was in stark contrast to everything else about her. He was about to respond, but she beat him to it. 'And if you've any thoughts that I had anything to do with their deaths, then you need to know, I've got a rather good alibi.'

'I'm not suggesting you had anything to do with their deaths. All I'm interested in is if you have any thoughts on who Q may have been blackmailing?'

For several moments, her gaze wavered between Jess and himself, then the half-amused look faded as if it had been no more than a façade. A cold look replaced it. Carver was surprised. To that moment he'd have sworn she was actually enjoying herself.

'Why should I help you? You ruined my life. Twice. Don't you think you've got a nerve even to ask?'

'I go where the information is Megan, you know that. And you're right. There is no reason you should help us. In your shoes, I'd probably think the same.' Sensing he was about to lose her, he switched tack. 'Tell me about the Upper Floor.'

She gave a derisory snort. 'Don't try and play games with me, Jamie. I invented them, remember?' The way she looked at him now, coolly, through narrowed eyes, he could almost feel her finger hovering over the trigger of some weapon in her arsenal. He stuck to his course but was ready to get to his feet the moment he sensed her cocking it.

'We believe that whatever Q was up to, it's connected with Josephine's, but everyone there claims they know nothing.'

She froze. 'You've spoken to the Hawthorns?'

As Carver wondered what nerve he had struck, Jess stepped in.

'They told us about an incident they think may have involved this Upper Floor group. But they say they don't know what it was.'

For a long time the dominatrix didn't say anything, but remained staring at Jess, as if locked in some inner debate. Then her face softened. When she turned to Carver, he was surprised to see concern there.

'You shouldn't have involved Gerald and Barbara.' She bit her lip. 'They're nice people. Look after them.' It was the nearest thing to apprehension he had ever seen in her. He latched onto it.

'Why? Are they in danger? We can only protect them if we know what it's about.'

Her eyes flicked left again. Carver followed the glance. The PO was still staring down.

Suddenly Megan laughed, loudly. Carver sensed it was forced.

'It's a shame you let those cerise folders of mine go missing before the trial.' Carver's brow furrowed. 'You never know, there might have been something there that could help you. Too late now.'

Something about the way she said it, her face, made Carver check Collette again. Her head was still down, but he had the impression she wasn't actually reading.

'And if you came here thinking I would point you in the right direction, you're a bigger idiot than even I imagined.' She rose to her feet. 'Goodbye Jamie.'

Without any warning, she started across the room. Collette was up and at her shoulder so quickly, Carver wondered if she'd been expecting it. At the door, Collette pressed the buzzer, signalled through the glass to her colleague outside. Megan turned.

'Do give my best to Rosanna. Tell her I think of her, often.' Then she added, 'And that other little bitch.'

Before Carver could respond the door opened and she was gone. Seconds later, heels thumped back up the stairs.

Jess turned towards Carver, a bewildered look on her face. 'She doesn't know you've still got all her records?'

'Oh, she knows alright.' Carver was still digesting it all, not least her final, '*little bitch*' remark. He shook his head. 'Let's go. I need to check something.'

CHAPTER 27

Jess had last seen Carver's ANACAPA chart a few weeks after he began working on it. Back then it was little more than a few lines and boxes. Now, its compelling complexity drew her.

'Oh My God.' Her eyes roamed all over it, checking off the names she'd managed to wheedle out of him the odd time. 'I know you said there was more than we first thought, but I never realised there was this many.'

'Top right quadrant.' He said it without looking up as he pulled another sheaf of papers out of the cabinet. He started to flick through them. 'To the right of the blue triangle.'

She didn't ask how he knew what she was looking for, but supposed anyone would who knew it was there. She found the blue triangle with its three letter acronym, HOL, easily. To its right, a square contained the name she'd been seeking. 'Fascinating.' Her finger tracked some of the lines running from it. After a few seconds she stopped. 'Blooody-Hell.'

Carver glanced up, saw where she had stopped.

'You never mentioned *him.*'

Carver shrugged. 'He's just a singer.'

'*Just* a singer? There's a generation out there think

he's a, *God*!'

Carver shrugged.

'But he's so… young. And innocent.'

He gave her a straight look. 'You know better than that.'

She shook her head. 'I'll never be able to listen to him again.' Tearing herself away, she came to join him. 'Have you found these cerise folders yet?'

'There are no cerise folders.'

'What?' She rocked back, as if he had pushed her. 'So what was Megan talking about? And in that case, what are you looking for?'

'Her source document,' he said, still flicking. 'It's here somewhere.'

'Whose source document?'

He ignored her. 'I think Megan was talking in code. Maybe because of that PO, Collette.'

'The "House-mother" person? What about her?'

'I *think* Megan didn't want her to know she was giving us a pointer.'

'She gave us a *pointer*?' She sat on the edge of the desk, watching him search. 'Okay, I surrender. I'm obviously missing something. Give.'

Even as she said it, he pulled a sheet out of the pile. 'Ah.' He perused it. 'This is it.' He handed it to her, then went and took her place in front of the chart.

Jess frowned. It was a receipt in the form of a letter on headed notepaper, addressed to Megan Crane at her home address. The banner across the top proclaimed, 'Wentworth Galleries' with a Chelsea address. *'In acknowledgement of receipt of £1450.00p as settlement of account re painting in oils, 'Blue Sun Rising'. With thanks.'* A distant memory of a mainly-blue picture above the mantelpiece in Megan Crane's elegant home came to her.

'What's this?' she said to his back. He was staring at the chart, cradling his chin.

'Check the signature.'

She tried to decipher the green scrawl. It began with a curved flourish but then the letters merged into a single line, impossible to read. But below it, in type, was, 'For and on behalf of Wentworth Galleries,' and underneath that, the signatory's name. 'Cyrisse Chaterlain.' She slid off the desk and joined him.

'Who's Cyrisse Chaterlain?'

Carver pointed at a square in his chart. 'Someone who knew someone.'

Jess closed on where he was pointing. 'Cyrisse Chaterlain…'. A single line led from the box containing the name. She tracked it. Though its position near the top edge of the chart suggested someone on the periphery of things, the line followed a circuitous route down through the maze of shapes and lines. It connected to a square close to the centre where several others also joined. She read the name within it.

'Oh, wow.'

CHAPTER 28

The colour drained from Barbara Hawthorn's face as she reached for her husband's hand.

'What do you mean, 'danger'?'

'We're not sure,' Jess said. 'She asked us to make sure you were looked after, but didn't say why.'

The older couple exchanged worried looks. Eventually Gerald stepped forward.

'I can't imagine what that woman would be thinking of. But since you called to say you were dropping in, Barbara and I have been worried sick. With what happened to Q and all. Can't you tell us what it's all about?'

Jess gave him a long look before shaking her head. 'If you don't know, Gerald then neither do we. We're on our way to see someone who might tell us something. But right now my advice is, be careful.'

'What sort of security do you have here?' Baggus said.

They all turned to him. He had addressed his question to Barbara. Jess had the impression he was as concerned for her as Gerald was.

'We have an alarm system,' Gerald said. 'And the usual door-chains, locks, that sort of thing. It's not state-of-the-art or anything.'

'Q had a sophisticated alarm system. Whoever killed him by-passed it.'

'So you *do* think he was murdered?'

Baggus didn't hesitate. 'I do now. And my guess is, it was professional. Jess is right. You need to be careful.'

For several minutes they talked security. Baggus said he would arrange personal attack alarms to back-up the ageing alarm system. When Barbara thanked him for his concern Jess saw the look that passed between them. She asked about Christo and Sally. Gerald confirmed they were still spending, 'quite a bit of time' there.

It seemed to irritate Baggus. 'If you have to have them around, put them on their guard,' he said. 'You don't have to tell them everything. Make up a story about some disgruntled member who's threatening to show up, or something. At least they'll be watching out.'

Before they left, Jess decided to give it one last try. 'You *are* telling us everything you know about all this? You're not keeping anything back?'

'Like what?' Gerald said.

'I don't know. Megan Crane obviously thinks you know something. Someone else might think the same.'

A noise from Barbara drew Jess's gaze, but her mouth was now a thin line. She shook her head.

'We'll call on our way back.' Jess said. 'In case you've remembered anything.'

The couple said nothing.

The detectives gone, Barbara Hawthorn turned to her husband. Fear showed in her face.

'Jess isn't stupid, Gerald. She knows.'

He crossed to the bar, started mixing drinks. 'She may suspect, but she can't possibly know.'

She came up behind and put her arms round him, hugging him to her. 'I know her Gerald. She isn't going to let it go. You heard what they said. We could be in danger.'

He turned, handed her a glass. She drank it straight down, passed it back for a refill.

'We could be in more danger if we start talking to the police,' he said.

Taking her drink, she sat on the edge of the sofa. As he passed in front, she grabbed his arm and pulled him down, next to her.

'I'm *frightened* Gerald. I think we should tell them. They're going to find out anyway.'

Gerald Hawthorn looked deep into his wife's eyes, and was shocked when he saw tears forming. It took a lot to rattle her. He hugged her to him. 'I'm not going to let anything happen. Believe me.'

'But what can you do? Look what happened to Q.' Suddenly the flood gates burst and she collapsed into his arms, sobbing. 'Please Gerald. Promise me you'll tell her.'

He held onto her, trying to control her shaking.

'Alright. I will. I promise.'

She sat up and took his face in her hands. 'Thank you.' She kissed him, softly, then returned to his arms.

As she laid her head on his shoulder, Gerald stroked his wife's hair - and wondered if he could keep his promise. He had faced danger many times in his life, though not so much recently. As skipper of a freighter plying the hazardous seas around Hong Kong he'd often found himself in tricky situations. Later, when he and Barbara ran their first club in Soho's back streets, he'd come up against many he would never turn his back on. But right now he realised, he was as scared as he could ever remember.

CHAPTER 29

Heading south on the M40, Baggus driving, Jess referred back to the discussion they'd had the day they visited Josephine's.

'What happened to your opinion that people like them are all, how did you put it, "weird"?'

His eyes flicked in her direction, but he didn't look at her.

'I never said, "all".'

Jess couldn't stop a wry smile. 'This change of heart wouldn't have anything to do with a certain blond lady some years older than yourself, would it?'

His stared at the road ahead. 'I've no idea what you mean.'

Jess studied his profile, saying nothing.

Eventually he said, 'Barbara's nice. I wouldn't want anything to happen to her.'

'Or Gerald of course.'

'I meant Gerald as well.' After a few moments he looked at her. 'What?' then turned back to the road. When she didn't answer he said it again.

She shook her head. 'I thought rugby's the love of your life?'

'I do have other interests you know. Besides, she's

old enough to be my mother. *And* she's married.'

'That wouldn't bother some people,' she said. 'You've heard of Oedipus I take it?'

'Who?'

She sighed. 'You really are one of life's innocents aren't you, Gavin? How you ever made D.I is beyond me.'

'Well not by shagging my way there, that's for sure.'

When she didn't respond, he turned to find her looking at him, pointedly, an eyebrow arched high. He reddened. 'I'm sorry. I didn't mean that the way it sounded. I just meant-'

She shook her head again. 'When this is over, Barbara and I will have to see to your education.'

'Okay, and in return I'll take you both to Kingsholm.'

'I can hardly wait. Mind, I suppose that'll depend on whether you decide to drive all the way to the Midlands instead of going to the match.'

He didn't speak again for a long time, and Jess didn't need to look at him to know he was glowing like a beetroot.

Like a child on Christmas morning whose attention keeps jumping from one toy to the next, Rosanna could barely stop talking. The connection wasn't the best and Carver was getting about half of it. But her final performance the night before had clearly gone well, the reception after also, by the sound of it.

'And Mr Berentes, he said-'

'Who?' During recent calls, he'd heard her mention several names. None had stuck. It didn't help that before she rang, his mind had been somewhere he didn't dare mention.

'Mr Berentes. Remember? Julio?' When he didn't

respond, she became impatient. 'I tol' you, Jamie. The man from Hemisphere? The recording company?'

'Oh yeah, him.' He remembered. Something about a possible recording deal. He'd assumed it was a line.

'He'd like me to try a studio-session-' - *I'll bet he does* - '- If I can stay a bit longer.'

'Right.'

He knew at once it wasn't enough. At the very least he should have *tried* to sound excited. Before her trip, she had mentioned the possibility that she may attract interest. He never voiced his thoughts. *Attracting* interest wouldn't be the problem. It was the *type* of interest that bothered him. Now it looked like she wouldn't be home for the weekend after all. As her continuing silence reinforced his guilt, he bit his lip.

Eventually she said, 'Is that all? 'Right'?'

'No. I mean… It's great. Well done. I'm really happy for you.'

'You don' sound happy.'

'I am. Honestly. It's just-'

'You want me to come home?'

'Of course I want you home. But if you have to stay a bit longer that's fine. If that's… what you want.'

'Is something wrong, Jamie?'

'No, I'm fine. Everything's fine.' He bit his lip. *Too many 'fine's.* But the last time they spoke he had mentioned the possibility that he may have to visit *Her.* She'd tried to talk him out of it. He told her about their visit to Stigwood.

'And were you…? Was it alright?'

'Yes. Better than I thought actually. But she… She hasn't changed.'

'She is the devil, Jamie. You must watch out for her.'

'I know. I will.'

They tried talking about other things, but a shadow had fallen. They said their goodbyes before either of them brought it up again. It was only after he'd hung up he realised she hadn't said when she would call again, like she usually did. As he reached for his glass, his hand passed over the latest pile of estate agent's flyers.

He was glad she hadn't asked about houses.

CHAPTER 30

Baggus could count on the fingers of one hand the number of times he had visited an art gallery that actually *sold* paintings. He'd certainly never seen prices like those the shaven-headed young man in the baggy white shirt quoted when he casually enquired about the solid green circle on the white background, just inside the door.

'Bugger me, he said. 'That's more than three season-tickets.'

From the look on the man's face, Baggus might have broken wind. 'Madame Chaterlain will be with you shortly,' he said, before retreating to the empty desk at the bottom of the stairs where he made a point of trying to look busy.

A minute later, a woman wafted in from the back of the gallery. Fortyish, she was dressed for business in a high-neck white blouse and black skirt. Her curly, dark hair was gathered in a ponytail held by a red clasp. Her skin was almost alabaster-white. She approached Jess, who was still studying the paintings Baggus had heard her mention were by some, 'Jake Vettrio-' person.'

'Mademoiselle Greylake?'

Jess flashed her warrant card out of sight of the man

behind the desk. The woman hesitated, glancing at Baggus as he sauntered over. Close up, he realised her outfit made her look older than first thought. *Thirty maybe?* Without saying anything, she beckoned them to follow. As they climbed the stairs, her bald assistant craned his neck until they passed out of sight.

She led them to a glass-doored office that was in stark contrast to the clean-lined gallery below. Small and cramped, it housed an oblong desk with a plastic chair behind and a couple more this side. The desk was way too big for the room, and was covered in catalogues of paintings, remnants of picture frames, and a host of what Baggus lumped together as, 'art stuff'. An ashtray contained several half-smoked stubs. The pungent odour of French cigarettes hung in the air. She closed the door, leaned back against it.

'If this is about the Michele Copin, I have already told the other officers. We could not have known it was-.'

Jess raised a hand, cutting off the almost perfect English. Baggus wondered if she played up her French accent when pursuing her other interests.

'We're not the Arts and Antiques Squad, Cyrisse,' Jess said. The woman looked surprised, then relieved. 'We're here to talk to you about someone you know.'

Becoming at once more relaxed, she waved them to sit. As they settled, she edged round to the chair behind the desk. 'And this person would be?'

'Megan Crane,' Jess said.

Baggus doubted she could have been more shocked had Jess told her they knew the truth about the Copin thing. She stared at Jess for several seconds before sinking, slowly, into the chair. Reaching across, she pulled a packet of Gauloises and a bic lighter from under some papers and lit up. She drew deeply, before blowing smoke back over her shoulder. In the cramped room, it made little difference. When she eventually spoke, her mood had darkened, her tone wary.

'What is this about please?'

Baggus thought that for one so young, she had the bearing and manner of someone much older. A woman of experience. Like Barbara.

'We'll come to that,' Jess said. 'But first, tell us about your involvement with Megan Crane.'

For several moments she puffed on her cigarette while regarding them, cautiously. Eventually, with a shrug, she sent it to join its brothers in the ashtray, and began.

For the next ten minutes Cyrisse spoke freely about her relationship with the dominatrix, emphasising at the start how she never dreamed she was capable of murder. 'I always found her to be perfectly balanced,' she said. She described how they first met when Megan came into the gallery looking for artworks. She recognised her for what she was immediately. Baggus had to work at not looking too gob-smacked when she spoke, matter-of-factly about dabbling in the Paris SM scene after finishing her course in Fine Arts History at the Sorbonne.

'As a dom?' Jess asked.

'Not always. I am that rare thing. A natural switch.'

Baggus nodded, sagely. Seeing it, Jess smiled, wryly, shook her head.

Cyrisse recounted how, when they met, she was on the point of giving up on that side of her life. But, as intrigued in Megan as she seemed in her, she accepted an invitation to visit her home to discuss her, 'artistic requirements'. More visits followed, often at weekends, when she sometimes helped Megan 'entertain' some of her friends, before things, 'fizzled out.'

'Why was that then?' Baggus said.

'She was into it more than I ever was. As I said, I'd given it up once. She was involved with a lot of people and I didn't want it to take over my life again.'

'Did you fall out?' Baggus said.

'Oh no,' Cyrisse said. She smiled at some memory, but then snatched it back, as if worried that warm thoughts about a multiple-murderer may be misinterpreted. 'We still used to meet for lunch occasionally, when she came to London. But I made it clear I didn't want any deeper involvement.'

'So you met some of Megan's companions?' Jess said.

'A few.'

'Anyone in particular?'

Cyrisse hesitated, eyes darting back and forth between the detectives. 'What is this all about?'

Jess mentioned blackmail, but not murder.

Cyrisse barely reacted. 'Oh yes?' She lit another cigarette. 'May I ask who it involves?'

Baggus hoped that the look he and Jess returned was sufficiently 'knowing.'

'Who do you think?' Jess said, timing it.

Instead of replying, Cyrisse smoked faster, flicking non-existent ash into the ashtray. Her gaze remained on Jess, but Baggus could see that beneath her makeup, she was starting to colour. They let the silence do its work. At one point she opened her mouth to speak, but then closed it. Eventually she said, 'This person is… someone in the public eye?'

Jess raised an eyebrow.

'Someone in high office?'

She raised the other.

Cyrisse's gaze switched between them. Eventually she took a last draw on her cigarette before stubbing it out and fixing Jess with another stare. 'It's Alistair Kenworthy, yes?'

Like Jess, Baggus took care to not react. Carver's analysis had been bang-on.

'Tell us about him,' Jess said.

Cyrisse shrugged. 'We met during a gathering at Megan's.'

'And you started seeing each other?'

'He called on me here. I accepted a dinner invitation.'

'And after that?'

An anxious look crept into her face. 'He asked if he could see me, regularly. To save him having to travel up to where Megan lived.'

'He's sub, I take it?'

Cyrisse nodded, but then her eyes narrowed, as if beginning to realise.

'Was payment involved?'

'He bought some paintings. Gave me the occasional gift.'

'So what happened?' Jess said. 'Why did you stop seeing him?'

As she bit her bottom lip, Baggus could sense her debating. *How much to say?* Perhaps sensing the same, Jess tried a different tack.

'Never mind, try this. Apart from his relationship with you, what would make Kenworthy susceptible to blackmail?'

Right then, Baggus saw the look that said Cyrisse knew she had been duped. She took another cigarette and threw the pack down, annoyed with herself.

'Why are you asking me these questions? Why don't

you ask him? I don't want to get involved.'

'You're already involved, Cyrisse.' Baggus said. 'You were a Government Minister's mistress.'

She looked at him, sharply. 'But that was before-'

As he watched her bite her lip again, Baggus felt a stir of sympathy. Cyrisse Chaterlain may have been a sometime-dominatrix, but she was no Megan Crane.

'Before what?' Jess said.

Her anxiety seemed to deepen and the eyebrows that, for a woman, were unusually thick knitted together. Baggus thought she looked trapped. She kept glancing at the door as if hoping for an interruption. Perhaps because she had given them a name, Jess eased back.

'Look Cyrisse. These are obviously sensitive matters. But we aren't here to cause trouble for you or your business.'

Cyrisse wiped her palms on her skirt.

'It's natural you are reluctant to talk about these things. But if you don't, you could find yourself being forced to give evidence at some time in the future. That would only make things worse.'

As Baggus watched, her anxiety seemed to morph into something else. *Fear?* Whatever it was, it seemed to confirm Jess's suspicions. She pressed on.

'Do you know a man called Quentin Quinlan?' The blank look and quick shake of her head seemed genuine. 'He was part of this circle. Megan Crane, Kenworthy, others. He was murdered a few days ago.'

At mention of murder, what little colour may have been in Cyrisse Chaterlain's face drained away. Any paler, Baggus thought, she would be a corpse.

'We believe others may be at risk because of this thing involving Kenworthy. We need to know what it was.'

Cyrisse fell back in the chair, looking dazed. 'Murdered…? I… That is awful.' Suddenly she sat up again, eyes wide. 'You think it was Alistair?'

'We are keeping an open mind until we know more,' Baggus said. 'That's why we're here.'

'But what makes you think I can help?'

Jess and Baggus exchanged glances before saying together, 'Megan Crane.'

Gradually, Cyrisse's blank stare gave way to a half-smile that seemed equal parts irony and resignation. And she nodded as she repeated the name to herself. 'Megan.'

During the silence that followed, Baggus sensed the fog clearing from her brain. Megan Crane's steer had not been without purpose. Cyrisse fingered another cigarette, left it. No one spoke. She clasped her hands on the desk, looked at them.

'There was a side to Alistair that scared me. He presented himself as a sub, but I always felt he was keeping something back. And his appetite for sex was… remarkable. He made me uneasy. Eventually I made up a story about meeting someone I was serious about and stopped seeing him.' She fell silent and her gaze slid away. For a long while her eyes were everywhere but on the detectives. Jess and Baggus exchanged glances.

'Cyrisse.'

Startled, her gaze snapped back to Jess.

'Tell us what happened.'

As the pair exchanged stares, Baggus saw something new come into Cyrisse's face. Jess had used the same tone the night she pressed the Hawthorns, and as the two regarded each other he wondered what was passing between them. He'd always prided himself on his ability to read witnesses during interview. Right now, he was struggling.

Cyrisse took a deep breath. 'Has anyone mentioned the name, Sylvie Tyler?'

CHAPTER 31

'DCI Carver?' the voice said. 'This is Lydia Grant.'

Carver swung his chair away from the screen. He'd been on the point of trying to track her down earlier that afternoon, but got diverted. After swapping introductions, he enquired about her Stigwood research. To his surprise, she seemed dismissive.

'You know what the Home Office is like. I'll spend six months writing it up. Then it'll sit on some Whitehall bureaucrat's desk for another six before getting shelved.'

Usually cynical about anything stamped, 'Home Office', for once, Carver was more positive. 'I'm not so sure. There's a lot of interest in serial-profiling right now. Is the Crime Faculty involved?'

She sounded uncertain. 'I… wouldn't know. This came direct to the University from the Prison Department.'

Ellen Hazelhurst had mentioned she worked at a Manchester university, but hadn't got round to saying which one. He was about to ask when she continued.

'Governor Hazelhurst told me you were interested in my research. You obviously know Megan Crane quite well. Perhaps we should get together sometime?'

'Sure.'

But before he could start talking dates she said, 'I'm afraid I'm really busy right now. Perhaps I can call you next week and we'll fix something up?'

'Of course, but-.'

'Good. Well I just called to make contact. Nice to speak to you Chief Inspector. We'll-.'

Realising she was about to ring off, he interrupted. 'Doctor Grant.'

She stopped. 'Please, it's Lydia.'

'Lydia, would you mind if I asked how you and Megan Crane are getting on?'

'No, I don't mind. And the answer is, quite well.'

'So she *is* co-operating then?'

'Very much so. In fact, she's an excellent subject.'

'Doctor Grant-. Sorry, Lydia. I-.' He didn't want to cause offence on their first contact, but if he didn't say anything and something happened, he would never forgive himself. 'Please don't take this the wrong way, but have you dealt with subjects like Megan Crane before?

There was only the briefest hesitation before she answered. 'Not exactly. This is my first inmate-based commission. Why do you ask?'

'Well I'm not sure how much you know about her, but I feel I ought to warn you-.'

'I've seen all the reports if that's what's worrying you. I know she can be very manipulative.'

'That's putting it mildly.' He suddenly wished they could get together sooner than next week. 'I'm sorry if this sounds patronising, but I've dealt with people like her before, and I can tell you, that of them all, she is the most-.'

She cut across him. 'I've read the paper you presented to the court, Chief Inspector. And I'm aware of your previous…. *experience* in these matters.'

Her tone was enough to make him look at his phone. *Was that a put-down?*

'But I can assure you, I am following all the protocols governing Institutional Research-.'

'I don't think the protocols have been written that take account of Megan Crane's capabilities.'

She barely hesitated. 'And Governor Hazelhurst has personally verified the regime I've adopted-.'

So, that's alright then.

'-So I really can't see there is anything we need to discuss until we meet, is there?'

He got the message. 'I guess not.' But before she could hang up he said, 'Can I just clarify something before you go?'

'If you can be quick. I have someone waiting.'

'Can I ask if the methodology you are using takes account of Professor Oxford's work on hyper-sexuality?'

'Of course. Now if you'll excuse me, I'll contact you during the next week or so.'

After, Carver stared out of the window next to his desk, not sure if he was being over-sensitive. No one was infallible, and there had been times when his instincts had played tricks on him. She was obviously busy, and after all, she had contacted him about arranging a meeting. So it wasn't as if she was avoiding him or anything. But busy or not, he would have expected her to put him right. Even a first-year Forensic Psychology student would have picked up on his mis-reference to the pioneering researcher who first linked hyper-sexuality with sexual deviance. All she had to say was, 'Oxford? Don't you mean Orford?'

So why hadn't she?

CHAPTER 32

The evening exodus from London is a frustrating experience at the best of times. For Jess, seething with anger and embarrassment, it was even more so. The anger was directed at the Hawthorns. She had thought she done enough to gain their trust. Clearly, she was wrong. The embarrassment was over having led Baggus to believe he could rely on that trust. Not since vomiting up her breakfast having fled her first 'Worshipper scene', had she felt so foolish. She waited until they were heading up the M1, before she rang Carver to report back on their meeting with Cyrisse Chaterlain, and ask if the name, Sylvie Tyler, featured anywhere in Megan Crane's archive.

'I've not come across it,' He said. 'And from what Cyrisse Chaterlain seems to be saying, I doubt I will. Kenworthy will have made damn sure there's nothing to link him to her.'

'Well Cyrisse Chaterlain obviously can,' Jess said. 'And maybe Q as well, and Gordon Halsall.'

'You could be right. Where are you going now?'

'Back to the Hawthorn's,' she said. 'And this time I won't be leaving until they've told us everything.'

'Do they know you're coming?'

'Not yet, but they will.'

'I'd leave it as late as possible,' he said.

'That's the plan,' she said.

Jess left it until they were nearing their exit off the M6 and through the worst of the late-evening traffic before trying Gerald on his mobile. She had thought about just turning up at their house on spec, but given the couple's lifestyle, she worried they could have, "company". Right now, the fewer who knew the Hawthorn's were receiving visits from the police, the better. When Gerald didn't answer, she tried Barbara's number. Nothing from her either. She rang their home number. Christo picked up.

'I need to speak with Gerald or Barbara,' she said, putting the call on, 'speaker'.

'I'm sorry Madam. They have both gone to the club.'

'I thought it's closed on Thursdays?'

'It is. But your colleague, Mr Gavin, called and asked me to tell them to meet him there.'

'You're mistaken, Christo.' She threw Baggus a look. 'Mr Gavin is with me. He hasn't called anyone.'

'With you?... But he… he *said* he was Mr Gavin.'

'When was this Christo?' She could see alarm, creeping into Baggus's face.

'Late this afternoon, about… five o'clock?'

She checked the time. It was coming on eight.

'Have you heard from them?'

'No.' His voice rose. 'Is everything alright Madam? Would you like Sally or I to go to the club, see if we can contact them?'

'You stay where you are. We'll go straight there.'

As Baggus swung onto the exit-slip he said, 'Which is the quickest way?'

The Hawthorn's Range Rover was parked outside Josephine's main entrance. Baggus pulled up next to it. There were no other cars.

The safety light at the top of the steps was on, the rest of the club in darkness. Baggus tried the front door.

'It's open.'

They made their way through to the lounge. A dim, security-light behind the bar shone through the shutter-grill, providing just enough light to see by.

'GERALD?' Jess called. 'BARBARA?'

Nothing.

'HELLO?' Baggus shouted.

Jess tried the door to the office. It was locked. She pressed her ear to it, knocked. 'Gerald? Barbara?'

At first there was only silence. Then, from somewhere, a metallic clinking sound echoed.

Baggus pointed to the double doors leading to the theme rooms. 'Through there.'

As they neared, they could see one of the doors ajar. Jess was about to walk through when he pulled her back. She turned. He put a finger to his lips.

Slowly, he pulled the door open, checked to the left. The corridor was in darkness but a chink of light showed under the first door on the right. Baggus remembered it from Barbara's tour - the 'dungeon'. A feeling of foreboding hit him. The clinking sounded again, louder this time. There was no mistaking where it was coming from.

They approached slowly, their steps muffled by the deep carpet. Baggus stopped at the door, checked behind him. Jess was a couple of paces off his shoulder. He could hear her breathing. He remembered that the door opened inwards. Baggus pressed his palm to it, then pushed it wide.

The light was coming from a small strip-light at the back, too far away for them to see clearly. Peering through the gloom, Baggus could just make out the outline of a dark shape hovering in front of him, a couple of feet off the ground. As he tried to focus, he realised it was turning slowly - and clinking.

At his shoulder, Jess moved to the wall where the light switches were. As the lights came on, he leaped back several feet.

'FUUUUCK.'

Beside him, Jess let out a scream and he jumped again.

Gerald Hawthorn's body hung before them, ensnared in a net of chains, the pool of blood beneath fed by the steady drip from his feet. The chains criss-crossed the length of his body from ankles to head, before ending in several turns round the bloody wrists from which he hung. Remnants of clothing hung in tattered strips through gaps in the chains. Where the flesh was exposed, deep slashes and cuts still oozed, testimony to the torture he had suffered before he died. Baggus was starting to register the dark patch surrounding his groin area when he remembered.

'BARBARA.'

He spun around. She was nowhere in sight. Behind him, Jess was staring up at Gerald as if transfixed, pressing a hand to her mouth, trying to suppress the gagging reflex. Seeing her, he remembered that towards the end of the Worshipper case, she'd come across a body in similar circumstances. But there was no time dwell on it. He called again, louder. 'BARBARA.'

He turned for the door, brushed past Jess. She tried to call to him, struggling to get the words out.

'Gav-. Wait…'

He stopped in the doorway, looked down. A trail of dark spots showed on the green carpet. He followed their track. They stopped at the third door along.

'Oh, CHRIST.'

He ran to the door. Behind him, he could hear Jess calling, but she seemed far away, the words dulled by the rushing sound in his ears. He grabbed the handle, hesitated, then turned it and threw the door open.

The hospital-style lamps were on, bathing the room in a clinical white light that only served to enhance the horror. She was strapped, naked, to the dentist's chair which was tipped back almost horizontal. A wide strip of crimson and white material was wrapped, tightly, round the lower part of her face. The blue eyes that had once been so full of life, stared up at the ceiling. They were still wide with terror.

Rushing to her, Baggus saw the ragged, white bundle - blood-spattered - beneath the chair, recognised it as the revealing dress she had worn the last time he'd called on her. It was then he realised what the killer had used to fashion her gag. And that what he thought was some crimson material was the white cotton, stained by whatever object the killer had stuffed into the once beautiful mouth and secured in place using the torn material.

At that moment he remembered the dark stain around Gerald Hawthorn's groin, and the dread realisation of what they would find when the gag was removed filled him with horror, and revulsion. Jess appeared at his side. She was shaking. But he was hardly aware of her as he cried out, 'OH GOD, NO,' turned away, and was violently sick.

CHAPTER 33

Carver arrived at Solihull Police Station shortly after seven in the morning. He'd taken Jess's call about the Hawthorns just before eleven, the night before. He didn't sleep after. Rising at five, he showered and headed down the M6. On the way, he rang and spoke with Jess again, for more details.

The place was already alive with support staff ferrying kit up to the station's designated Major Incident Suite on the third floor. He signed-in, and was escorted up by a passing detective who led him past the station's main briefing room - soon to be the Murder Incident Room - and showed him to an office. The door was ajar. Stuck to it, was a sheet of A4 on which someone had scrawled, in black felt-tip, "DEPUTY SIO." A voice sounded within, loud and Brummie. He knocked once, and walked in.

A man was standing behind the desk. He was on the telephone. Tall, with a beer gut and in need of a shave, he looked like someone who'd been dragged out of bed by a phone call five minutes after his head hit the pillow, and had worked through the night. Carver knew the feeling. Seeing Carver, the man beckoned him in, but kept talking. The conversation was animated and littered with references to LAN points, network ports, line capacity, and other tech-terms of the sort Carver had heard before, but had little understanding. From the frustration in his voice, and his references to, 'Whichever tosser signed the MIS Plan off before making sure it could carry a double-homicide," Carver guessed he was talking to someone in IT. For all the pre-planning and exercises, it's nearly always the IT/Coms that delays the MIR go-live. A minute later the man signed off with a grumpy, 'I'd be fucking grateful if *someone* would,' and slammed the receiver down. For several seconds, he continued to stare at the telephone, as if confirming to himself the next problem that needed his attention, before turning to his visitor.

'Are you Carver?'

Carver nodded.

The man stuck out a hand. 'Craig Whitewell, DCI. Your DI, Jess, said you were coming.'

'How's it going?'

Whitewell blew out his cheeks. 'Slowly,' he jerked a thumb at the telephone, 'As you heard.' He gave Carver a straight look. 'I gather this is a right bag of worms? Something to do with that job of yours a while back involving that dominatrix woman?'

'*One* possibility.' Carver said.

'You're not sure?'

Carver rocked a hand. 'I'm keeping an open mind. Can you point me to where I'll find my team?'

'Sure. Next floor.' He pointed at the ceiling. 'Right above us.'

Before leaving, Carver said, 'Who's the SIO?'

'Andy Gilleray. Superintendent. Know him?'

Carver shook his head. 'What's he like?'

Whitewell pondered. 'Good, but he can be a ballbreaker. He's still at the scene. He says he wants to speak with you soon as he gets back.'

'I can imagine'

'One thing.'

'Yes?'

'The other one-' He nodded at the ceiling.

'Gavin? Baggus?'

'He's rambling on about this MP, Kenworthy. You may want to reign him in a bit. Mr Gilleray wasn't too impressed being told who he ought to be arresting before we've even done the scene.'

Carver nodded. 'Noted.' He made his way up.

Outside the door marked, 'Rest Room', he paused to listen, but the voices were too low. He went straight in. Jess was squatting in front of Baggus, slumped in an armchair, head in his hands.

Speaking to Jess on the way down, Carver had guessed things weren't good when she was spare with the facts and gave a wary, 'Rather upset', when he asked about Baggus. Suspecting others were present, he hadn't pressed. But he hadn't expected to find him *this* bad. The week before, Jess had joked about Baggus developing a soft-spot for Barbara Hawthorn. Now, looking at him, he suspected that 'soft-spot' wasn't the half of it. As he came in, Jess stood up. Like Whitewell, she too looked washed-out. Her face told the story.

Problems.

'You okay?' he said. She tried a wan smile, nodded. 'As bad as…?' Even now, he couldn't say Angie's name. Jess would know what he meant.

She took a deep breath, nodded. 'Maybe… worse.' She checked Baggus. He was out of it. She mimed a chopping motion at groin level, then raised her hand to her open mouth.

Jesus Christ. Carver looked over at Baggus, then back to Jess. She shook her head. *Not Good.*

Coming forward, he laid a hand on Baggus's shoulder. 'I'm sorry Gavin. I know how you feel, believe me.'

It took a while, but eventually Baggus dropped his hands, turned his face up. Tears mingled with the bitter anger that was all too plain to see.

'The *bastards.* The fucking *bastards.'*

Carver nodded.

'You know what they did to her?' His voice rose. 'Do you?'

'Yes,' Carver said. 'And you're right. They *are* bastards.'

Baggus grasped at it. 'It was Kenworthy. Did Jess tell you what the Chaterlain woman said, about the Tyler girl?' He started to ramble. 'It must be him that Quinlan was blackmailing. He must have decided to silence the Hawthorns as well.'

Carver nodded. He kept his voice even. 'You may be right. We'll put it together, see what we've got.'

Baggus began to fidget. 'I don't need to put it together. I already know what we've got.' He looked up at Carver. 'And I'm going to have the cunt before the day's out.' He made to rise, but Carver pressed him back into his seat.

'Easy, Gavin. In good time.'

Baggus tried to shrug himself free from Carver's pressing.

'*FUCK* in good time. We need to pull him before he knows we're onto him. I'd be there now if Jess hadn't said to wait for you.' Baggus twisted round to look up at the man whose grip was preventing him going anywhere. 'What's wrong? Don't tell me you're scared to arrest him.'

Carver and Jess swapped glances. Hers said, *Told you.*

Carver pulled a chair round to sit in front of Baggus, met his stare.

'I'm not scared to arrest him. And we will. If it's him.'

'IF IT's-?'

'A couple of points.' Carver cut across. He counted them off, thumb first. 'One. This isn't our case. It's the West Midlands' decision who to arrest, and when.'

'Fuck them,' Baggus said. 'We told them the score and they're just sitting round on their arses. That bastard Superintendent…,' He turned to Jess. 'Whassisname?

'Gilleray?' Carver offered.

'That's him. He more or less accused Jess and me of being *involved* with the Hawthorns. Like we're *into* that stuff.'

Carver looked over at Jess. She nodded, bit her lip.

'Soon as I mentioned Megan Crane he backed off. Said he wasn't going to stand for, 'all that crap' and told us to wait here until he's finished at the scene.'

Carver nodded. He could imagine how it might sound to an SIO, woken in the night to be told he had a double-murder on his hands, and a horrific one at that.

Jess continued. 'I tried telling him about Quinlan and everything, but he didn't want to know.' She paused, before adding, 'He's no Duke.'

Few are. He returned to Baggus. 'Two, we can't just waltz in and arrest a Government Minister, even a junior one, without some evidence. And if we don't have Chief Officer support when we do, we'll be off the case before you can say, Jack Shit.'

Baggus turned to Jess, the beginnings of a sneer showing. 'I thought you said he's okay?' He came back to Carver. 'I thought the man who locks up serial killers follows his instincts? I didn't realise you're an arse-licker who can't make a decision.'

Carver let out a long sigh. But he didn't avoid Baggus's stare and let the moment hang. He'd dealt with situations like this before. They are never easy. However much detectives know they shouldn't get personally involved, sometimes they just can't help it. *Like me.* But Baggus was as bad as any he had seen. He continued.

'Three. Coming down, I got Special Branch to liaise with the Met and check yesterday's Westminster List. Kenworthy spent yesterday afternoon giving evidence before a Parliamentary Sub-Committee. He left around six to come home for a Constituency Party Meeting today. He arrived home shortly after nine last night. Whatever you may like to think, he did not kill the Hawthorns.'

Baggus didn't waver. 'So he got someone to do it for him. Let's bring him in and put him through the wringer. He's a politician. He'll soon start talking.'

Carver sat back, gave the younger man a hard stare.

'Get real, Gavin. You know as well as I do that won't wash. He's alibied to the hilt. His solicitor will be there. We wouldn't get past the first detention review.'

It worked, of a sort. Baggus slumped back in his chair, muttering oaths that were littered with the words, 'bastards' and 'bullshit'.

The initial crisis averted, Carver turned to Jess. 'Anything from the scene?'

Jess shook her head. 'Not the last I heard.'

'What about the phone call this Christo bloke took?'

'I've not spoken to him. I think they've brought him in, but no one's said anything.'

'We need to find him,' Carver said. He turned to Baggus. He was bent forward, head in hands. 'We'll be back soon, Gavin. Don't go anywhere.'

Baggus nodded, but didn't look up.

CHAPTER 34

They found Christo and Sally in separate interview rooms on the ground floor. Sally was giving a statement to a woman detective. Through the door panel they saw her taking tissues from a box while the detective looked on, sympathetic. But Christo was alone, slumped over a table, head on his arms, a polystyrene cup and ashtray beside him. As they walked in he stood up, looking hopeful.

'Miss Jessica?' But seeing Carver behind, he became wary. 'What is happening? They will not tell me anything.'

Carver thought he seemed even more distraught than Baggus. *This Barbara Hawthorn must have been some woman.*

After introducing Carver, Jess asked Christo about the phone call that had lured the Hawthorns to their deaths.

'He said he was your friend, Mr Gavin.' His eyes flicked to Carver. 'He has telephoned Mistress Barbara a few times.' Jess and Carver exchanged glances. 'He told me to tell Master Gerald and Mistress Barbara that they were to meet him at the club, and that he would be there. I gave them the message, and they left.' He burst into tears. 'I…. I didn't see them again.' Reaching out, he grabbed Jess's hands in his. 'Oh Mistress Jessica.'

Carver started at the familiarity. He hadn't realised they were on anything more than nodding terms.

'They were such beautiful people,' Christo said. 'I loved them so much.'

She leaned into him. 'Think, Christo. It wasn't Mr Gavin, so who else might it have been? Was there anything about the voice you recognised? Have you heard it before? On the phone? At the Club?'

He shook his head, full of grief. 'If only I'd gone with them.'

A few minutes later, Carver looked back through the window at the man who was still trembling so much he was having difficulty lighting another cigarette. 'You'd think he's lost his parents,' he said.

'In a way, that's what they were,' Jess said. 'Gerald told me he latched onto Barbara, the first time they met. Whenever he was there, he hardly left her side. Gerald called him, "Her pet".'

'Obviously has a thing for strong women,' Carver muttered. As Jess turned to him, he looked away. 'Let's get back to Gavin.'

When they returned to the Rest Room, Baggus wasn't there, but Whitewell was, together with another man, whom Carver guessed was the SIO, Gilleray. The man who would lead the investigation into the Hawthorn's murders was stood at the window, legs apart, hands on hips. As they came in, he turned to face them. Gilleray had a good few years on Carver, was about the same height, but bulkier. His spiky grey hair somehow made him look older than he probably was.

Carver approached, extended a hand. 'Mr Gilleray? Jamie Carver.'

As they shook, Gilleray eyed him with what Carver read as suspicion.

'So you're the man I keep hearing about. The young lady,' - he swung a nod towards Jess but didn't look at her - 'Said you were mixed up in this. I hope you aren't thinking of turning this into another magazine story.'

Carver remembered Jess's comment about Gilleray being no Duke. In his place, he'd have more welcoming towards someone who may be able to shed light on a double murder. Behind Gilleray, Whitewell looked slightly uncomfortable. Carver stood his ground.

'If by, "mixed up in this," you mean someone who may be able to help, then you're right.'

Gilleray glared back at him. 'From what I gather so far, your help has landed me with two bodies.'

Carver tried again. 'If you'll let us talk you through everything, we may be able to give you a pointer.'

'So your other colleague said. A Government Minister is it? Great. My Chief will love hearing that. Well bring your man in. Let's hear it again.'

Carver stiffened. 'Wasn't he here when you arrived?'

'We thought he was with you.'

He turned to Jess. She was already making for the door. 'Back in a minute.'

Over the next few minutes, Carver's willingness to help started to wane. Before he could even begin, Gilleray insisted on knowing why someone attached to a Regional Intelligence Unit was involved in a suspicious death enquiry. 'Isn't your area supposed to be organised crime?' Carver explained that he was simply advising, using his background knowledge of Megan Crane and her network. But Gilleray showed little interest in listening. Carver sensed an agenda.

Jess returned, looking grave -faced. Coming straight

over to Carver, she whispered in his ear.

'His car's gone and he's not answering his mobile.'

Carver jerked round. The look in her face, she was thinking the same as him.

'Something wrong?' Gilleray said.

Carver stared at Jess. 'Shit.'

CHAPTER 35

Carver wasn't sure if it was good or bad that Alistair Kenworthy's home constituency was less than an hour's drive from Solihull nick. Being close meant they might make it in time to stop Baggus doing something stupid. But if it had been further away, he may have been less inclined to rush off in the first place, giving him time to think things through. Maybe.

The Aylesbury Constituency Offices are located in the Westcott Exchange building. A former Victorian school house on the fringes of the town centre, it houses a range of community and local business support enterprises. Jess's mobile took them straight there. As they pulled onto the car park, Jess pointed to a red, Mazda SUV parked near the entrance. 'That's him.'

Carver parked next to it.They made their way inside. The lady receptionist was dealing with a couple of visitors. Over by the stairs, a burly security guard was checking passes. Carver went straight to him, showed his warrant card.

'I'm looking for a colleague of mine who-'

An outburst of shouting echoed from above. It was followed by the wah-wah-wah of a personal-attack alarm.

The guard reacted at once. 'What the-?' Turning, he started up the stairs, Carver and Jess right behind him.

As they raced up, the guard used his radio to alert his control. On the first floor landing, they were joined by another guard. The shouting grew louder as they carried on up to the second floor. Amongst several voices, Carver recognised one. His heart sank.

On the second-floor landing, a middle-aged man in a dark suit and wearing a panicked look was holding the security door open. On the guide-board behind him, Carver glimpsed, "Aylesbury Parliamentary Constituency Offices". The man pointed down the corridor. 'He's attacking the minister.' Carver hoped he was exaggerating, even if it was understandable given the experience of recent years.

Halfway down, a group of people hung in a doorway. They all looked fearful. Carver followed the security team straight in.

Baggus was leaning over a desk, jabbing a finger in the face of a man Carver recognised at once as Alistair Kenworthy. Either side of Baggus, two be-suited men were grabbing at his flailing arms, while behind, an older, silver-haired woman pulled at his jacket. Carver's immediate thought was that Kenworthy seemed remarkably calm for a man under attack.

'You lying bastard,' Baggus yelled. 'You know exactly what I'm talking about.'

The security officers rushed to take over the restraint, pulling Baggus's arms behind and dragging him away from the desk. For several seconds there was chaos as people shouted and Baggus raved.

'CALM DOWN.'

'Who is he?'

'HE DID IT.'

'Get him out of here.'

'He's a, FUCKING MURDERER.'

'Are you alright minister?'

Carver forced himself through to stand in front of the struggling detective.

'GAVIN. STOP IT.'

Baggus stopped. Everyone froze, surprised by the stranger's intervention. But then he started up again, directing his words at Carver.

'I was right. The bastard did it. He knows them. He knows the Hawthorns.' He tried to wrench himself free from the guards' restraining grips. Twisting round, his voice took on a threatening edge. 'Let go of me.'

Carver pulled him back round. 'STOP it, Gavin. This isn't the way. You're making it all worse. Calm DOWN.' Jess appeared next to him. She looked close to tears.

'He's right Gavin. Please, just stop.'

It worked. Baggus stopped struggling, stared at her, then folded. Anger gave way to the despair of someone who knows he is beaten. 'Aahh, FUUuuck.' He hung his head. 'Barbara, I'm sorry. I'm so sorry.'

Sensing control being brought to bear, the mood of those present started to change, anger replacing fear.

'Who is he?'

'How dare he barge in like this.'

'This is outrageous.'

'A police officer? Which force? Who's his Chief Constable?'

Carver went to work. Holding his warrant card high, he shouted above the clamour. He needed to divert them from Baggus, and quickly.

'I'm sorry everyone. I'm afraid this is my fault.' Turning to the Security Guards, he invoked the authority he used only rarely. 'It's alright. He's not a risk. He's a colleague. Go easy on him.' Carver gambled it was probably their first genuine major security alert, and would follow anyone who looked like they knew what they were doing. He was right. Easing down, their fearful looks changed to ones that said they were ready to take orders. 'Jess?' He looked to find her at his shoulder. 'Go with them. Take him somewhere quiet,' then whispered in her ear, 'For God's sake, calm him down.'

But before she could move, an older man in a grey pinstripe stepped forward. 'Just one minute.' Though shaken, his bearing spoke of someone used to being listened to. Ex-military, Carver guessed. 'Before anyone goes anywhere, I want to know what the hell is going on? On whose authority are you-'

'I'm sorry sir, Detective Chief Inspector Carver, I'm with the National Crime Agency. He hoped it would carry enough weight to forestall further questioning. 'I need to speak with the minister, privately.'

The man began to bluster, 'And *I'm* not sure-.' Carver lifted a hand, cutting him off. 'Carry on, Jess.'

As he turned back to Kenworthy, now flanked by a younger man and the woman who had been holding Baggus's jacket, he saw the MP's gaze fix on Jess as she turned to the security guards and said, 'Where can we go?' The way she said it, Carver knew she would have no trouble.

As they filed out, Carver saw Kenworthy following her confident stride. At the door, she turned and threw a piercing look back. It seemed aimed mainly at Kenworthy.

The intruder gone, the crowd turned on Carver, demanding answers. The man in grey looked like he was about to start again. Carver knew he had one chance. Looking beyond the faces, he locked eyes with Kenworthy. 'Can we speak minister?'

During the seconds that followed, the mute communication between the two men worked its way into the others. For the first time since it had all started, silence descended. As Kenworthy broke a half-smile, pinstripe seemed to sense what he was contemplating.

'Minister, I must caution you that-.'

'Thank you, Thomas,' Kenworthy said, his relaxed manner signalling the danger had passed. 'I don't think there is a need for any further alarm. I'm familiar with DCI Carver. I'm sure I'll be quite safe in his hands.' He turned to the others. 'It's alright everybody. Please carry on. Thank you all for your help.'

Everyone began to withdraw, still muttering.Kenworthy turned to the formidable-looking woman who had hung onto Baggus's jacket. 'Some tea, Elizabeth, I think.'

The way she glared at Carver, he had no doubt she would defend her boss against the SAS if asked to. Reluctantly, she crossed to the door to an adjoining office, but her gaze stayed on him until the door closed behind her. The only person remaining was the younger of the two men Carver had seen grappling with Baggus when he first arrived. The way he had positioned himself, close to his minister, Carver guessed he was his First Secretary. He whispered into Kenworthy's ear.

Kenworthy nodded and gave several grunts, acknowledging whatever advice he was being given. Eventually he said, 'Yes, alright, Hugh.' He sounded impatient. 'But I am quite recovered enough to speak with Mr Carver. Don't worry, I'll call you the moment he starts to become unhinged.' He winked at Carver.

Carver didn't return it. He was picturing his

ANACAPA Chart, and wondering if Hugh's surname began with a 'G'.

After Hugh had gone, Kenworthy regarded Carver the way he might a prospective opponent. Eventually, he came around the desk, indicating the red-leather Chesterfield under an old portrait of some statesman Carver didn't recognise.

'Shall we sit, Chief Inspector? I'm sure we have much to talk about.'

CHAPTER 36

Following his success in the Ancoats Rapist case, the College of Policing Crime Faculty sponsored Carver on a 'Series-Crime Investigation Exchange' trip to the US. It included a stop-over at the FBI Academy at Quantico, Virginia. There, he undertook an assessment similar to the one Doctor Maureen O'Sullivan of the University of San Francisco used during her research into Human Lie-Detection Abilities. It was O'Sullivan's research that gave rise to the term, 'Wizard' to describe those rare individuals whose abilities are such they can outperform any polygraph. Carver's score didn't place him in the, 'Wizarding', percentile, but he was borderline-exceptional. In the weeks and months following Megan Crane's conviction, he pondered long and hard over how it was, given his supposed skills, that he failed, repeatedly, to see through the dominatrix's web of deceit. Eventually, he settled for convincing himself that, apart from that first day when she denied keeping records of her 'encounters' - there was a lot going on in his head at the time - she never lied, directly, to his face. Deep down, he harboured the suspicion that, like all her victims, he'd simply let himself be distracted. He also wondered if the skills involved - reading microexpressions and other tell-signs – simply fade in the absence of regular use, as they do in other areas. Such thoughts were in his head as he listened to Alistair Kenworthy describing his past involvement with the Hawthorns, and Josephine's.

Kenworthy's initial response on hearing what had befallen the couple - shock, distress, horror - were as Carver would have expected. Pupil dilation, accelerated breathing, gaping mouth, (rapidly corrected), pallor. But Carver was aware they were all capable of being faked. As a politician, Kenworthy would be more practised than most in using masking behaviours. He claimed not to have visited Josephine's for several years - around the time his political profile began to rise - and Carver knew of nothing in Megan Crane's archive that showed otherwise. During the time he was a regular frequenter, he did so under an assumed name, his identity known only to those, 'I became close to.' It rang true. Any hint of a Member of Parliament and Minister of the Crown frequenting somewhere like Josephine's, would bring the curtain down on a political career. But over the years, Kenworthy would have grown used to hiding his predilections. It all meant that Carver was struggling to gauge how much of what came out of his mouth was truth, and how much was something else.

For his part, Carver had little choice but to condemn Baggus's 'unprofessional overreaction', though it felt like he was knifing Baggus in the back. He referred to how the young DI had grown close to the Hawthorns during the time he'd known them. He didn't mention how short a time that was.

'I can understand that, Chief Inspector, 'Kenworthy said. 'The Hawthorns were lovely people. But whatever put the thought in his head their deaths may have something to do with me?'

Carver took a deep breath. Baggus's disastrous decision to confront Kenworthy, however understandable, left him with no choice but to disclose at least some of what they knew. *You've got a lot to answer for, Gavin.* Keeping as much back as he could, particularly their steer from Megan Crane, Carver referred to Quinlan's death.

'I heard about it,' Kenworthy said. 'I understood it was an accident.'

'We're still looking into it.'

'You think it could be something else?'

'Until we're sure, we're keeping an open mind.' Even as he said it, Carver wondered how many more times he would use the line.

Kenworthy paused, taking a long look at Carver.

'Bearing in mind your colleague's behaviour, *and* what's happened to the Hawthorns, do I take it you're looking at the possibility that Q was also murdered?'

'Like I said, we're keeping things open.'

Kenworthy ignored it. 'You must have a theory, surely?'

Carver said nothing.

Kenworthy's eyes narrowed. 'Blackmail.'

Carver made sure not to react. 'What about it?'

'You think Q was blackmailing someone.' He paused again. 'And you suspect that someone was me, or at least your colleague does.'

Carver tried to not react. It was not uncommon for a suspect to pre-empt an accusation in the way Kenworthy had just done. It eliminates the risk of a subconscious reaction when it is eventually put. But while it always begs the question, *Why?,* it can't be relied on to indicate guilt. *Thanks again Gavin.*

'It's one hypothesis,' Carver said

Kenworthy grinned in a way that, had it come from someone other than a politician, Carver might have read as, *You prove it.* He'd known the man less than ten minutes, but he already knew he was the sort he could easily dislike. The wink, earlier, had a lot to do with it. Kenworthy was a showman who liked to hide his true nature behind a veneer of polite reasonableness. *Too damned clever by half.*

Carver switched tack. 'Tell me about Cyrisse Chaterlain.' He hoped that dropping her name may prompt something. But Kenworthy's nonchalant shrug gave nothing away. He seemed impervious to embarrassment.

'I haven't seen her in a long time.' But there was a moment's hesitation as Kenworthy's gaze wavered, before steadying again. 'But I won't prevaricate. We had a relationship, as I did with Megan Crane.'

Another pre-empt, Carver thought.

'I assume that if you're aware of my association with Cyrisse, you must also know of my contact with that woman. I followed the reporting of her trial, and your exploits in bringing her to book with great interest, as I am sure did many others.'

Carver said nothing. The man was working hard at showing he had nothing to hide.

'As you know, such relationships involve nothing illegal. Nor do they constitute a threat to national or parliamentary security. If you have cause to suspect otherwise, then I must ask you to disclose what you know, as I am obliged to notify my Permanent Secretary and the Chief Whip of such matters.' He paused then added, 'Unless, of course, you have already done so?'

Nicely done, Carver thought. Straight down the

middle. He returned in kind.

'I haven't mentioned these matters to anyone in Government. And I wouldn't want to embarrass anyone by saying too much too soon.'

'After your colleague's behaviour today, Mr Carver, I believe it may be rather late for that.'

'For which I have already apologised.' Carver looked at him squarely. *And that's the last time.* Baggus's assumption that Kenworthy was behind the killings may be speculation, but that didn't mean he was wrong. 'Nevertheless, I'm sure that as a Crown Servant, like myself, you will want to assist the police in any way you can.'

A hint of a smile played about Kenworthy's lips. 'That may be expecting rather a lot.'

'Let's see how far we can get.' Carver said. 'You knew Megan Crane through Josephine's and met with her several times. Correct?'

'Correct. But that was before she started murdering people.'

'I don't actually know when that was. Do you?'

The smile vanished. 'I can only go off what I read in the papers.'

'Of course. And you met Cyrisse Chaterlain through Megan?'

'She was at Megan's home once when I was there.'

'And afterwards you started seeing her?'

'Chelsea is more convenient than Cheshire.' The smile again, as if it were simply a question of economics.

'Cyrisse introduced you to a friend of hers. Sylvie Tyler?'

For the first time, Kenworthy seemed less sure of himself.

'The name sounds familiar….' He reached for his teacup.

'Let me help. She worked for Cyrisse. She was young.'

'Ah yes, I remember now. I did meet her, a couple of times.'

'When did you last see her?'

'I would think… two, maybe three years ago.'

'Any idea where she is now?' Carver made it sound casual, but was keenly interested to see how the man would react. If he had something to hide, it was an obvious jumping off point. He jumped.

'This seems to be heading somewhere specific, Chief Inspector. You must understand, that part of my life is behind me. I am happily married.' As he said it, his gaze turned, briefly, to a photograph on his desk. It showed an attractive, dark-haired woman.

Carver glanced at it, then came back to him. 'I understood you were married when you met these women?'

In the act of returning his cup to its saucer, Kenworthy looked up sharply. 'I'm sorry, Chief Inspector. I thought I was being cooperative?'

'For which I am suitably grateful.'

'But if my motives and actions are going to be made subject of comment, then I think I must take advice before answering further questions.'

'That is your prerogative,' Carver said. 'But I only have one other. Has *anyone* contacted you in the past month concerning your involvement with any of the people we've spoken about?'

'No one.'

For several seconds the two men regarded each other in silence.

Eventually Carver stood up. Kenworthy rose with him.

'Sorry, I do have one last question. Who is VR?'

The response was quick, his face a blank mask. 'VR? Is that a name or are they initials?'

'Initials.'

Leading Carver to the door, he made a show of trying to think. 'I'm sorry, I don't know any "VR". My assistant, Hugh, will take you to your colleagues.'

As he opened the door, a woman sitting in the outer office rose to her feet. Carver recognised her from her photograph.

'Alistair? Are you alright? Hugh told me what happened.' Behind her, the man called Hugh was speaking into a telephone.

'I'm fine my dear. But it wasn't as bad as I am sure everyone is making out.' He introduced her to Carver.

As they shook hands her eyes narrowed. 'Have we met?'

Carver returned her a smile. She seemed very different from her husband. 'I don't think so.'

'You've probably seen his face in the papers,' Kenworthy said, throwing Carver another wink, which he ignored. 'That case the beginning of last year. The woman who committed those awful murders?'

'The ones involving all those prostitutes?'

'Not prostitutes, Mrs Kenworthy,' Carver corrected. 'They were dominatrices.'

She pulled a face. 'Isn't that the same thing?'

'No.' But he wasn't sure if the glint in her eye was from the sun streaming through the windows, or something else. Though the years had not treated her as kindly as they may have done, she still had some of her former model looks about her.

'Mr Carver should know, darling,' Kenworthy said. 'He's something of an *expert* in these matters.'

Carver turned back to him. 'I'm sure I'm not the only one, Sir.'

Kenworthy dropped it. He turned to his assistant just as he came off the phone.

'Apparently, the Area Police Commander and a Special Branch officer are on their way.' Hugh said. 'They'll be here in ten minutes. They want to speak with you, Minister. You too, Chief Inspector.'

Great, Carver thought.

Kenworthy turned to his wife. 'If you don't mind delaying lunch, my dear, I'll join you as soon as I can.' He ushered her to the door. 'Don't worry, Chief Inspector. I shan't be making a formal complaint.' As he led his wife away, Carver heard Anne Kenworthy asking about what had happened. 'I'll tell you all about it over lunch,' he said. 'It's all rather amusing.'

Carver resisted the temptation to let her know that the matter her husband found, "amusing", involved the murder of two people. He turned to Kenworthy's assistant.

'Right, Hugh. Where are my colleagues?'

He needed to get to Baggus before the lynch-mob arrived.

Carver and Jess watched from the doorway as the Area Superintendent, stormed off down the corridor, the Special Branch DI following. Baggus was still slumped in the chair. He'd barely moved throughout the inquisition. As it went on, the Superintendent had become increasingly angry, both at Baggus's uncommunicative state and Carver's answers - which told him next to nothing. Eventually, he'd had little choice but to call it a day.

'Something about this stinks,' he said, rising. 'And if you won't speak to me then you can speak to your own Chief. You're just damn lucky the Minister doesn't wish to complain, though God knows why not.' He stomped to the door, followed by the SB DI who hadn't opened his mouth since introducing himself. 'Now bugger off back where you all came from.'

'Charming,' Jess said as the pair disappeared. She had also paid the Superintendent scant attention. Rather than charm him round, the way Carver knew she was capable, her concerns had stayed with Baggus. 'Still, it could have been worse.'

Carver pulled a face. *Not so sure.*

She pulled him round into the corridor. 'He could have suspended him,' she said.

'It could still happen,' Carver said. If there's one thing Chief Officers won't stand for, it's being embarrassed in front of politicians, especially senior ones. 'At least he managed to stick to the plot.'

Jess harrumphed. 'I'm not sure he believed your story about Gavin misunderstanding your instructions.'

'Maybe not. But it buys us time. We need to get back and sort out Gilleray, and a double murder.'

'Christ, I've been so worried about Gavin, I'd forgotten all that.'

As they made ready to leave, she asked about his meeting with Kenworthy. He waited until they were in the lifts and on the way down - Baggus standing mute behind them - before giving her a summary. After they signed out and left the building, she picked up the conversation.

'What do you make of him?'

He glanced over his shoulder as if expecting to see

Kenworthy watching from his office window. 'I think he found a reason to clam up when I mentioned Sylvie Tyler.'

'Why?'

'My guess is, because that's when he would have had to start lying.'

Alistair Kenworthy watched, hidden behind the window blinds, until the detectives rounded the corner and were lost to sight.

Behind him, Hugh Gubby said, 'Did he say how much he knew?'

Kenworthy turned back to his desk. 'Of course not. He was just fishing. He doesn't even know what they're looking for.'

'But they're not going to give up, are they? Not now. Not after… what's happened.'

Kenworthy let his irritation start to show. 'Let's not start again, Hugh. They will.'

'How do you know?'

'Trust me. I know.' He headed for the door. 'I'm going for lunch. Make sure everyone knows it was simply a case of the police getting their facts wrong, again.'

CHAPTER 37

By the time Jess returned from her soak, Baggus was asleep on the couch. Leaving the Midlands, she'd insisted he come back and stay the night at hers. He'd tried to argue but she cut him off. He didn't try again. Reaching down, she prised the glass from his fingers. The bottle of Jack Daniels next to him, and which she'd opened new, was less than a third full. For almost a minute, she stood looking down at him.

She would never have imagined him reacting the way he had. But then, Barbara Hawthorn *was* special, even to her. His belated realisation, on the way back, that his actions had only made things worse didn't help. As they headed up the motorway, with him in the passenger seat, staring out into the dark, she'd actually checked to make sure the locks were set. It was a ridiculous idea, but it made her feel better.

They still needed to resolve things with Gilleray and the West Midlands. A meeting had been fixed for the next morning which should provide an opportunity. She'd learned of it in a late phone call from Jamie. But when she voiced her hope it might, 'Get things moving in the right direction,' he'd responded with a mysterious-sounding, 'Don't count on it.'

When she told Baggus - he'd only just started on the JD - he promised he would, 'Get my act together,' in time. In truth, she would rather he wasn't there at all, and knew Jamie felt the same. But Gilleray was insisting apparently, talking of 'serious matters needing to be discussed.' She could guess what they were. Word of their visit to Kenworthy's office had already circulated. She'd also heard from The Duke earlier. Someone in the West Midlands was baying for blood. It would be nice to think that by tomorrow, people may be in a better frame of mind to listen to what they had to say about the Hawthorns' murders. But she wasn't optimistic.

Kneeling beside Baggus, she brushed a lick of his hair off his forehead.

'Who'sssat…?' but didn't wake.

She regarded him through sad eyes. 'Come on Gavin,' she whispered. 'You're better than this.'

With a sigh, she rose and fetched a blanket from the airing cupboard. She tucked it round him, then headed for bed. But at the door leading through to her bedroom, she turned to look back at him. He looked peaceful, at last. It was then that the memory came. Baggus, dressed in black tie, standing in the middle of Josephine's busy lounge, almost strutting with pride as Barbara, dazzling as ever, hung on his arm.

As she turned to the bedroom, her eyes were wet again.

'Bastards,' she spat.

CHAPTER 38

Ellen Hazelhurst knew that the sort of London-based postings she had her eye on, invariably go to Governor grades seen as having, 'operational credibility,' and to be, 'feet on the ground,' types. For that reason, she'd always made sure to devote some of her time to being seen 'at the sharp end'. It gave her the chance to both see what her staff were getting up to, and listen to their complaints. She did this by turning up, unannounced and at all hours of the day or night, either on the wings, or at one the prison's other 'operational' units. She wasn't so naive as to think it gave a her a handle on *everything* that was happening on the ground, but it was better than sitting in her office being fed only what her Management Team wanted her to know.

But to have any worth, her visits needed to be unpredictable, which was why she took care to ensure her intentions remained secret until such time as she presented herself at wherever she had chosen to visit. On one occasion, she turned up on E-Wing at two o'clock in the morning when she was, supposedly, holidaying in Ireland. Another time, now famous, she smuggled herself back into the prison in the rear of a food delivery van only an hour after finishing work for the day. Two-and-a-half years into her term, the occasions when she caught her staff doing something they shouldn't, had fallen to single figure percentages.

Ellen had last visited Cloverbank only nine days before, during a busy, 'visiting day'. On that occasion, she came away satisfied that, on the surface at least, the Annex was being run and managed as it should. The admission protocols were being followed and the visit-supervising processes were by the book. Those inmates not receiving visits were either properly secured in their 'rooms' – The Minnesota Scheme didn't allow for 'cells' - or properly booked out to whichever part of the prison they were assigned for educational, rehabilitation, or work purposes.

Two things niggled, however. First, the Minnesota Trial meant there were times when the Annex operated differently not just to the rest of the prison, but also her and her staff's, experience. It was also subject to regular review-monitoring by a specially-appointed cadre of Prison Visitors. God forbid that the next review may discover that the scheme's aims were being subverted in a way that reflected badly on Ellen and her team. Such a stain would take long to fade. The second niggle was, of course, Megan Crane. At their last meeting, Ellen thought she had seen signs that the woman was beginning, at last, to accept the need for compliance on her part with the rules, written and unwritten, that are essential to maintaining good order and discipline - the prerequisites for a smooth-running prison. But she was ever-mindful of the several Assessment Reports she had read about her. They all highlighted her propensity for duplicity, especially when it comes to misleading, 'establishment authority figures'. Which was why Ellen's instinct was to not take anything for granted.

And which was why she had decided to visit Cloverbank again. Tonight.

Ellen had never visited the same unit twice within such a short period. She'd once visited The Special Operations Unit twice in sixteen days, but the problems they were encountering meant it warranted such attention, and in the end it had proved justified. Having been given a 'clean bill of health' only nine days ago, no one at Cloverbank would be expecting another visit.

Unpredictability. That was the key.

She knew something was wrong the moment she swiped herself through to the vestibule-reception and found the mini-control behind the glass security-screen empty. Barring a fire or similar emergency - which she would know about - it should never be left unattended. Cameras covered the path leading up to the front door. It meant either, that no one had been there to witness her approach – a security breach of the utmost seriousness, and therefore worrying. Or the duty officer had seen her coming, and had rushed off to tell someone, which was also worrying, but in a different way.

She was about to radio through to the Prison's main Control Room when the door at the back opened and the duty PO slid round to return to her post. Her face was red. She was breathing hard and appeared flustered.

She's been to warn someone.

'G-good evening Ma'am,' the woman stuttered. "We, er- We weren't expecting you.'

Ellen was on it at once. 'Why were you out of the room?'

The woman's colour deepened. 'I just went to let PO Bright know you were here.'

Ellen started. According to the duty roster, the Cloverbank Housemother should have signed off duty at six that evening. It was now approaching nine-thirty.

'Collette's still here?'

The PO nodded. Eye contact seemed a problem.

Ellen thought about asking why she had thought it necessary to alert her supervisor, but that wasn't the priority. 'Let me through,' she barked.

'Yes, Ma'am.' The PO reached across for the Visitor Log. 'I just need to ask you to-.'

'NOW.'

The PO jumped, pressed the door release. There was a buzz and a click. Ellen stepped through into the communal area, and stopped dead.

Cloverbank's compliment of eight residents – not 'inmates' - were arrayed around the sofa and chairs in a way that put Megan Crane at the centre. Plastic cups and mugs littered the coffee table. Out in front of them, as if making some presentation, was Collette Bright, the other night-duty PO next to her. Ellen's thought was, it all looked laughably-staged. Behind the attempts at innocent expressions, she sensed tension. Whatever she had barged in on, it was not one of the standard, 'House Meetings,' the programme allowed for.

Collette Bright did her best to look and sound casual when she turned to her and said, 'Good evening Ma'am. Welcome to Cloverbank.'

Ellen was in no mood to play along. Her instincts pricked. 'What's going on Collette?' She pointed to her watch. For all its concessions, the Minnesota programme conformed to standard, 'Bedding Down', procedures, which require that inmates be in their rooms by nine.

'House Meeting, Ma'am. I'm afraid it's, er, gone on longer than I expected.' But the crack in her voice and her nervousness gave the lie to it.

Ellen stepped forward. 'What's it about? Why wasn't it notified to my office?' But before Collette could answer, Ellen raised a hand - 'What's that?' - and pointed.

On the sofa, half-hidden under the woman to Megan Crane's left, part of a silver-metal object protruded. The woman, Toyah Devine, a Manchester Moss Side crackhead, looked down, but didn't stir. Ellen held out her hand. Reluctantly, Toyah drew it out and handed it over. It was a pair of handcuffs - and not standard prison issue. Ellen stared at it. She opened her mouth to say something, but no words came. She turned to Collette but as her gaze swept over Megan Crane she spotted something else. Stashed behind the sofa was a black cloth bag, with a draw-string. Ellen froze. She had no idea what might be in it, but her brain started conjuring images of the scene in the room moments before she arrived. How close to accurate they were she had no idea, but they triggered others, amongst them a Sunday Red-Top headline - the lurid sort that can spell doom to a career professional. "*Scandal Of Prison S&M Parties*" She wondered about what was in the mugs and cups. Eventually she found her voice.

'PO Bright.'

She turned to find the woman at her shoulder. About to address her, she saw Collette's nervous gaze flick in Megan Crane's direction. Spinning round, Ellen saw that Megan was sitting in a slightly different position than before, the expression on her face, way too innocent. *She's just slipped something over the back of the sofa.* She turned back to the waiting House Mother. *Not for much longer.*

'Collette, WHAT, the HELL-'

'MADAME GOVERNOR?' a voice said.

Ellen turned to it. Megan Crane was regarding her with the sort of calm but firm expression Ellen herself liked to use during her dealings with Prison Officer Association reps.

'May I have a word?'

Ellen stayed firm. 'In a moment, Megan.' She needed to get things under control before listening to whatever spin the dominatrix would no doubt seek to put on things. But before she could resume addressing the waiting PO, Megan persisted.

'I think you may wish to hear what I have to say before proceeding further.'

About to fend her off again, Ellen paused. There was something about the look in the dominatrix's face - pleading, but also demanding - that sowed a seed of doubt. She wondered if she was in danger of misreading the situation. If she over reacted to something that turned out to be entirely innocent, word would get around. Megan seemed to sense her hesitation, and took her chance. She was full of contrition.

'I'm sorry, Governor. I'm afraid what's happening here is all my fault. Please, do not blame P.O. Bright. The ladies-' -She made a sweeping gesture, like a speaker at a W I meeting - 'Have been badgering me to share some insights into my, er… area of expertise?. I asked P.O. Bright for permission to give a talk to them about some matters I thought they may find entertaining. I'm afraid I got my timing all wrong, which is why we are still here.'

Ellen only half-heard the words. As the dominatrix had been speaking, the other residents had risen, quietly, and, ushered by the other PO, filed down to the other end of the room, giving them space. At the same time, Ellen was thinking about the options now facing her, the scenarios that could be about to unfold. They centred on the black bag behind the sofa.

So far Ellen had not drawn attention to it. If she did so, investigated, and its contents were innocuous, she would be free to deal with the situation in whichever way she saw fit. Whether she believed Megan's story or not, she could either invoke sanctions in respect of the breaches of discipline that were so far apparent - her favoured course - or she could deal with matters less formally, which risked her appearing 'soft'. But if the bag's contents matched her suspicions - a pair of handcuffs could be the least of it - then she would face a dilemma. A full investigation, which would include reviewing that evening's CCTV footage, could reveal things that would reflect badly on Stigwood's managerial regime - which meant Ellen herself. And given Megan Crane's involvement, the chances of keeping any whiff of scandal away from the media may prove impossible. The implications didn't bear thinking about. But if she chose not to initiate the investigation that a bag of SM paraphernalia found in a supposedly secure unit warranted, it could well be interpreted as a cover-up. Her authority would be undermined to the point where her career aspirations could be in jeopardy anyway.

She fixed her gaze first on Megan Crane, then PO Bright. The former was calm, smiling, the latter, apprehensive, fidgety. As Governor, the decision as to what happened next was hers. All the power was with her. It didn't feel that way.

She made her decision. Swinging round to face the PO directly she said, 'PO Bright, get everyone to bed. Then come and see me in my office.'

'Yes Ma'am.'

But before anyone could move Megan stepped forward. Ellen was shocked to feel her hand on her elbow as she leaned in to speak softly in her ear.

'I'm sure I can imagine what may be going through your mind, Ellen. But may I suggest that you give yourself time to reflect on things before making any hasty decisions, particularly if they involve PO Bright? We all think very highly of her here. And of course, I can assure you that none of this would ever reach the ears of Doctor Grant. You can rely on my discretion.'

Ellen froze as the intimation within Megan's words hit her. For long seconds, she stood there, gaze switching between Megan and her Housemother. Finally, she turned away from Megan Crane.

'On second thoughts, PO Bright, I will see you first thing in the morning.'

'Yes, Ma'am.'

Ellen waited as the POs ushered the House-mates out the door and upstairs. As Megan Crane filed past, Ellen made sure her gaze was elsewhere.

She left the unit a minute later, having made no mention of the black bag to anyone.

CHAPTER 39

'THIS IS BULLSHIT,' Baggus declared.

Martin Gardener, the West Midlands Police's Assistant Chief Constable Operations and the meeting's chairman, interrupted his address to gaze down the table at the young DI. It wasn't the first time. The way Baggus met his stare, head on, Carver sensed he'd given up any pretence at self-restraint in favour of outright attack, though most of those present probably wouldn't notice the difference.

The meeting comprised those who were, or had been, involved in investigating the Quinlan and Hawthorn deaths. Present were, Baggus and his boss, Robinson, Gilleray and his team, and Carver, Jess and The Duke.

Within minutes of them gathering round the table on the fourth floor of Birmingham's Colmore Circus, Police HQ, Baggus had delivered his opening salvo. It wasn't so much a request, as a demand that they all, 'Stop wasting time, recognise that Q's and the Hawthorns' murders are connected, and arrest the man we all know is responsible, Alistair Kenworthy.' He'd made other contributions since, most in similar vein – a mix of implied-criticism and insolence-bordering-on-insubordination. His message was clear. For whatever reason, Senior Officers were failing to recognise what, 'any detective worth his or her salt could see.' Furthermore, their continuing reluctance to what needed to be done was, in Baggus's view, due to the fact it involved a Government Minister.

As the meeting progressed, Carver had found himself cringing inside every time Baggus spoke. He'd tried sending him silent messages of the, 'Wind your neck in,' variety, but to no effect. It was as if Baggus had decided the only way to get them to listen, was to goad them into kicking him out. And while Carver understood his frustrations, he also knew that as a strategy, it was doomed to failure. Senior police officers don't like being lectured to by their juniors. They especially resent any inference that their decision-making is subject to political influences.

Only the fact that Gardener was showing extraordinary levels of patience, restraint and understanding, explained Baggus's continued presence. It was clear from the outset that he wasn't objective, and his determination to deride any attempt at forensic analysis of the facts, was coming across as simply, unprofessional. Carver suspected that by now, most around the table would be wondering why the ACC wasn't living up to his reputation for no-nonsense efficiency. The previous summer, his forthright handling of the Birmingham City riots had played well in the media, social as well as mainstream. But it was not a surprise to Carver. Gardener was making sure that if he ever had to face questions about how they arrived at their decisions, he could show he'd been open to dissenting points of view. And only Carver knew why.

Now, everyone watched in silence as the ACC leaned forward to peer over his wire frames at the younger man down the far end of the table.

'Excuse me?' he said.

Baggus was champing. 'After everything we've heard, I can't believe you're going to decide there's no connection. I mean… Jesus *Christ.*'

Gardener remained unruffled, though he couldn't stop his voice betraying a hint of sarcasm. 'I'm sorry Mr Baggus, I don't think I said there was *no* connection.' He checked for dissenters, there were none. 'What I said was-' He paused while he checked his notes. '"There is not, as yet, sufficient evidence supporting the notion of a connection to justify a joint enquiry."' Satisfied he had quoted himself accurately, he looked up. 'As your own Superintendent has pointed out-' He gestured at Baggus's Gloucestershire boss, Wilf Robinson, next to him. 'There isn't even any evidence to show that Quinlan's death was anything other than an accident.'

'What about what Blackstone told us about the incident involving some of Josephine's members? Quinlan knew about it, and even Megan Crane hinted the Hawthorn's could be in danger because of it. Now they're dead.'

Wilf Robinson leaned forward, so Baggus could see him. Had others been looking at him, as Carver was, rather than waiting for Baggus's next salvo, they would have seen the glaring look he sent his Acting DI. 'Gavin,' Robinson began. 'I think it would be best if you left it to me to-'

'It's alright Wilf.' Gardener rested a hand on Robinson's arm. 'It does no harm to challenge our own thinking. After all, these are important matters. It's just a shame we didn't do so before we started harassing Government Ministers.' Before anyone could pick up on it, he turned his attention back to Baggus, still showing the patient smile that was devoid of humour. 'I understand your concerns, Mr Baggus. But before I can sanction a joint enquiry, I need something more than suspicion and gut feelings. We've not seen or heard anything that proves that this so-called Megan Crane network even exists. As far as I can see, the only thing you have is rumour and conjecture, and much of that comes from a dead solicitor with perverted sexual interests, and an art dealer who I believe is known to deal in stolen paintings. I'm sorry, it's not enough.'

Carver watched Baggus carefully, ready to jump in if he looked about to give anything away. As their eyes met, Carver shook his head, slowly. *Don't do anything stupid.*

Earlier the four of them, Baggus, Jess, The Duke and himself had met to talk about what they could and could not disclose about Megan Crane's archive. After listening to what Carver had to say, The Duke was clear. Right now, any disclosure might prove counter-productive, if not downright dangerous. As well as ACC Gardener, Carver's own NCA Director, Nigel Broome, would also be present, though he had no idea why. Any reference to Megan Crane having kept records, would inevitably give rise to demands they be produced, followed by awkward questions as to why they had remained 'suppressed' for so long. Carver wasn't overly-concerned about answering such queries. From an intelligence point of view, he could argue his case. But he wasn't ready, yet, to see the information disappear. On this point they were all agreed. It was better to say nothing, than risk losing their only route-map to Megan Crane's labyrinthine network. Carver was yet to share with them his other reason for saying nothing in this particular forum, though he intended to do so as soon as the meeting was over. He was relieved when Baggus backed off and sat back in his chair, though it was obvious to all, he was fuming.

'DCI Carver.'

Carver turned to give Gardener his full attention.

'We've not heard from you yet, and I'm still not clear what your present involvement is. Is the Worshipper Case still under investigation?'

Carver was ready. 'The Operation Kerry file was marked, 'closed' after Megan Crane's conviction. At this moment it remains so.' Carver turned to the Duke as if seeking confirmation.

'That's right,' The Duke nodded.

Gardener's eyes narrowed. 'In that case, what exactly was your purpose in continuing to question Mr Kenworthy after DI Baggus left?'

Unlike Baggus, Carver didn't question why Gardener kept harking back to the events at Kenworthy's constituency offices. He recognised a smokescreen when he saw one.

'I was aware of my colleagues' enquiries at Josephine's. In view of the information about Mr Kenworthy having once met Megan Crane, and given his position, I wanted to establish if that was the case before the press or someone else got hold of it. In view of my knowledge of the case, I thought it best that I do it myself.'

'Did it not occur to you to seek approval for such an approach?'

'What was there to approve?' Carver said. 'No one is accusing the minister of anything. And though DI Baggus acknowledges that his initial approach to the minister on my behalf may have been over-enthusiastic-.' He made a point of meeting the gazes around the table. 'Anyone who discovers someone they know in such horrific circumstances, as he did, is bound to be affected. If Gavin was on edge when he spoke to Mr Kenworthy, then it's not hard to understand why.'

Around the table, heads nodded. Robinson's and Gardener's were not amongst them.

The Duke leaned forward. 'And if Jamie *had* mentioned to me his intention to speak with Mr Kenworthy, I would have approved it. It's just background. I don't see the problem.'

'The problem is, John,' Gardener began, dryly. 'We have a Government Minister complaining that he was subjected to a barrage of questions about his private life by two officers who-.'

'Whoa. Just a minute Martin.'

Gardener turned to the source of the interruption. Carver's NCA Director, Nigel Broom's hand was in the air, like a soccer referee waving a yellow card.

'As far as I'm aware, the Minister has not laid an official complaint against either DI Baggus or DCI Carver.'

Gardener hesitated. 'That's correct, Nigel, he hasn't. But he says-.'

'You've spoken with him?'

Gardener became wary. 'He isn't complaining as such. It's just that-.'

'So you *have* spoken with him?'

Carver locked eyes on the pair. He could imagine warning bells starting to ring in Gardener's head. Stamping on Detective Inspectors was one thing, but a fellow, former Chief Officer was something else. Gardener would know where Broom was going. He played it calmly.

'As you know Nigel. Whenever a Government

official is interviewed, their office contacts the home force to verify the investigation. It happens all the time.'

'But DCI Carver works for me, not you.'

'A simple mistake on the part of the Minister's office, I'm sure. Now if we can get back to-.'

But Broom wasn't finished. 'I'm sorry, Martin. In view of your disclosure that you and the Minister have spoken about this matter, can I have your assurance that what you discussed has no bearing on the outcome of this meeting?'

'Absolutely,' Gardener said, more eager to convince than even Carver thought necessary. 'This meeting was called simply to consider the question of whether there is a need to establish a joint investigation.'

'Which has nothing to do with Government Ministers.' Broom cemented his point.

'Uh, of course not.'

Broom had said little throughout the meeting, but Carver could tell his boss was deriving some pleasure from reminding everyone of his former status. And he for one, was happy to let him do so. Forced to give way, Gardener let the matter of the visit to Kenworthy go and turned to other matters.

Ten minutes later the meeting was declared over when Gardener used his casting vote – Carver, Jess and Baggus had no say - to confirm the decision that there would be no joint investigation, '*at the present time*,' As Gardener swept from the room, Gilleray following in his wake, Carver thought he looked relieved, but also angry.

He looked across to where his Director was packing his briefcase and nodded his appreciation. As Broom made his way round the table towards him, exchanging comments with some of those he passed, he looked entirely relaxed. But as he reached Carver and the two men shook hands, his smile had an assassin's quality about it. He closed on the man who was second in command of his North-West Branch-Office so only he would hear his words.

'Whatever the fuck it is you're doing in that office in Salford, you've got one week. Then I expect some straight answers.'

Before Carver could even respond, Broom was gone, heading for the door. As he watched his present boss departing, his former one's low growl, sounded in his ear.

'We need to talk about where this leaves us.'

Carver turned to The Duke. 'And I need to show you something.'

CHAPTER 40

The Duke stared at his copy of the sheet that Carver had produced to support his theory. 'Where are we supposed to be looking?'

'Middle left,' Carver said. 'To the right of the 'Cooper' box.'

As they followed his direction, Carver lifted his glass and checked around again. Tucked away in one of Birmingham City Centre's quieter corners, The Blue Barrel isn't the sort of place he would expect to bump into anyone from Colmore Circus. Still, he was taking no chances.

'There,' Baggus said. He leaned across to point it out to Jess, next to him.

'MG,' Jess said. She gave a weary sigh, shook her head as if to say, *How many more*? 'Who are the Coopers, and what makes you think it's Martin Gardener?'

'They're a couple Megan Crane met a few times. He's an accountant. She's a journalist. They contacted her to offer to be her subs. Later on they asked if she would be interested in meeting a friend of theirs. They refer to him as 'MG,' and mention he has to be careful because he's, "someone senior in public service." They talk about him working in Birmingham, but living between there and Cheshire. Gardener lives near Telford. They also mention he can supply his own handcuffs.'

As always, The Duke was cautious. 'Coincidence?'

Carver rocked a hand. 'After his performance this afternoon, I don't think so. I had the impression his mind was set from the start.' The Duke nodded his agreement. 'He certainly swung the decision for no joint investigation. And if he is MG, the last thing he would want is anyone digging deeper into Megan Crane's affairs. It would also explain why Gilleray was so wishy-washy. He's got no choice but to go along with what Gardner says.'

'How long have you suspected?' Jess said.

Carver sat back. 'Megan hinted about a senior police officer several times, but never elaborated. After the Hart trial, before she ever came on the scene, I gave a presentation at a College of Policing seminar. Afterwards, Gardener button-holed me in the bar. It didn't strike me at the time, but I remember he quizzed me, in some detail, about the Hart case. He'd heard about our accomplice theory and was interested in how far we'd got. Looking back, I think he was fishing to see if we'd picked up anything about Megan. When I came across the, 'MG', reference, I checked where he lives and… Well, make up your own minds.'

'So why not confront the bastard?' Baggus said. 'My guess is he'll tell us anything we need to know if we show him this.' He waved the sheet of paper.

The Duke cleared his throat. 'I think that's called blackmail, which is probably what started all this.'

'Besides,' Carver chimed in. 'It would give away where we are getting our information. And if word gets out, people will start covering their tracks, which is exactly what we want to avoid.'

'So what *do* you suggest?'

Carver saw the sharp look Jess sent Baggus's way. The impatience he'd displayed in the meeting was still there. 'More digging,' he said. 'But low key. What happened to the Hawthorns is a warning. Someone wants something to stay hidden, and is prepared to kill to keep it that way.'

The Duke put down his glass. 'Which suggests others may be at risk.'

Carver nodded as he drank his beer.

'Cyrisse?' Jess said.

'Possibly. We need to warn her. Make sure she's protected.'

'I'll do it,' Baggus said.

But Carver shook his head. 'After today, Robinson will expect you back at your desk. If you're not there, he'll want to know what you are doing. We need him, and Gardener, to think we've stopped probing.'

'No fucking way,' Baggus said. 'Not until we've caught this bastard. I saw the bodies, remember?'

Jess rested a hand on his arm. 'You must, Gavin. Jamie and I will-.'

'This is my case. I'm not bowing out.'

In the silence that followed, Baggus's glare dared someone to deny him. Carver and The Duke locked eyes as they drained their glasses. The Duke broke the impasse.

'I'll tell you how it's going to be. Jamie, I'll speak with Nigel Broom and try and get him to give you some slack.' He turned to Jess. At then end of the meeting, she'd been given a 'liaison' role on the Hawthorn enquiry. She was now their only 'in'. 'I'll give you Alec Duncan. See what you can dig up between you.'

'And me?' Baggus said.

The Duke looked stern. 'Like Jamie said. You go back to Gloucester. We can't afford to have Robinson rocking the boat.'

Baggus turned a pleading look on Jess. She didn't say anything, but placed a reassuring hand on his arm. He shrugged it off. He rose to his feet, knocking his stool over. He glared down at her. 'Thanks.' Her expression didn't change. He turned to Carver and The Duke. 'Thank you all, a fucking lot.'

He headed for the door.

'Gavin,' Jess called.

'Let him go,' Carver said. 'He's not going to like it, whatever we say. He needs time.'

The pub door banged. A moment later Baggus's shadow passed the window.

'We need to keep an eye on him,' The Duke said.

'Don't worry,' Jess said. 'I intend to.'

As she finished her drink, Carver thought he'd never seen her look so concerned about anything.

CHAPTER 41

'So when *are* you coming home?'

Standing at the living room window, waiting for Rosanna's answer, Carver watched the he two men going in and out of the flat opposite. The white rent-a-van had been there when he arrived home. Now, looking at the stuff they were bringing out - table lamps, stools, cardboard boxes with cables hanging out - he guessed the heavy stuff must have gone during an earlier trip. It was late for a family with young kids to be moving. The street comprised mainly rented properties, like theirs. The thought came they were doing a flit.

'I am not sure,' Rosanna said. 'He says a few more days. The studio is booked. He can only get an hour, here and there.'

Carver sighed. *A few days?* Wasn't music recording supposed to be fairly simple these days? He'd even heard there were apps that can do the job. But after thirty-six hours with little sleep, his guard was down. Before he could stop himself, he let his thoughts show.

'Who is this, Berentes, guy anyway? What's he after?'

Her voice lowered. 'I tol' you. He owns the record company. He wants to hear how I sound in the studio.'

A clinking noise sounded in the background.

'Where are you?' he said.

There was a moment's hesitation. 'I'm having dinner.'

He checked his watch. 'Isn't it a bit late to be eating?'

He heard her sigh. 'It's Lisbon, Jamie.'

A thought came to him. 'Are you with him? Now?'

There was another pause. When she spoke again, her voice was at normal pitch. 'Julio and I have been working this evening. He was kind enough to offer me dinner.'

'Well, that's nice of him.' As the mute seconds passed, Carver realised. Suddenly he felt stupid, *and* guilty. 'I'm sorry. It's been a long day.'

'Again?' She wasn't for letting him off the hook. The days were often long. It never used to cause problems.

He wondered about telling her what was happening, but thought better of it. It would seem manipulative. As the two men across the street reappeared, this time carrying a bicycle and what looked like a box of children's toys, he turned away from the window. He didn't want the conversation to end like this. He remembered what he had been doing before he called her. He seized on it.

'Look, I think I may have found somewhere.' He reached for the leaflet on the table, shaking off the crumbs from his sandwich.

'You have?' She brightened, willing to forget the spat, he hoped. 'Where is it? Tell me.'

He hesitated. He needed to be careful. 'It's in North Wales. Near Conway. One of those barn-conversions.'

'Isn't that a bit far from Manchester?'

'Only an hour or so. It's a good road.' *No need to mention now what the A55 can be like in summer. When she gets back.* 'The house is pretty isolated, but there's a village nearby. Property's cheap out there and there's some land with it.' Hearing only silence, he tossed the bait. 'There's a big kitchen. One of those with the cooker in the middle. You know, one of those island things?'

'Have you seen it?'

'This weekend, if I can get free.' His hope had been she would be home by then.

'I thought you said you are not working his weekend?'

'I'm not but…. Well, you know, things come up.'

'Yes, I know. And I know you as well. What is happening?'

So quick. 'Nothing particular,' he lied.

She let it go. 'Is there a picture? Can you send it?'

He lied again. 'It's… er… not very clear. I'll ask for a better one. Anyway, you'll see it when you get back.'

'I cannot wait. I will ask *Julio* if he can make things go quick.'

The way she said his name, Carver imagined her smiling at him, getting ready to work on him. It gave him a strange feeling. 'Do that.'

A minute later, Carver stood, mobile in hand, staring at the agency leaflet. A rumble from outside made him look up. The van was pulling away. It was followed by a rattling Ford estate, stuffed to its roof with the young family that had lived opposite, and scores of plastic bags containing their effects. As they drove away, Carver saw that the ground floor flat was in darkness, curtains gone, windows bare. Already, it looked like no one had lived there for months.

He looked back at the picture he had been wary about sending. He probably should have mentioned that the renovation wasn't quite complete. According to the estate agent woman, the seller had had to abandon the project halfway through. 'Financial difficulties,' she said. His thought had been they would enjoy finishing it together. But as he'd stared at the half-finished project – the end containing the kitchen, study and living area looked promising – he'd worried she might not go for it. He was still thinking about it when his phone signalled an SMS.

He didn't recognise the sender's number, and when he opened it he had to read it twice before he understood it. When he did, he had to work at not panicking over the fact that she, someone, had managed to get his number.

The message read, *MC wants to CU. Alone. Be ready.*

CHAPTER 42

Baggus stared out into the darkness beyond the window of the office he shared with Peter Kent, Gloucester's second DI. Had it been daylight, he would have been looking out over the dock basin. Right now, all he was seeing was the mental image of a plush office, a man behind a desk with a leering smirk stitched across his face. The sort of smile guilty people wear.

That the Secretary of State for Community Affairs had blood on his hands, Baggus was in no doubt. He had seen the sneering, 'You prove it,' smile the moment before he pressed the button behind his desk, summoning his aides to restrain Baggus – not that he needed any restraining. It was only when he realised that Kenworthy's ploy was to prevent him having to respond to his accusations, that he 'lost it'. The MP had paled when Baggus put to him that he was out to silence those who knew of his involvement in whatever had tempted Quentin Quinlan into blackmail. Only guilty people pale.

A knock on the door wrenched Baggus back. He turned.

Katy, one of the young CID-Aides – uniform trainees – hung in the doorway, not yet confidant enough to enter the DI's office without an invitation. Away down the corridor, voices echoed. Earlier that evening, there had been a bad stabbing in The Saddle and Stirrup. The DC at GRH was saying it was looking like it could prove fatal. The rest of the CID trying to track down the injured man's drunken girlfriend, last seen staggering away -probably to find more alcohol. After checking that the night DS had everything under control, Baggus had wandered back to his office to resume his bitter musings. Now, seeing Katy in the doorway, Baggus thought she'd come to let him know the victim had died. He was wrong.

'Excuse me, sir,' Katy said. 'Someone's asking for you at the front desk.'

Baggus made his way down the three flights of stairs - his only source of exercise lately. On the ground floor, he poked his head into the draughty reception-waiting area. There was only one person there, sitting on the single bench, swathed in a long, black coat, head down. The coat's hood was up and a few blonde curls peeped round its rim. Baggus looked across at the station clerk, who nodded towards the visitor.

'Can I help you?' Baggus said.

As she sat up, Baggus recognised the grief-stricken face that still bore traces of tear-streaked mascara from the day before. It was Sally.

CHAPTER 43

Cyrisse Chaterlain's home was an edge-of-Highgate Village cul-de-sac mews-house, overlooking London. As Carver rounded the corner, he could see the police car parked outside. The uniformed PC who stepped out to meet them was quick with his warning. 'Just so you know, she's not happy,' - as they discovered the moment they stepped inside. She was at them at once, addressing Jess directly.

'Please explain, what is this all about?' She waved out the window in the direction of the police car. 'When you said you were arranging for someone to, "keep an eye on me", I did not realise it would be so obvious. Do you not have the… les policiers-?' She waved a hand. '-Detectives, for this sort of thing?'

For a split-second, it reminded Carver of his and Ros's early days, when her sometimes-tortuous English used to make him laugh. But he was too slow masking the memory.

She turned on him, eyes blazing. 'You think this is funny? Do you not think that neighbours like to gossip?' She turned back to Jess. 'Who is this sniggering idiot?' Hearing Carver being called an idiot, Jess made the same mistake, which only made things worse. Throwing her arms in the air, Cyrisse went to the window and peered out. 'Where is your other friend? He did not make fun of the way I speak.'

Carver showed his palms. 'My apologies-' *Madame or Mademoiselle?* '-Ms Chaterlain. If you'll let me, I'll explain.'

She glared at him - 'Hmmpph,' - then turned to take a cigarette from the pack on the mantelpiece.

As she smoked, Carver told her who he was, and explained how he was there to hear her story for himself. Travelling up, Jess had rung her to let her know about the temporary protection arrangements they were putting in place through the local DI. But she already seemed to know more about the Hawthorns' murders than had been released to the media. She wouldn't say how.

'Is it true Gerald was….' She gestured below her waist.

Carver nodded.

'And they put it…?' She did the same, in the general direction of her face.

He nodded again.

Her face paled. She dropped into an armchair. 'Mon Dieu.'

When she had recovered, Carver asked first about her relationship with Kenworthy, before moving onto Sylvie Tyler. Over the next ten minutes, he listened as she repeated the story she had told to Jess and Baggus two days before.

Sylvie had worked for Cyrisse as a gallery assistant. A Middlesbrough girl, she was around twenty when Cyrisse took her on. Very pretty, but with no great ambitions, she was, nevertheless, interested in. 'bettering her position.' And she made no secret of the fact she was happy to use what God had given her, rather than having to work for it. At that time, Cyrisse was still seeing Kenworthy. He used to drop into the gallery on the odd occasion, which is how he and Sylvie met. It was only later, after Cyrisse stopped seeing him, that she pieced it all together. He must have called at the gallery one day she was not there, and talked Sylvie into seeing him. The first sign anything was amiss came when she didn't turn up for work for several days. When she returned, she looked awful, like she was sick. Sylvie said it was a virus, but Cyrisse saw bruising beneath the heavy make-up, also marks to her arms and legs. When Cyrisse asked, she said something about having fallen down some steps. A month or so later something similar happened. Some weeks after that, Cyrisse sensed Sylvie worrying about something, and followed when she finished work. She saw Kenworthy pick her up in his car. The next day she was absent again. When she returned to work, Cyrisse asked her outright if she was seeing Kenworthy. She denied it, and became angry when Cyrisse said she'd seen him pick her up, insisting it was just a coincidence and he'd simply given her a lift. Cyrisse said that one of reasons she had stopped seeing Kenworthy was because he kept pushing her to go further than she was prepared to.

'In what way?' Carver said.

'He never said, specifically, but I know that group sex, and heavy BDSM, turned him on.'

'What happened with Sylvie?' Carver said.

'I warned her to stay away from him, but she wouldn't listen and insisted she wasn't seeing him. She was lying. For a while everything seemed okay and I hoped it had stopped. Then she went missing again. After a few days I tried to contact her but she wasn't answering her phone. I went to her flat but she wasn't there. I was on the point of going to the police when she rang to say her mother had fallen ill and she was giving up her job to go home to look after her. I didn't believe it, and asked if she was in trouble. She was evasive and nervous. She sounded close to tears. I told her to ring me back in a few days and she said she would.

'She called back a week later. She sounded scared and spoke in whispers. She said she was in some sort of trouble. I asked if it involved Kenworthy, but she wouldn't say. She started to talk about me contacting someone but then hung up suddenly. That was the last I heard from her. I gave it a week and when I couldn't reach her on her mobile, I went to the police.'

'And?' Carver said, though he could guess.

'They weren't interested. They said there was no evidence of anything suspicious and when I mentioned it involved an MP, and of course I had to tell them we'd been involved, they more or less laughed me out of the station.'

I can imagine. 'What about her family? Did you have any contact with them?'

She shook her head. 'Sylvie never spoke of them and I had no details. I got the impression she'd come to London to get away from them.'

'And no one has spoken to you about her since?' She shook her head again, looking sad. 'Do you think her disappearance may be something to do with Kenworthy?'

She lit another cigarette, drew on it, then leaned forward, staring into his face. Close up, he could see she was younger than she looked. 'I have this... *feeling*.' She narrowed her eyes, as if she needed to convince him. 'You know? When you just *feel* something?'

'I know.'

He turned to Jess. Her enquiring look said, *What do you think?* In truth, he wasn't sure.

Cyrisse organised drinks and for several minutes they spoke about other matters - her business, her background – she was originally from Renne – how she liked living in Highgate. As they talked, Carver prepared himself. If she wasn't happy about the police car outside, his next suggestion would go down like concrete diving boots. He told her that Kenworthy knew she had been visited by the Police. He didn't say how.

'Good,' she said, full of haughty confidence. 'I hope he remembers-.' She stopped and they could see her working it out. She half-turned towards where the police car stood sentinel, outside. 'That is why they are here? Not because of what happened to the Hawthorns?'

'Maybe both,' Carver said.

'Am I in danger?'

Carver took his time answering. He took a deep breath. 'We think you may be safer living somewhere else for a little while.'

Half an hour later, as Carver returned from the bathroom, Jess was looking up at the ceiling. The sounds of wardrobe doors and drawers banging shut accompanied Cyrisses's heavy stomps.

'It wasn't as bad as I thought it might be,' Carver said.

'Bad enough,' Jess said, then added. 'At least you got her to agree.'

'With your help,' he said. 'I think she likes you. Probably recognises a kindred spirit.

She gave him one of her stares. 'So what's this flat in Manchester?'

'It's an NCA safe house. They use it for supergrasses, witness protection, that sort of thing.'

'How have you managed that?'

'The Manchester branch DCI is an old mate. He owes me.'

'Does he know what's involved?'

He didn't reply but gave her a look that said, 'Don't be stupid.'

Ten minutes later, as Carver sent the police car away, Jess helped Cyrisse carry her bags out. She was still protesting, even as they loaded them into the boot of her BMW cabriolet. Carver was keeping out if it. So far, he had managed to avoid her questions about compensation for lost business while she was away. He hoped that once she calmed down, she would recognise that staying safe was compensation enough.

Jess called to him from the car's passenger door. 'We'll meet you back at Longsight nick.'

Cyrisse glared at him from the driver's seat.

Waving his acknowledgement, he got into his Golf. But as he switched on the engine, he saw movement in the driveway of the house across the road. A dark figure moving into shadow. Seconds later, a man emerged from the drive, pushing a wheelie-bin which he placed at the kerbside. Several others were already out - collection day tomorrow. The man turned and headed back up the drive.

Shaking his head at his own nervousness, Carver waited while Cyrisse drove off, then followed.

As the Golf's lights disappeared around the corner, the man stepped from the shadows to which he had retreated after his narrow escape. Eager to hear where they were taking her, he had made the mistake of being seen. If it hadn't been for his quick thinking with the bin, things may have become awkward. His client had not mentioned about the police being here, and it made sense that he should report back and confirm instructions before continuing.

He certainly hadn't expected to see the detectives back on the case so soon. They must have decided to continue their investigations, unofficially. And their spiriting the French woman away would now mean a short delay before he could tie things up - if that was still what was required. Of course, had he been given the full story right at the start, he would have suggested it there and then. Clean-up operations always work best when all likely targets are identified at the outset. This sort of step-by-step approach nearly always means you end up having to rush around doing what could have been done earlier, and with much less hassle.

It didn't worry him that all he had managed to catch was, 'Longsight'. He knew enough to know it was in Manchester. He could still pick them up on the motorway if he wished, though that would mean rushing things again. And besides, he was certain now that the little deception he was planning – partly, he had to admit as a bonus for the risks he was taking - would enable him to track her down without too much difficulty, provided he had lost none of his charm.

He smiled to himself then, taking one last look at her house – no point in looking in there now – headed back to the pub car park where he had left his car.

CHAPTER 44

As Alistair Kenworthy listened on the house phone, he tried to work out where his wife was. There were three other phone points in the house, and though he doubted she was imaginative enough to listen in, he would rather be sure. Since the incident in his office she had been showing more interest in his affairs than usual. As he'd come through from the garage he'd heard her saying, 'Well if you can't tell me what it's about, I'm not sure I should let you speak to him.'

He took the phone off her and shooed her away, but wasn't sure she believed his assertion it was just, 'Committee business.' He hoped she wasn't beginning to suspect anything. The last thing he needed was for her to start poking her nose in things.

For several minutes he listened in silence.

'That sounds in order,' he said as the man finished. It was good to be dealing with someone who knew how to handle things - unlike Hugh who just went into a panic at every little hiccough. 'Are you sure that will be the end of it?' After listening to the answer he said, 'Good. Keep me informed.'

As he rang off, Anne re-appeared from the breakfast room. It crossed his mind she could have been listening from behind the door.

'Who was that, Alistair? I didn't recognise the voice.'

'Just one of the committee's researchers,' he said. 'A new chap. You've not spoken to him before.' He stopped there. No need to overdo it.

'Are you in, or out tonight?' she said.

He glanced at her before turning back to the draft of the speech he was pretending to be revising. The question seemed innocent, but given the nature of the evening's business, he couldn't be sure.

'Out,' he said. 'I'm meeting with Clive. Shouldn't be too late.' It would sound right. Clive Abram was a generous party supporter. They met regularly to discuss party affairs, mostly over a drink. Not that he would be doing much drinking tonight. 'Have you anything planned?' he countered. She had been out twice in the past week, which for her was a lot.

'Not really,' she said. 'I'll see how I feel later on.'

He wasn't sure what the, 'not really', meant, but didn't want to arouse any suspicions by asking. She sometimes complained about him not showing interest in her affairs. If he started now, she may wonder why. She and a friend, Jane, liked to go to the cinema together. It was probably that.

He threw her a smile. 'Better get on with this speech.' He headed for his study.

Behind his back, Anne Kenworthy watched his departure. She continued watching until the study door closed.

CHAPTER 45

For her 'liaison' role on the Hawthorn murders, Jess had been allocated a corner desk in the Murder Incident Room. She'd taken it rather than share an office with Whitewell, though she had thought carefully before passing on his offer. With Gilleray seemingly determined not to acknowledge a link between the Hawthorns' and Q's deaths, it may have been useful to be close to the heart of the enquiry. But while Whitewell seemed okay, Jess was learning to like Gilleray less each time she met him. It was why she'd decided to stick with her corner. At least there, she didn't have to spend time in his company.

Officially, her role only related to Josephine's and any possible Megan Crane connection, though Gilleray had intimated that her background knowledge of, 'All this weird stuff the Hawthorns were into,' might prove useful. She was sure he'd meant it as a put-down when he mentioned it during a team briefing, though she suspected it's effect was the opposite. She was aware of the rumours that were flying, the stir her presence around the team was creating. So far, the tally of detectives seeking to discover if there was any truth in them stood at three. One in particular, a DS named Carl, had seemed particularly keen to demonstrate his familiarity with both, BDSM terminology - 'top', 'bottom', 'switch', 'safe-words' - and the world with which they were associated. 'I've met a couple of doms in my time,' he said, as if proud of the fact. Whatever he was after – she was sure it wouldn't stop with finding out about her connections with Josephine's and the Hawthorns – he left as empty-handed as the others. Far from embarrassing her when he spoke of his experiences during some Hamburg stag-night, she made a point of asking, 'So are you dom or sub?' at the same time urging him to describe the scenarios - 'Hardcore or vanilla?' - he played out with the girlfriend he mentioned. 'Are you straight by the way, or bi?' It took only a couple of minutes for the not wholly-unlikeable detective's delivery to dissolve into a nervous stutter. When she suddenly switched her attention back to the statement she'd been reading when he showed up at her desk - just like that - Carl got the message. As he slunk away, wordlessly, Jess wondered what story he would give his mates.

Now, for once, it was quiet around the MIR. Gilleray had ordered a sweep of Josephine's members. Most of the teams were still out. She had tried telling him it would prove counter-productive but he wouldn't listen. Josephine's members were mostly professional types who would not hesitate to complain - or sue - if they felt they were being harassed. In all her visits, Jess had never witnessed anything unlawful, not even drugs, though it was obvious some members were regular users. But Gilleray seemed to prefer to believe that the sort who frequented Josephine's would be bound to be, 'into other things.' She'd heard him speak of paedophiles, 'and worse', though she couldn't think what 'worse' might be. He'd also spoken about searching homes and seizing computers to uncover material that, 'would set tongues wagging.' When she asked Whitewell what was recorded on the Informations being laid to obtain warrants and search authorities, the response came back, 'Not your concern,' so she left it. In her mind's eye however, she could already see the illegal-search and wrongful-arrest writs being drafted. She certainly didn't intend being around to bump into anyone the teams may bring in. She had met some of those on the list and it would only make things worse if people spotted her - *Jess, tell them. You've been there.* She had nothing to hide, but she had better ways of spending her time.

She turned to the last statement of the batch she'd picked up to work through, and came upright as she realised it was Christo's. Though they had spoken in the interview room the morning after, she had never read his actual statement. She did so now. And as she went through it, a frown developed. It was barely two pages long, surprisingly brief considering he was the only witness known to have had direct contact with the killer - or an accomplice. Midway down the second page she tutted, and shook her head. 'This can't be right.' Reaching the end, she looked up, staring off into space. She was still musing on it a few minutes later when a DS she remembered only as 'Stuart' appeared in the doorway.

'Ah! You're here, Ma'am. Great.' Unlike some, Stuart hadn't assumed she was happy with first names. 'I've got this kid's TV presenter, Simon Caffery, in the interview room. He says he knows you, and that-'

'Sorry Stuart,' she said, already rising. 'Got to go. Give Simon my regards.'

She brushed past him, and was gone.

CHAPTER 46

The PO, Collette Bright, was off to Carver's right, Megan's left. Soon after sitting down, he'd realised that if he turned his head slightly, she dropped out of his field of vision altogether, allowing him to imagine they were alone. But it gave him an eerie feeling and after trying it a couple of times – he still had a perverse interest in observing the way she affected him - he stopped doing it.

This time, Collette seemed more attentive to her charge than previously. The book was gone and he felt her, following every step of their conversation.

He still hadn't worked out what was going on. Megan's opening words - 'I don't know why you're here, Jamie. I said all I had to say last time,' - threw him, and made him wonder if he was being set up. The SMS that had brought him had come from a pay-as-you-go mobile, bought in Sheffield and used only once. He had no idea how the sender might have got his number. It still worried him.

But as he wrestled with it, something in the way Megan had positioned herself, angled slightly away from Collette, registered. The striking face that was capable of saying and deceiving so much seemed to be sending him another message. He read it as, *Play along*. And so they had sat as before, her on the sofa, him in the chair facing as he began to feel his way forward. He started by asking if she had heard about the Hawthorns. She tutted, as at some minor inconvenience.

'It was always a risk, running a place like Josephine's. Still, it was a damn shame. They were a nice couple.'

The words were the sort someone might use about some far-off tragic event, like an earthquake in China - sympathetic, but not heartfelt.

At once, Carver knew his instincts had been right. From her position, Collette could not see the sadness and anger reflected in Megan's eyes - the windows to her true feelings. The way her eyebrows arched and her eyes glistened, Carver sensed she was fighting to keep her emotions hidden.

But why? What difference would Collette knowing make?

Deciding to be patient, he played along, making up questions that fitted with him pumping her for information. Did she know anyone who had a grudge against the couple? How often had she visited Josephine's? Had she ever come across anyone who got off on dismemberment, cannibalism, and so on. For her part, Megan batted them off in the manner of someone not only disinterested in helping, but resentful at being asked.

'No,' she said to his first question. 'And even if I did know someone with a grudge, what makes you think I would tell you?' Her other responses were in similar vein. 'That's none of your business,' and, 'Don't be ridiculous. I would never dream of having anything to do with such people. What sort of person do you think I am?'

It was an impressive performance, and as it went on, Carver had to keep reminding himself it was an act. Nevertheless, he began to recognise that whatever she was leading up to – 'Be ready,' the SMS had said – there was a thread of truth running through whatever script she was following.

Carver had never forgotten that while the psychiatric reports had differed in several respects, they all agreed on one thing. In Megan Crane's psychotically-skewed view of the world, one person alone was responsible for her downfall and the loss of her hedonistic lifestyle - him. During her several recorded interviews - he only managed to sit in on one before he was barred in case his involvement was ruled 'prejudicial' - she baited him over his relationship with Angie, knowing he would listen to them. She used oblique asides and cunningly-disguised phrases that only he would pick up on, references to small incidents and disclosures he didn't realise he'd made until they emerged from her lips. It all seemed intended to show how much she hated him for what he had done to her - and before her, Edmund Hart. The strange thing was, despite knowing about him and Angie, she didn't expose him, as she could have done. It was as if she preferred to dangle her knowledge, tantalisingly, keeping him guessing as to if, or when, she may let the rest of the world in on it. It was a subtle but effective mode of torture, one that fitted with everything he knew about her. And he'd had no choice but to live with it, though in recent weeks he'd thought he was dwelling on it less, having almost convinced himself that the nights when he used to wake up, soaked with sweat, may be over.

But as he listened to Megan's sham responses to his

questions, he realised. It was all still there, locked in her head, ready to be released when the time was right, when she was ready to exact her revenge. And as they continued to play out the charade Megan had drawn him into, he had to force himself to stick with it, to carry on asking meaningless questions, listening to the dismissive replies with their tiny bullets as he waited for her to disclose what her real purpose was.

They had been talking for nearly half an hour, during which time her mocking derision at his attempts to extract something meaningful had taken their toll. He was beginning to think he was mistaken after all, that she had lured him there for the sadistic pleasure of simply reminding him of what she was capable. He was sweating and his heart rate was up as she told him, for the umpteenth time, how sad it was that he, Jamie Carver of all people, should be reduced to begging help from someone whose only interest was in seeing him dead.

It was too much.

It was time to let her know that whatever she had got him there for had better happen soon because he wasn't going to sit there and take this crap much longer.

'Megan. I think we ought-.' But she held up a hand. That look in her eyes again.

'Yes, I think we ought as well, Jamie.'

The finality in her tone confused him more.

'You've wasted enough of my time. It should be clear by now that I have no intention of helping you with this or any other case you may think gives you an excuse to renew our acquaintanceship. Those days are over. I thought you knew that. You will have to find someone else to obsess over.'

He gawped at her. What the hell was she talking

about?

He was about to voice angry protest when she stood up, catching him off guard again. He rose after her, but saw her quick glance towards Collette, also now rising. Megan's body language said she was ready to go, the discussion over. They were facing each other, only a couple of feet apart, the coffee table between them. Suddenly her face changed, the sort of look someone gives a sick puppy.

'You know Jamie, it's such a shame.' His puzzlement drew a sympathetic smile. 'You, I mean. To look at you, anyone might think butter wouldn't melt in your mouth. But I know what you really like, deep down.' He brindled at the gibe. She *was* taking the piss. The eyes flashed a warning. 'If only you weren't so damn, *nice.*'

Suddenly she was on him, hands gripping the lapels of his jacket, pulling him forward so he was off-balance over the table, clamping her mouth to his, eyes closed. As Collette shouted, 'MEGAN,' her tongue encircled his, then it was down his throat, almost triggering a gag reflex. What was she doing? He coughed into the kiss, spluttered and, beginning to panic as he felt himself choking, pushed her away.

He half-expected she would hang on, so forceful, so *determined* was the assault. But, to his surprise, she didn't resist, letting him push her back as Collette leaped between them, a horrified look on her face.

'BACK OFF MEGAN,' she shouted, shoving her away and putting herself between them.

Carver saw Colette's eyes sweep over the front of his shirt, then the rest of him. If she'd had a blade…. As he stepped back, hand still up to his mouth, struggling to contain the coughing fit, Megan smiled the sly, knowing smile he had seen before. *Next time….*

'Don't worry, Collette,' Megan said. 'If I'd wanted to stick him, I'd have done it long ago.' She turned her attention back on Carver. His fit was under control but the shock was still with him. Her expression was questioning. *Yes?* But what she said was, 'I'd forgotten what you taste like, Jamie.' The dark eyes twinkled. 'I must say you're as scrummy as I remember.' She laughed like a schoolgirl, tossing her head back so her hair swung round her shoulders.

'Goodbye Jamie. I don't expect they will let us meet like this again.'

Then she was marching towards the door, Collette scampering after her.

'Wait, Megan.' Collette called, trying to impose herself. 'You know contact isn't allowed. It means I've got to-.'

'Oh stop fussing, Collette. It was only a little kiss.'

Then Carver was alone in the middle of the room, still too stunned to move, listening to their thudding footsteps sounding up the stairs.

As he climbed into his car, Carver was still shaking. He wasn't sure if it was what she'd put him through, or her unexpected lunge and the momentary panic he experienced as he imagined a knife in her hand. Then again it could have been the shock of feeling her body against his, something he never, ever, expected to experience again. Or it could have been the choking fit that had nearly killed him. As he gripped the steering wheel, taking deep breaths, giving himself time to recover, his thought was, *All of the above.*

Eventually his breathing steadied, the shaking eased. He was certain now she *had* used the occasion to indulge herself. To demonstrate how, even under her present circumstances, she could still put him under the wheel. He hoped it would be the last time, and he knew he would never tell anyone about it. Certainly not Rosanna.

He reached into his jacket pocket and took out the cling-film wrap he had pocketed after coughing it up into his hand. Collette was concentrating so much on making sure Megan wasn't planning any further moves she hadn't even come close to seeing it. If it hadn't been for the look in her face just before she lunged, reminding him of her, 'be ready' warning, he might have spat it out as soon as the gagging reflex brought it up.

'Crazy bitch could have killed me,' he muttered, which made him wonder if just such an outcome might even have been a secondary, if subconscious one on her part.

For nearly a minute he stared at the glistening object in his hand as if it might contain poison, or some rare virus that would infect him and pollute his life even more.

Then he remembered. She had alluded to it several times. If she wanted to harm him, she could do so any time.

He began to pick at the thin layers of plastic.

CHAPTER 47

Through the dimpled-glass panel in the door, Jess saw his lean outline approaching from down the hallway long before it opened. As it swung back, the face registered disappointment. It was replaced almost immediately by surprise, then delight.

'Miss Jessica?' Christo ushered her in. 'Why- What are you doing here?'

'We need to talk, Christo. About the statement you made to the police.'

His face fell. 'Oh.'

'Is Sally here?'

The disappointed look returned. He shook his head. 'She has gone.'

'Gone? I thought you were…. What happened?'

He read her assumption. 'We were never… partners, or anything. We just got together for the-. For Barbara and Gerald.'

Jess made an, *I see*, sort of face. It explained some things.

'I thought you were her. Coming back.'

Hence the disappointed look.

In that moment, Jess saw something childlike in him - despite his very adult interests - and was sympathetic.

First Barbara, now Sally. He was having a rough time of it, though she resisted the impulse to mother him.

He led her through to the lounge and they sat down. She was surprised to find it sparsely furnished, devoid of any of the sort of personal items, pictures, ornaments or other paraphernalia you usually find in someone's home. It had the impersonal feel of a furnished let. But then remembered how he liked to spend his spare time. *Probably stays more at other people's homes, than his.*

In his statement he had described himself as a software-designer. Knowing what they can earn, she was surprised to find him living in a block of flats behind a suburban shopping centre just outside Coventry. Her face must have betrayed her thoughts as he cast a derisory eye around.

'This is just temporary, while my place is being done up. I'm in the process of renovating it, but it's taking longer than planned.'

Jess nodded, though the thought of him decorating houses jarred with how she'd come to seem him.

'When we saw you at the police station, the morning after…?' He nodded. 'You told us the person you spoke to on the phone sounded like Gavin, my partner?'

'A little. But it was mainly the way he spoke. Official, you know? And the two of you had been speaking to Master Gerald and Mistress Barbara earlier in the day. I just assumed it was him.'

'You told us you weren't sure if you would recognise the voice again. And that you couldn't say if he had an accent.'

'That's right.'

'Yet in your statement you describe the voice as-.' She checked her notes. '…having a north of England accent. Definitely not a southerner.'

A puzzled look came into Christo's face. 'That cannot be right. I did not say that.'

'It's in your statement,' Jess said. 'You did read it before signing it?'

The way he stared at her, she wasn't surprised when he said, 'I am not sure. I think they just asked me to sign at the bottom. I was upset at the time and probably wasn't paying attention.'

Jess stared at him, taken aback. A witness to a murder and they don't even bother to read his statement back to him? What the hell is going on? She sat back in her chair, frowning.

After a while Christo said, 'Why would someone write that if I did not say it?'

She looked up. The sad eyes that, since Barbara's death, looked like they might burst into tears any moment, stared back at her. 'That's what's puzzling me.' She thought on it some more, but nothing came. She stood up. 'Don't worry, Christo. I'll get to the bottom of it.'

He got to his feet, but didn't move to show her to the door. The way he looked at her… He seemed awkward.

'What is it Christo?'

'I wonder-,' he began. 'I wonder if I might ask you something, Miss Jessica?'

Jess hesitated. He was looking at her the way he had done the first time she met him, as well as the night she and Baggus visited Josephine's. *Surely he doesn't think I'd...*

'Of course, Christo,' she said. 'What is it?'

Baggus wasn't used to dining by candlelight, and certainly not at home. It wasn't the only 'new' experience he'd come home to recently. After agreeing to let Sally take his spare room - *'just while I get myself sorted.'* - the past week had seen other changes in his routines. Like arriving home to a prepared meal, served at the table, place mats and everything. But while such pampering made a nice change to ready-meals and take-aways, he still wasn't sure how he felt about the arrangement, or how long "temporary" might be. And he was conscious that the conflicted feeling that had come soon after she arrived, was growing stronger.

Thee was no denying that the first couple of days, her being there did him good - her as well, he liked to think. The horror and sadness of Barbara and Gerald was still raw, for both of them. And while Baggus never found it easy talking about, 'feelings', just knowing that she was there, and going through something similar, helped.

As did the sex.

He still liked to think that that first night, his resolve to not get physically involved with the woman in the bed the other side of the wall from his, and whom he remembered once dressed in a French maid's outfit, was genuine. But it disappeared the moment he heard a noise, and looked up to see her naked silhouette framed in the doorway. He was fairly certain now that the couple of hours that followed - again since - was more a case of letting natural urges and passion achieve what hours of talking might never, rather than the start of something.

Nevertheless, he was conscious that whatever spin he put on it, Sally was a witness to a crime. He wasn't yet certain what sort of witness - maybe to no more than the Hawthorns' movements in the days and hours before, but a witness all the same. And though he was no longer part of the investigation - which meant no conflict of interest - he knew that was just semantics. As far as he was concerned, he *was* still involved - and would be until such time as Kenworthy, or whoever, was in the cells and charged. Which meant that whatever the benefits of her being there - and they were considerable - complications would, eventually, loom.

But it had been another long day, involving a crisis in the middle of a Crown Court trial which he had to get involved in resolving, and a gang-related, drive-by shooting. Whatever issues may need resolving in the future, right now, he was just grateful for the opportunity to enjoy a pleasant meal with someone whose appearance had already sparked the odd thought about what her later intentions might be. Right now however, it seemed her thoughts were still on the conversation that had dominated as they'd worked their way through her pasta bake, as her next question confirmed.

'So you're not thinking of doing anything yourself then?'

He looked up at her. The candles had burnt low and the flickering flames danced in her eyes as she regarded him over her wine glass. All through dinner, the questions had kept coming. Was he planning to do anything more about Kenworthy? What was Jess Greylake doing? Where they any nearer catching anyone? He'd tried batting them away, but each time there was a lull in conversation, she came back at him. She would make a good detective if her interrogation skills were anything to go by.

As he sat back in his chair, feeling full, he pushed his glass round on its coaster, trying to get his thoughts in some sort of order. Fosters never gave him this fuzzy feeling.

'Dunno yet,' he said, finally responding to her question. 'I just want to see the bastard caught.' He drained the last of his wine.

'Me to,' she said, reaching over to re-fill his glass. 'So you *were* only joking about going to the papers?'

He shrugged. 'You never know, it might make some rats start thinking about jumping the sinking shit. Sorry, ship.'

She made a lop-sided smile. 'Wouldn't that get you in trouble?'

He gave a dismissive grunt. 'I know a couple of reporters I'd trust to not reveal their sources.'

She became serious. 'Listen Gavin. I know I've gone on about it, a lot.'

He shrugged, amiably. 'No more than me.'

'And I know we both feel the same about what happened to Barbara… and Gerald.' He frowned, took another drink. 'But I think you ought to leave it to the others. It could be dangerous.'

He looked at her, puzzled. 'I thought you were concerned that nothing's being done? Well maybe you're right. Some press interest might start to make things done… happen.'

She leaned forward, giving him another good view of the cleavage that had caught his eye several times already. 'I just want to know that someone is doing *something*. Not for you to get involved again. Remember what happened last time.'

'What do you mean, "last time"?' He tried to think straight. He wasn't sure if he'd mentioned the hoo-hah that followed his visit to Kenworthy.

'I meant with all the frustration and worry you've gone through. You don't want to put yourself through that again, do you?'

Now it was his turn to fix her with a not-too-steady gaze. 'If it means showing Kenworthy for the bastard he is, then it'll be worth it. Even if we can't prove anything enough for court, it'll ruin the cunt.'

'That's just alcohol talking,' she said.

He raised his glass - 'Well bottoms-fucking-up.' - and drained it of its contents.

CHAPTER 48

Carver ended the call, then reached for the glass he'd had to run under a tap before using. The JD had fortified him during the early days of his analysis, but since then it had languished, untouched, in the desk's bottom drawer. His conversation with Jess had been a long one. She was as intrigued by Megan's note as he was over Christo's apparently inaccurate statement. If that was someone's attempt at diverting attention in the wrong direction, then it would only ever have lasted until the first twenty-eight-day formal review, when all statements are rechecked with their makers. Okay, he was already suspicious of Gardener's motives in not allowing a joint enquiry, but doctoring a witness statement hinted at some more deeply-rooted conspiracy, and he was always sceptical about those. He'd never wavered in his belief that Lee Harvey Oswald was nothing more than a lone gunman.

He savoured the whisky, enjoying its soothing effect after a day that had set his nerves on edge. Picking up the slip of creased notepaper he read it over again – maybe the twentieth time he had done so. The three short lines were giving him plenty to think about.

I am being watched

Find the VR. Watch it
Anne Kenworthy is The Key

As he read the middle line again, he gave another self-derisory snort. Jess had said he shouldn't be hard on himself. That all riddles are like that - obvious once you know the answer. But he should have at least considered that 'VR' may be a 'what', rather than a 'who'. He'd been too focused on names and initials, and probably distracted by ones he recognised. But if it *was* a Video Recording, as it now seemed, was it the one that had already caused him so many sleepless nights, or something else? And this was assuming Megan Crane wasn't playing games, seeking to lead him on. As far as he could tell, her passions for cruelty and deviousness hadn't changed. As he had told Prosecuting Counsel during a pre-trial meeting, 'If she'd been around in the fifteenth century, she could have tutored Lucrecia Borgia.'

But he was clear on two points. First, her grief, not to mention anger, over the Hawthorns, was genuine. After her sham dismissal of their deaths, the echo of the sadness had stayed, even when she was pretending to bait him. Second, while they were together - and he had spent enough time in her company to know when it was happening - she had been sending out a signal. Hidden deep, for sure, within the barbed words and dismissive gestures, but a signal nevertheless, clear and consistent. *Catch the bastards.* For all she may hate him, she hated whoever killed the Hawthorns at least as much. And she wanted him to find him, or them, which, presumably, was where her note came in.

He was yet to come up with any credible hypothesis that might explain why, or by whom, she was being watched. More than one of her assessments described her as suffering 'paranoid delusions'. But as the line runs, '*that doesn't mean they aren't out to get you.*' He had seen for himself how PO Bright had changed since last time. Then, she had barely paid them any attention at all. This time she had watched Megan Crane's every movement, as if half-expecting something may happen. It could, of course, just be an internal prison matter. Or it could be that someone beyond the prison's confines was taking an interest in Megan's activities, whom she was meeting, and why. He wondered if Ellen Hazelhurst or Lydia Grant might shed light on it, and scribbled a reminder to speak with them.

But what excited him more, was the reference to Kenworthy's wife.

Apart from confirming his suspicion that Kenworthy, or something he was connected to – the Video Recording? - was at the heart of the puzzle, it re-opened what had begun to look like a dead end. With Kenworthy himself on alert and further approaches declared 'out of bounds', the suggestion his wife may be key to unlocking the mystery spurred Carver's thought processes.

Seeing her that day at Kenworthy's offices, his impression was of a quiet, dignified woman, one in thrall to her husband. Getting her to reveal what she knew would not be easy.

He looked up again at the chart projected on the wall. The VR reference appeared next to several names. It could mean they were all possible suspects. None were as high profile as Kenworthy, but it didn't have to be someone with a public profile to protect. As he rolled the glass between his hands, he weighed options.

So far there had been three deaths, four if Gordon Halsall was part of it. There could yet be more. He thought of Cyrisse Chaterlain, presently drumming her heels in a Salford safe-house, insisting she wasn't going to stay there much longer. Who else may be at risk? He thought about approaching the other names linked to 'VR'. But if any were connected to the murders it would put them on their guard - if they weren't already. He thought about the Hawthorn enquiry. Presently, Gilleray seemed focused on causing maximum embarrassment to the membership of Josephine's. Not the best tactic to get people to talk about things they may balk at disclosing to their closest friends. He wondered when he would wake up.

As he took stock, Carver felt his instincts kicking in. It was a good feeling, one he'd missed of late. They told him that right now, their best chance of finding the Hawthorns' killer and preventing other deaths, lay in Megan Crane's note. Not for the first time, he reflected on how he was about to put his trust in a woman whose life was characterised by sexual perversity, a twisted love for a serial killer and an appetite for causing mayhem - not forgetting what she tried to do to him and Rosanna. With a final shake of his head, he drained his glass, and rose from the chair. Tomorrow was Friday, the weekend looming. Cyrisse needed pacifying, and if he was to start looking at Anne Kenworthy, things couldn't wait. Just as well Rosanna was still away.

Which was when he remembered his planned weekend excursion to look at the unfinished project out at Conway.

'Ahh, fuck.'

CHAPTER 49

Ellen Hazelhurst was adamant. 'I'm sorry Lydia, it's out of the question. And frankly, I find it hard to imagine that Megan Crane feels constrained by my POs being present.'

'I can only interpret what I see, Governor.' The researcher placed her mug on the desk and shrugged, matter-of-factly. 'My first reaction was the same. But I have to say, I do have the sense she's holding something back. As if she wants to talk to me about something, but doesn't feel able.'

'Such as what?' Ellen said. The memory of her last visit to Cloverbank, and Megan's visit to her office the following day, was still vivid. It had made her cautious about anything and everything concerning the woman. The idea of allowing her to meet with the researcher, unsupervised, made her uncomfortable in the extreme.

'I can't be sure,' Lydia Grant said. 'It could be something personal. Or it may be something from her past, something she still feels guilty about. Or maybe-' Seeing Ellen's doubtful looked, Lydia shrugged an acknowledgement. *Perhaps not.* 'It could just be something she wants to share with me, but is scared of the consequences.'

'Megan Crane? Scared?' Ellen shook her head. 'I very much doubt it.'

But the psychologist was less quick to dismiss the idea. 'You know as well as I do that prison does strange things to people. Look at Billy The Kid.'

Ellen nodded, acknowledging the point.

The case of the man who had changed his name by deed poll to that of his childhood Western hero, William Bonney, was once tagged as one of the most dangerous characters in the prison system. Now a gibbering wreck in Liverpool's Ashworth Mental Hospital, he woke up one day, convinced that everyone with whom he came into contact was in the pay of the notorious Nottingham family whose son he had beaten to death in prison, years before. Overnight he changed from the system's most notorious hard-case to an insecure, whimpering jelly, though some suspected - and still did - it was simply an act aimed at doing easier time.

'Even so,' Ellen said, still cautious. 'I'd be worried she may try something. She could-'

It was then Ellen remembered the call that morning from the detective, Carver. He'd wanted to know if she was aware of any reason why Megan might think she was being watched. It hadn't meant anything at the time, but in view of what Lydia was saying-

The other woman interrupted her thought processes.'There is another factor in this.'

Ellen waited.

'There's some research I've been following in the US. They're looking at psychosis being linked to the physical make-up of the brain.'

Ellen looked askew. 'Sounds a bit Frankenstein-ish.'

'Maybe, but it's attracting interest. Have you heard of someone called, LaPierre?' Ellen shook her head. 'He's shown that in some cases, the pre-frontal cortex of psychopaths' brains differ from normal people. And it's well known that psychopaths show a measurable difference in skin conductivity and heart rate in response to fear. There's growing support for the theory that violent behaviour can be predicted through biology.'

'Why are you telling me this?'

Lydia bit her lip, hesitating. 'If I could get Megan to my lab at the University, I could do an MRI and some other tests. She's the ideal subject. Intelligent and self-aware, but with a marked disconnect from reality in some very specific areas.'

'Like with that detective, Carver, you mean?'

'Exactly. She's created an alternate reality round her perception of his motivations. She's convinced he's obsessed with bringing her down. I believe it's why she targeted him in the first place.'

'Does he know?'

'Only part of it. Some things are only just starting to come out. That's why I'm interested in getting her into a safe environment. She's so egotistical, I am certain I could get her to open up.'

Ellen hesitated, uncertain. 'What might these tests show?'

'We won't know until we run them, but whatever the results, I'd publish the research.' After a moment, she added, 'Under joint names of course, yours and mine.'

Ellen pondered. Eventually she said, 'Tell me about your lab. What sort of security does the university have?'

CHAPTER 50

Carver parked facing out across the dock basin towards Salford's Quays. A quarter-mile away, the Lowry Theatre and its accompanying Outlet stood, silhouetted against the night sky. Their lights and those of the surrounding restaurants reflected on the dark waters. As he cut the engine, Jess let out a sigh.

'D'you think I could qualify for Protected Witness status?'

Carver sent her a wry glance. 'You're expendable.'

'Tch. Shame.'

As they got out, he saw her eyeing the banks of apartment blocks that overlook the former docklands area and imagined what she was thinking. 'The flat faces the other way,' he said. 'The NCA's budget doesn't run to waterfront properties.'

'Shame,' she repeated. 'Which one is it?'

He pointed at a path running between two blocks of apartments. 'Through there.'

As they crossed towards it, a sporty red-saloon car pulled onto the car park, heading towards them. They stopped to let it pass but it swung into a vacant space before it reached them. They carried on.

If Jess was impressed with the location - most 'safe

houses' are in far less salubrious areas - Cyrisse Chaterlain was not, and wasted no time letting them know.

'All night you can hear the music from the bars.'

'Close the windows.'

'I've been here two days and I've had three letters from some Neighbourhood Watch person about cars being stolen off the car park, mainly Mercedes and BMWs. If my car goes missing does your insurance cover it?'

'I'll look into it.'

'What are you going to do about the smell?'

'What smell?'

'In here. This horrible stale, stink. Can't you smell it?'

Carver sniffed. 'I can't smell anything.' He looked at Jess, who shrugged. Cyrisse was adamant.

'I have a sensitive nose and I can smell it. It is awful.'

'We'll get you some air freshener.'

Cyrisse gave him a pointed look.

Jess sorted coffee while Carver listened, as patiently as he could, to Cyrisse's complaints about the kitchen. The washing machine was broken. There was green stuff growing in the fridge and there was no dishwasher. When she paused for breath, Carver asked her what she knew about Kenworthy's wife.

'I never met her. What does she have to do with anything?'

'I'm not sure yet. Did he ever mention her?'

'I didn't know he was married until after we'd met a few times. Then it was the old story. My wife doesn't understand me, you know?'

'Would she know about Sylvie Tyler?'

She thought on it, shook her head. 'I doubt it. As far

as I know, he did not tell his wife about me.'

Carver tried digging deeper, but Cyrisse apologised, saying she knew little about her. Having vented her frustration, she seemed more amenable.

'When will I be able to go home?' she said. 'I told Andrew I would only be away a few days.'

'Andrew?' Carver said.

'My assistant. He's looking after the gallery.' She turned to Jess. 'You met him.'

Jess nodded. 'The chap in the white shirt.'

Carver stayed non-committal. 'I'm sorry Cyrisse. I need you to stay here a while longer. Things aren't clear yet.'

'How long is, "a while"?'

'I can't say.'

She turned to Jess again. 'Is he always this decisive?'

Jess threw Carver a glance, stifled a smile. 'Not always.'

Cyrisse read what passed between them. 'You two have worked together long, yes?'

'Not that long,' Jess said.

'But you are close. Lovers perhaps?'

Carver gave a weary look, not rising to it. Cyrisse wasn't the first. 'No. We're not lovers.'

Cyrisse switched target. 'The other detective then. Perhaps he is your boyfriend?'

As Jess took her turn at giving a pointed look, Carver sensed Cyrisse warming to company.

'You're being mischievous, Cyrisse. You know he isn't.'

Cyrisse turned back to Carver. 'She is mysterious, this girl. She denies, but does not give anything away.'

Carver stood up. His thoughts on Jess were his own. 'I think it's time we went.'

Before they left, he showed Cyrisse the personal-attack alarm he had brought for her, instructed her on its use. Then he ran through the flat's alarm system with her again, just to make sure.

Five minutes later, Carver checked over his shoulder before reversing out of the space. Off to his right, Old Trafford's floodlights set the sky aglow. Though it was the wrong shaped ball, it made him think of Baggus and how he was managing, distanced from the investigation.

'I like her,' Jess said. 'She's straight.'

'Straight, how?' Carver said, pulling away

'Says what she thinks. Doesn't hold back.'

'Hmm. We said that about someone else once.'

She didn't reply.

As the Golf passed behind the red saloon parked close to the exit, the man in the driver's seat slumped low, then watched as it slowed, before turning right to head back into the City. He waited a few seconds, before stepping out into the fresh night air, stretching away the stiffness that had come into his limbs during the hour's wait. He craned to check down the road to make sure they were gone, before turning and setting off down the path between the two apartment blocks from where he'd seen the two detectives emerge.

CHAPTER 51

Carver followed Anne Kenworthy through to an airy kitchen-family room. Seeing the worktops covered with sheets of newspaper, flowers and cuttings, he thought he ought to play the reluctant visitor one more time.

'Are you sure you wouldn't rather that I come back when your husband is here?'

She flicked her wrist. 'It's alright Chief Inspector. If I can help, it will save everyone's time, won't it? Just give me a minute while I put these lilies in water.'

As she went back to splitting stems with a knife, Carver took the opportunity to study the woman with whom he'd spoken for only the second time earlier that morning. In these surroundings, she seemed very different to the woman he'd met at her husband's offices. Then, she had seemed the typical politician's wife, well-to-do and a bit stiff. Someone whose life revolved around her husband's. But the way she was now, looking at ease in a light summer frock that showed her figure better than the staid affair she'd worn then, and with her hair down, he sensed this was closer to the real Anne Kenworthy. And while grateful for the chance to speak with her alone, he'd been surprised by her enthusiastic insistence over the phone that he should visit, despite her husband being away in Paris for the weekend - 'Cultural exchange talks, or something.'

In truth, he'd set things up in the hope that they might just fall this way, making out he happened to be in the area, and that he needed to clarify a couple of matters about her husband's constituency organisation, 'for the record.' When she confirmed what he already knew, having checked with SB, - that her husband was away - his disappointed, 'Damn', followed by a thoughtful, 'I wonder if you might know-' prompted the response he was looking for.

'If you think I may be able to help, then feel free to call round. I'm not doing anything this morning.'

He tried to sound conflicted. 'It wouldn't be fair to ask you. I should wait until Mr Kenworthy returns.'

But her response - 'Nonsense. He won't mind. I often get involved in helping with his affairs. And if you are in the area, it would be silly not to,' - sealed it.

Now, as he watched her putting the finishing touches to her flower arranging, he was conscious that she could have offered to provide the 'clarification' he claimed to need over the telephone. That she didn't, intrigued him.

'Right,' she said, pulling off her gloves. 'How can I help?'

Carver debated it one last time. He had thought long and hard about how best to manage conversation so it would appear to fit with his cover story. In the end, he had decided to wait until he saw her, then rely on his instincts. But as she waited, regarding him through sparkling-blue eyes that were alive with intelligence and curiosity, he knew it wasn't going to be as easy as he had imagined.

'Before I begin,' he said, 'May I ask what know about the incident at your husband's office?'

She shrugged, matter-of-factly. 'Not a great deal. He said it was just a case of mistaken identity. That the officer who barged in had put two and two together and made five.'

Carver feigned surprise, then discomfort. She read it.

'Was that not the case? Is there more to it?'

He made a show of not wanting to be too revealing, so she would know there was. 'In one sense, your husband was right. On the other hand, it's not *quite* as simple as a case of mistaken identity.'

Intrigued, she led him to the sofas in the adjoining conservatory. They sat across from each other.

'I'm sorry, you'll have to explain.'

Carver looked uncomfortable. 'Did he tell you we are investigating some suspicious deaths?'

'He said something about a solicitor who'd died? But that it was an accident?'

'Ah.' Carver hesitated, and set his face to reflect some inner conflict.

'Is there something I should know Chief Inspector?'

He hesitated. He'd reached this point sooner than expected, and knew that getting her to reveal anything would mean a gamble. He reasoned that if it all went wrong and his visit later drew a complaint from Kenworthy - *if* his wife told of it –then it would help to be able to show that *she* had pressed *him*. He'd even thought about wiring himself, but that would show duplicity from the start, so he ditched the idea. He hoped his logic remained sound.

'That's not for me to say Mrs Kenworthy. I just assumed that, if it *was* all a mistake, he'd have told you the full story.' He made to rise. 'Perhaps I ought to-'

She put out a hand. *Stop.* He sat down again.

'What do you mean, *if* it was a mistake? What *is* the

full story?'

He adjusted his tie - not all his discomfort was sham - before meeting her gaze. 'A few days ago, a couple, a man and wife, were murdered. They ran a private club.'

'What sort of private club?'

'An adult club. The sort where people go to… play games.'

For long seconds, she stared at him. Eventually she said, 'Do you mean some sort of sex-club?'

He hesitated. 'Yes.'

She nodded, slowly, as if matching it to some prior knowledge. 'Does it involve-' She gave a little shudder. 'I think they call it, BDSM?'

Carver did his best to mask surprise. 'In some cases, yes.'

As she sat on the edge of the chair, hands clasped in her lap, an older version of the English rose she'd once been, Carver could see she was fighting to maintain her composure. Eventually she gave a resigned sigh.

'Carry on, Chief Inspector.'

'We've been speaking to people connected with the club in the past. Or who know people connected with it.'

She looked at the ceiling. 'I see.'

He waited, but after several seconds realised she couldn't bring herself to ask. *To hell with it*. 'We needed to talk with your husband.'

She spotted the evasion. Her eyes narrowed. 'Are you saying that Alistair was connected with this place? Or just that he knows someone who is?'

He strung the silence out, knowing the effect it would have. 'I'd rather not say.'

After several seconds, she turned away to stare out through the patio doors at the lush garden. Carver waited, wondering what was going through her mind. A minute passed before she turned back to him.

'What, exactly, is this 'minor matter' you said you wanted to speak to my husband about, Chief Inspector?'

Carver pursed his lips. He had a choice. He could either continue to hedge round it, hoping that she may, eventually, reveal something. Or he could take the more direct route, which risked Kenworthy knowing he was under the microscope, and which could make things more difficult than ever. But as he pondered, the certainty grew in him - he wasn't sure where from - that Anne Kenworthy *did* know things about her husband that he needed to know. He made his decision.

'What do you know about your husband's private affairs Mrs Kenworthy?'

On the face of it an odd question, he knew she would understand. MPs spend more time away from their wives than most. She could either continue the conversation, or throw him out.

'How Alistair spends his time when he is not engaged on government business, concerns no-one but ourselves Chief Inspector.'

'Not even if it leaves him open to blackmail?' She froze, colour rising through the slender neck. 'I'll put the question another way. Do you know if your husband was ever involved in anything that he, or someone else, wouldn't want made public?'

'Everyone has secrets, Chief Inspector, even you, I'm sure. It doesn't necessarily mean anything.'

It was a measured response, but he could see how she was pressing her hands into her lap to hide the shaking. She still hadn't asked him to leave.

'I'm told you aren't like other ministers' wives, Mrs Kenworthy. Is that right?'

She blinked, caught out by the sudden change of

direction. 'I'm sorry?'

'You only visit The House when you have to. And whenever possible you avoid the receptions and grand occasions most MPs' partners like to be seen at.'

She pulled a face. 'Such things simply aren't for me. And if you know that much, then you also know I find my charity work much more rewarding.'

Carver acknowledged it with a nod. The profile he had drawn up after receiving Megan's note said as much. It hadn't taken long to pull together. Kenworthy's relatively low-key Community Affairs portfolio drew less media attention than some of the grander Ministries. However, the fact that his famously-puritanical, industrialist father-in-law, Logan Hartley, was worth a fortune, *and* harboured extreme political views, ensured occasional press interest. Most often, it concerned how Kenworthy's political ideals squared with his father-in-law's oft-quoted pronouncements about why the country was going to the dogs. And given Anne Kenworthy's photogenic qualities, it was no surprise that she sometimes also featured. So far, the profile was proving accurate - apart from her lack of surprise over her husband's, 'interests'.

He pressed his point. 'Am I right in thinking you don't have much regard for politicians?'

She allowed a half-smile. 'Does anyone, these days?'

He lowered his voice, reinforcing the conspiratorial element that had crept into their conversation. 'You know what I mean.'

She did the same. 'In that case, then yes. I find most politicians two-faced and, for the most part, vile creatures.'

'Which must be hard, seeing as you are married to one.'

She fixed him with a stare. 'What is it you want from me, Chief Inspector? I'm sure you already knew Alistair was away when you rang.'

Touché.

But before answering, he ticked off what her face and posture were telling him. The crossed legs pointed at defensiveness. The flush in her face and chest, anticipation. Shallow breathing and the ticking muscles in her cheeks, tension. They all spoke of someone preparing to face something they feared. It was now or never.

'I'd like you to tell me about the video recording.'

Her efforts to mask her reaction were wasted. 'What video recording?' Her Adam's-apple was suddenly more prominent.

'The one that could destroy your husband's career.' Mentally, Carver crossed fingers. He was reaching.

She stood up suddenly, visibly agitated. She looked about her, out the windows, through into the kitchen, anywhere she didn't have to look at his face. 'I think you should go now, Chief Inspector.'

Two minutes later, getting into his Golf, he heard the front door slam and he looked back over his shoulder. There was to be no cheery send off. But as he turned away, he saw again, parked under the car port at the side of the house, the Aston Martin Vantage he had admired on his arrival.

'It belongs to a friend of Alistair's,' she had said when she answered the door and saw him admiring it. 'He lets him borrow it now and again, just for fun. They share an interest in classic cars.'

As he drove away, Carver was wondering what sort of friend loans out one-hundred-thousand-pounds-worth of motor car to a Government Minister, 'just for fun.'

CHAPTER 52

Baggus parked on the main road, a little way down from Jess's flat over the shops. He then spent five minutes trying to decide whether to call her, or just cross the road and ring the bell. He'd been debating it all the way there, which he thought was a symptom of the very issues he needed to talk to her about, though the knowledge of it didn't help. Eventually, after nearly ringing then putting his mobile away several times, he decided. 'Fuck it.' Reaching for the handle, he got out.

A minute later, standing at her front door and now hesitating over pressing the button, he realised. She may not even be home. What does a girl like Jess do on a Saturday morning when she isn't working? Shopping? The gym? He hadn't thought to check around the back to see if her car was there. *Jesus Christ. You're definitely losing it.* Nor did he know how she would react to him suddenly turning up unannounced. The last couple of times they had spoken she had sounded … different. It was one of the reasons he was so reluctant to call her. He needed to *see* her. That way he would know what she was really thinking. Besides, she wasn't the sort who would be fazed by an unexpected visitor.

He rang the bell.

But it wasn't until the third ring he heard movement above. A door slamming, her voice, raised. It sounded like 'Stay there.'

Fuck.Company. The one thing he had never considered. Idiot.

When she opened the door, his first thought was she was getting ready to go somewhere. She was wearing a long dressing-robe, her make-up was… different, and she seemed a little breathless. Seeing him, she made no attempt to hide surprise, nor to put on a welcoming face.

'Gavin? What are you doing here?'

'I, er-' he began. 'I'm sorry. I should have called.'

She glared at him. 'Yes. You should.' For several seconds she stayed, rooted in the doorway, arms wrapped, protectively, round her as she regarded him. He could sense her debating whether to invite him up or not. In those seconds he realised the mistake he had made. He was about to bail out, admit it and tell her he would ring again later, when she heaved a long sigh.

'Oh for fuck's sake. You'd better come in.' She stepped aside, opening the door wide.

As he passed, Baggus caught a whiff of fragrance and recognised it as the one she'd worn that night at Josephine's. Looking down, he glimpsed dark hose, black court shoes. Possible scenarios came to him. In one, she was getting ready to go somewhere, someone's wedding perhaps? Another, made him think of her, 'Stay there,' command.

She directed him upstairs and into the kitchen. She threw the switch on the kettle.

'I take it this a bad moment?' he said, trying to sound apologetic.

She shook her head, more in weary resignation, he thought, than denial. She leaned back against the counter, keeping the robe tight about her.

'Why are you here, Gavin?' she said. 'What's wrong?'

Conscious of her gaze, he turned towards the living area with its bay window looking down on the high street. The couple of times he'd stayed over, he'd sat there, looking out… He marshalled his thoughts before turning to face her.

'I thought it might-.' He started again. 'I need your advice.' She arched an eyebrow. He closed his eyes as he forced the words from his throat. 'I'm fucked-up, Jess. I'm a mess.'

Almost at once the fierce gaze wilted, replaced by one of sympathy. The kettle boiled and neither spoke as she made coffees. She handed him a mug then took him by the sleeve, dragged him into the living area and sat him down.

'Tell,' she said.

For the next few minutes he talked non-stop. First about Robinson and how he was trying to edge him out. Then about him lying awake all night thinking about what had happened to Barbara - and Gerald. He spoke about his growing obsession – even he recognised it for what it was - with doing something about Kenworthy. His fear that if he didn't, no one would. 'From what I hear, the enquiry isn't getting anywhere.' As he talked, Jess drank her coffee, regarding him with a steady look tinged with pity that reminded him of the way Barbara had looked at him that first night she'd shown him around the club. He was conscious of how pathetic he must sound. 'I hardly knew Barbara, yet I can't get her out of my mind. The job's *never* got to me like this before. I don't know what's wrong with me.'

She put her mug down, looked at him squarely. 'There's nothing wrong with you. For a start, we don't usually know the victims. For another, people like Barbara, they-.' She hesitated.

'They what?' he said.

She took a deep breath. 'I know you thought Barbara was special. And in some ways she was. But you do know what she was, don't you?'

'What?' A nervousness stirred in him.

'She was a pro. On the game.' Seeing him about to speak, she cut across him. 'Before she met Gerald I mean. A good one too. Classy. People like her are skilled at making men think they love them. That's what they do. Barbara was better at it than most. That's why you think she was so special.'

Anger welled in him. 'You're wrong. It doesn't matter what she used to be. What I felt was….' He stopped, unsure of himself.

'Real? Is that what you were going to say? Come on Gavin. Don't mistake infatuation for something else.'

He bridled at her. 'It wasn't infatuation. Barbara and me, we-.' He stopped. He hadn't come to discuss his feelings for Barbara. But now Jess was giving him that pitying look again. Like he was too naive to understand. 'I know Barbara's dead, and I know I can't do anything about it.'

'But you think you can do something about whoever killed her. And you're obsessing about getting back at Kenworthy. If you're not careful, it will destroy you. Believe me, I know.' She saw his look. 'Don't be surprised. When Jamie and I first got involved with Megan Crane- Let's just say we both had our problems.'

'Carver?'

She nodded.

'What sort of problems?'

'You'll have to ask him. All I can say is, he's not as

detached from things as he sometimes appears.'

He thought about it. Eventually he said, 'My trouble is I'm just no good with women.'

She gave him a half-smile. 'Oh I don't know. This down-to-earth rugby-fan thing you do has its charm.'

Her teasing reminded him of the problem he was yet to mention. 'You might be right. But that's not what I came to talk ab-'

The noise of a door opening made him turn towards the bedrooms. A man came into view, bare from the waist up, sweating, like he had been working out. As he came through into the living area, he stopped, as if suddenly realising they were there. He turned to them.

It was Christo.

'Hello Mr Baggus. Nice to see you again.

CHAPTER 53

During the first two weeks of a murder enquiry, detectives know to not even think about days off, unless someone is in the cells and charged. And though Carver wasn't, officially, part of the Hawthorn investigation *and* his present role didn't require that he work Sundays, he intended to follow the maxim – at least in spirit. His plan was to grant himself an 'out-of-office' day so he could see to some urgent, personal business, while being still contactable in the event something broke.

The 'personal business,' consisted, firstly, of having an early run out to the Welsh hills above Conway to look over the barn conversion he hoped might still be a runner. Secondly, he needed to be on hand to pick Rosanna up from Manchester Airport – when she messaged to confirm which of the two Lisbon-Manchester flights scheduled to arrive that afternoon was hers. The previous evening, she'd confirmed that she and "Julio", had finished doing whatever they had been doing, and she was coming home. He was glad. Their last few conversations had been difficult. When she'd spoken about looking forward to getting back and seeing him, he wasn't sure she sounded convincing. But whatever doubts he had about how things would go when they met, his plan for that Sunday was a good one.

It never got off the drawing board.

Shortly after six, he was roused from sleep by a call from his NCA boss, Nigel Broom. Within seconds of listening, he came wide awake, and a long, 'Fuuuck,' escaped him.

Afterwards, he sat on the edge of his bed, staring out of the window at the breaking dawn, trying to get his head round the implications of what he'd heard. However long he stayed there, it wasn't enough. Shaking his head, he stood up.

'*Jesus fucking Christ,*' he said, then headed for the bathroom.

An hour later, Carver stood in two inches of water, looking down on the charred remains of what had once been Megan Crane's archive. The room itself, like most of that side of the building, was a burnt-out and smoke-blackened write-off. Around him, the process of relocating the Regional Intelligence Unit and its associated NCA support functions to a temporary, but hopefully-more-secure base, within Greater Manchester Police's Training campus was already underway.

When he'd arrived on-scene and parked behind the melee of emergency vehicles out on the main road, he'd congratulated himself for not rushing to remove the Wellingtons from the car's boot. His present responsibilities didn't involve examining dead bodies in muddy fields. But by the time he made his way inside, and saw the extent of the damage, his smugness disappeared, quickly.

Now, Carver watched as the man squatting over in the corner, sniffed at the spoonful of charred debris, before sealing it in a plastic container. Carver didn't need to ask what he was testing for. The smell of petrol still hung. And he didn't need a Fire Investigator to tell him he was looking at the seat of the fire. Apart from the smell, this was where the damage was at its worst.

As the fire officer stood up, a cracking noise came from his knees. Turning to face Carver, he winced. In his late forties, the man had introduced himself as Tony McAteer, Greater Manchester Fire and Rescue Service's Senior Fire Investigation Officer. Carver couldn't tell whether the burnt-cardboard texture to his skin was job-related or the result of plenty of holidays in the sun.

'What was in here?' McAteer said.

'Not much,' Carver said. 'Table, chair, laptop. And that.' He pointed at the twisted plates of metal that had once been a filing cabinet.

The FIO nudged at one of the drawers that lay scattered around with his flame-retardant boot. 'What was in it?'

'Papers,' Carver said. 'Some computer discs.' He'd already confirmed they were missing.

The FIO considered the information, then turned his attention to the doorway. The outer door was still hanging off its hinges in the corridor, the inner one flat on the floor inside the room. Its outer face bore the boot marks of the firemen who had fought to bring the blaze under control. McAteer bent to examine the buckling next to the inner door's hinges. His knees cracked again as he straightened up.

'Must have been important papers.'

Carver said nothing. While respecting the man's experience, he wasn't going to expand further. It was clear enough what had happened. Right now his thoughts were on where it left him, what he needed to do. Though they were yet to work out where and how they had entered the compound - the CCTV recordings someone was already trying to get off the remote server should do it - the bits of kit left behind told enough of a story. The hydraulic jack used to force, first, the side fire entrance doors downstairs, then the doors to this office, still lay where it had been abandoned in the corridor outside. Similarly, the bolt croppers and charred, heavy-duty angel-grinder over in the corner, showed they had come properly equipped to get into the filing cabinet. The jagged edges of the casing indicated where they had cut the sides off, so the drawers could be taken out. The sodden ashes littering the floor were all that remained of their contents. Carver didn't yet have a theory as to how they'd come by the information. Only The Duke and Jess had ever been here. But it was obvious that somewhere, somehow, insider knowledge had to figure. In what form and from where it originated, was yet to be determined. And he was still coming to terms with what the attack might signify. *If they're desperate enough to try this....*

'What sort of facility was this?' McAteer said. 'Don't you lot work nights anymore?'

Carver recognised McAteer's attempt at fishing, though he suspected the man could probably hazard a guess. Hell, he'd probably had a hand in the Fire Risk Assessments.

'Non-operational,' Carver said. 'Admin and records-storage, that sort of thing. There's no one here at night, and not much goes on over the weekend either.

'So they'll have had plenty of time to weigh the job up then,' McAteer said.

'Looks that way.'

As Carver watched, the FIO took out his camera and

started taking pictures. Standing over the ashes, he stirred them with the toe of his boot. But there was nothing to see. Not anymore.

From along the corridor, voices and the flashlights cutting through the smoke-haze drew Carver out. With the lights in his face, he almost didn't recognise the two men in front. The first was Manchester's ACC Crime. A gruff north-easterner, they'd met when Carver presented an assessment on the Northwest's people-trafficking problem. Next to him was Barry Tudor, the Detective Chief Superintendent head of the force's Major Crime Unit. Carver knew him well. Behind them were a man and a woman dressed in the all-whites of Forensic-Analysts. The circus had arrived.

'Are you Carver?' the ACC said in thick Geordie.

Obviously made an impression then Carver thought. 'Yes sir.'

'Is Broom here?'

'Not yet. He's on his way up from London.'

'In that case, I hope you can explain what the fuck this is all about. Our Chief's going ballistic.'

CHAPTER 54

Cyrisse Chaterlain sat at one of the coffee-shop's outside tables, watching the stream of Sunday-shoppers bustling past and wondering what the hell she was doing. She hated shopping unless it was for art-works, and never, ever, visited out-of-town shopping centres such as the Trafford Centre. Yet here she was, in the middle of what a sign she'd seen billed as, "The UK's Second-Biggest Shopping Emporium", surrounded by people she was finding it hard not to categorise in ways that fitted with a Capital-dwellers prejudices about "Northerners".

The table wasn't actually, outside. In this case, 'outside' meant out on the mall, amongst the shoppers. But at least the centre's glass roof let in natural light - unlike that dreadful place near Thurrock she'd once visited. *Never again.* As she sipped her cappuccino she wished more than ever she was outside Highgate's Pavillion Café, enjoying the village's laid-back ambiance under a warming sun. It made her wonder, again, about how much longer they expected her to kick her heels in a place that was so alien, she could be on Mars.

But it was a measure of her frustration – and

boredom - that she had chosen to come here. Just off Manchester's M60 Ring Road, her hope was it would prove a diversion, and would at least provide some contact with people. If she had to spend much longer alone in the dreary flat the two detectives seemed to think she should be grateful for, she was sure she would go mad.

Unfortunately, her plan wasn't working out as hoped. While she'd found the centre without too much trouble - following the directions Carver had given the previous evening when he'd rung to check on her - it took her another thirty minutes to find a parking space. And while she had indeed found people, they were not at all the sort whose company she craved. As the seemingly endless procession of young mothers pushing overloaded baby-buggies and groups of excitable teenagers filed past, she had to work at suppressing her own prejudices. She would see the same, she was sure, in any shopping centre anywhere in the country of a weekend. The same blind-rush to spend money on items she regarded as little more than 'tat', and which would do nothing to enhance the buyer's quality of life. The looks on faces that suggested that, for many, an outing to a place such as this was the cultural highlight of their week, month, maybe even year, God forbid.

But as her gaze tracked right, following the young woman who could look attractive were it not for the clothes and makeup that made her look like something from a disaster movie, the feeling of panic she had experienced several times already that morning came back in a rush. Once more, she had to fight against the impulse that made her want to grab her bags and race back to her car - wherever that was.

He was there. Again.

This time he was across the far side of the upper mall, peering through the window of a men's fashion shop. At least that was what he *appeared* to be doing. His back was to her, so she could not see his face. But she recognised the brown bomber jacket and black baseball cap. And the angle he was standing, she knew he would be able to see her reflection in the glass. Then she realised, that also meant he could also see her staring his way. She turned away, sharply, though keeping him in her peripheral vision. It could, of course, just be coincidence. The Trafford Centre is, essentially, one long mall. It would be quite normal to encounter someone more than once during a visit. But Carver's warning about staying on her guard and keeping her sunglasses and hat on, 'Just in case,' had made her jumpy.

She'd first noticed him in Reiss. As she stood in front of a mirror, idly measuring herself against the dress that had caught her eye, she spotted him lingering behind her. He was staring at her back, or so it seemed. When she turned to give him a look, thinking he was one of those who like to lurk around women's changing rooms, he turned away, quickly, and left the shop. When she came out he was gone. But later, in Boots, as she waited in line to pay for mascara, she saw him again, trying to appear nonchalant as he sauntered passed. A few minutes later, as she made her way towards Selfridges, some instinct caused her to look up. She was certain now it *was* his brown jacket she'd seen slip behind one of Upper Mall's wide pillars. What made him stand out, to her mind, was that though he had followed her route - whether deliberately or not - from one end of the centre to the other, he hadn't bought anything, at least nothing so big as to need a bag. Now, seeing him across the mall again, worried her more than she cared to admit.

She swung her gaze, doing her best to make it appear natural, as she looked to see if he was still there. For a moment her tension eased when she didn't see him. But then, as she extended her sweep, she spotted his cap poking out above the shoppers a few shops further along. Having picked him up again she turned away, quickly, in case her searching glances drew his attention.

Her first thought was to ring Carver. 'Ring me any time,' he'd said, and she remembered him mentioning that his office was, 'not far' from the Trafford Centre. Instinctively, she made to reach for her mobile on the table, but stopped. The thought of him being somewhere close brought some reassurance, and as her initial panic receded - she was in no immediate danger, and was safe around so many people - she decided to wait.

Cyrisse had always been proud of the fact that she wasn't the sort who panicked just because some stranger pays her attention. She had come across, and dealt with, men who would terrify most women in her time. She needed to consider, before calling Carver over something that may be nothing at all. The likelihood was, she was overreacting. The man's recurring appearances could well be coincidental. Apart from his initial lurking in Reiss - where he only *seemed* to be looking at her, and then only for a few short seconds - he had done nothing that proved he was taking a particular interest in her. Nevertheless, she would feel a whole lot better if she saw him head off down the mall and keep going.

Having paid her bill inside, she made ready to leave. Gathering her bags, she rose, at the same time looking across to where she had last seen him. He wasn't there.

She widened her search, but still couldn't locate him. She began to relax. Setting off in the direction she hoped would take her to where she had parked, she made her way back along the upper mall until she reached the central atrium and escalators. She lingered there for several more minutes, mingling with those waiting to rendezvous with partners, families, friends. Eventually, seeing no further sign of him, she became more confident that she *had* been imagining things. Pleased with the way she had kept her nerve, she headed for the car park.

The Trafford Centre's lower-level car park is the size of several football pitches. Unfamiliar with the lay-out, and still a little distracted, Cyrisse spent fifteen minutes marching up and down the rows, looking for her car. She was beginning to think it had been stolen when she finally stumbled across it. Heaving a sigh of relief, she got in, manoeuvred out of the space, then spent a further frustrating few minutes going around in circles looking for the exit.

'Merde,' she fumed, as she passed down the same line of cars for the third time. 'Who designed this place?'

But she drew comfort from the fact that she wasn't the only one finding the lay-out confusing. The young man in the red car she was passing for the third time, seemed to be having as much difficulty finding the exit as she.

Eventually, she found it. As she drove out, she spotted an overhead sign that read 'Salford' and followed it, heading in the direction she hoped would take her back to her temporary home.

CHAPTER 55

Carver was on the phone to The Duke when the knot of senior police and fire officers exited onto the car park to compare notes. Not wanting to be drawn in, he slipped around the corner, out of sight.

'It's a professional job alright,' he continued. 'And it wouldn't have come cheap.' As The Duke digested what he had been told so far, Carver glanced back around the corner. The fire officers were talking amongst themselves while the police team were still discussing jurisdiction. Earlier, he'd heard, Barry Tudor pushing for the investigation to be left in the hands of the local CID, referring to the number of investigations his Major Crime Team were already conducting. But his ACC was talking Security Breaches, Special Branch and Professional Standards. Everyone was aware there could be some sort of, 'inside angle'. Carver stayed out if it. He had other things to think about.

When The Duke asked about how the attackers had entered, Carver described the scene and the abandoned equipment. 'I've spoken to the first response officer. He was on-scene at five-oh-four, twelve minutes after the alarm activated, but didn't see any drive-away. Whoever it was, they knew exactly what they had to do, and how long they had to do it.'

'Twelve minutes?' The Duke said. 'That's bloody tight.'

'But long enough,' Carver said. 'They obviously knew they had that sort of time. The site is tucked away at the back of a business park.'

The Duke listened as Carver filled him in on the rest of the details. 'Let me know when Broom gets here. You may need some support.'

'Thanks,' Carver said. 'In the meantime, I'm sticking to the line it was an NCA archive and that some Crime Target must have contracted it.' He checked again to make sure no one was near. 'The worrying thing is, how they knew about it in the first place.' He hesitated, reluctant to voice his conclusion. 'There's a leak somewhere, John.'

'If that's right, and I think it is, there's something else you need to be thinking about as a priority.'

'What?' Carver said. He had already thought of several things.

'Someone's pulling out all the stops to prevent things coming out. A fire bomb might just be the start.'

It took Carver a couple of two seconds to catch on. When he did he wondered why the hell it hadn't been the first thing he'd thought of.

'*Christ*. Cyrisse. I'll get back to you, John.'

Ending the call, he brought up her number and hit 'dial'. It rang out, unanswered. 'Shit.' He peered around the corner again. Someone pointed at him and he snapped his head back. He started jogging, clumsily in his boots, to where he'd parked. Somewhere behind a voice echoed.

'Hey, Carver.'

He ignored it.

CHAPTER 56

By the time Cyrisse pulled onto the car park, she was tired, stressed and looking forward to a long, hot bath. She'd missed her turn on the M60 and ended up driving all the way round before even realising. With what should have been a fifteen-minute journey taking nearer two hours, the day was close to being a complete disaster. Hopefully the bottle of Rioja that was her last purchase before leaving the Trafford Centre, would go some way towards saving it.

Before she got out, she rang Andrew again. He had called just after she left the car park and they had spoken several times since. He'd wanted to speak with her about the deal with LaFayette, and she needed to tap into his knowledge of Manchester's daunting road network. His Fine Arts degree was from Salford University. He picked up at once.

'It is alright, *cheri*. I am home, at last.' In response to his enquiry she said, 'No-no, I am fine,' then laughed. 'It was not your fault. I should have been paying more attention to where I was going. I will call again tomorrow.'

Leaving her car, she headed towards the walkway between the blocks. As she neared the path, she passed a red sports car that seemed somehow familiar. Tired and anxious to get in, she didn't give it another thought.

Eventually, Cyrisse stopped trying to juggle the several shopping bags while she wrestled with the door key. After weeks of non-use, the lock was still stiff - another of the flat's many annoyances. She put her bags down and tried again. After several attempts it turned, and she pushed the door open. She stepped into the hallway, swung the bags in off the step, and went straight to the alarm panel on the wall just inside the kitchen.

About to key in the number, she stopped. The System Status indicator read 'Standing by.' For several seconds she puzzled over it, trying to remember if she had forgotten to set it on her way out. She took a deep breath, exasperated by yet another hiccough in her day's routine. Which was when she noticed the smell. It wasn't the one she had come to associate with the flat, and definitely hadn't been there before. Her senses pricked up at once and some instinct led her to suddenly dredge up an image of the red car she had seen on the car park below. As she focused on it for the first time, she suddenly remembered why it had seemed familiar. In that moment another image came to her.

A young man in a red car, like her, searching for the car park's exit. But as they pass, he turns his face away. There was no sign of a baseball cap. But the collar of his jacket was- brown.

She froze. The flat was deathly quiet. The nearest room was a bedroom, on the right, a few yards down the hall. But before that, was a storage cupboard, the door of which was hanging open slightly, the catch not engaged. She had run the vacuum round before she left that morning and she was sure she had shut it properly.

She remembered having to shove the door hard, against the hoover to get it to close. It could have sprung open, she supposed, but then remembered the alarm.

Her breath caught in her throat as she reached into her handbag, feeling for her mobile. She was unsure what her next move would be. Thoughts of flight conflicted with those telling her she was imagining things again. But she needed the reassuring confirmation that she was only the press of a button away from Carver's voice. Her hand touched cold plastic but it felt unfamiliar. She pulled it out and saw not her phone, but the personal attack alarm Carver had given her. Then she remembered. After speaking to Andrew, she'd put her phone back on the passenger seat as she reached into the back for her shopping. It was still there.

She looked at the alarm again. The smell she'd noticed as she came in, seemed stronger now. She looked round. The door to the cupboard was opening, slowly.

As Cyrisse screamed and started to turn, the door swung wide. She ran for the front door, her only means of escape. But she had forgotten her shopping bags, still on the floor. As her feet tangled up in them, she started to fall. Even as she did, she pressed her thumb to the alarm's red button.

Nothing happened.

She hit the floor, hard. But before she could move to get up, something heavy landed on her, crushing her down again. The smell was all around her now, and as she felt something loop and then tighten around her throat, she tried to scream again.

But this time no noise came.

CHAPTER 57

Carver didn't bother with the car park but stopped behind the two police cars parked nose to nose right outside the apartment block. As he ran into the lobby two concerned-looking residents, a middle-aged man and an older woman were stood in their doorways, talking to each other. They stopped as he rushed in and watched him take the stairs three at a time. On the first-floor landing, a uniform PC was speaking to a small group of people.

'DCI Carver,' Carver said, brushing past the officer's outstretched arm. For a moment, the PC looked as if he might try to stop him, but he read the look in Carver's face and didn't.

In the doorway, Carver stepped over the tangle of shopping bags and their strewn-about contents and went straight in. As he came through into the living room, two police officers, a man and a woman, jumped up, alarmed by his sudden arrival.

'How is she?' he said. 'Is she alright?'

Cyrisse Chaterlain was on the sofa, with her legs up. As she turned towards him, his breath came out in a rush. *Thank Christ.* He gulped air as the woman officer answered.

'She will be.. sir?' She tried to look reassuring, turned to Cyrisse. 'How you feeling now, love?'

Cyrisse nodded, weakly. Even paler than normal, he could see she was still in shock. Her hands shook as she tried to raise a glass of water to her lips. The WPC reached over to help steady it.

Carver moved round the sofa so Cyrisse could see him. 'Can you tell me what happened?'

She opened her mouth to speak, but then doubled up as the shakes took her and she put a hand to her face.

'Give her a couple of minutes,' the WPC said. 'She's still coming round.'

Carver nodded. Across the room, her partner caught his eye, nodded to the door. Carver followed him out onto the landing.

'From what we can gather,' the PC said. 'She sussed someone was in the flat when she arrived home.' He pointed to the cupboard. 'Seems he was hiding in there. She tried to run but he jumped out and grabbed her. There was a struggle, here.' He indicated the scattered shopping. The old guy next door heard a scream and came out just as her attack alarm went off.' He gave a wry grin. 'Nearly gave him a heart attack he said. My mate's in there now taking his statement. The bloke ran off soon as the alarm sounded.' The PC had it in his hand, passed it to Carver. 'She says it didn't go off at first. I think the battery mustn't have been connecting properly and the jolt of her hitting the floor set it off.' He gave a rueful stare. 'She's a lucky woman.'

'Tell me about it,' Carver said, running his hand through his hair. His mind was racing. The PC said something Carver didn't hear.

'Sorry?'

'I said, all we could get out of her was that you put

her up in the flat and we were to call you.' Carver nodded. 'Witness, is she?'

Carver looked at him but said nothing. Neil Booth would go ape when he heard his safe house was blown. He dug out his card and handed it to the PC. 'Thanks for what you've done. But I need to move her, now. Can I leave you to carry on here while I do the necessary?'

The PC took the card, read it. He was young enough to be impressed. 'No problem, sir. The local CID are on their way as well. I'll let you know what we come up with.'

About to move back inside, Carver stopped, turned back to the PC. 'Hang on. How did she know someone was inside?'

'The smell,' Tim said.

Carver looked puzzled and Tim beckoned him back into the hallway. He opened the door to the cupboard and sniffed. Carver leaned in and did the same. It was faint now, but there was no mistaking it.

Petrol.

'Where're we going?' Cyrisse said. It was the first time she'd spoken since he'd sent her off to pack, "just the essentials".

'My place.' As he answered, he checked his mirror for the umpteenth time. He was taking no chances.

After a few minutes, she said, 'I heard you talking to the other officer about something else that's happened today? What was that?'

He glanced at her, then turned his eyes back on the road. 'Nothing you need to worry about. But it looks like the worms are coming out of the woodwork.' He caught her mystified look. 'They're coming out into the open.'

'So they came for me?'

He pressed a hand over hers, on her lap. 'Don't worry. From now on I'm going to make sure someone is with you at all times.'

A minute passed. 'How long will this go on?' she said

All he said was, 'We'll see.'

Twenty minutes later, Carver remembered to go before her as he showed her into his flat. It gave him the chance to grab the couple of beer cans and near-empty bottle off the table next to the sofa, and remove the un-ironed shirts from the back of one of the chairs. As he took them into the kitchen he called back. 'Sorry about the mess. I didn't get a chance to tidy up before I went out this morning.'

'Don't worry,' she said, smiling weakly. 'My mother always complained that I could not possibly be her daughter.'

As Carver returned from the kitchen and saw her standing there, looking vulnerable and scared, he felt the impulse to give her a reassuring hug, but decided against.

'The second bedroom isn't much, but it will do for tonight. Let me show you.'

As he squeezed passed her, he caught a whiff of her perfume. Close to, she was even more attractive than he'd thought.

After pointing out the bathroom and fetching her towels from the airing cupboard, he left her to make herself comfortable. Before leaving the Salford safe house, he'd rung The Duke and Jess and brought them up-to-date. Now he called them again, arranging a meet the next day to agree their next move. Speaking to Jess, the thought occurred she sounded distracted. But when he asked, all she said was, it was disorienting that they had no way of knowing what might happen next. Carver agreed. Even when chasing down Edmund Hart, or trying to make sense of the Worshipper Killings - before Megan Crane's unmasking - he'd never experienced such a sense of not being in control, of having to sit on the side-lines while the game went on, waiting to see what might happen. It wasn't a pleasant feeling.

As he put his phone away, Cyrisse appeared from the bedroom. She'd changed into some sort of all-black lounge-wear comprising leggings and a polo-neck top. She was brandishing a bottle of Rioja which she handed to him.

'I don't know about you, but I could do with a drink.'

He managed a half-smile. 'That's a damn good idea.'

Moving to the kitchen, he dug out a couple of glasses. Pouring the second glass, she said something he didn't quite catch. Picking up the glasses, he returned to the living room and was surprised to find her standing in the middle of the room, looking uncomfortable.

'Sorry,' he said, offering her a glass. 'I missed that. What did you-?'

The words died as he realised she was looking over his shoulder, at something behind him. He turned.

The front door was open, Rosanna standing there, bag in one hand, suitcase on the mat next to her. She was staring at Cyrisse. Only then did he remember. In all the excitement, he'd forgotten to check his messages for details of her flight.

'Ros,' he said, and though he knew he'd done nothing to be ashamed of, he felt himself colouring. 'Oh God, I'm sorry.'

He scrambled for the right thing to say next, but even had he managed to think of something, it wouldn't have done any good.

Without taking her eyes of Cyrisse, Rosanna lifted her hand in a gesture that said, 'Stop.'

'Don't tell me,' she said. 'Let me guess.'

Carver saw it coming. *Don't,* he thought. *You mustn't.*

But she did.

'You are one of these, *dominatrices*. Yes?'

CHAPTER 58

It was late in the evening by the time Baggus left Gloucester Central. He was week-end off, but after spending the morning churning over his visit to Jess the day before, he craved some form of 'normality.' Sally was away somewhere, 'Visiting friends,' she'd said. His first port of call was Gloucester's Social Club. But with no home game that weekend, it was dead, so he headed into the office. Weekends are often lively and right then, work - any work - was better than skulking around at home, feeling sorry for himself.

Sure enough, a vicious tie-up burglary out at Abbeymead had everyone running around, not least because of the suggestion that the daughter of the house had been assaulted - though the R-word hadn't been mentioned yet. After authorising an extra team of detectives to be called out and nipping in the bud a dispute with Social Services over who had priority call on the Rape Suite - 'We do. No arguments,' he'd said – he called Peter Kent, the weekend duty-DI, and filled him in. Kent's first question was, what was he doing there?

'Just dropped in,' he said, as if it was what everyone does on their day off.

When Kent arrived, Baggus briefed him up, then hung around to see if there was something he could usefully do. There wasn't. Eventually, seeing his colleague well on top of things, he realised he was surplus to requirements and in danger of getting in Kent's way. As he left the office, he imagined them all thinking, *Sad bastard.*

Driving out the station yard, he knew his getting-stuck-into-work ruse had failed when his mind went straight back to where it had been since he'd left Jess's. Ruminating over Barbara Hawthorn and what, if anything, he could do about Kenworthy, what he *was going to do* about Sally, and also now, what he *should do* about Jess, and her unexpected lodger.

The last thing he'd expected was to find Christo there. And though he'd given her plenty of opportunities to explain, if she'd wanted to, why someone who Barbara kept around to do her bidding was staying with her, she didn't - not even if when he told her, briefly, about Sally. 'Looks like we're both harbouring refugees,' she said, ruefully. When he remarked on it being a strange coincidence how they had both ended up taking in the Hawthorn's former 'servants', she gave a shrug, and challenged him to come up with an alternative explanation. He couldn't. Then she started talking about, 'getting Sally and Christo back together,' which he wasn't sure was what he wanted to hear. Eventually, Jess seemed to realise he was in two minds, if not more, over what to do about Sally. She appeared to have no such confusions over Christo, but made it clear she didn't want to talk about it while he was around, which suited Baggus. It was around then that Christo started floating in and out, making it even more difficult for Baggus to talk freely. He found himself wishing Jess would tell him to fuck off, so he could really open up to her, but she didn't. Likewise, it meant he wasn't able to talk to her about Kenworthy either, though she seemed to pick up on his train of thought when he mused, idly, that, 'Something needs to happen.'

She threw him a piercing look. 'Whatever you may be thinking, Gavin, stay out of it.'

Which was exactly what Sally had said over dinner.

Eventually, he realised. With Christo around, he wasn't going to get what he'd come for. In fact by the time he was ready to leave, he had more questions than when he'd arrived and was thinking he'd wasted his time coming.

But as she showed him to the door, Jess mentioned that Christo had told her he wouldn't be there the next day, and made him promise to call her, 'So we can talk more.'

'Yeah. Right,' he'd said. He realised now, he must have sounded like a petulant schoolboy.

Leaning forward, still clasping her robe about her, she'd kissed him, lightly, on the cheek and ran her hand through his hair. 'You should stick with rugby, Gavin.'

Great, he thought. *Just what I need to hear.*

By the time he pulled onto the small car park across the road from his front door, he was more certain than ever that the weekend had been a complete waste. He still craved the normality that had eluded him, and had already decided that the next day he would ring round some of his mates - the single ones at least - and try and arrange a session in the Cat and Lion so he could get well and truly pissed. Bugger what Sally thought about it.

Passing the bushes that shielded most of the car park from the row of houses opposite, he heard a rustling from somewhere behind and to his left. Before he could turn, something hit him, hard, on the back of the head and he went down. He tried to raise himself but couldn't. Everything was spinning and he felt sick to his stomach. The pain in his head was excruciating. He tried calling out, but either his mouth, or his tongue, or *something,* wasn't working. But he was still conscious enough to realise he was in trouble. It was as if his limbs were stuck in some thick gel that clawed and sucked at him. Suddenly a dark shape – he was too far out of it to make out detail - materialised at the edge of his vision. A second later he felt himself being lifted under his arms and dragged. Bit-by-bit, his senses were going as he slipped further and further towards unconsciousness. However, his sense of smell - always the strongest - was working enough for him to recognise the faint odour that came to him. Petrol.

Then he felt himself falling, but slowly, like in a dream. As he hit the ground again, the little breath left in his lungs was forced out and he lay there, gasping. Nevertheless, feeling the road's rough surface beneath his cheek, his survival instincts kicked in and he realised the danger was still there. Summoning what strength he could, he managed to lift his head enough that he could see his front door, less than the width between rugby-posts distant. It may as well have been a pitch's length. He made one more, supreme effort to raise himself, to drag himself to it. He couldn't. He imagined Sally, inside, waiting for him. He tried to call to her. All he could manage was a barely audible, '-*ally*.'

Somewhere, far away, there came a roaring sound. His confused mind pictured a lion, which made him wonder if he was at the safari park where he used to go with his brother and parents on summer weekends. But then his faculties returned enough for him to recognise it for what it was. An engine, revving. He tried to look towards where the noise was coming from, and as it grew louder he saw a dark shape, bearing down.

The roar turned to thunder.

Baggus's world turned black.

He saw no more.

CHAPTER 59

Jess sat at the window, staring out at the darkening, late-summer sky. Her face was blotchy, her eyes red and raw. The rivers of tears had run dry hours ago. How long she had been there, she had no idea. Time had lost all meaning since the phone call from Whitewell the previous morning telling her about Gavin. She'd been with The Duke, Carver and Alec at the time. An early meet at The Duke's office to agree what to do following the attacks on Carver's office and Cyrisse. As they settled, juggling coffees, notes and printouts, they could not have known that the worst was yet to come. Which it did, ten minutes later. And while right now she was struggling, she had experienced something similar before. During the last, horror-filled twenty-four hours of the Worshipper Enquiry, Megan Crane had claimed the Enquiry's second ASIO, Gary Shepherd, for her penultimate victim. Even now, the impact it had on her, and everyone, was clear in her memory. Shattering, devastating, galvanising.

It was as nothing compared to this.

Shepherd had not been a friend. In fact, he was a scheming, disloyal, misogynistic bully of the worst kind. An enemy of both her and Carver, though he certainly didn't deserve to die, especially that way.

But Gavin Baggus *was* a friend. No, *more* than that. Thinking about it, she wasn't sure how to describe what he was to her. But in the few short weeks they had known each other, she had come to regard him with something more than the simple affection one often has for a colleague. She'd never thought to analyse it, though she was now. There was no escaping their obvious differences, which probably lured them both into thinking they would never be anything other than friends. At heart, Baggus was a down-to-earth rugby-fan who, for all his laddish qualities, was a damned good detective. Yet he was also naive in a way she'd found endearing. She on the other hand, was- Well. that was another good question. Six months ago, she would have known exactly what she was. A right-on, modern-thinking, self-assured young woman with no hang-ups and a promising career beckoning. Someone who had proved herself capable of working alongside the best, was still eager to learn, but whose recent experiences had provided insights into aspects of human behaviour she found both fascinating, and abhorrent. She knew that those experiences had changed her, but how exactly, and what that meant for her future, she was still discovering. In recent times, she'd heard comments from those closest to her - her mother, Carver, Alec Duncan even – implying they could see changes in her. But what those changes were, exactly, they never made clear. The occasions she had tried pinning them down, all she got back was the likes of, 'Dunno really. Just… different.' She didn't press. To do so risked embarrassment, or worse - for them as well as her. She didn't like to think that aspects of her behaviour may be giving rise to concerns amongst those she knew. Nor was it nice to think they might be talking about her behind her back. But there was no denying that the thoughts that had been coming since she'd learned about Gavin, were at odds with the person she thought she was, especially the Jess Greylake that believed, strongly, in the Criminal Justice Process. They concerned those responsible for the Hawthorns, Gavin, maybe others, and what do about them. Alistair Kenworthy featured. It all meant that right now, she was struggling to come to terms not just with what had happened to Baggus, but also its impact upon her.

That she was sad went without saying - devastated more like. But the hole that had opened-up and which was now eating away at her was deeper, darker, than she would expect for someone who was just a colleague. Not for the first time since leaving work early that afternoon, tired of failing to focus on the stuff she knew she should be focusing on, she found herself wondering what may have happened if things between them had run their course - assuming she'd let them run their course, which was by no means a 'given'.

Shifting her gaze to the mobile next to her, she touched a finger to the screen. It lit up with the image she she had found herself being drawn back to more and more over recent days, even before the latest, awful news. Now especially, she wanted - needed - to have it close to hand.

It showed the two of them, arm in arm in Josephine's, the night she first took him there. She, showing off the look that had taken her hours to achieve, him just standing there looking awkward and uncomfortable, but unquestionably the handsomest hunk in the place.

At that moment, the river returned, and burst its banks.

CHAPTER 60

Carver waited for The Duke to finish talking with their Deputy Chief Constable. Over the past minute, his responses had shrunk to 'Yes's, 'No's, and 'Right's. He wanted to get on. They *needed* to get on. Eventually, with a final, 'Will do, Sir,' he hung up. He stayed staring at the phone for a few seconds, then looked up.

'That's it then. As from tomorrow, I'm taking overall charge. Quinlan, The Hawthorns *and* Gavin. Gilleray and Robinson's replacement will assist.'

The previous afternoon, rumours about Robinson had begun. Someone high-up in the Gloucester force had finally rumbled his, 'lack of rigour'. Word was that his first response to the news about Baggus was to suggest, 'it might just be a simple failing-to-stop.' Later, they'd heard that he was to play no further part in the investigation.

Carver kept his response to The Duke's announcement to a muted, 'Fair enough.' Though he'd been anticipating something like it since the attack on Cyrisse - the only question being, when? - now was not the time for smug point scoring of the, '*Should have listened to us to begin with,'* variety. Gavin deserved better. What was needed was that they get on with what needed doing. And with The Duke in charge, it would happen. It was just a shame it had taken an attack on one of their own to get Chief Officers to recognise they needed an SIO willing and able to pull the strands together. To Carver, it had been obvious from the start.

'I'm to meet with the West Mids and Gloucester teams tomorrow to set up a joint enquiry,' The Duke said. He hesitated. 'Do you want to be there?'

Carver shook his head. The night before, lying in bed following another difficult evening - Cyrisse was still there, though not for much longer, hopefully - he'd decided what he had to do. Even before the news about Gavin he'd been considering it. Now, his mind was clear. But having decided, he needed to keep his head down, give things time to settle. Seeing The Duke looking at him, waiting, he remembered. His former boss was always suspicious when he said little.

'Better if I'm not there,' he said. 'At least to begin with. You'll need time with Gilleray and the others. If I'm around, they may see me as spy.'

The Duke gave a slow nod. 'My thoughts also. But I want you there when we start looking at possible connections, and that won't be long.'

'I'll be ready,' Carver said. 'It'll give me time to see what we've still got.'

The day before, between waiting for more news about what had happened, he'd confirmed to the others that while the paper part of Megan Crane's archive was gone, he'd taken the precaution of backing up some of the data - videos, photographs, scans of letters, other documents - including his charts and analysis. And while they'd lost much - including, sadly, the 'France' folder he'd been about to turn to next, and which had looked particularly interesting - there was still material he hoped may yet shed light on some of those linked to Josephine's, Kenworthy, and maybe others yet to feature.

He was making ready to leave when a knock came on the door.

Alec Duncan popped his head round. Seeing them both, he said. 'A couple of things Guv'ner?'

The Duke beckoned him in. Alec took the chair next to Carver. He looked uncomfortable.

'First, I'm not sure if you need to know this, or even if it's relevant to anything. In fact I'm not sure if-'

'Tell us Alec,' The Duke said.

He took a breath, looked at Carver. 'I was going to have a word yesterday, but then we heard-'

'FOR FUCK'S SAKE-'

'Right. Jess mentioned yesterday that she spoke to Gavin on Saturday, and that she thought he was still struggling. About the Hawthorn woman, and him being taken off the enquiry and everything?' Carver and The Duke nodded. 'Do you know how she spoke to him?'

Carver thought about it, shrugged. 'Telephone I assume, why?'

'Actually, he visited her flat.'

'How do you know?'

'Because Gavin rang me later on that evening. He sounded pissed and said he was worried about something and wanted someone to know but didn't think he should ring you and wanted my opinion.'

Carver frowned. 'Worried about what?'

Alec sat forward. 'When he got to Jess's, that Christo bloke was there. You know, the one who-'

'I know him,' Carver said.

'Gavin said he was staying there. He didn't know how come or anything, and Jess didn't say, but-'

The Duke flared up. 'She never said anything yesterday about him staying with her. They're not shagging as well are they?' The previous day, Jess had mentioned about Baggus, 'taking Sally in'. He turned to Carver. 'What the fuck's going on?'

Carver took his time. For Sally and Christo to both end up staying with the two officers at the heart of their former employers' murders, was a strange coincidence, if it *was* coincidence. He'd always trusted Jess's judgement, implicitly. Yet over the time they'd worked together, particularly the last twelve months or so, he'd sensed changes in her. Small things mainly. Some to do with her appearance - hair, makeup, clothes - others her manner. She was a lot more self-assured these days, though he'd expect that given her growing experience. He remembered the state Christo was in the morning after the Hawthorns.

'I'm not sure,' Carver said to The Dukes question. 'Maybe she's just helping him through a difficult time.'

Hearing Alec's cough, they turned to him.

'Gavin said Christo came out of Jess's bedroom. He said he was, "hot and sweating."
Apparently, he kept hanging round when they were talking, like he was trying to pick stuff up. Gav said he wasn't happy him being there, that it didn't feel right.'

'Jealous?' The Duke said.

'Could be,' Carver said. 'But so far, Gavin's instincts have been spot on, every time.'

As The Duke stared at Alec in stony silence, Carver could almost hear the cogs whirring. A detective getting involved with a murder witness, for any reason, was never good. And he should know. It was why he'd rung The Duke on the way back to his house with Cyrisse. In her case the circumstances warranted it. But he wasn't sure about Jess taking Christo in, nor Baggus and Sally. In the silence that followed, the three men looked from one to the other.

Eventually, Carver said, 'Leave it with me. I'll speak with her.'

The Duke nodded. 'Good. What was the other thing, Alec?'

Alec turned to Carver. 'That Aston you asked me to check out? The one from Kenworthy's?' Carver nodded. 'It's registered to a car dealership owned by a bloke called Eddie Sullivan. He owns a string of garages in and around London. Some are on record with C-Eleven as being a bit sus. Car-ringing, that sort of thing. He's got form for a bit of violence and thieving going back, but nothing recent. He appears straight now, but he's known to still have connections to some pretty bad people. Traffickers, pimps, suppliers, you know.'

'A fixer-type,' Carver said.

'Exactly,' Alec said. 'So I spoke to a mate of mine in The Met and asked him to do a bit of digging.'

'And?'

'And he's just come back to me. It seems Sullivan has been suspected of brokering contracts in the past. Gangland hits mostly, but not always.' Carver's eyebrows lifted. 'He says Sullivan was supposed to know someone who specialises in-' Alec paused for effect. 'Accidents.'

Ten minutes later, as Carver left Warrington to get back and see how Cyrisse's latest re-location was going, his mind was full of questions. Some were around Jess and Christo, but mostly they were to do with Alistair Kenworthy, and Eddie Sullivan.

For the final time, Megan Crane leafed through the

pages of the book she'd got Collette to order for her off the net, rather than go through the Prison Library system. For the time being at least, she preferred that her reading list remain private. Lawrence Taylor's, 'Born to Crime' had proved a fascinating, if difficult, read. Still regarded as one of the seminal works on the biological predisposition of people to kill, she wished she'd known of it years ago. Given what it said about how repeat-killers share similar motivational responses to non-offending schizophrenics and corporate high-achievers, she was more convinced than ever that what her instincts had always told her were correct. The only difference between her and the high-libido-index scorers Taylor studied was, she was open about believing in the morality of summary justice – up to and including the death penalty. As Taylor pointed out, it was the accepted way in feudal times. Even today, it is the mainstay through which some societies maintain family and social traditions. And if it's good enough for them, then it was certainly good enough for her.

When she first researched background reading to give her some idea of what to expect – and therefore how to prepare herself – for her forthcoming excursion to Lydia Grant's lab, she had no idea of how stimulating such dry academic volumes could be. True, Taylor's work was probably the most graphically-written of the several studies on psycho-biology now stacked neatly on the shelf above her bed, but that didn't detract from its relevance.

Replacing the book in its allotted place – she would not need to refer to it again - she checked herself in the mirror one last time before heading down to join the others.

CHAPTER 61

The room was painted in plain pastel-pink and simply furnished - green-leatherette armchairs, arranged around a circular coffee table. Carver and Jess were waiting by the window when one of the room's two doors opened and the gangly figure of Baggus's Gloucester DI colleague, Peter Kent, came in. He held up a large brown envelope.

'Sorry to take so long,' he said. 'Took me a while to track it down.'

Returning to their seats, Carver said, 'Thanks for this. I know some of your team think that if he hadn't come to us, it would never have happened.'

Kent waved it away. 'Bollocks. Gavin knew what he was doing, and he's been proved right. Wasn't you ran him over.'

'Even so, we appreciate it.'

'Besides,' Kent said. 'Gav would want me to give you any help you need. From what he said, you're the only one knows how it all fits together.'

'He said that?

Kent nodded. 'Spoke to him Sunday night, just as he was leaving the office, before… He was still hoping you might get something out of that Megan Wottserface.'

Despite everything, Carver managed a half-smile. Kent's affability was a welcome change to what they'd had to put up with from Robinson. But Kent's words surprised him. Since the day he'd blocked Baggus's plea to drag Kenworthy in, he'd assumed the younger man had written him off.

Carver and Jess sat forward as Kent emptied the envelope containing Baggus's 'personal effects' onto the table. They consisted of a Seiko watch, a calfskin wallet, some cash in a plastic envelope, a signet ring, a gold chain and a wedge of papers. Carver went for the papers, Jess his wallet. The papers were mainly receipts, along with some match-ticket stubs, and several hand written notes on pages torn from a notebook. But as he leafed through them, disappointment began to take hold. He'd been hoping he might come across something that would have meaning only for him. He shook his head. 'Nothing,' he said, flatly.

'Nor here,' Jess said, equally disappointed.

'There is one thing,' Kent said. He fished in a pocket, drew out a photograph. 'We're still doing his mobile. This is a picture we've taken off it. We're wondering if you may know who it is?' He showed it to them.

Taken during dinner, a blond woman raising her glass to the camera.

Carver cast his mind back. He had seen her only once, and then briefly, through an interview room window. But she looked different somehow. He turned to Jess. 'It's Sally isn't it?'

Jess nodded. 'Yeah, but she looks a lot older. A mature woman I'd say.'

'Who is she?' Kent said.

'The girl who was staying with him,' Jess said

'What girl? There was no girl there when we arrived.'

Jess stared at him, then recounted what Baggus had told her about taking Sally in.

Kent shook his head. 'There's been no mention of her, far as I know.'

Carver said, 'Wasn't it her rang the police?'

'His next-door neighbour rang it in after he heard the bang'

Carver looked from Kent to Jess. 'So where is she?'

'You think something could have happened to her as well?' Kent said.

'I don't know, but someone ought to be considering the possibility.'

Kent jumped up. 'I need to ring this into the MIR.' He held out a hand. 'May I?' Jess passed across the photograph.

After he'd gone, Carver turned to Jess. 'I thought they knew about Sally?'

'So did I,' she said, puzzled.

Reminded of the Hawthorns servants, Carver remembered his last conversation with The Duke. The one about her and Christo. They'd travelled down in separate cars. This was his first chance to speak with her. 'There's something I need to talk to you about.'

She turned to him. 'Like what?'

'I believe that you and-'

The door to the adjoining room opened. An Asian man wearing a white coat appeared.

'We've finished now, if you'd like to come back in?'

Jess looked at Carver. He shook his head. *Later.*

They followed the man back through. The room was in semi-darkness, the only light coming from the small reading lamp above the bed, the bank of monitors next to it.

Carver looked around. 'Where are they?'

'Gone to get something to eat,' the man said.

Carver nodded. He'd met the family - parents, brother and sister earlier. Some or all had been in attendance since it happened. As he stood at the foot of the bed, looking down at the figure on it, with its several IV tubes and wires running off, Jess moved round to the side. She placed a hand on the one resting on the sheet, ran her fingers down his cheek. The man in the white coat, Doctor Anwar Singh, Senior Neurosurgeon at Bristol's Frenchay Hospital, came to stand at Carver's shoulder. Carver had heard he'd not left the hospital since he'd operated on the Monday morning.

'How is he Doctor? Any changes?'

'He remains stable, but still critical.'

Carver nodded. *Bastards.* 'Is there anymore yet about how he might be if- When, he comes out of it?'

Singh rested a hand on his shoulder. 'Like I told the family, right now we're concentrating on keeping him stable. When we're ready, and he's strong enough, we'll start to try to bring him out of the induced coma. But it will be a slow process, and until he's awake we can't begin to assess brain damage.'

Jess looked up. 'You mentioned the extent of the skull fractures. Does that make permanent damage more likely?'

Even in the semi-dark, Carver could see the tears that had never been far away the last few days.

The doctor looked sympathetic. 'It really is impossible to say. I've seen more serious injuries where there was no permanent damage at all. But also the reverse. You can't always tell.

'And his kidneys?' Carver said.

'The one we managed to save is functioning at about seventy-percent. If we can get it up to ninety, it will be enough.'

Jess sniffed, nodded. 'Thanks, Doctor. We know you are all doing everything you can.'

'And we will continue to do so.' he said.

After the surgeon had left, Jess continued to stroke Baggus's cheek. A minute later she bent down and whispered something in his ear. Carver couldn't hear above the hisses, clicks and hums of the equipment keeping him alive, but wasn't about to ask. A minute later she came to stand next to him, looking down on the young man clinging on to life.

'We're going to have these bastards,' she said.

Carver turned to her. He'd never heard that tone in her voice before. Seeing the steely determination in her face, he remembered their interrupted conversation. But it wasn't the moment to start quizzing her about her private life. Still sniffing, she began searching through her bag, but found only a scrappy tissue.

'Back in a few minutes,' she said.

Alone with Baggus for the first time, Carver regarded the man whose dogged refusal to take 'no' for an answer, had catapulted him back into the darkness that surrounded Megan Crane's affairs. He did so without resentment. Since first meeting the young detective whose enthusiasm for stone-turning reminded him, in many ways, of himself, Carver had been conscious that he would soon have to start shedding light on that darkness. For too long, people had used it to their advantage. Some had done so simply to preserve their privacy, and there was nothing wrong with that. But others had used it as a blanket, to keep hidden from the world activities, behaviours - crimes - that rightly needed exposing. Well the time had come.

Standing there, alone in the semi dark, he made his

oath.

'Like she said, Gavin. We're going to have them. Starting now.'

Drawing out his mobile, he made the call.

CHAPTER 62

As Carver waited for the man on whom he'd called to return - 'Excuse me, I need to take this call,' - he used the time to gauge what, if anything, the study's contents said about its owner. His conclusion was, *not much.*

The mix of rosewood - desk, bookcases - and green leather - swivel chair, Chesterfield - put Carver in mind of the sort of adverts that appear in the back pages of Sunday newspaper magazines. The sort, self-styled executives look at and think, *that's so me,* without realising it says nothing at all, apart from that they've more money than sense. Even the books – some literary fiction, glossy travel, volumes with titles including words like, "Policing", "Crime", "Society" - looked like they'd been chosen to portray a rock-solid professional, but one not wholly obsessed with work. It made him think of his own, former-Chief Constable-father's 'den' at their old house. 'Shabby chaos' was how Carver remembered it, but it said more about Peter Carver than the carefully-orchestrated display around him.

One exception. Amongst the bric-a-brac, funky matchbox-toy cars and policing memorabilia on show, was a six-inch high ebony figurine of a naked woman. Kneeling with her head bowed and wearing a blindfold, her hands were restrained behind. Carver had seen such artefacts before, either in places like Josephine's, or the homes of those who don't care if the world knows their interests.

He'd just completed his search for similar items - there weren't any - when his host came back.

'My apologies,' Martin Gardener, said as he returned to his chair. 'There's a firearms incident brewing.'

The way he wafted a hand, like it was no big deal, Carver saw it as more image-management. *Firearms Incidents? Ten-a-penny.* But then he reminded himself. He oughtn't be biased.

'Now,' Gardener said, making a point of seeming relaxed. 'What's so sensitive you thought we should meet here, rather than my office?'

Carver saw it for what it was - an act. Gardener would know full-well, at the very least suspect, the reason behind Carver's visit.

'We need to talk about your relationship with Megan Crane. And your past associations with Josephine's.'

Gardener didn't so much freeze, as simply become slower in his reactions and movements – much slower.

He met Carver's gaze, and his tone was even when he said, 'That's a huge statement, Mr Carver. I hope you have something to back it up.'

'I nearly didn't. But thankfully, not everything was lost in the fire.'

Gardener's response took longer coming than it should have done.

'What fire?'

Carver sighed. 'I'm not trying to trick you into saying anything. When the time comes, the facts will speak for themselves. But you need to know, I know about the Coopers.' The lines about Gardener's mouth tightened.

'And I know what they were into, and who with.' His jaw jutted. 'I know they introduced you to Megan Crane, and that you used to call on her.'

Gardener hesitated, then reached for the tea-cup his wife had brought in along with Carver's coffee, soon after Carver arrived. He drained the dregs, then returned it to its saucer. For a moment, he appeared to sink down into the chair, his large head settling deep between his shoulders. *Accepting defeat? Already?* But Gardener hadn't fought his way to ACC by not being resilient. Suddenly, he drew himself up, sat forward and faced Carver, squarely.

'Have you ever done something you've always regretted, Mr Carver?'

At that moment, Angie's face swam before Carver eyes. He did his best to ignore it. The mistake that would stay with him forever hadn't come out during Edmund Hart's trial. And though Gardener might, possibly, have learned of it through Megan, he doubted it. Even during her trial, she had not shared the knowledge to which only three people - now only two - had ever been party. Carver had never worked out why.

As if guessing his thoughts, Gardener said, 'I'm sorry. Silly question.' He moved on, 'Megan Crane is an incredible woman, don't you think?'

''Incredible' isn't the word I'd use.'

Gardener twitched a smile which Carver assumed was meant to be ironic. 'Perhaps not. Nevertheless, she is capable of some remarkable things. Such as getting people to do things they would never normally contemplate.'

Carver held his gaze. 'I'm not here to judge. I'm just trying to resolve things.'

Gardener looked up at the ceiling, then back to

Carver. 'And there's the difficulty. How *do* we, resolve it? How does someone in my position disclose that he was once involved with a woman who was killing people, and whose boyfriend was killing even more?'

'I'm not asking you to disclose anything. I'm here to tell you to have no further involvement in the ongoing investigations.'

Gardener looked sceptical. 'And how do I do that? I'm ACC Ops for God's sake.'

Carver shrugged. 'Pass it on. Declare a conflict of interest. Take some leave. Whichever suits.'

'And what difference would that make? It would come out anyway.'

Carver found Gardener's fatalism surprising. For the first time he wondered if he might be missing something. 'We live in liberated times. A taste for adventurous sex isn't the career-killer it used to be.'

Gardener snorted. 'For someone who's supposed to be expert in these things, you're very naive.' Suddenly he checked himself, as if a thought had come. When he looked up, there was a wariness in his eyes that hadn't been there before. 'Apart from my relationship with Megan Crane, what else do you know?'

Sensing Gardener about to haggle, Carver suddenly realised. It wasn't just his association with Megan Crane he was worried about. There was something else. As Carver pondered, he saw Gardener drawing strength from his silence, as if thinking he might ride it out. Carver's instincts took over.

'I know about the video.'

Gardener barely managed to stop his face crumbling. After a few moments during which he looked like he was hoping Carver might retract his words, he slumped back in the chair. Carver's mind raced as he saw the effect of his gamble. *What the hell does it show?*

Eventually Gardener looked up, and as Carver saw the look in his face, he wondered if the man had ever worked CID. An experienced detective would have at least considered the possibility of a bluff, and tried to call it. Carver was glad he hadn't.

'You've seen it?' A note of resignation in his voice.

Carver rode his luck. 'Let's just say, I know about it.'

Gardener breathed long and deep. 'For what it's worth, I didn't want them to do it. I told them they didn't have to.'

Carver didn't dare say anything. For almost a minute he watched as Gardener stared at the top of his desk, rubbing his chin between finger and thumb. Eventually he looked up, out of options.

'You can have the Hawthorn Investigation, Mr Carver. It doesn't matter anymore.'

'What about Kenworthy?'

'What about him?'

'How far is he involved in all this?'

Gardener looked thoughtful. 'I'm not sure where a response to that question would leave me. Let me think on it.'

Carver resisted the temptation to push further. He couldn't risk showing how little he knew. Nevertheless he wondered what Gardener needed to think on. *Let him stew.* He moved to rise, satisfied he'd loosened the first brick. With luck, the rest would soon follow. But as he stood up another thought came to him.

'When did you last have contact with Megan Crane?'

Gardener's eyes narrowed. 'A couple of years ago. Why do you ask?'

'Do you know about the research she's involved in?'

'Research?'

'Someone's researching profiling. For the Home Office. She's the subject.'

The way Gardener stared at him, blinking but saying nothing, Carver sensed cogs falling into place. But for once the ACC managed to keep his thoughts hidden. 'No, I didn't know about it.' Then, almost as an aside, he added, 'But I wouldn't bank on seeing any result.'

As he said it, Carver thought he saw a flash of something - *amusement?* - before the serious look returned.

'Why do you say that?'

'Let's just say I'll be surprised if it ever gets finished.'

Carver pressed him to say more, but Gardener had said as much as he was going to say and ushered Carver to the door.

'Goodbye, Mr Carver. I'll let you know about Kenworthy.'

As the ACC's converted-farmhouse-home receded in his mirror, Carver's mind was alive with questions. Not about Gardener giving way on the Hawthorn investigation, nor the mysterious video recording the man clearly knew was damning. Nor even, about Kenworthy. His thoughts were around why Gardner doubted that Lydia Grant would ever get to complete her research.

CHAPTER 63

When Carver arrived home, Rosanna was already in bed. It wasn't eleven o'clock yet. She was a night owl. Most nights she stayed up long after midnight, reading, listening to her music. Clearly, she was as tired of arguing as he was. Since her return, they had barely stopped.

The trigger, of course, was finding Cyrisse there when she arrived home. That and the fact that he was, in her words, 'involved with these women again.' It got worse when he told her he'd been back to see Megan Crane - a misplaced attempt at openness that rebounded when she whirled on him and said, 'What is it about that woman, you cannot keep away from her? Have you forgotten what she did to me?' And his attempt to claw back some moral high ground by mentioning the time she had spent with, *'Mr Berentes'* while away - but in a way that inferred something he knew he had no right to infer - was clumsy, inept and just plain wrong. The look she sent back signalled it was a grave misstep. The accusation was rooted, he knew, in his own frustrations, fuelled by the doubts he always suffered whenever the subject of his, 'relationship' with Megan Crane cropped up. But his *relationships* weren't the only issue. His confession that he had not yet got around to looking at the house in Wales as he had promised, allowed her to resurrect the topic he could never counter. His work always took priority over their private lives. This time, her, 'And you are not even a real detective anymore,' cut deep.

Now, alone in the dark, Carver wondered if the frustrations of the past weeks were a pointer to the future. There had been a time - after all the broo-hah died down, her voice had recovered and enough time had passed for the memory of that awful night to be less vivid - when he thought they were getting back to where they were before it all began, before he ever heard of Megan Crane. He didn't have that feeling now.

It wasn't his only worry.

Digging out his mobile, he rang Cyrisse. Another late-nighter, she picked up at once. He checked first that the City-Centre Hotel they had moved her to was as comfortable as it needed to be, considering what she had been through. Second, he checked that the Close Protection Team were doing their job. She demonstrated they were by opening the connecting door to her room so he could hear the reassuring, 'Everything okay?' from their Team Leader. Carver didn't need to speak with him to reinforce the need to stay alert - they'd been briefed by The Duke himself - but he did anyway. Finally, he did his best to reassure her that her situation would be resolved so she could return to a normal life, 'soon'. She didn't ask when 'soon' would be, which probably meant, either she'd resigned herself to waiting 'as long as it takes', or she no longer trusted his word, - and he wouldn't blame her for that. At least her, 'Thank you for calling,' as he rang off, suggested she hadn't totally written him off, yet.

He poured himself a JD - a large one - then sat and pondered his other worry. It too involved a woman. Jess.

Something about her promise to Baggus that afternoon - 'We're going to have these bastards' - had stayed with him, even though he'd endorsed it. Driving back, he'd put it together with other snippets. Things he'd seen, Conversations over the past months, mostly with The Duke, but not always. Alec had seen things as well. That she was different from how she'd been, was not in doubt. Anyone who knew her two years ago, would tell that just from looking. But the *ways* in which she was different - apart from her appearance - and what it meant in terms of what went on in her head, he could not assess. The Jess he'd first met was relatively simple to figure out. Independent, free-thinking, ambitious to succeed in her chosen profession. He also pegged her as someone who, while keen to see justice done, believed strongly in 'due process', in playing by the rules - at least as far as the 'big stuff' was concerned. After six months working together, he'd felt he understood her enough to share things he'd never shared with anyone - including Rosanna. At that time, he could have predicted how she would react in any given circumstances. That certainty was no longer there. In its place was a nagging suspicion that, first the Hawthorns' murders, now the attack on Baggus, had affected her in ways they wouldn't have done previously. Apart from the obvious grief and sadness, he had no idea what she was thinking, deep down. He certainly couldn't see the Jess he'd once known getting involved with someone like this Christo character- if she *was* involved. Carver had always had a vivid imagination. When he remembered the thought that had come when he saw her looking down at Baggus, swathed in bandages and kept alive by tubes and wires, he hoped it was a case of it running away with itself.

Jess? *No way.*

After several more minutes of, 'what-if', he realised he needed a diversion. Digging out his mobile, he did something he'd only learned to do when Kayleigh Lee showed him how, some months before. He opened-up her feed in the app she'd set up on his mobile one time he called in for coffee. By now he knew more about how it all worked. Both his sisters were big users, and Rosanna used it occasionally, though only for gigs, events, and stuff. His only interest was seeing she was okay. He didn't lurk, nor creep. He didn't even pay particular attention to her posts, the people she was mixing with, or the things she got up to. All he needed was the reassurance of knowing she was getting on with her life. He had no idea what he would do if he ever saw something that gave him real cause for concern. A face he recognised. A reference, verbal or visual, to activities that could spell trouble, now or in the future. Up to now it hadn't happened. If it did, then Hell, he'd deal with it then.

Scrolling through her last few posts, he could see she was still working, communicating with those few she called, 'friends', and concerned about the directions some TV series he'd never heard of was heading. The latter was about the only, 'normal girl stuff,' he knew she was into. Satisfied she seemed to be doing okay, he came out.

He'd only scrolled back a few days. Had he gone further, he may have felt differently.

CHAPTER 64

Assistant Chief Constable Martin Gardener, QPM, put down his pen, folded the paper over and ran his palm, slowly, along the crease. It wasn't a long note, just enough so that the addressee would know what to do. She would be grateful. It had gone on long enough. Placing it into the padded envelope along with the item already there, he ran his tongue along the flap, sealed it, then made sure with cello-tape.

The doorbell rang.

Rising, he went to answer it. As he passed along the hallway a voice drifted down the stairs.

'Who is it Martin?'

'Just work dear,' he said. 'Go back to sleep. I won't be long.'

She didn't enquire further. Wendy Gardener was well-used to the disruptions that came whenever her husband was duty-Chief Officer.

As he opened the door, the yellow-jacketed police-motorcyclist made a half-salute against his helmet.

"Evening Sir. You have some urgent corrie?'

Gardener held out the package. As the PC stepped forward to take it and Gardener saw the big BMW on its stand in the middle of the gravel turning circle, his mind went back to his own brief stint on Traffic. They'd used BMWs back then as well. R80s. Noisy, but fun.

'It needs delivering tonight,' he said. 'It's out of county, but I've authorised it with Control Room. It's not expected so you'll probably have to wake someone.'

Despite the helmet, Gardener saw the glint that came into his eyes as he read the address. The prospect of a long ride through the night clearly energised him.

'Don't worry sir. I'm good at that.'

'I'm sure you are constable. Goodnight, and thank you.'

"G'night, Sir.'

Gardener watched as he mounted his machine, kicked it to life, then took off down the gravel drive with just enough wheel-spin as would look the part, without prompting later adverse comment to his Inspector. As the bike's lights and roar faded into the night, Gardener wondered what it must be like, doing what you love - in this case biking - and getting paid for it. Closing the door, he returned to his study.

Sitting at his desk, he glanced at the framed photograph he'd always kept there. He had done so several times while awaiting Carver's arrival, more since he'd left. His father's retirement-day picture, it showed him in his Inspector's uniform, looking commanding, powerful, as Inspector's were in those days. Back then, an Inspector was God, Chief Constable, just some mythical figure who, when not playing golf, put in occasional appearances at Headquarters between meetings with County Councillors and luncheons with High Sheriffs. Everyone knew it was the Inspector who really ran things. It was the burning desire to match his late-father's achievements that had driven Martin Gardener's thirty-two-year career

The trouble was, by the time of his appointment, things had changed. By then, the Inspector was little more than a shift manager. Superintendent was, The Big One. And that process continued, all through his service. Chief Superintendent, then ACC. Nowadays it seemed like only the rank of Chief Constable itself brought the degree of respect and deference he remembered his father receiving around the market town where he'd grown up.

He knew now he would never make it. His chance had come and he'd blown it. Truth was, he'd probably blown it two years before when his Operations Team let him down so badly that day the Prime Minister visited. He still felt he'd been unjustly blamed for the security breach that allowed three, 'Fathers for Justice' to get close enough to drape their banner round him in front of the cameras. And he suspected that the public dressing-down the Chief got from the Crime Commissioner, together with the more private rebuke sent by the Home Secretary, meant his name would never find its way back onto the *List Of Prospective Chief Constables* kept in the Home Office. Even if, by some miracle, that were not the case, it soon would be. Once everything came out and those Westminster bastards had something juicy to point at, he would be hard put to resist the calls that would come demanding his resignation. And that was assuming the DPP ruled, 'Insufficient Evidence,' on any criminal charges.

To be fair to the detective, Carver, he hadn't threatened to expose him. He didn't need to. Chief Officers are appointed for their supposed ability to see the 'big picture', to be able to sense where things are headed. 'The Helicopter View' some call it. Now, from his own, lofty position, he could see, exactly, where the whole debacle that began with Quinlan and had since escalated way beyond anything anyone had foreseen was headed. With people named, secrets exposed, lives ruined. Martin Gardener QPM amongst them.

As he reflected on it, he shook his head. What comes of allowing himself to be sucked in during the heat of the moment – *Though what a moment.* He had learned since how such things have a way of coming back to bite you. He'd seen it himself, many times. Too late now.

As he studied the picture before him, he imagined the man in uniform looking down on him accusingly, face tinged with disappointment. He thought about the woman asleep upstairs, unaware that the life they had made together, would soon be coming to an end.

Rising, he went over and closed the study door.

CHAPTER 65

Carver was at his desk in his new, temporary office, listening to the young man with the Irish lilt who was trying to talk him through what he had to do. After a minute, Carver said, 'Hang on, Liam. I didn't understand any of what you just said. All I need to know is, how do I find the backup file?' He listened again, shook his head. 'I'm sorry. As far as I'm concerned, a cloud is something in the sky, and a server throws a tennis ball in the air. Tell you what, why don't you come down here, and show me?' He listened as Liam explained, his problem. 'Dublin? So how do we get on-site support?' He was beginning to glaze over when his mobile started ringing. The Screen showed, 'Duke'. 'Never mind. I'll call you back.' He hung up, pressed 'answer'.

'John. How're things? Are you-'

'You've obviously not heard. Martin Gardener's killed himself.'

An hour later, Carver was still in his chair. He hadn't moved since finishing his thirty-minute conversation with The Duke. Much of it concerned the recriminations already flying around the West Midlands Police HQ, some of which would be heading his way. The Duke had called from Warrington. He'd dropped in there before heading down to Gloucestershire. He'd been about to hit the road again when Gilleray rang to tell him Gardener had shot himself. Gardener's wife was saying that Carver was the last person to see her husband alive. Carver could tell that The Duke wasn't happy to learn of it that way.

It took Carver less than five minutes to satisfy himself that in this case it really was suicide, rather than another 'Q'-style set up. Gardener's wife heard the bang around three, but sounding like it was outside, went back to sleep. She wasn't concerned about her husband not being in bed. She assumed he was still dealing with the firearms incident he'd been taking calls about through the night. It was only when she went downstairs to make some tea, that she found him, in his car in the garage, along with his shotgun.

The Duke understood why Carver had kept his visit to Gardener quiet. He even admitted once manoeuvring a Chief Officer into early retirement himself. But suicide was something else. The Duke was anticipating that the next twenty four hours would see all kinds of accusations and inferences, and not just against Carver. His new position as SIO, meant everyone would look to him for explanations. He could only give them if he knew what was happening.

Carver knew he was right, which was why he offered up the only apology he could muster. 'I'm sorry, John. I never saw him as the type to blow his brains out. He must have been in deeper than even I realised.'

'Then you were wrong,' The Duke said. 'Mind, since all this started, a lot of people have been wrong about a lot of things.'

The let-off went some way to easing Carver's

conscience, but not much. He remembered Mrs Gardener's friendly welcome when he'd called on her husband, her nice smile. And the graduation-day photographs on the wall in the hallway. A boy and girl. He was the spit of his dad.

But sympathy for the family and the likelihood of blow-back on himself, weren't all he had to think about. Apart from anything, Gardener's suicide represented yet another dead-end – a literal one in this case. He had hoped that after sleeping on their meeting, Gardener would see sense and call to say he was ready to talk, particularly about Kenworthy. Now he had to look elsewhere, again. Given a free hand, he knew where he would start. A search of Gardener's study, a trawl through his lap-top and an analysis of his mobile data would, he was certain, reveal some clue, however small. But whilst The Duke was of similar mind, he wasn't hopeful.

'Right now, I'd say the chances of getting someone to sign a warrant are about zero. Hell, I'm not sure I'd sign one myself on the basis of what we can prove.'

And though Carver tried pushing it, his instincts told him he was on a loser. 'So what about Kenworthy?'

'What about him?'

'It seems every avenue is being blocked off. I'm beginning to wonder if Gavin wasn't right after all.'

'Pull him in you mean?' Carver stayed silent. It was a big ask. 'If that's all we're left with, then it has to be an arrest. I can't see him, 'helping police with their enquiries,' can you?'

'No,' Carver said. 'I can't'

'So, what have you got?'

Carver thought about it. Good question. What have I got? Tittle tattle from the likes of Cyrisse. A missing girl - Sylvie Tyler - who may, or may not, have something interesting to say about what he did to her. If they tried they could probably find a couple of Josephine's' members willing to describe some of the adventures Kenworthy and they got up to. But, so what?

Eventually, after minutes spent going round in circles, Carver ended with, 'I'm trying to get into my backup files to see what's still there. When I do, I'll look for something we may be able to use, then come back to you.' But he wasn't optimistic. If he'd come across anything that clear during his early trawls through Megan's archive, it would be jumping out at him by now.

But thoughts of Megan's archive had triggered another strand. Starting with the fire-bombing, things had been happening so fast, he'd barely had time to assimilate them. He had a nagging fear more would soon follow. But who, when and where, he couldn't yet say. One thing was for sure. Megan Crane's cryptic-clues showed that she, at least, could say more - if he could get her to. He also remembered Gardener's mysterious allusion to Lydia Grant not being able to complete her research. What was that all about? He didn't waste time trying to think it through. If he did he would end up thinking about Rosanna, and other things that would only distract him. Right now, things were complicated enough.

He brought up Ellen Hazelhurst's number, rang it. After several rings it dropped into voicemail. He left a message asking her to ring him back, then returned to thinking about the permutations that might flow from Gardeners suicide - not least those that may impact on himself. He was still doing so when Alec Duncan rang, from Warrington.

'A woman has just walked into the nick. She's asking to speak to you and says she won't speak with anyone else.'

'Who is it?'

As he liked to do, Alec hesitated, for effect. 'Sylvie Tyler.'

CHAPTER 66

Megan Crane was sitting in front of her mirror, putting the finishing touches to her hair, when Collette Bright appeared, framed in the doorway.

'Ready Megan?'

'I'll be right down.'

For a moment, Collette looked like she might linger, regarding her charge with the strange mix of envy, love, fear - maybe even hate - that Megan knew so well. She had seen it, or most off it, the very first day she arrived at Cloverbank. She knew right then that her stay at HMP Stigwood would not be without hope.

Megan stared, pointedly, at the PO's reflection. She hated being observed whilst getting ready, unless it was part of a scene and the watcher was there only to serve, be sat on, played with, or otherwise used as an accessory. Collette saw the look, hesitated as if not sure, then took herself off back down the stairs.

'Two minutes,' she threw behind her, as if Megan would take any notice.

Megan allowed herself a smile. It was another of the little victories that had fed her hunger these past months. It served to remind her of who, what, she was. Though minor compared to past triumphs, she'd been happy to settle for them, while awaiting the opportunity she knew would one day come. And as she ran through her mental checklist for the final time, her excitement grew. The last week had dragged, expecting to hear any moment that her trip to the University had been cancelled, or that some problem had arisen. Something to do with security, or Prison policy, or Lydia Grant's busy schedule.

But as the day drew near with no sign of any disruption, her confidence had grown. The opportunity she'd known would one day come, looked set to arrive sooner than even she'd expected. She needed to be ready.

Listening out for Collette, she took the bottle of nail-fix from her makeup case, rose and went over to her bed. Reaching down, she felt along the underside of the metal frame. Finding what she was looking for, she picked at the strip of silver duct tape then pulled it away. Stuck to it were the cash-card and craft blade that had arrived only that week, secreted within the covers of the latest addition to her Research Library.

Taking off one of her flat shoes - she wasn't expecting she would be doing any running, but you never know - she pulled back the in-sole, pressed the tape with the card and blade to the underside, then used the nail-fix to glue it back down. Replacing the shoe, she tested it, making sure she could walk without obvious discomfort.

Satisfied, she checked herself in the mirror one last time, as she always did before going out. The white t-shirt and blue jeans were ideal for a university campus, diverting enough for anyone she may come across, but not so much as might draw too much attention.

'Perfect.'

Pausing only to cast her eyes over the room that had been 'home' these past eighteen months, she turned, and headed down to join her escort.

CHAPTER 67

Carver arrived at Warrington Police Station just as The Duke was getting out of his car. Carver's former boss had got as far as Stafford, on the M6, when Alec rang to tell him he needed to return to Warrington to meet Carver, and why.

They found Sylvie upstairs in the CID interview room, where Alec had been plying her with coffee and cake while awaiting their arrival. Once attractive, she now had the drawn, hunted look of a junkie. Her scraggy blond hair, thin face and sunken cheekbones reminded Carver of some of the crack-hounds he'd come across. When he introduced himself, she insisted on seeing his warrant card, taking it off him to study it closely, before handing it back.

'He says I'm not to speak to anyone but you,' she said, eyeing The Duke suspiciously. As she spoke she sniffed and swiped the sleeve of her ragged cardigan across her nose.

Carver explained who The Duke was. 'You can trust him as much as me,' he said.

Eventually, she nodded, though he could see she wasn't sure. He batted on.

'What do you want to tell me, and who is 'he'?'

She met his reassuring smile with a challenging look that told him two things. One, she wasn't about to be rushed. Two, whatever had hold of her, it wasn't just drugs. He could see she was teetering on an edge. He needed to be careful that he didn't scare her off. Eventually, she reached down to the tan shoulder bag at her feet. Pulling out a buff, padded envelope, she handed it to him. It was addressed to her, at a Liverpool address.

'He said I'm to answer any questions you ask me.'

The envelope contained a sealed envelope addressed to "DCI J Carver", a folded sheet of note-paper bearing Sylvie's name, and a CD/data disc in a plastic case. He opened the note, saw it was signed "Martin".

He looked at her, sharply. 'When did you get this?'

'Last night. A police motorcyclist brought it.'

Last night? The last thing he did. He checked the disc. There was no label or marking to indicate its content. His heart thumped. *Could it be..?* He read Gardener's note to her.

Beginning, 'My Dearest Sylvie,' it told her how to find Carver, and instructed her to give him the disc and the envelope. There was reference to money - five hundred pounds - in the envelope, and more that would come her way eventually. The rest of it was a rambling, heartfelt plea for forgiveness, together with assurances that Carver would see she was, 'looked after.' They were the words of a man racked with guilt, but who had settled himself to making amends. He opened the envelope bearing his name.

"By now you will know what has happened. I'm leaving it to you to tell Sylvie. She'll be upset, I think, but not too much. I cannot keep her safe any longer so I'm sending her to you. Look after her. She doesn't know

what she knows. Work it out." It signed off with, *"Fuck you, Carver."*

He passed the letter to The Duke. After he read it, the two men stared at each other, recognising the prospect of an unexpected breakthrough.

At that moment, Carver's mobile rang. The screen read, "Ellen Hazelhurst."

He showed it to The Duke. 'I'll be right back.' He stepped outside .

'Ellen. Thanks for coming back to me. I'm just in the middle of something but I just wanted to let you know. I may need to come and see Megan Crane again.' He remembered about Gardener's doubts concerning Lydia Grant ever finishing her research. 'There's something else I need to talk to you about as well, but I'll tell you when I see you.'

'That's fine, but if you're thinking of coming today, I'm afraid you won't be able to.'

'Why's that?'

'She's just left to go to the University.'

Carver's first thought was he'd misheard her. 'Say that again? It sounded like you said she's gone somewhere.'

'I did. She's with Doctor Grant, under escort obviously. She's putting her through some neuro-psycho testing for her research.'

'WHAT? Where?'

'The University. At her laboratory.'

It took Carver a couple of seconds, then, 'Please tell me that's a joke.'

'Pardon me? There's no need to-'

'You're allowing Megan Crane out, to be examined at a *University?'*

'Don't make it something it isn't, Chief Inspector.

You know full well that prisoners are often allowed out, for all sorts of reasons.'

'Yes, but not-'

'There's no need to be concerned. We've done a three-hundred-and-sixty RA. Route, Site, Objective and Contingencies. It's a Standard Operating Procedure. There's no need-'

'The University's an open site. How the hell can you predict-'

'The Campus Security Manager was involved in the Risk Assessment. He and his team are quite confident that-'

'Ellen, they work at a University. They're not equipped to deal with the likes of Megan Crane.' His frustrations started to boil. 'Christ, I don't believe this.' About to delve deeper into the hows and whys, he realised. It wouldn't change anything, and the clock was ticking.

'How many escorts?'

'Two.'

'Both female?'

'She isn't a big woman, Mr Carver. She hardly needs-'

He breathed deep, bringing his voice down. 'Would you mind giving me the details?'

She hesitated, reluctant now, he was sure. But if she refused, and something did happen…

A minute later, he had what he needed. 'Thank you.'

'If you are thinking of doing any-'

He rang off.

He returned to the interview room, popped his head round the door. 'John? A minute?'

The Duke joined him outside. Carver briefed him on what he'd learned.

'A University laboratory? You're kidding.'

They returned to Sylvie. She looked worried. 'Is something wrong?' she said.

'Nothing you need to be concerned about.'

He picked up the plastic case, handed it to The Duke. He was desperate to know what was on it. It would have to wait. He squatted beside the girl, took her hand.

'Sylvie, I need you to do exactly as I say. Go with John here,' he nodded to The Duke. 'He will look after you. Don't worry about anything. I will be back as soon as I can.'

She looked up at The Duke, probably wondering if he was as intimidating as his size suggested. She sniffed again, nodded.

'I'll let you know,' The Duke said waving the plastic case.

'Me to,' Carver said. Pausing only to give Sylvie a last reassuring smile, he left. As he closed the door, he heard The Duke saying, 'When did you last have a proper meal?'

Heading into Manchester on the M62, Carver kept telling himself he was overreacting. That his paranoia over Megan Crane was driven by the memory of what she had once tried to do to him. He had no plan, nor even a clear idea as to why he was rushing there in the first place. But since first coming across Ellen Hazelhurst's 'Minnesota' Regime and learning of Lydia Grant's research programme, a tick had been pulsing in his brain. Concerns over Lydia Grant's experience, or lack of it, had made it grow. He was still awaiting a call-back from Mike Stapleton, the avuncular head of Manchester University's Police Studies Unit, confirming her background and credentials. Mike's first, a few days before, had simply clarified that the Salford-based researcher was on some sort of retainer from the Prison Department. He was yet to come back with the more detailed CV he'd promised.

Even with no plan, he needed to satisfy himself that whatever Lydia Grant was up to, whatever security arrangements were in place, they'd taken proper account of who they were dealing with. All Megan Crane needed was for someone's attention to wander, if only for a few seconds. He remembered how easily she had led the Worshipper Enquiry Team on a merry dance.

All the way into Manchester, Carver's stomach churned.

CHAPTER 68

The late-evening sun was making a final effort to break through the conifers at the bottom of the garden, but the last thing on Alistair Kenworthy's mind was the colourful sunset. Martin Gardener's suicide was a development he could never have anticipated. Weren't policemen supposed to be made of sterner stuff? But though he had once counted Gardener amongst his friends, he was not wasting time on regret. In recent times, their relationship had reduced to something that was more symbiotic than social, each relying on the other for support when and where needed. Still, his death raised issues needing serious consideration.

One immediate problem was, how he would now keep in touch with what the police were up to. But Hugh was looking at that, and hopefully the incentives on offer meant the gap would soon be plugged. More problematical was that Gardener's selfish act all-but guaranteed that the police would continue delving into Q, and the Hawthorns. And whilst he was happy to pit wits against any policeman – including Carver – given enough time, even they could blunder into things. Kenworthy had never understood why people worried about not being able to stick to a story. It wasn't as if the police had some magical means that proved duplicity the way ultra-violet light shows up cum stains - the one useful thing he remembered from his opening the new Thames Valley Police Scientific Support Unit building. Nevertheless, he was thinking about ringing round again, to make sure people were still, 'on message'.

Of more concern, was what Gardener might have done before he blew his head off. Who had he spoken to, what had he said? He knew now that the only note left was a brief one to his wife of the 'Please forgive me', variety. In that respect, the call to Gardener's overly-tearful secretary to offer his condolences, had been risky, but necessary. Between sniffs, she had assured him that everyone was, 'mystified'. *Not everyone,* he thought, as he hung up. But with Gardener gone, there was no one to give him a clear steer, which meant that for the moment, he was unsure which way to jump.

Most worrying, was the damn thing that had started everything. He had always assumed that Gardener was lying when he said he no longer had a copy. Others had said the same, until persuaded to tell the truth - the benefit of learning long ago how it helped to know certain people. It had amused him at the time. What did they think? That he was just going to accept their word, sit back and wait for the day when the shit hit the fan? No. That wasn't how the Right Honourable Alistair Kenworthy MP did things. He liked to make sure. Leave nothing to chance. Which was how he felt now. But what to do, and how?

He weighed priorities. The first thing was to establish if his suspicions were right. To find out if Gardener had kept a copy. But how?

For several minutes he stared into the gathering

darkness, chewing his nails as he always did if Anne wasn't around to stop him. Thoughts of her made him wonder, briefly, what time she would return from her theatre trip. She had left nothing out for him to eat. And slowly, as he considered options, an idea formed. It wasn't without risk, as Hugh would have been quick to point out if he'd been around. It could even blow up in his face. But Kenworthy had always been proud of the fact that he never shirked from a course simply because it involved risk.

The memory of her that day at his office, came to him. She was actually quite attractive. Not what you'd call 'beautiful', but nevertheless-. And she seemed so sure of herself, or so she thought. As he always did when he imagined such things, he stirred.

He brought his focus back to where it was supposed to be. Normally, the difficulty would be making direct contact without alerting anyone. But the way things had gone, that would not be a problem. He thought it through one more time. The possible return made the risk acceptable. Definitely.

He reached for his mobile.

CHAPTER 69

Salford University's Bio-Sciences Research Institute lies in the Frederick Road Campus's Allerton Building, close to the heart of the city. Carver had been there once. A day seminar. Something to do with Behavioural Science. Traffic snarled as he neared the city centre. It was gone half-six by the time he pulled onto the small car park at the side. There were few students about. The Union building was around the corner. He imagined it bursting.

The portly, black security officer on reception looked up from behind the counter and swung his feet down as Carver entered and headed straight for him. He could have been monitoring the CCTV, but the nearest football stadium was City's Etihad - too far away for the chanting to carry.

'In a bit of a rush lad?' he said, as Carver approached.

'I'm looking for the Neuro-Science Centre?'

'Second floor.' The man nodded towards the flights of stairs that zig-zagged their way up the side of the building, next to the lifts. 'But I'm not sure anyone's there now. Is someone expecting you?'

Carver flashed his warrant card. 'There's a group from the Prison here, with Doctor Grant?'

The security man registered, nodded. 'Ah, right. That was them was it?' His apparent uncertainty did nothing to ease Carver's jitters. 'They arrived half-an-hour ago. But I'm not sure Doctor Grant was- Hey, you'll need to sign in.'

Already heading for the stairs, Carver called back, 'I'll do it on my way out.'

On the second landing, he checked the signs for, 'Neuro-Science Research Centre.' He followed the arrow through the double doors and along a corridor, then through another set and along an even longer corridor. It was in semi-darkness and smelled of hospital. Doors on both sides bore the names of doctors, professors and various support departments. They were all shut. Those with windows were in darkness. All was quiet, apart from the distant hum of what sounded like a floor cleaner. No voices or phones ringing. None of the normal buzz of a busy educational facility. Halfway down, another corridor joined from the right. A sign pointed to "Laboratories; EEG; MRI;" He followed it. It was as quiet as the one he'd just come from. He felt himself tensing. Surely he should hear *something*. Ahead, on the left, one of the double doors to another corridor stood open, a light showing. As he neared, a muffled cry echoed from it. It was followed by a metallic crash, then another – like crockery smashing.

As the echoes died away, he called out. 'Doctor Grant?' There was no reply.

He started running.

CHAPTER 70

Jess was making slow progress on the M5 northbound. Nearing the junction with the M6, traffic slowed to a crawl. It didn't matter. Her brain was whirring anyway, as it had been all day.

She'd arrived at her 'liaison' desk in the Gloucester MIR early that morning and was there when the news first broke about Gardener. It meant she had a ringside seat from which to observe the ensuing maelstrom. But unlike most, for whom news of Gardener's suicide added just another layer of confusion, it merely helped Jess see things more clearly than ever.

The clarity had started to come the day before, as she'd stood looking down on Baggus's broken body. To begin with, the thoughts were vague, unformed. Just a sense of an idea, rather than something sharp and clear. They sprang from the realisation that despite all their efforts, they were as far from uncovering what lay behind Q's death and events since, as the day Gavin first came to see her. In fact, Gavin's comatose state, and now Gardener's suicide, probably meant they were even *further* from the truth than they had been. At least, that was the way things seemed - from an *Investigator's* point of view. From the Investigator's perspective, everything they had unearthed so far fell under the definition of hearsay, or circumstantial evidence. There was no direct evidence of the sort a judge would allow to be laid before a jury. It meant that in prosecution terms, they were nowhere.

But the *Investigator's* perspective wasn't the only one.

As an *individual*, Jess knew full well what the truth was. She might not yet know all the details, the specifics of what had happened, or to whom, when or where. But one thing was clear. Everything that had happened could be traced back to Kenworthy. Baggus, of course, had known that the moment Cyrisse Chaterlain first said his name. That much was clear from his reaction to the Hawthorn's murders. And whilst they had all tried to dissuade him from following up on his instincts, they had done so from their positions as *Investigators*. In their hearts however, as *individuals,* they knew he was right all along. He'd been right on day one when he refused to accept Q's death as an 'accident', and he was right when he stood in front of Kenworthy's desk jabbing a finger in his face and accusing him of murder. But there was a difference between knowing something, and being able to do something about it, without prejudicing the investigation, or subsequent court case. Which was why, to begin with, Jess's thoughts were confused, hazy.

But the more she mused on it, the more she began to realise, the problem only existed, when looked at it from the perspective of an *Investigator*. If she looked at it again, but as an *individual*, then suddenly the problem no longer existed. As an *individual*, she could take any action she wanted. All she needed was to have no regard for - a willingness to accept - the consequences of her actions. Alistair Kenworthy was a man, nothing more. A Government minister and Senior Politician sure, but still only a man. And as a man, there was no reason to believe he was any less amenable to certain influences as other men. Some men value their reputation, or their loved ones. Some are more focused on money, power, material possessions. But *all* men value their *life.* And right now, Jess knew that, if she chose to act as an *individual,* rather than an *investigator*, she could deal with Alistair Kenworthy however she liked.

She could call on him. She could speak to him. Thinking about it, she could, she believed, influence his behaviour. Most of all, she could *hurt* him. It was this last, 'could', that had been in her mind the most since seeing Gavin, lying in hospital. News of Gardener's death had focused her thinking even more. An investigator would see Gardener's death as another setback. But as an individual, knowing of his association with Kenworthy, well, it just made her desire to take action more acute. Now, as she crawled through the evening traffic, her thoughts had progressed to where she was thinking about what form that action might take.

That was then her mobile rang. It was Christo.

'I'm sorry I've not rung,' she said. 'It's been a busy day.' She heard the thrum of traffic down the phone. 'Where are you?'

'I'm just doing some shopping. I wasn't sure when you'd be back and thought I better let you know. Someone's left a message on your home phone. He says he needs to speak with you urgently, but in private'

'My *home* number? Did he leave his name?'

'A Mr Kenworthy?'

'KENWORTHY?'

'You know him?'

'Kenworthy is-.' She stopped herself. By instinct, she'd avoided mentioning names to Christo. He wouldn't know he was the man who may have ordered the murder of his former 'employers'. 'Did he leave a number?'

He had. A mobile. Jess tapped it into hers.

'When will you be home?' he said.

'Not sure now. I could be late.'

'Oh.' He sounded disappointed.

'You can wait up for me if you like. I may need cheering up.'

'Okay.' Brighter.

After ringing off, Jess shook her head at the coincidence. 'Now is that a sign, or what?'

She rang the number, then sat like a statue for a full minute, listening to it ring out. She ended the call.

'Damn.'

For the next couple of minutes, she drummed fingers on the steering wheel, running options. She thought about ringing Jamie, but dismissed the idea at once. She didn't dare involve him, not for what she had in mind. Then she remembered. The HOLMES database contained details of everyone who figures in the investigation - for *any* reason. She rang the MIR and when the duty clerk answered told him she needed an address.

'Who would that be, Ma'am?' the clerk said, recognising her.

'Alistair Kenworthy.'

CHAPTER 71

Carver stopped to listen again. His heart was thumping but not from exertion. He'd covered less than twenty yards since hearing the crash. He strained for the slightest sound. There was none.

He called out again. 'HELLO?'

No answer. Where *was* everyone? Even if the University's staff had finished for the day, where were the escorts? If he heard the crash, then so must they. He geared himself. Ahead of him, the corridor joined with another. He jogged to the junction, looked left. It was empty. He turned to the right - and froze. Halfway down, a body lay across a doorway. He recognised the garb of a Prison Officer.

'Shit.'

He ran to her. As he got there, he realised the wet patch on the floor wasn't blood, but whatever she had been drinking when she collapsed. Her finger was still hooked in the handle of the shattered mug. He recognised her at once. Collette Bright.

It took him a few seconds, but was relieved when he confirmed she was breathing, though only shallowly. He was wondering how the hell Megan might have managed to doctor her escort's drink, when a thought came to him. He span round, half expecting to see some menacing accomplice, creeping up on him. There was no one.

He stood up. He'd heard Collette's fall less than a minute ago. She couldn't have got far. He looked up at the sign pointing to a room on the left. It read, 'E.E.G. Lab'. The door was closed but a light showed beneath. Even as he saw it, there came another crash from within, followed by some commotion.

Leaping over Collette's prostrate form, he burst into the room, only to be knocked sideways as something heavy hit him, full on. As he fought to stay on his feet, he caught a fleeting glimpse of the body swinging back on its pendulum arc, just inside the door, frantic legs, thrashing. Off-balance and distracted, he didn't see the chair he'd heard being up-ended seconds earlier. His legs tangled with the chair's, then he was going down. As he put out an arm to save himself, his cheek hit against something hard. At the same time a sharp pain exploded in his wrist. His eyes must have closed, instinctively, because he didn't see where she came from. He only knew that before he could even begin to raise himself, she was on him, driving her full body weight through the knees that hammered into his back, flattening him to the floor, forcing the air from his lungs. His right arm was trapped under him and as he put his other hand down flat, intending to lever himself up, another excruciating pain shot up his arm. As he tried to look round, he saw the legs swinging back over him, still thrashing, though less frantically now. Something thin flashed down through his line of vision to close round his throat. As it bit, his air cut off.

Not again.

An image of Rosanna flashed before him, alone,

vulnerable. He knew he had only seconds.

His right arm was still trapped and he could feel her forehead levering against the back of his head, pushing him to the floor as she pulled on the ligature. He had one option. He pressed his injured hand flat to the floor. Willing himself not to recognise the pain, he marshalled what strength he had, and heaved upwards.

He was bigger and heavier than her. Under normal circumstances he would have lifted her, easily. But winded, with a weakened arm and his strength ebbing, he almost didn't make it. He just managed to raise himself onto all fours with her still clinging to his back, they way a child does playing 'horsey'. With one last effort, he reared up, twisted right then dropped his left shoulder, just like his father used to do with him all those years ago. *Bucking-broncos.* He felt some of her weight slide off, and though whatever was round his throat stayed, it gave enough for him to manage one final breath. As it bit again, he channelled his remaining strength into something he had never done before.

Rearing again, he twisted round as fast as he could, but to his left this time. As he did so, his blurring vision searched for the target he knew was there somewhere. Sighting on it, he just had time to adjust the trajectory of the balled fist following on behind so that it smashed, squarely, into the middle of the triangle formed by her eyes and nose.

There was a crunching sound, a scream of pain, cut short, and, as the pressure on his throat disappeared, something wet on his knuckles. As her head flew back, an arc of blood streamed out and up from the shattered nose, maintaining its curve until it splashed and sprayed up the wall next to him. The force of the blow carried her away so that she landed on her back, skidding across the polished floor to crash into the side of a metal cabinet. She didn't move and Carver knew from the dull ache in his hand – the right one this time - she wouldn't be getting up any time soon.

He stood up, gulping air as he steadied himself. Then, as fast as his shaking legs could carry him, he crossed to the figure whose legs were no longer kicking. Looking around, he saw scissors on a desk, grabbed at them. It was then he noticed the third figure on the floor the other side of the room. He knew without having to check it would be the other escort.

But it was when he righted the chair and stood on it, reaching up to cut her down, that he realised what was bothering him. It had been nagging since the moment he'd burst through the door and freeze-framed the body as it swung towards him, the split second before she sent him sprawling. But he hadn't had time to get it straight in his mind until this moment. He threw a confirming glance over his shoulder at the still-inert figure of his attacker, as he worked the scissors. But it was an instinctive, rather than studied look, driven by the forces working, furiously, inside his head to make sense of it all.

Then the part of the rope he was yet to cut through was shredding, spiralling, parting, and she fell. He tried to catch her, but had no chance and they both crashed to the floor, she landing, awkwardly, on top of him. His left wrist hurt like hell again, but no more than before. Then it was like his brain had split in two.

One half directed his actions as he loosened the knot in the rope that was tight round her throat, tilted her head back and pulled her jaw open. At the same time the other half of his brain posed a question, *Why the hell are you doing this?*

As he clamped his mouth over hers and started to blow, he peered to the side, trying to get a better look at the blood-spattered face that seemed vaguely familiar. And as he struggled to remember if he had bumped into Lydia Grant before somewhere, he was acutely aware of the irony that lay in the fact he was now giving the kiss of life to Megan Crane.

CHAPTER 72

Before following the ambulances and paramedics to Salford Royal, Carver made sure there was an ARO riding alongside each casualty Their respective partners joined the convoy in their Armed Response Vehicles. Before they left - after the Senior Ambulance Officer in charge of the chaotic scenes within the Neuro-Science Centre confirmed Megan was, 'stabilised enough to travel' - he'd taken the two officers aside and spoken to them, briefly but urgently. When they realised who and what they were to watch over, they exchanged glances, before swinging their Heckler and Koch G36s across their chests as if to confirm their readiness. 'Understood,' they confirmed together, before stepping up alongside the paramedics.

But with his damaged wrist – Carver had told the paramedic who wanted to look at it he would get it checked out at the hospital - it was all he could do to drive, let alone carry on his telephone conversation with The Duke.

'She's on a respirator,' he said in response to The Dukes question. 'We'll see how she is at A and E.'

'What about this Grant woman?' The Duke said. 'Who the hell is she?'

'According to Security, Lydia Grant has been on sick-leave receiving cancer treatment the past three months. Whoever's behind this went to a lot of trouble to set things up. They must have been targeting Megan from pretty early on. Probably as soon as Q started putting the squeeze on and they decided people may need shutting up. I'll have a better idea when they clean her up and I can get at her. Tell me about the video.'

He listened as The Duke described what he'd been watching as Carver was fighting for his life. But the 'eureka moment' he was expecting didn't come. When The Duke finished he said, 'So Kenworthy doesn't appear at all?'

'Not so's you would recognise. He might be one of the guys wearing a mask, but you'd never know.'

Carver thought on it. *So what the hell has it all been about?*

'What does Sylvie say?' he asked, then groaned when The Duke told him Sylvie wasn't saying anything. 'For Chrissakes, I told her she could trust you.'

'She twigged something had happened when I got dragged out the office to take your first call. Now she's clammed up until she sees you in the flesh. She's scared to death.'

Carver's mind raced. 'I need to see it myself. I'll get back as soon as I've finished.' He mentioned that he needed close protection for Megan Crane, as well as, 'Lydia Grant'.

'Leave that with me,' The Duke said, then rang off. Carver was grateful. He had enough to think about, and the pain in his wrist was growing worse.

At the hospital, Carver peeled off from behind the ambulances to park in a bay marked 'Emergency Doctor Only'. As he got out he was thinking about whether he would ever tell Rosanna he had saved Megan Crane's life - if she lived.

Megan was first through the doors. Her gurney was rushed through to a room where Carver heard a doctor calmly giving out instructions to the Emergency Resuscitation Team, like they do in TV dramas when it's never clear who is supposed to do what. Then the doors banged shut and Carver realised that if she didn't respond, he would never see her alive again. He didn't allow himself to dwell on the feelings the thought triggered in him, but turned his attention back to the woman who, for the last few weeks had posed as Lydia Grant, even going so far, it seemed, to purloin a supply of her personal letterheads. He wondered what Ellen Hazelhurst's reaction would be when she learned how thoroughly she had been duped.

For the next quarter-hour, he stayed out of everyone's way by letting a nurse examine, then dress, his throbbing wrist. 'It's just a bad sprain,' she said, after seeming to enjoy twisting it, painfully, in all directions. 'Nothing broken.' She said it like she thought he was a wuss for even mentioning it.

But he was determined not to let the woman who was his only link to the conspiracy out of his sight, even allowing for the armed officers watching over her. As the nurse strapped his wrist and forearm, he resisted getting up and going to see where the cushioned pads were coming from as the staff seeing to, 'Lydia Grant' worked on her. By now the two Prison Officers had also been brought in and were being treated in adjoining cubicles. The occasional drowsy muttering and vomiting suggested they were recovering, slowly, from whatever substance 'Doctor Grant' had slipped into their drinks, before giving the same to Megan Crane.

As soon as the nurse was finished, he crossed the floor to get a better look. The imposter's shattered nose meant she was having difficulty breathing and even as they worked to clean her up they kept the oxygen mask on. He was yet to get a good look at her face. Finally, knowing how much could be riding on it, he could wait no longer. He nodded directions to the two PCs who waited until the nurse seeing to her turned away for some fresh swabs then stepped into the gap between her and the bed-trolley. As she turned back she came up against a black wall of solid PC.

'What do you think you are-. HEY.' The PC's edged aside, taking her with them, and letting Carver in.

Still only half conscious, the woman on the bed barely responded as he pulled the mask away. Bloody bubbles came from her nostrils and she breathed noisily. As her head lolled and her eyes wandered, Carver got the impression she was half-aware of what was going on, but too concussed to do anything about it. For a moment, he stared at the face, non-plussed. Then he realised. It was the makeup that was throwing him, rather, the lack of it. In fact, he had seen two versions of her. One in real life, but only from a distance and in profile. Then, the heavy makeup had made her appear younger than she was. And without all the stage-padding that filled 'Lydia Grant' out, she was much slimmer. The second time was in the photograph they found on Baggus's phone, showing them taking dinner. For the woman on the bed was, undoubtedly, Sally.

'What do you think you are you doing?' the Indian doctor said, as he forced himself to his patient's side. Alerted by the nurse to what was happening and out to restore control, he pushed Carver back with his elbow as if he didn't want to lay a hand on him. 'This is disgraceful,' he said. 'This woman is a patient. Move away.'

Still stunned, Carver didn't resist, but allowed himself to be pushed back by degrees. But as the doctor ranted about patient rights and police 'heavy-handedness' Carver didn't hear a word. He was staring at the woman whom first the Hawthorns, then Baggus, had taken into their homes, only to be set up for death.

'Fucking BITCH.' he spat.

The doctors, nurses and the two porters nearby froze, shocked by his outburst. The two PC's looked at each other, wondering what had so suddenly consumed the man on whose orders they were acting. Carver was reddening by the second.

'You okay, boss?' the more senior of the pair said. He seemed suddenly uneasy, as if he and his partner might be about to face another, 'situation'. Carver flinched, as if to move toward the woman, but the PC who had seen Carver's hands balling into fists moved quickly to put himself between Carver and the woman on the bed. 'I said, Are You Okay Boss?'

Slowly, Carver eased himself back, unclenching his fists and breathing deeply. He met the PC's steady gaze.

'Yes,' he said. 'I'm fine. Carry on.' He moved away, letting the medical staff in to crowd around the bed, as if protecting their charge from the maniac policeman they'd thought was in charge. Seeing their suspicious looks, he realised he was distracting them from what they had do. He backed away some more. The two PCs were now stood on either side of the bed, ready. The older of the pair glanced at Carver and nodded. *She's going nowhere.*

Carver turned, looking for a sign for the Gent's. He found it some way down the corridor.

He opened the door to the cubicle just as his insides decided they'd had enough and he was heartily sick.

When he returned, Megan was still being respirated, yet to regain consciousness, while Sally/Lydia Grant/whoever, was being taken for X-ray. He watched her go, relieved to see the two PC's marching alongside her. The still-irate doctor told him she would be a while, which gave him the chance he needed to turn his attention to other things. Digging into a pocket, he took out 'Lydia Grant''s mobile. One of the paramedics had taken it from her pocket as she lay, unconscious, in the University lab. With no clue to her true identity, he'd already set in motion the laborious PACE procedures that would allow her DNA and fingerprints to be taken. In the meantime, he hoped the object in his hand might shed light on the conspiracy that was now looking more sophisticated than he had ever imagined. He was disappointed. There were no Saved Contacts and the Call-Register was empty. Whoever she was, she was careful about leaving data trails. He pondered his next move, which is when the thought finally came that he knew should have come the moment he recognised her as Sally.

Christo.

Christo and Sally were an item. In what way, he wasn't yet sure. But if Sally was part of it, then so was Christo. And Christo meant… Jess. A knot of fear grew in his stomach. *Oh God.*

After speaking to The Duke earlier he had tried her but got no response. He'd rung Alec and asked him to track her down. He rang him again.

'I was about to call you,' he said. 'She's still not picking up so I rang the MIR to see if they know where she is. Apparently she left around tea-time-'

'In which case she should be home by now, so where-'

'There's more,' Alec said. 'She rang in an hour or so after she left. She asked for Kenworthy's home address.'

Carver froze. 'Why would she want his address, and this time of night?'

There was a pause before Alec said, 'I don't like to think.'

The knot in Carver's stomach tightened. 'Me neither,' he said.

CHAPTER 73

Carver and Alec met up at the M6 Keele Services. It took them another hour to get to Kenworthy's. Given the way things had gone so far that day, Carver fully-expected to see a blue light appear in his mirror anytime, then to lose time explaining who he was and why he was driving like a maniac. As it turned out, the Road Policing units must have been busy elsewhere.

Even before they were in sight of the gateposts, Carver's old beat-craft skills kicked in. He switched off the lights and, as soon as they were on the straight, the engine too. The car coasted to a stop fifty yards short of the house. They jogged the rest of the way to find the gates wide open. The day he'd visited Anne Kenworthy, she had buzzed him in through the intercom and electric gates that made him wonder if they'd been installed by the same company Megan Crane once used. Cloud cover was sparse and the half-moon threw enough light for them to see by. As they came up the drive, Carver's heart fell as he saw what he'd hoped he wouldn't. Jess's Toyota was parked off to the side.

As they approached the front door, Carver saw chinks of light between the curtains in one of the front rooms. Through the glass in the front door, another light showed towards the back of the house. He checked the door. It was unlocked. He opened it, stepped inside, listened. Nothing. He remembered the layout. Reception rooms and study at the front, kitchen-family room and utility rooms at the back. He indicated for Alec to check the front room to the right while he took the one where the light was on. He pushed open the door, peered inside. A sitting room, it was empty. He turned round as Alec came out of the other room, shaking his head. They checked the study, also empty.

A noise echoed through from the back of the house. Someone coughing, followed by running water.

Carver led the way through to the kitchen. As they came in Jess was standing at the sink, splashing water on her face. Hearing them, she span round.

'Jamie? Alec?'

Carver couldn't tell if it was the shock of seeing them there, but as she stood in the middle of the kitchen, swaying from side to side, her face turning a deep shade of red. She looked spaced out. He took a step forward. Strangely, she moved away from him.

'You alright, Jess?'

'Yes. No. I'm not sure.' She seemed disoriented. 'What are you doing here?'

He frowned at her. 'Never mind us. What are *you* doing here? Where's Kenworthy?'

The questions seemed to throw her, like he had no right to ask. And the way she cast her eyes around the kitchen, it was as if she expected he may be standing in some corner and they hadn't noticed.

'I don't know. Have you seen him?'

The fear that had been nagging at Carver all the way there kicked in again. This wasn't like her at all. He went to her, held her by the arms, looked into her face.

She turned away, as if avoiding his gaze. As she did so, he caught a whiff of the pungent, semi-sweet smell he'd grown to recognise. Then her head came round, and as her eyes found his, it was as if she was seeing him for the first time. *She's well out of it.*

'Jamie? Why are you here? I'm supposed to be doing this on my own. You shouldn't be here.'

Then her eyes rolled up and he just had time to tighten his grip as she collapsed into his arms.

'Bloody hell,' Alec said, rushing to help.

Between them, they carried her to the sofa. As Carver brushed hair off her face - she was hot to the touch - Alec went to the sink and returned with a wet cloth, pressing it to her forehead. After a minute or so, she started to come round. Seeing him, she started to panic.

'What's happened, Jamie? Have you found him?'

For some reason, Carver found her confusion worrying. He looked at Alec.

Alec shrugged and shook his head, lost.

'Found who? Do you mean Kenworthy? Calm down, Jess. Take a breath.' She closed her eyes and when she reopened them, seemed calmer. 'Right.' He started again. 'Do you know where you are?' Her eyes slid round the room and she nodded.

'Kenworthy's.'

'Okay. Why are you here?'

She blinked several times. 'He asked me to come.'

'So where is he?'

She looked confused. 'I'm not sure. No one answered when I got here… The door was open so I came in… I called out for him, but there was no answer..'

He waited. 'Go on. Then what happened?'

'I'm not sure.. I think… Yes, I remember coming in. I

started checking rooms… I… 'Oh God.' She put the back of her hand to her head. 'What the fuck am I doing?'

Carver eased back. 'Okay, just take it one step at a time and talk me through it. When did he ask you to come here?'

She squeezed her eyes shut, concentrating. Or appearing to. 'Christo rang me on my way home. He-.'

'Christo?' Carver said. 'Was he here?' But his interjection seemed to throw her and he had to wait as she gathered her thoughts again.

'Christo picked up a message from Kenworthy earlier... He said he needed to see me… alone.'

Carver forced himself to be patient. Every sentence seemed an effort.

Alec tapped Carver on the shoulder. 'I'll take a look round.' Carver nodded.

As he left the room, Jess continued. 'Like I said, there was no one here when I arrived, so I started checking round. I think I… Yes, I remember now. I was checking one of the rooms… I heard something, behind me. Then I felt something over my face. I think it must have been-'

He nodded. 'Chloroform, or something.'

She closed her eyes, gagged at the memory. Carver thought she was going to faint again and gave her the damp cloth. When she revived she continued. 'It put me out… I woke up here. Then you arrived.'

Alec poked his head round the door. 'Nothing down here. I'll look upstairs.'

'Okay.' He returned to Jess. 'Are you sure there's nothing else you remember? There was definitely no one here when you arrived?'

She shook her head. 'I think so…'

At that moment, lights reflected into the kitchen from the hallway. The sound of a car drawing up at the front drifted through.

'Stay here,' Carver said.

He opened the front door in time to see Anne Kenworthy getting out of the Aston Martin's passenger seat. The driver was a heavily-built man of a type Carver recognised. It had to be Eddie Sullivan. They both stared up at him.

'Who the fuck are you?' Sullivan said. 'What are you doing?' His buzz-cut went with his bullish manner.

'Detective Chief Inspector Carver. Mrs Kenworthy knows me.'

Sullivan glanced at her, but she was already coming forward.

'Why are you here? What's happened? Is it Alistair?'

Carver raised his hands in a calming gesture. 'Nothing's happened. Come inside and I'll explain.' He stepped to one side, at the same time trying to work out what the story would be.

But as Anne Kenworthy stepped through the door, Alec's voice bellowed down

'BOSS. UP HERE. FUCKING JESUS.'

'Stay here,' Carver said to the couple, but seeing the alarm in Anne Kenworthy's face knew she wouldn't.

He raced up the stairs. Alec was hanging out of a bedroom doorway. His face was ashen. He nodded into the room. 'In there.'

Carver burst in - and stopped dead. 'Oh, *Jesus*.' And as the memories of events two years before swam before his eyes, he knew that for once, Baggus had been wrong.

The scene that greeted him was a familiar one. It should be. He had seen several like it during the period

Megan Crane practised the signatures that fed into the profile of the bogus serial killer the media came to call, The Worshipper Killer. And a glance was enough to tell him they were all present and correct. The careful arrangement of the ropes binding the victim's wrists, torso, legs and ankles. The way the arms were suspended in front by the rope tied to the top-surround of the four-poster bed. The hands, joined together in the 'praying position' by the super-glue that Carver could smell, even from here. And last, but by no means least, the length of black ribbon round the neck that was biting deep and had forced the blackened tongue to protrude between the gap in the cloth gag. There was only one difference. All Megan Crane's dominatrix -victims were female, and were dressed accordingly. And though the corset, stockings and shoes followed the pattern, Alistair Kenworthy was clearly not female.

No sooner had Carver taken it in than Anne Kenworthy burst into the room, followed almost immediately by Sullivan. She stopped next to Carver, and it was a measure of the shock that had taken root, that it took him a couple of seconds to react when she started screaming like he had never, in all his service, heard anyone scream before.

CHAPTER 74

Nicholas Whitely, Thames Valley Police's Deputy Chief Constable, was some years younger than The Duke, several inches shorter, and half as wide. To his credit, he wasn't giving way to someone whose investigative experience far outweighed his own, the way some Chief Officers might.

'I'm sorry, Morrison. I *am* insisting.'

Looking out of the French windows, Carver waited. Over the last couple of minutes, the difference of opinion had flared to full-on confrontation. When he didn't hear The Duke coming back at Whitley, Carver guessed he was biting his tongue. He turned to face the room. The DCC's back was to him, so he could see The Duke over Whitely's shoulder. Suspecting his former boss could do with a steer, he gave a quick shake of his head. The smaller man must have spotted the slight shift in The Duke's gaze and turned, but by then, Carver was looking out the window again. The Duke picked up on Carver's plea.

'And I'm sorry as well, Sir. But they're my team and they answer to me.'

Whitely's voice rose several decibels. 'I don't give a flying fuck who they answer to. This is my patch, and in case it had escaped your notice, that's a Government Minister up there. People want answers and I need to hear what, "*your team*" have to say.'

'And as I've said. As soon as they've briefed me I'll be quite happy to….'

Still trying to process everything that had happened, Carver tried again to tune out of the hubbub that was growing in intensity as time passed. There was little to see through the window other than the slanted rectangle of light it cast across the patio and which framed his shadow like some film-noir poster. Beyond that there was only darkness. But over to the right, was the brightly-lit conservatory. There he had a clear view of Anne Kenworthy, distraught, on the sofa. He had been observing her on and off, knowing that the table lamp in the conservatory that was between them, would obscure him from her view. A female PC was crouched beside her, one hand on her knee, the other her shoulder. Behind them, Eddie Sullivan hovered, his stony features unreadable.

Carver still hadn't managed to question Anne Kenworthy about what she knew of her husband's intentions whilst she and Sullivan were out, visiting the theatre that evening. He was conscious that if he didn't do so soon, it may be too late. There is a period, usually only an hour or two, following news of devastating personal loss, when those most affected are still lucid enough to answer questions, hard though it is to ask them. But as shock sets in, withdrawal begins, usually accompanied by disorientation and, quite often, memory loss. Usually temporary, in the worst cases it can last weeks. During that time the person is, effectively, lost to an investigation. And it doesn't come much worse than discovering your husband dressed in woman's lingerie and ritualistically murdered in your own bedroom. But Carver couldn't get to her until the two men behind him resolved their differences.

Thankfully, The Duke arriving before Whitely, meant they'd had a chance to swap information. Carver told him about finding Jess there and her confused state. The Duke updated him regarding what they had found out so far about the woman who had stolen Lydia Grant's identity. The Fingerprint Bureau had turned up a possible match with a Katrina Muller. A one-time eco-terrorist-turned armed-robber with a reputation for the art of disguise, an entry in NCA Intelligence had her as someone known to take on, 'Contract Work' . There was a cross-reference to a boyfriend-lover, Alessio Rossi who sometimes worked with her. The Duke also gave him back Sylvie's disc, though his accompanying, 'Buggered if I can see what it's to do with Kenworthy,' gave Carver little hope it would tell him anything. When The Duke asked what had brought Carver there in the first place, Carver answered, 'It's complicated. We need to speak privately.' It was enough to signal that there was a possible problem. He'd been about to expand further, when Whitely arrived.

The Duke had tried to buy Carver time by guiding the DCC into the study to, 'bring him up to date,' while Carver ran the disc through the laptop he'd brought with him. His hope was, by the time The Duke returned, he would have what he needed. He didn't. The Duke's sketchy answers weren't enough to hold Whitely long, and when he stormed back into the room ten minutes later, Carver just had time to close the laptop before Whitely zeroed in on him, Alec and Jess. Jess was in an armchair, Alec on the sofa next to her, keeping a watchful eye. She hadn't said a word since Carver told of Lydia Grant's attack on Megan Crane, and didn't stir when The Duke arrived. Her vacant stare and unusual silence was the first thing The Duke noticed when he walked in. But alerted by Carver's warning looks, he avoided asking.

'I believe it was you who found him?' The DCC said, before insisting Carver tell him everything. At which point The Duke objected.

'I'd rather they brief me first, Sir. If you don't mind.'

Which was when the argument started.

Now, as Carver stared across at the conservatory again, he was beginning to come to terms with the fact that his gamble had failed, that he would soon have little choice but to tell what he knew. Which wouldn't be enough.

Far from shedding light on things, the video clip had told him nothing. Had it done, he may have been able to postpone explaining how they came to discover the crime - at least until such time as he had worked out Jess's part in things. That she'd chosen to visit Kenworthy without telling anyone, hinted at an agenda of her own. He didn't know what it was yet, but some of the possibles occurring were enough to pull the knot in his stomach even tighter. The way things stood, if he had to disclose to Whitely that one, maybe two, investigating officers had become involved with possible suspects, he would likely evict them all in favour of a whole new team. Suspensions couldn't be ruled out.

Carver wasn't concerned for himself, but he was desperate to keep things moving while they were 'hot'. If they didn't, he feared that the truth about everything that had happened since Q's death, would remain a mystery. Katrina Muller - if it were she - would be convicted of Megan's attempted murder, provided she lived. But if she was indeed the 'professional', she was supposed to be, she would almost certainly say nothing about the identity of her paymasters. The enquiry would grind to a halt - again.

As the two men behind him continued to argue – Carver could tell that for once, The Duke was going to lose - he thought again about the video clip.

That it was still the key to everything, he was in no doubt. Everything pointed to it. Megan's cryptic messages, Cyrisse's suspicions, Gardener's suicide, Sylvie's nervous reappearance. But without Sylvie to interpret its hidden message - assuming she could - Carver was groping in the dark. The younger of the two women was Sylvie, that much was clear. Though the mask over her face and the distance – about twenty feet – made identification difficult, you could see it if you knew who you were looking for. And though he had only met Sylvie once, he had little trouble matching her slim figure and bleached-blond hair with the naked young woman led into the room at the beginning of the scene. Not so the other woman. Older, taller, fuller of figure and also masked, it wasn't Megan, or Cyrisse - wrong colour hair - which left the men. But apart from the scenes showing the women being shackled, unresisting, to the tables by two, naked-from-the-waist-up body-builder types who were also masked, the men were shown only from the rear or, when the action focused on what was happening on the tables, from below chest height. Carver assumed one of them had to be Kenworthy, but which one, it was impossible to tell. More easily identifiable was thc corpulent figure of the solicitor, Q, and, if he wasn't mistaken, the heftily-built ACC, Martin Gardener. Carver still wasn't sure how many men there were altogether. He'd stopped counting at twelve. But as each came forward to take their turn, before moving round to the head of the table – an accidental pun he needed to remember to avoid in future – he'd looked for identifying marks or characteristics which those attending Kenworthy's post-mortem might look for. But he saw none, and the way the film was shot and cut, the line of eager participants could have included a good friend, and he would never have known. The only characteristic he had managed to spot through the whole film was the tattoo – image enhancement would show it properly – on the back of the older woman's shoulder.

Whatever it was, Carver knew there had to be something damaging enough in the film to lead to murder. And though it wasn't as heavy, violent, or plain sickening as some he had seen – far from the women being forced they seemed willing, at least to begin with - he could see why anyone with a reputation to protect would want to ensure it never saw the light of day.

As he mused on it, staring into the blackness beyond the French window, Carver could tell that behind him, the argument was all but lost and he would soon need to turn his mind to other things. Such as what, exactly, he was going to tell Whitely.

Suddenly the DCC stopped mid-sentence. 'Whose *bloody phone* is that?'

Everyone stopped to listen. This time Carver heard the low buzzing that twice before had interrupted Whitley's flow. Each time it had stopped before it could be located. Once more everyone whipped out mobiles, but again, no one owned up. When the buzzing cut off a few seconds later, Whitely waited, then resumed delivering what sounded like his final word on the matter. 'If you want to see it that way then yes, Chief Superintendent. It does come down to me pulling rank.'

Carver started to turn, the battle lost, and as he did so his gaze fell again on the conservatory where Anne Kenworthy and Sullivan still waited. The policewoman wasn't in sight and for the first time since they had arrived back at the house Sullivan had strayed from Anne Kenworthy's side. He was across the other side of the room, his back to her, looking at his mobile, putting it to his ear, then looking at it again. Carver stopped, halfway through turning. His eyes narrowed.

The Duke gave a defeated sigh.

'Sit down, Jamie. Let's go through it.'

'Just a minute,' Carver said.

He went over to the corner where his jacket lay across a chair. He picked it up, returned to the window.

Whitely was impatient. 'Time's pressing, Mr Carver. We need to get on.'

Carver held up a hand. 'Sshhh.' He needed to think. Across in the conservatory, Sullivan was back at Anne Kenworthy's side, his large hands cradling hers.

The DCC reddened. 'Don't 'sush' me Chief Inspector. I'm-.

Carver's head snapped round like he was on a spring. 'Shut the fuck up a minute, will you?'

The Chief Officer's jaw dropped and he turned to The Duke as if to say, *Either you bring him to heel, or I will.* But The Duke's raised hand simply echoed Carver's command. Exasperated, the DCC turned back.

Carver delved into the jacket's pockets. *What are the chances?* His fingers closed round the object he was seeking. In all the excitement, he had forgotten about it. He drew it out. The screen on Lydia Grant/Sally's mobile read '3 Missed Calls.' He started pressing buttons.

It all depended how she had set the phone up. But while she may have cleared the Call Register regularly, there was no reason for her to suspect her deception was about to come apart. Settings showed the ring-alert set to 'vibrate'. He navigated to the missed calls list. A number showed. He selected 'return call', and put the phone to his ear. A ring -tone sounded. His heart thumped in his chest.

Across in the conservatory, Sullivan remained still. Carver's heart sank. He gave it another few seconds and was about to end the call when Sullivan suddenly shot off the arm of the sofa as if he'd been electrocuted. Moving to the other side of the room, he fished into a pocket. He took out his mobile, checked the screen, then spoke into it, his voice clear in Carver's ear.

'Where the hell have you been? What's happening? Hello?'

In that moment, Carver knew that the link they had been hunting since the morning Quentin Quinlan had been found, asphyxiated in his luxury apartment bedroom, was, literally, in his grasp.

A weighty hand landed on Carver's shoulder and he turned. The Duke stood next to him. Carver put a finger to his lips, nodded out of the window and held the phone so The Duke could listen.

'Katrina? Are you there?'

The Duke's eyes went wide and Carver was about to end the call – they needed to move quickly – when Sullivan did something Carver hadn't expected. He turned around.

Up to that moment, Carver had been focusing so closely on Sullivan he had paid scant attention to Anne Kenworthy. But now he saw her, arm stretched out towards her companion, the cupped hand beckoning. *Give it to me.* Sullivan handed her the phone. She spoke into it.

'Katrina? Talk to me dammit. Is the job done?'

But even as she spoke she looked up, alerted by Sullivan's hand on her arm, his other pointing across to where Carver and The Duke were framed in the French window. Seeing them, she screamed and dropped the phone.

Like a cheetah after prey, Carver sprang across the room and out the door, The Duke following.

'What's happening?' Whitely yelled, then span like a top as Alec Duncan exploded out of his chair to follow after his bosses. Alec would have no idea what was happening, but knew a strike when he saw one.

Nearing the kitchen, Carver heard a crash and Anne Kenworthy crying and yelling. 'Oh no, Eddie, no. *Do something.*'

Sullivan's voice was harsh, fierce and desperate. 'Shut up you stupid bitch. Fucking CHRIST. How do you get into this fucking thing?'

Carver burst into the kitchen, round the breakfast bar and into the conservatory to find Sullivan clawing at the mobiles cover. Gangster or not, he knew enough that his only chance was to destroy the sim-card. Carver stopped in front of him, breathless, but ready for anything as other officers, responding to the rumpus, arrived behind. Calls of, 'What is it?' and 'Take it easy.' rang in his ears.

Face full of fury, Sullivan squared up to Carver. 'You fucking smart-arse. You think that was clever? Well one fucking phone call means nothing. You've got fuck all. Do you hear me? Fuck all.'

'I hear you, Eddie,' Carver said, calm but ready, in

case the bigger man kicked off. 'But what we have and haven't got will be a matter for the CPS.' Reaching out, he took hold of the mobile in Sullivan's hand. There was a moment's resistance, before he gave it up.

As The Duke appeared at his side, Sullivan's 'come and get me' stance seemed to wilt and Carver saw he was forcing back the words that threatened to spring from his lips. But he'd said and done enough, as had his accomplice.

A whimper from behind them made them turn. During the confrontation, Anne Kenworthy had backed off and was now crouched in the corner of the room, as if trying to hide herself away. Her fists were balled in front of a face streaked with tears once more. Only this time they were tears of fear, rather than the crocodile ones of grief she had shed thus far this night.

'Don't let them take me, Eddie,' she cried.

'I *told* you,' Sullivan snapped. 'Keep your mouth shut. Don't say a fucking word.'

But as she looked up at Carver, he could tell she wasn't hearing him. Anne Kenworthy may have conspired to murder, but she was no hardened criminal

'Stand up, Mrs Kenworthy,' Carver said. But as he offered her a helping hand, she cowered away, like a rabbit from a fox. Before Carver's eyes, the sophisticated woman who coped as well with state occasions and government receptions as she did church jumble sales, changed into a simpering, whimpering, little girl. She looked up at him, pleadingly.

'Please don't tell daddy. Promise you won't tell him?'

'Stand up, Mrs Kenworthy,' he repeated. This time he went to her and placed his hands, gently on her shoulders to guide her up. Suddenly he stopped, frozen in the act of bending forward. His head dropped and he let out a long sigh that those behind heard, clearly.

'Jamie?' The Duke said.

Carver heard him, but didn't answer. At that moment his mind was occupied, piecing together the myriad pieces of the jigsaw, the cover image of which had just been revealed to him in the most unexpected way.

Unlike most women in her position, Anne Kenworthy had never seen being married to a government minister as a particular mark of 'success', nor even something she may one day look back on with pride. Borne into a family where 'civic duty' meant little, Anne Hartley had been taught by her entrepreneurial but puritanical father that, in life, only one thing matters. Security. And security, means money. It was a lesson that Logan Hartley probably spent years drumming into her. But in comparison to the way she was brought up, even a government minister's salary promised little in the way of security. Which was why the inheritance that would one day be hers was so important to her. Such a fortune would ensure that no matter how the vagaries of politics affected her husband's income, she would always have the means to do whatever she pleased. But she also knew that her father's religious and moral convictions were such he would never allow the fruits of his pious labours to pass to someone exposed to the world as a 'fallen woman'. All this came clear to Carver as he bent over the woman who had started to disintegrate the moment she realised who was on the other end of the phone - and he happened to see her reflection in the window.

For her theatre trip that evening – the perfect alibi – Anne Kenworthy had chosen an elegant black dress with a rather daring, 'v'-shaped back. And as Carver glanced at her cowering reflection, he saw, peeping out from under the strip of material that covered less than half her left shoulder blade, a tattoo. In that split-second he knew, beyond any shadow of doubt, that when forensic enhanced the one in the video clip, it would prove identical to the one on the shoulder of the woman cowering before him - the woman with the seemingly insatiable appetite for sex in all its forms. The woman the video showed being serviced by as many men as could fit around the table on which she lay.

She didn't resist as he lifted her from her corner refuge, and led her into the safe hands of the waiting woman PC. As she passed, he was able to get a better look at the uniquely identifying design her husband should never, ever, have allowed to be captured on camera. Seeing it, Carver was surprised no one else had seen the possibilities long before Quentin Quinlan chanced upon the means by which he imagined - foolishly it turned out - he could end his money problems. The tattoo was in the form of a key entwined with roses. The sort of old-fashioned key that would fit some ancient gate's lock or a dark dungeon. At that moment Carver had no way of knowing it's meaning. Perhaps it referenced some significant event, person, or memorable period in her life. It didn't matter. What mattered was that Carver knew, precisely, its significance.

And as he reflected on how they had all been wrong to assume that Alistair Kenworthy was the blackmail victim, Carver finally understood the true meaning of the words in the note from Megan Crane that had almost choked him. *Kenworthy's wife is The Key.*

Carver turned to the two people who had set out to ensure that Logan Hartley would never have cause to change his will.

'Anne Kenworthy and Edward Sullivan, I am arresting you for conspiring to murder Quentin Quinlan, Barbara Hawthorn, Gerald Hawthorn and Alistair Kenworthy. You do not have to say anything…

At the back of the room, the slight figure of the Thames Valley Deputy Chief Constable, who had thus far failed to find a gap through the throng of policemen and detectives, could barely believe what he was hearing.

CHAPTER 75

'She's faking,' Carver said.

Mr Phillip Sturton, Senior Consultant at Salford Royal's Neurology Department, pushed his rimless glasses back up his nose and looked at Carver the way he might a dog that had just urinated on his two-hundred-pound Loakes.

'I'm sorry?'

Carver moved round to the other side of the bed. There were fewer drips, wires and hoses there. He bent to take a closer look. 'I said, she's faking.'

Sturton checked to see if the others - The Duke, Jess, Ellen Hazelhurst and the Junior Doctor overseeing the patient's care - found the suggestion as amusing as he did. There were no smiles.

'Oh, I *see*,' Sturton said. 'You must be one of those policemen who are qualified in the field of neurology, yes?'

Carver took his time replying, so Sturton would know goading would not work. He leaned further, bringing his face within a few inches of the woman lying, peacefully, between the white-cotton sheets. *Is that perfume?*

'I don't know anything about neurology. But I know a

great deal about, *Her*.' He straightened up, said it again. 'She's faking.'

As Sturton glowered at Carver, the junior doctor, observing from the other side of the room, folded his arms and lifted a hand, casually, so it came level with his mouth. At the foot of the bed, The Duke and Jess stayed still and silent. Ellen Hazelhurst looked unsure what to make of any of it. Sturton tried again.

'I assure you, Chief Inspector. Oxygen-Deprivation-Induced Metabolic Coma is common in cases of asphyxiation trauma. There is no reason to believe her condition isn't genuine.'

Carver looked from Sturton to The Duke and back again, before contorting his face in a way that showed scepticism. Returning his gaze to the woman in the bed, he said, 'Let's get this straight. Her brain function reads as normal?'

Sturton nodded.

'No evidence of brain damage?'

'None we can diagnose so far.'

'She has some, you say limited, response to pain, and certain other forms of external stimuli?'

'Yes.'

'And she's breathing on her own?'

'All correct.' Sturton said it as if Carver's re-stating of the facts proved his diagnosis.

Carver waited a few seconds more before turning to Ellen Hazelhurst. 'She's faking.'

Sturton gave an affronted, 'Harrumph.'

Carver ignored it. 'The card and blade in her shoe, show she was planning an escape. I'm telling you, if she stays here, you'll lose her. And if she goes, you'll not get her back. You know the sort of friends she's got. Right now, they're lining up to whisk her out of the country, the first opportunity.'

It was too much for Sturton.

'This is ridiculous.' He turned to The Duke. 'Are you going to let this officer denigrate my diagnosis and advice? If so then I'm afraid I've no alternative but to complain to your Chief Constable, in the strongest possible terms.'

The Duke gave Carver a weary look – *Now look what you've done* - before replying. 'DCI Carver is expressing a personal opinion. It's not the official police position.'

Carver shrugged, moved away a little. He was remembering the night he burst into her playroom just in time to, 'save her from death', at the hands of the unfortunate William Cosgrove. She'd been pretty damn convincing then too. But the Duke's reassurance wasn't enough for Sturton.

'In that case, perhaps you wouldn't mind confirming what is the *official* police position. I take it you don't concur with what this officer is saying?'

The Duke studied the prostrate figure for what seemed a long time. Eventually he turned back to Sturton. 'Let's just say that, officially, the Police are not qualified to comment on Megan Crane's medical condition.'

Sturton gave a derisive snort. 'Well I am, and I can tell you, she remains our patient. If you try to move her against medical advice, then we'll be involving our legal department.'

Turning, he strode out of the room. The junior doctor threw The Duke and Carver a look that seemed a little less certain than his senior, before scurrying after.

As their footsteps receded down the corridor The Duke turned to Carver. 'You know, sometimes you can be a real pain in the arse.'

Carver shrugged, again.

The Duke turned to Ellen Hazelhurst. 'Can we have words please, Governor?' He took her by the elbow and started to lead her away. 'If she *is* going to have to remain here, then we need to discuss security….'

The pair strolled off down the corridor, leaving Carver and Jess alone with the woman in the bed. Outside the door, two prison officers, a man and a woman, hovered.

Carver stood at the end of the bed, staring down at the woman who could have been taking an afternoon nap. *She still looks-*

'Jamie.'

He turned to find Jess looking at him, disapprovingly.

'We can't do anything here. Let's go.'

At the door, Carver stopped to speak with the POs. They had their chairs ready. Beside them were bags Carver knew would contain books, devices, magazines.

'You heard what we were saying in there?' They both nodded. 'Good.'

He turned on his heel and walked away, leaving Jess to cast a last, doubtful look at the figure on the bed, before following after. She caught up with him by the lifts.

'When's your next interview?' he said.

So far, Anne Kenworthy had been interviewed three times. Each time she had said nothing, 'On the advice of my solicitor.' That morning, out of the blue, she had asked to see Jess again – without her solicitor being present. Carver knew Jess was looking forward to it.

'Four o'clock. I'm calling in to see Gavin first.'

'How was he last night?'

She tried to sound positive. 'They say it's a bit like after a power cut, and you start throwing all the switches back on? Only in the case of the brain, the lights come back on slowly, one by one. Some take more time than others. Some may not come back on at all.'

Carver saw the glistening in her eyes. He gave her arm a squeeze. She looked at him, nodded, forced a smile.

The lift arrived. As they got in Carver returned to the matter of the woman behind it all.

'Is she going to cough?'

Jess was running the tip of her little finger under her eye-liner. She pushed her bottom lip out. 'More likely she wants it on record that Kenworthy made her do it. The gang-bang I mean. In the hope her father will believe it.'

'She doesn't look like she's being forced.'

'No, but a woman trying to please her husband can be very convincing.'

'True,' he said. Then he added. 'She'll try to throw the rest of it on Sullivan.'

'I know,' she said. 'But it will do me. With Katrina and Sullivan saying nothing, I'll be happy to let the jury make up its own mind.'

The rest of the way down and out of the building they talked about other things, statements, outstanding enquiries, forensic. Still much to do, coordinating things between several police forces wasn't proving easy. As they neared the car park there was a lull. It allowed her to switch subject.

'What does Rosanna think of the house?'

'She liked it. We put in an offer and they've accepted. Its vacant possession so we're hoping it will all go through quickly.'

'Does that mean you'll be applying for Welsh citizenship?'

He chuckled. 'I'm not sure I'd pass the interview.'

Their cars were at opposite ends of the car park and they lingered before parting. He suspected what was in her mind, but didn't raise it in case he was wrong.

'Any word on this Rossi character yet?' she said.

Here we go, he thought. There weren't many opportunities for them to be alone together these days.

'We've got prints and DNA matches with samples from Christo's flat, so that's one job sorted. I spoke with the German police last night. He and Katrina operate out of Hamburg. They're hitting some addresses as we speak.'

'We could do with him turning up.'

'He'll come, eventually,' he said. 'Give it time.'

'I'd rather it be sooner, if it's all the same.'

He sighed. Time to face it. 'You don't have to prove anything, you know?'

She looked him square in the face. 'Yes I do.'

'Why do you say that?' But he knew the answer before she said it.

'Because you're still not one hundred percent about what actually happened to Kenworthy.'

'Yes, I am.'

'Don't lie. But don't worry, once Rossi's locked up, then you'll see.

'You don't have to convince me, Jess. I'm on your side.'

'Okay.' She turned on him, suddenly determined. 'Convince me. Why would Anne Kenworthy and Sullivan have got Christo to kill Kenworthy? He would never have exposed her.'

Carver sighed. Right now, he would rather not be treading this particular path. Still, he owed it to her to try. 'Because it was always part of her plan. Revenge for all the things he supposedly got her to do when they were regulars at Josephine's. And to free herself up for Sullivan.'

She gave him a doubtful look. 'Hmm. Alec told me about your Beauty And The Beast theory.'

'There're plenty of examples if you look for them.'

'Maybe, but they don't last.'

'But they do for a while, and that's the point.'

She nodded, as if half-accepting it. But he could tell she wasn't yet done. She wouldn't be until Alessio Rossi came.

'But how do you *know* it wasn't me? You knew I was going to see him. And the Worshipper pose thing. Why would Rossi have done it like that?'

He gathered his thoughts. Time to draw a line under it.

'Two points. Then we drop it, agreed?'

'Agreed.'

'First off, I believe Christo- Rossi, always intended to muddy the waters with Kenworthy, to throw us off the scent. But after you and he….' She arched an eyebrow. 'After you agreed to put him up for a few days, he saw an opportunity to *really* confuse things. Which is why he sent you to Kenworthy's with a story about a phone call.

'So he tried to set me up?'

'Basically, yes.'

She looked at him as if trying to gauge how far he believed it. 'The second point?'

He moved close to her, looking deep into the hazel eyes. 'The second point, Ms Greylake is….'

'Yes?'

'You aren't capable of killing someone.'

For a long time they stood there, staring each other out. Eventually she could keep the smile at bay no longer. Breaking the spell, she leaned forward and kissed him, lightly, on the cheek. 'I believe you, now.'

He returned the smile. For all the complications it may bring, he missed her as a partner.

'I'll let you know how Gavin is,' she said.

She turned and headed towards her car, stilettos click-clacking, noisily, on the concrete.

As he watched her go, Carver felt the ever-present knot in his stomach tighten another notch. And as he turned to look for his car he tried not to think of the apocryphal story about a woman on her death bed calling to the husband she had long suspected of infidelity.

'If you really love and respect me, you will tell me the truth. Have you ever cheated on me?'

Looking deep into her eyes, the wayward husband knew he had no choice. 'No,' he lied.

The woman died happy.

Carver got into his car, gunned the engine and, wheels spinning, headed back to the office.

CHAPTER 76

Carver could remember a time when the successful end of a murder enquiry was invariably marked by a, We-Got-The-Bastard-style piss-up. Nowadays, they are more muted affairs. When they do happen, the emphasis is usually less on raucous letting-hair-down, than making sure no one does anything the media may get hold of, and put a spin on. When drink flows, it's easy to forget that the 'celebrations' trace back to someone's violent death.

As it happened, the gathering in Stockton Heath's Red Lion that evening was never going to be celebratory, despite the fact that the key essentials were present and correct. Bastards-duly-got, and investigation successful. -Ish. For a start, there were only four present, Carver, Jess, The Duke and Alec. For another, the shadow of Baggus's continuing battle still hung over everything. The latest news - he'd come off the respirator - was encouraging, but they all knew that the bigger test was still to come. Waking him up. But while no one was ignoring it, the mood was more reflective, than sombre. Like after Megan Crane was unmasked as the Worshipper Killer, they all knew that matters remained that would need further, serious attention over the coming weeks. Some, Carver knew, would be fairly easy to resolve, such as establishing why the links between the various strands weren't picked up sooner. In this regard, and with Gardener gone, he suspected that Wilf Robinson last few months' service may prove 'challenging'. Others, such as putting together a precise time-line for Alistair Kenworthy's murder may prove more problematical. Fortunately, none of it was for tonight, other than remembering the man who wasn't there, but should have been.

'To Gavin,' The Duke called the toast. And none held back their response.

'TO GAVIN.'

Over the next couple of hours, Carver downed just one proper pint. After that he went onto some alcohol-free concoction that smelled like wet socks and tasted much the same. Alec had offered to run him home when his wife came to pick him up - she was standing by for the call - but it was far out of her way and Carver wouldn't hear of it. Rosanna had also offered, but they were still working on things. Right now, asking her to drive fifty miles, just so he could have a couple of pints, was probably not, a good idea. Besides, they were due to visit Jason the next day. While they were there, he would talk Susan Kendrick - and Paul - through his decision. It was important, they understood his thought processes. A clear head would be needed.

By ten o'clock, he'd had enough. Downing the dregs of whatever was in his glass, he rose. 'I'm done,' he said.

Reaching across, he shook hands with each of them, firmly, and with enough eye-contact to reaffirm those things that bound them together. The look he gave Jess was particularly meaningful, as was the one she returned. As he headed for the door he heard Alec say,

'We'll hae one more, then I'll gee the missus a ring.'

Out on the car park, Carver breathed deep, enjoying the reviving night air. He was still suffering the fuzzy, not-quite-all-there feeling which comes with not enough sleep over too long a period. He was beginning to wonder if it would ever go away.

Before setting off, he put on Rosanna's CD and skipped to Track Ten. While his appreciation of her Fado was broadening, slowly, *'Povo Que Lavas No Rio'* remained his favourite. To his ears, Rosanna's rendition was every bit as good as the Amalia Rodriguez version she'd introduced him to soon after they met.

Traffic was light that time of night. He'd just joined the M62 at Winwick, heading for Manchester, when the double beep that broke into his listening told him he had a message.

'Read,' he said, to the question on the display.

He didn't recognise the sender's mobile number that preceded the message, and his first thought was it would prove to be spam. But when he heard the message content, he came upright and much of the fuzziness blew away. *"Number-thirty-eight-Wilfred-Street-Bewsey-Warrington-Cheshire." It was followed by the post.*

Kayleigh Lee's address.

'Whaaat?' Why was someone sending him Kayleigh's address, and at this time of night? He knew it well enough already.

As he continued heading east, he mused over possibilities. Mistake was most likely. It was probably meant for someone else. But Kayleigh wasn't the easiest person to get to know. Those she wanted to know her address would, in all probability, already have it. It could be something official. Maybe someone from the

Housing Trust needed to visit and someone else was just passing along her address. But surely they would know it as well? He racked his brain to think of any outstanding 'business' left over from Megan's trial. But that had all been put to bed around the time they sorted her house. Besides, in Carvers' experience, the sort of 'officials' with whom Kayleigh still had occasional contact, weren't the sort likely to be working on their client lists this time of night. The one exception would be Rita Arogundade, though he'd heard recently that she was no longer involved with the Lees either.

Puzzled, and a little disquieted, Carver felt the need to put his mind at ease. Bringing up her number on the screen, he hit 'call'.

It rang out several times, and he was about to end it when she answered.

'Jamie?' She sounded sleepy.

'Sorry, have I woken you?'

'Yeah, but it's okay. What's wrong?'

'Nothing's wrong, I was just- You haven't just sent someone a message, have you?'

'No, I'm in bed. What sort of message?'

'I've just received a text showing your address. I'm not sure who's sent it.'

'Not me. Why would someone be sending you my address? You already know it.'

'That's what I'm trying to work out. You okay? No problems there?'

'No, I'm fine. I don't know who would have my address to send it, apart from you, or Rita. Should I be worried?

'Not at all. It'll be a mistake. Some social worker's database mix-up. Go back to bed.'

'Okay. I'm sorry I didn't get back to you about *are*

Billy. I meant to ring but-'

'Don't worry. We'll talk the next time I see you. Maybe drop in for a coffee next week, eh?'

'Cool. 'Night Jamie.'

"G'night.'

As he drove, he reflected on the call. She'd sounded fine. No problems at all, she'd said. So why hadn't it set his mind at rest? What could there be to worry about? Nothing he could think of. Yet someone was sharing her address with a third party. Who?

The hundred-yard marker posts for the East Warrington exit flashed past. In the middle lane, he yanked the wheel left, and swerved onto the exit approach - then realised he was lucky no-one was coming up on his inside. He had no idea why he was turning off, or what he was going to do next. But at that moment, his gut was telling him it didn't want to be stuck on the motorway, putting more distance between him and Kayleigh Lee.

At the roundabout at the top of the slip, he pulled left onto Birchwood Way, and stopped. He took out his mobile, brought up the message, stared at it. It told him nothing he didn't already know. He thought about ringing the sender's number, but for some reason, decided against. He wasn't sure why. He looked out at the darkness round him. He hadn't felt like this in a long time, and didn't know why a simple SMS should trigger the feeling.

What happened next Carver would later recall as, like an out-of-body experience.

Suddenly he was a detached observer, watching himself pull a three-point that brought him back to the roundabout. To his left, the slip road back onto the motorway was sign-posted, 'M62 Manchester'. *Home.*

He saw himself, staring at it, blankly. After something close to a minute he said simply. 'No.'

Gunning forward, he navigated the roundabout and took the slip road taking him down onto the M62 Westbound, back the way he'd come.

CHAPTER 77

Carver's mind and body re-joined as he came off the M62 at the A49 Winwick exit. Realising he was again operating blind - no plan, still uncertain what was wrong - he pulled into the first lay-by he came to. He looked in his mirror.

'What's the fucking problem?'

He had no answer. He needed to eliminate possibles.

He thought about ringing Kayleigh again, but what could he tell her? He thought about Christo, still out there somewhere. But Kayleigh would never have been on his radar. In fact as far as he knew, the only person he would ever place in the 'risk' category as far as Kayleigh was concerned, was Megan herself, for spoiling her Grand Plan. But right now, Megan was out of the game, so how could-?

A thought came.

'You're being paranoid.'

He tried to think, *What else?* But it continued to prick at him. He'd never believed in ESP, premonition, or any of that garbage. But right now-

He picked up his mobile. Called the number. It rang twice.

'Hotel Echo One,' the man's voice said.

After identifying himself, Carver asked who he was speaking to.

'Graham Potter, Sir.' he came back. 'What can I do for you?'

Carver remembered the name, but struggled for the face. Megan's Close Protection Team comprised six officers working twelve hour shifts. Two off on any one day.

'Is everything okay there, Graham? Any problems?'

'No,' he said. 'We're fine. They've done us some hot chocolate and someone brought in some pies so we're set for-'

'This isn't a welfare call. I'm talking about your subject.'

Potter's voice changed as he realised his error. 'Sorry, Sir. No, everything's as per protocol this end.'

'Are you two-up?'

'Yes Sir. Me and Lizzie Yarwood.'

'Good. How about the prison staff?'

'Two of them as well. They're along the corridor.' His voice lowered. 'Waste of space though if you ask me. They seem to think that because we're here, they can nod off.'

'Well, don't let them. She's their prisoner. You're just there to protect her.'

'Yeah, well I did try to have a word with their boss while she was here, but she ignored me.'

'Which boss was that?'

'There was a PO Supervisor here when we took over at ten. Apparently, she called in to check on the subject. She's gone now.'

Carver hesitated. 'A PO Supervisor? This late? There's no medics around are there?'

'None I've seen.'

'Was it their Governor? Short, blond-haired woman?' He remembered hearing how Ellen Hazelhurst liked to make random drop-ins on her staff.

'No, this was a dark woman. I think I heard one of the PO's call her Collette.'

Carver froze. Last he heard, Collette Bright was on suspension, pending investigation.

'What was she doing there?'

'Other than visiting the subject, I've no idea. She was in with her when we arrived. She left a few minutes after.'

'She's definitely gone? You saw her leave?'

'Absolutely.

'Did you speak to her?'

'No, but we saw her come out of the room. Then she went straight off.'

'When you say she went straight off, did she speak to the duty POs first?'

There was a pause. 'Actually, she didn't. One of them called her an ignorant cow for not saying goodnight.'

Carver stared straight ahead. *Not possible.*

'Is Lizzie with you now?'

'Yes Sir.'

'Outside the room?'

Yes.'

'Right. I need you to go in and check on the subject.'

'Really? What for? Are you-'

'And it needs to a tactical entry, with weapons.'

'*What?* But there's no one there apart from her.'

'Do it Graham. There may have been a breach.'

'But we can just-

'DO IT, Graham. Draw your weapons. NOW.'

'SIR.'

As the CPO jumped to, background hiss replaced his

voice. Carver heard him alert his colleague, '*Lizzie,*' followed by rapid movement. He imagined them conversing with hand signals. He heard rapid breathing, adrenalin already starting to course as always when an ARO draws their weapon. There was a moment's silence, then a whispered, 'One, two *three.'*

The next few seconds played out in Carver's mind's eye, as he matched the scene to the sounds in his ear.

A sharp squeak - one of them flinging the door wide.

Heavy footfalls as they entered, weapons leading. Him first, her following.

Nylon rubbing on webbing as they swung around, checking corners and shielded areas.

'All clear, Sir, There's no one here.'

'The subject?'

'Present and correct.'

'Have you checked her?'

'I can see her from here. She's asleep.

'CHECK HER.'

'Right.'

It was the extended silence that gave Carver the first sign. Then came, 'What the- FUCK.'

'What is it, Graham?'

'Ahh, *CHRIST.'* Lizzie's voice.

'WHAT IS IT? What's happening Graham?'

'It- It's not her, Sir. It's another woman. I- I think it's the PO Supervisor... And she's- Is she?' A short pause as Lizzie checked vitals. 'She is, Sir. Holy fuck. I think she's dead.'

For the second time that night, Carver froze. Then he reacted. 'Call the medics. Tell Lizzie to preserve the scene. Don't let anyone in, especially prison staff. Contact Hospital Security. Tell them to lock the hospital down. They're looking for Megan Crane.' But he already knew. An hour ago? *Well gone*. 'Then call it in to Control Room. They'll tell you what to do next. Got it?'

'Yes Sir.'

He cut the call, re-ran the calculations he'd been making even as he'd been instructing the CPO.

Colette's arrival was no random event. Megan had planned it all. *What else?* She'd walked out of the hospital an hour ago. She would know exactly where she was going. There'd have been a car, waiting. He received the SMS soon after she left the hospital. Salford Royal to Warrington is around a thirty-minute journey this time of night.

It may already be too late.

As he set off, he rang the Control Room, told the female operator who answered who he was, that it was an emergency, that he needed to speak to the Duty Inspector. After a short pause, a voice said, 'Mr Carver? It's Kevin Deacon. What have you got?'

'There's a possible Number One in progress at a Warrington address, Kev. I'm five minutes away. I need back-up, including AR and a dog.'

'What's the address?' He passed it, waited as the Inspector logged it.. 'Sir, in view of what you've told me, I need to tell you not to-'

'Yeah, I know, I'm not to enter until AR are on scene.'

'I'm sorry, Sir, it's-'

'I know, Kev. Procedure. Don't worry about it. Just get them there.'

'I'm already on it.'

He floored the pedal.

CHAPTER 78

Bewsey is one of Warrington's older districts. Wilfred Street comprises two-up-two-down Victorian terraces. At night, cars line both sides, nose-to-tail. Carver stopped in the middle of the road outside thirty-eight, checking it out before looking for a space. The house was in darkness. He dropped the windows, listened. Nothing except the distant hums and whines of Warrington's night-industry. For the moment satisfied, he drove down until he found a gap he could squeeze into, wheels up, half-on, half-off, the pavement. As he jogged back to Kayleigh's he rang her again. She didn't pick up.

At her front door, he was in two minds whether to ring the bell, or force entry. He remembered the Control Room Inspector's safety warning. *Fuck that*. And when he saw the narrow gap between the door and the frame and realised the door was open, he didn't hesitate. He pushed it back. The stairs were right in front of him. He bounded up, yelling. 'KAYLEIGH? IT'S JAMIE.' If he had it all wrong, and scared the shit out of her, tough. At the top, he rounded the post and made for the front bedroom, guessing it was hers. At the door, he groped for the light switch, found it.

As the room lit up, Carver's mind went right back to the moment two years before, when he finally realised the bloodied corpse hanging from a rafter was Angie, not Megan Crane. Kayleigh was lying, sprawled across the bed in her pyjamas, arms out, hair hanging down. A black ribbon was about her throat, the ends trailing on the floor.

'No-no-no-nooo.'

In that moment, as he stood in the doorway looking down at her, the enormity of his failure hit him. At their recent meetings, Kayleigh had asked him, begged him, for reassurance that she was safe. And he had given it to her. 'Don't worry,' he'd said. 'She can't get you now.'

LIAR.

He'd failed her just like he'd failed Angie - and, almost, Rosanna.

Seventeen. That's all she is. *Seventeen... Innocent.*

As he bent to her, fighting to stay in control, his mind raced. How long had it been since they'd spoken? Twenty minutes? Thirty? For all he knew, Megan could already have been in the house, waiting for her to finish her telephone call so she could strike. At the same time, he was trying to remember how long after the heart stops, CPR can still be effective? He'd heard of people pulled from water being revived as long as forty-plus minutes after. But that was where there was a rapid drop in body temperature. In normal cases, brain cells began to die after around five minutes. Any longer, and even if the heart starts beating again, the damage to the brain is already done.

He had to at least *try.*

Grabbing her shoulders, he pulled her round onto the bed - and got the shock of his life when a low groan sounded from her throat. His heart hammered.

'KAYLEIGH?'

Was it her, or just death rattle? Then he realised. The ribbon round her neck, wasn't biting the way he'd seen in others. And her face colour was near normal, no sign of the bloating or swollen tongue he would have expected. *Could it be?*

He pressed his fingers to the side of her neck. It took a second, but - *There.* A pulse. Low and slow, but definite.

'Kayleigh? He shook her, trying not to be too rough, trying to work out what might be wrong - *If not dead, then…?* Holding her shoulders, he put his cheek to her mouth to check her breathing. As he did so, he smelled the pungent, sickly-sweet odour again. Hope surged in him. He checked around, searching for a water bottle, a glass. On the dressing table, next to the bed, was a crushed gauze pad, the source of the smell. But it was the sheet of note-paper next to it, propped against the mirror by a bottle of nail-polish remover, that drew his attention. He recognised the hand-writing.

You saved my life, I'm giving you hers
Now we're even. Don't try to come after me
If you do, all bets are off.
Remember, I still owe you for Edmund
M.C.

As he read the words, his skin crawled and the hairs on the back of his neck pricked against his collar. She'd *been* there. The thought sent a shudder through him. What she *could* have done.

Turning back to Kayleigh, he pulled the ribbon from her neck - window dressing from a sick mind. As he did so, she began to stir. Another groan, followed by a whimpering sound, like a distressed kitten.

'It's me, Kayleigh. It's Jamie. You're okay. You're-'
A noise sounded outside. A car drawing up, engine, revving. Easing her down, he crossed to the window. As he passed the foot of the bed, he almost tripped on a pile of clothes. Looking down, he saw a gillet, bearing the distinctive crest of the Prison Service. He'd once seen Collette Bright wearing one just like it. Next to the window was a wardrobe. The door was open, clothes scattered, off hangers.
He looked out at the street below. The car was stopped right outside, facing to his left. Showing no lights, all he could make out was its dark shape. Even as he watched, a light came on inside, spilling out as the offside-rear passenger door opened. From the shadows of the houses opposite, a figure stepped out, and stopped at the kerb.
Wearing a long coat with the hood pulled up - he recognised Kayleigh's Parka - she waited a few seconds, before tilting her head back, slowly, to look up at the window. And as the hood fell back and the light from the nearby street lamp fell on her, Carver found himself, once again, face-to-face with Megan Crane. As ever, the expression was implacable. A raised eyebrow. A hint of a smile. And while in that moment Carver found it unreadable, in the weeks and months to come he would ascribe to it meanings that varied according to his mood.
I win.
It's over.
It was nice while it lasted.
We'll not meet again.
Things could have been different.
Her hand lifted. Fingers wiggled up at him. *Farewell.*
Then she was off the kerb, stooping into the car. The door slammed, the engine revved and, with a slew of its

rear end, it sped off down the street and out of view - which was when the trance broke enough for him to react.

Spinning around, he leaped over the bed, and back towards the door. *There might still be time to-* But as he was half out of the room, a low moan sounded behind him. He stopped. For brief seconds, he debated within himself. Then he realised. *It's too late.* Closing his eyes, he stood rock-still in the doorway, listening to the sound of Megan Crane, disappearing into the night.

When she was gone, he turned, went back to the bed. Kayleigh was stirring more now, beginning to come out of it. Lifting her gently, he held her to him as he sat on the edge of the bed, stroking her hair, speaking soft words of reassurance to her slurred attempts at speech.

'Jamie…? Issatyou?'

'Yes, I'm here. You're safe now.'

'I had a horrible dream, Jamie.'

'I know.'

'She was here. In my room. She was-' She lifted an arm, tried to point to the end of the bed, couldn't quite make it. 'Right, there.'

'I know. She's gone now.'

'She won't come back, will she Jamie?'

'No. She won't come back. Like I said, she's gone.'

'Forever?'

'Forever.'

'Promise?'

'Promise.'

And with that, she heaved a long sigh, and burrowed into his chest, like she was trying to bury herself inside him.

In that moment, Carver felt his heart rip.

Never again.

He didn't try to move her, but stayed, rocking her like he would an infant, stroking her hair and whispering calming words until the roars of engines heralded the circus arriving.

The street blazed with blue flashing lights that bounced off the walls of the bedroom. Brakes and tyres squealed. Doors slammed.

Seconds later, a voice shouted up.

'ARMED POLICE. DCI CARVER, ARE YOU THERE?'

The end

Coming in Spring 2018 - the third and final part of, The Worshipper Trilogy

A killer in hiding
A climactic confrontation
But who will survive?

Like a preview? Read on for the prologue and opening chapter of OUT OF AIR

Don't miss out. Keep up to date with news about release dates, and offers and competitions by signing up to my VIP mailing list at http://robertfbarker.co.uk

Want to know how st arr etadti l ?

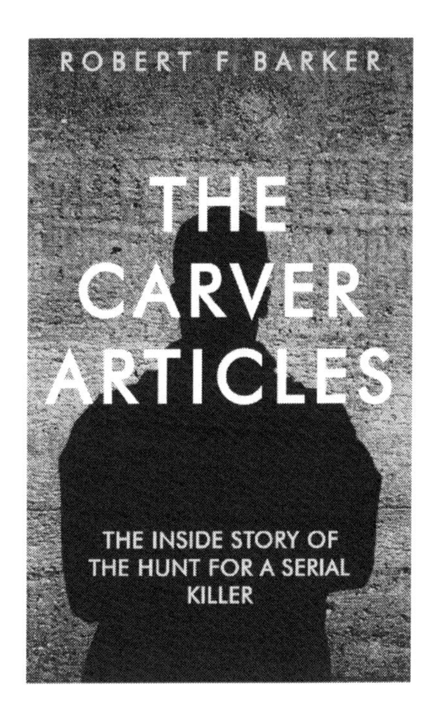

Sign up for the author's V.I.P. mailing list and get a free e-copy of, *THE CARVER ARTICLES,* the series of articles that kick-started it all - as featured in LAST GASP

To get started, visit:-

http://robertfbarker.co.uk

OUT OF AIR

One City - Paris
Two killers - one known, the other not.
A young couple - bewitched into the most deadly danger
An English Detective - who must find them all, before the worst happens.

DCI Jamie Carver is in Paris, laying out the bait he hopes will appeal to his Nemesis's warped tastes and draw her from hiding. Only when she is back where she belongs can he resume the life that has been on hold these past months. But when a young couple fall into Megan Crane's clutches, Carver knows he has only so long to save them, before tragedy strikes. At the same time he is lending his expertise to the local police's hunt for a brutal killer stalking the city's streets. The victims are all provincials, visiting the capital for the same purpose - to purge themselves of a guilty secret. But what is it, and how does it link them to the killer?

In the third and final part of The Worshipper Trilogy, Jamie Carver finds himself torn between the need to catch a killer whose brutality matches anything he has seen so far, and recapturing the woman whose shadow has blighted his life far too long. What he cannot know is, the two are fated to come together in the most horrific way imaginable, bringing with it bloody, violent death.

But for whom? The Paris Killer? Megan Crane? Himself? Or all of them?

Prologue

The room is pitch black. The boy sits on the middle of the bed, hugs his knees to his chest and rocks, back and forth. He is crying, though silently, in case he misses the sounds he is straining to hear. The ones that tell that tonight, like other such nights, there will be no respite from the evil.

It is later coming than usual. From his bedroom at the back of the house, the boy can just hear the church clock in the town. It chimed the half-hour some time ago. And while he knows he cannot escape the evil that is a part of his life, he cannot ignore the flicker of hope that sparks every now and then. The hope that tonight, it will *not* come. That something has happened to stop it. An accident of some kind. Perhaps the unexpected arrival of an unlikely saviour who, even now, is making ready to bear him away somewhere safe, somewhere the evil cannot reach.

But the boy's eleventh birthday draws near. By now the experiences of birthdays past lie on his bony shoulders like a shroud, restricting expectation, suffocating hope. In any case, hope has blossomed before – probably every time, truth be told - only to be dashed on the rocks of reality that seem to rise like devil's teeth as the inevitable storm hits.

A bright boy, he knows what date it is, its significance. Over the past weeks his thoughts have turned more and more to what this day will bring. Rather, what the night will bring. During those times he has thought often of running. Of spiriting from his plate such scraps as might not be missed until he has sufficient to sustain him long enough to reach the city, many days travel hence. Perhaps there, he imagines, he will find refuge from his pursuer.

For there lies the problem.

If he runs, the evil will follow after. And when it catches him, as it surely will, he will suffer even more. By not running, he knows that at least tomorrow the evil will have passed, at least until the days run their course and the time comes round for it to show itself once more.

So instead he rocks, back and forth. And cries.

Eventually there is a sound. A metallic scrape. A click, then another click, followed by a rattle. A key in the lock.

It is here.

He stops rocking.

He tries to stifle the sobs. His breathing slows to a sort of panting-gasp. 'Huhh… huhh…. huhh….' He keeps listening.

The creak of a hinge in need of oil. The scrape of boots on tile. The first heavy planting of foot on stair, followed by others, slow, steady.

He counts the thuds. One, two, three… In his mind's eye he observes the evil's ascent as clearly as if he were standing on the landing, witnessing its approach. The count stops at thirteen. For several moments there is only silence. But not entirely. As he strains, the sound of laboured breathing comes to him, mixed with the low throaty rattle that in those not used to physical exertion, speaks of too much drink.

The pause lasts almost a minute. During it the heavy breathing dies and the boy stares, through the darkness towards where he knows the door is. The sound of shuffling steps is followed by the squeak of a handle, turning. A crack of dim light appears. For a moment it remains just a crack, as if tempting him to hope the door will shut again. But he is not fooled. He knows it will not. This is the way it happens. Every time.

The crack widens.

A whimper escapes the boy's throat and he scuttles back on the bed until he reaches the wall and can go no further. A man's head and shoulders, huge it seems in the now semi-dark, appear round the door. Guttural breathing and the odorous smell of stale beer fill the room. The figure is silhouetted against the light behind, so the face is in shadow. Even so, the boy imagines the flabby lips and drooling mouth, twisted into the black-toothed snarl that passes for a smile as he hears the greeting that marks the evil is upon him once more.

'Hello boy. Happy Birthday.'

Chapter 1

Marianne Desmarais stood at the kerb, arms stiff at her sides, eyes closed, mouth set in a thin line. She was fighting against the voices in her head telling her she should abandon her mission, that she should return to her hotel, immediately. All she had to do was cross Plâce Madelaine and two hundred metres up on the right was St Augustin Station. From there she could catch the metro straight back to Montmartre. She could be checked out and on her way to Gare St. Lazare within the hour. By late evening she could be home, safe in the arms of her husband, Guy, her children, Marie-Rose and Thierry, at her side. But warming though the thought was, Marianne rejected it. To give in now meant abandoning them all to the ruination she had brought upon them. How could she carry on knowing she had come this far and given up with her goal in sight? No, she had planned too long, travelled too far to even think such a thing. Steeling herself, she turned to face her enemy.

The stretch of grey cobble stared back at her, waiting. Though the sun had now broken through, damp patches from the morning showers still showed between the brickwork. On the other side of the railings to her left, the broad flight of steps led up to the church's great bronze doors. In her conflicted state, Marianne imagined the cobbles themselves daring her to make another pass, to attempt once more what she had failed to do three times already.

On each of her previous tries, the cobbles had defied her intentions, carrying her past the gate through which she meant to turn. The thought came that perhaps the stones were imbued with some divine power by which they could see into people's minds and deny access to those deemed unworthy. Even as it formed, Marianne recognised it for what it was, a faint-hearted attempt to cast blame from where it truly lay. She knew full well that the enemy was not the ground beneath her feet, but her own fear. But by transposing her guilt onto the inanimate stones, her hope was she might strengthen her resolve. She clenched her fists.

'This time,' she said. 'This time, I *will* succeed.'

A particular cobble opposite the opening, slightly raised above the others, marked the point at which she should make the turn. Fixing her gaze on it, she set off once more. As she bore down on her target, Marianne felt the familiar wave of panic beginning to rise. Her heart pounded. Her breathing quickened.

Please God, give me the strength to do what I must. She did not dwell on what would happen if her prayer went unanswered. She would not find the resolve for another attempt. *It has to be this time... It must be.. Now.*

Suddenly, she was mounting the steps. One foot in front of the other, advancing towards her goal. Finally, her legs had responded as she had willed them to. A joyous feeling came over her, banishing the doubts of a few short seconds ago. She *was* going to succeed. As she neared the top step, exhilaration almost drove her to break into a run, but she controlled it. For all that she was young at heart, her forty-fifth birthday had come and gone. In France, Paris especially, women of such years do not *run,* certainly not into church.

Gaining the plateau at the top, Marianne joined with the tourists and worshippers filing through the high portal. As she crossed the threshold, a shudder of anticipation rippled through her. Stopping just inside, she waited, letting her eyes adjust to the sudden gloom. Before her, the wondrous interior that many of those around had travelled far to see, stretched in all directions. In that moment, the fears and doubts she had carried with her so long melted away.

For the first time since arriving in Paris, Marianne Desmarais relaxed, confident in the knowledge that she had, for once, made the right decision.

She had no way of knowing how wrong she was….

****

An hour later, Marianne Desmarais blinked and squinted as she stepped out into the bright sunlight. The morning clouds had cleared and as she looked up to the cobalt sky she experienced a lightness of spirit she had not felt in a long time.

Since arriving in Paris, two days before, she had spent much of her time casting furtive glances at people on the bus, the train, in the hotel. Over the past week, her guilt had built to the point where she was convinced that despite the city's vastness, she was certain she would bump into someone from her home town. They would, she was sure, have heard about her grandmother's 'sudden illness.' They would ask her why she was here, in Paris, instead of tending to the old lady's needs in Provence.

But now, buoyed by her new-found feeling of freedom, those fears were gone. She was even looking forward to her final night in the capital before catching the morning train home.

Such was her good-heart, Marianne had no thought

for others as she almost skipped down the steps that earlier had proved so troublesome. Even if she had, she would not have given the figure in the long, dark coat, halfway down on her right a second glance. Holding a mobile/camera at arm's length, the figure's only interest seemed to be in capturing the perfect symmetry of the view down the Avenue De Medici and across the river to the imposing, Assemblée Nationale. But once Marianne was passed, the arm lowered. A second later the device disappeared into the coat's side pocket.

At the bottom of the steps, Marianne turned left in the direction that would take her back to her hotel. The figure waited until she rounded the corner, into the Plâce and out of sight, before descending rapidly and following in her footsteps.

About The Author

Robert F Barker was born in Liverpool, England. During a thirty-year police career, he worked in and around some of the Northwest's grittiest towns and cities. As a senior detective, he led investigations into all kinds of major crime including, murder, armed robbery, serious sex crime and people/drug trafficking. Whilst commanding firearms and disorder incidents, he learned what it means to have to make life-and-death decisions in the heat of live operations. His stories are grounded in the reality of police work, but remain exciting, suspenseful, and with the sort of twists and turns crime-fiction readers love.

For updates about new releases, as well as information about promotions and special offers, visit the author's website and sign up for the VIP Mailing List at:-

http://robertfbarker.co.uk/

Printed in Great Britain
by Amazon